BLOOD LINES

DCI JOHN DRAKE
BOOK 3

M. R. ARMITAGE

zenarch books

Find out more about the author and other forthcoming books at: www. mrarmitage.com

For my parents,
Richard and Rosemary

SPOILERS WARNING

This book is the next instalment in an ongoing storyline and there are spoilers throughout regarding Book 1 and 2.

If you have not read Book 1, *The Family Man,* or Book 2, *The Ties That Bind,* then I strongly recommend starting with those before reading any further.

To find out more, scan the QR code.

1

I gasped, my eyes snapping open as I came to.

My body felt strange, alien, as though my consciousness had forced its way back inside an empty shell. I tried to get my bearings from my slumped position on the floor, forcing my stinging eyes to focus until a series of blurred shapes began manifesting in front of me: a sink, a bath and a mirrored medicine cabinet, all highlighted in a stark, white light.

A-A ... bathroom? How ...

Confused, I bunched myself up further against the door, drawing my knees in close as I tried to rub the bleariness away. There was a strange familiarity to the space that I couldn't quite put my finger on. Had I been here before? If so, when?

Taking a deep breath, I looked up again, the breath catching in my throat at the imagery in the cabinet's reflection.

A white door, streaked with blood.

The very same door which I was propped up against, the crimson smearing down toward me.

I scrambled to my feet, desperate to understand, and even

more desperate to see. But nothing could have prepared me for what I saw when I peered into the mirror.

A face, drenched in blood. Dark, crusted, stinking, coppery blood.

My face.

I shrieked, stumbling back into the bloody door with a hollow thump, unable to tear my eyes away.

And it was then that I beheld the horror that was *me*.

It wasn't just my face that was covered in blood, it was *everything*. My hands, my chest, my clothing. I was completely drenched, the whites of my eyes peering through the gore.

This isn't real, this can't be real. It can't be!

I tried to shield my eyes against the nightmarish reflection as I slid down to the floor again in a heap, hoping to banish what I'd seen out of my head. Instead, strobing flashes of my bloodied, *smiling* face assaulted my mind, each momentary image making my brain feel like it was going to burst.

I continued to whimper; hands now clamped at my temples. Tears running down my bloody cheeks.

No. Stop, please!

My fingernails dug deeper into my skull with each pulse of pain.

Stop! Please. Please, stop!

It ceased instantly, like someone had flicked a switch in my brain. My ears rang amidst the abrupt new silence. My mind felt incapable of processing what I'd seen, at what must have happened to me. Or what I must have done.

Blood. So much blood . . .

The persistent thought caused me to scramble over to the pristine white of the wood-panelled bath and retch violently, but nothing came. I began sobbing, each sniffle painfully punctuating the dry retches. If only something would come, if only I could purge whatever darkness was within me, I could start to heal, to rid myself of the pain. But my body *refused*.

The image of my bloody face flashed across my mind again and the pain returned, as though to mock me. I slumped against the bath, sobbing in frustration, and put my hands back to my temples. I needed to get a grip. I had to. If not for myself, then for Ben and Cari, at the very least. They needed me to be strong for when I returned. It had already been so long.

Figure out where you are. Figure out what you can do. You can do this.

I took a deep breath and held it in, my cheeks bulging, child-like, while I listened intently. But the silence was all-encompassing and there was nothing to see. Nothing that gave even the faintest hint as to my situation. No sounds, nor movement outside to indicate someone had followed me back to finish what they'd started. No banging on the door to show I was going to pay for whatever I'd been involved in.

Just awful silence. And my own bristling panic.

I picked myself up and paced the bathroom, raking my face with my nails in frustration. 'What did you do, Andrea? What. Did. You. Do?'

I can't remember . . . Why can I never remember? Why did it have to be like this? Why?

I gripped the edges of the basin and stared intently at my reflection, my grimy hands bloodying the porcelain surface. Tears and sweat streaked my ghastly features, and the voids of my eyes stared back at me between strands of damp hair.

'What did you do, Andrea? What did you do? What did you do?'

My grip tightened on the sink.

'What . . . Did . . . You . . . *Fucking . . . Do . . .* ?'

2

Detective Chief Inspector John Drake stared out of the window of the flat on the eighth floor. A bright spring day looked back, lending him the visibility to see for miles. The Thames, languid and dirty, snaking through the glistening city, the various cranes and buildings looming large. The constant streams of people as they went about their daily lives. Taking it all in, he focused beyond the centuries-old buildings of London, encircled by the more modern tower blocks, toward one of the newer structures, The Shard, and a memory of a time when he'd taken Becca and Eva out for the day. The 360-degree view from the observation deck, the River Thames weaving its way through the heart of London, the chug of the boats making their way downriver, the swell kicking out behind. The hustle and bustle of city life playing out below at a near microscopic level. Eva with an ice cream, Becca with a much-needed - though incredibly overpriced - glass of red wine. He couldn't believe how much could change in three years. Still couldn't. His wife had been dead for almost eighteen months. How time flies when you're not having fun.

Drake's scarred hand pulsed, the damaged skin still prominent. The memory of the kitchen tiles and the ping of the knife making him wince as he ran an index finger over the scar. At his age, his healing powers weren't quite what they had been.

'Mr Drake?'

The young woman's raspy voice cut through his melancholy. He turned to greet another of the reminders of his recent past.

'Cari, come on. You know you can call me John. You're a member of the family now, for all intents and purposes,' he said, leaning back against the window frame, the sunlight casting a long shadow into the room.

The corners of her mouth twitched faintly. But a smile wasn't forthcoming. It hadn't been since the incident with her parents, nor since she'd moved in with him and Eva in their temporary new home a few months past. 'Sorry, Mr—er, John. I'm just being polite, I guess. I'm a guest in your home.'

'You're not a guest. You live here, same as we do. Least for now we do, anyway – don't think I can afford the rent on this flat for much longer,' he joked, trying to lift the mood. 'London prices being what they are.'

'I did say I could help. I could pay my way. You know, use my inheritance now it's been released to my account . . .' Her voice tailed off at the memory of the events that had led to that money in the first place.

'Cari, that won't be necessary. I was just joking.'

'But—'

'Dad, are you trying to pinch her money again. Seriously?' Eva said, sliding noisily into the room, her slippers skimming across the lounge's smooth wooden floor.

It still took him aback how similar the two girls were physically, even now when they were sixteen. They both had long, dark hair and were of a similar height, waif-like and with dark brown eyes. But that's where the similarities ended; where Cari had been beaten down by life into being quiet and considered, Eva had grown increasingly loud and obstinate. And where Eva was logical and excellent in a debate, Cari was, he was told, more of a creative creature. Eva said the creativity had become darker in nature during the time she'd known Cari, and with what the girl been through, Drake wasn't surprised. The scar at her throat was a constant reminder of the death of her father, Ben, at the hands of her mother. Drake felt the familiar pang of guilt he got whenever he saw the Whitman girl. He still hadn't told her about the phone calls he'd been receiving. That her mother wasn't *quite* so missing anymore.

He sighed at his daughter. 'Eva . . .'

Eva plucked an apple from the coffee table's fruit bowl in the middle of the modern, sparsely furnished lounge and sprawled on a grey futon, while her best friend took up a perch on the back corner.

Eva took a noisy bite and spoke with her mouth full. 'Has there been any progress on the house yet, Dad?'

'You know I've not made a final decision on that,' he said, frowning.

"The house", their family home in Barndon, had stood empty apart from his brief visits to his study since Becca's death. His one failed venture into the kitchen where Samuel Barrow, 'The Family Man' serial killer, had butchered her was the only time he'd even come close to facing up to what had happened there. He didn't think he had it in him to go back again.

Drake winced inwardly at his cowardice. 'Besides, I seem to recall the agreement to sell up was made when I was under the influence of very strong painkillers,' he continued. '*And* under considerable duress, might I add.'

'Dad. Don't give me that shit.'

'Eva. You know your Mum wouldn't like you talking to me like that. Nor do I, for that matter.'

'Dad. Come on . . .' She crossed her arms.

Cari gave a small sigh. 'Eva, give him a break. It's not just you who lost someone, remember? That house must have lots of other memories for your dad. Not just bad ones . . . It's a big decision selling it.'

Drake nodded at her. 'Thanks, Cari. You're right, it does.' He paused. 'But, Eva, you're right too. I know I need to make a decision. It's just . . . I can't right now, okay?'

'Okay.'

He huffed, appreciating the effort it must have taken for her to back down. 'So enough with the jibes?'

'Yes. Fine. Anyway, how're you feeling today? Less sore?'

'Pretty much back to normal. Thank you, love.'

The beating and broken ribs he'd received at the hands of the killer siblings Jack and Fiona Spencer had left him barely able to move and next to useless for a few weeks after he'd been taken off the pain medication. But it had given him all the time in the world to think about his phone call with Cari's mother, Andrea. Only it hadn't been Andrea, not then; the chilling voice he'd listened to had belonged to Miray, Andrea's psychopathic mother persona.

'. . . Dad?'

'Sorry?'

She continued to chew loudly as she devoured the apple. 'You spaced out for a moment there. So, what's the plan then? Not the house, just in general?'

'Oh.' He looked back out over the cityscape for a few moments before turning back. 'I'm going to go back to work in a couple of days. Get back in the saddle, as it were. Then, we'll talk about our next steps. Okay? It's early March now, so you've got, what . . . ? A few more months of college? Plenty of time before we figure out next steps, I'd say.'

Drake got up to go to the one remaining spare room.

'Cool. Got it,' she said, her eyes following him while Cari looked down at her feet, like the weight of the world was on her shoulders.

He'd find the girl's mother if it was the last thing he did.

3

DS Ellie Wilkinson perched at the edge of the ruined retreat's mezzanine balcony, the sweat pouring off her face. Her knee pounding with pain, she caught a glimpse of the jagged piles of wood and debris below. Before she had a chance to act, Fiona Spencer hurtled in her direction, slamming Ellie back into the corner of the balcony doorway and leaving her on the brink of falling.

The moment suddenly froze in time: Fiona's sneering face, the look of satisfaction at having bested her opponent, Ellie teetering on the brink.

Despite everything else being frozen in place, the crazed woman's face moved, and she started speaking.

'I know what you did. You made a choice, you disgusting pig. You *chose* to kill me. You *chose death*.' Fiona spat, her features screwed in hatred as rivulets of blood began pouring from her nose and mouth.

Ellie shut her eyes to the horror in front of her. 'No-no—no! I wouldn't. I couldn't have. You gave me no choice!'

Fiona screamed. Ellie opened her eyes, in time to see the

deranged woman being impaled by the wooden beam with a sickening thud, the sound echoing around her.

'Ahh!' Ellie gasped and started up from the sofa, her heart beat going through the roof as she readied herself for a confrontation. But nothing came, only the void of the television stared back and the tick of the mantelpiece clock.

There was no-one there. Fiona was dead. Ellie was alone.

She clamped her legs and exhaled loudly. 'Oh, sweet Mary, mother of God.'

'Ellie? You okay down there?'

She heard Len bound downstairs as she slumped back down and began rubbing her forehead.

'Yeah. Sorry.' Ellie waved a dismissive hand at her husband as he entered the room. 'Just another dream. Honestly, it's nothing.'

He peered at her from the doorway, his kind face a picture of concern. 'That's the third time this week, Ellie. It's not nothing, and you know it.'

She knew he was right, despite her protestations to the contrary. The nightmares had become a common occurrence since she and Drake had encountered the Spencer family in the woods that night. She insisted outwardly that she was fine, but the pretence was beginning to wear her down. She shouldn't be scared of falling asleep. But that's what things had come to; she was so exhausted lately, she was crashing out on the sofa without even realising.

'Okay, okay,' she said, slumping back further into their gargantuan sofa. 'I get it. I'll handle it. I've been through worse – not just in SMT – and you know that. Remember that time I got beaten by that drug addict with a metal pipe?'

He winced. 'Yeah?'

She looked at him guiltily as she admitted: 'Well . . . I had flashbacks for months.'

He inhaled sharply. 'You didn't tell me!'

'I didn't want to worry you, Len.' She shrugged. 'It's just one of those things. Part of the job. I didn't want to worry you then, and I don't want to worry you now, either.'

Len moved from the doorway and sat down beside her, his lean frame dwarfing her. He took her hand in his. 'Ellie, that's not true. You shouldn't have to suffer like this. You're not even *at* work. It's not right.'

The clock whiled away the seconds as they sat in silence. She didn't get a chance to reply before he spoke again. 'I'm not happy, Ellie.'

Her heart lurched. 'What? What do you mean?'

'I'm not happy with the dynamic right now.' He let go of her hand. 'How *we* are. How things have been since you've been working with DCI Drake in that team of his.'

'Of *mine*,' she corrected him. 'Len. We've been through this.' She paused, trying her best not to sound as agitated as she felt. 'Now is not the time to rake over old ground. I'm tired. I just want to be able to rest and go a day without arguing with you about my job. You've always had my back before. What's changed?'

He took her hand. 'This . . .' he said, passing a finger over her scar. 'Oh, and this,' he pointed at her knee, which was finally back to normal, or so she led him to believe. 'And most of all, this.' Len made a particular point of pointing at her temple.

She shrugged again. 'People get hurt. It happens.'

Len flung his hands up in frustration. 'You're my wife. I can't lose you. *Bella* can't lose you.'

'You won't. You haven't so far, have you?'

He paused for a moment, pursing his lips before continuing quietly. 'There only needs to be one time, Ellie. You know that.'

She paused, stopping a retort from passing her lips. Her

husband was right, she knew it. But this was her job, her new career. It was only just getting started, after all.

'Those were one offs. Freak occurrences,' she remonstrated. 'As I've said time and time again, Drake's been doing this for years. He's still around.'

'His wife isn't, though.'

'Len . . .'

'I think you should see someone. Or at the very least, *speak* to someone. Or I will.'

'Okay, okay. I'll think about it. I promise.'

'Good.' He stood up and went over to the dining table, shifting his laptop mouse to wake the device. He scratched the back of his neck. 'I've got a meeting starting in a minute. Do you mind?'

'All right, I can take the hint. I was off out soon anyway,' she said, hauling herself up from the sofa.

'Oh?' He sat down at the table, and reached for his glasses.

'Yes, I'm going to see Drake. Seeing as we're both starting back soon, I felt I should check in with him.'

Len sighed and shook his head. 'This will only end one way eventually, Ellie.'

'Everything will be fine, Len. Just you wait.'

Ellie headed upstairs to their bedroom to get changed, leaving the plastic child gate open behind her. She didn't like being home without Bella around these days. It left her with an uneasy weight in the pit of her stomach; the concern that the school would phone to tell her that her girl had been taken. She knew it was irrational; the Spencers were either dead, locked up, or in Gemma's case, in a coma. There was no danger there anymore.

And Andrea Whitman was hardly likely to go after her, either – she barely knew Ellie enough to give rise to anything, surely?

Despite the bright sunlight shining through the window, the bedroom was cold, the heating having not kicked in yet to stave off the remnants of winter. The chilled air caused her knee to ache. Yet again, she'd said one thing to her husband, and was feeling another.

Ellie pulled on her favourite purple work jumper, along with a pair of high-waisted black jeans and looked herself over in the mirror. She raised her eyebrows, nodding approvingly at her reflection. 'Looking good, if I do say so myself.'

The muscle at the corner of her right eyelid twitched and she rubbed at it irritably, glaring at the mirror. She didn't need to see the evidence of her sleepless nights and ongoing stress reflected back at her. She needed to speak to someone, she knew that, and for a moment, she thought about Drake. But her boss had enough to deal with, and she didn't want to burden him with her nonsense. Nor would raising it to anyone else be particularly good for her career. Even in this day and age, with its increased awareness about mental health, Ellie knew it could still be used against her if the circumstances warranted it, irrespective of the virtue signalling.

No. I'll keep it to myself. I'll be fine. Just need more time.

Ellie nodded determinedly to her reflection and headed back downstairs to make her escape.

4

Leaving the two girls gossiping in the lounge, Drake quietly unlocked the door to the spare room he'd commandeered as his office space, and closed it behind him. He secretly welcomed the noise and hustle and bustle about the place that came with them being there. It certainly made a change to the miserable living circumstances he'd endured in recent times. Drake had only partly been joking about the cost of the flat, however. He genuinely couldn't afford it for much longer. He didn't want to touch his savings, so he needed to get back to work. He owed it to the girls to look after them.

Drake glanced down at the small pile of papers on the bedside table nestled next to the bare mattress. His office – if he could call it that – was a pitiful sight, amounting to little more than said bed and side table, coupled with an unyielding chair that hadn't done much to aid his recovery. Though that was probably more his fault than that of an inanimate object.

He settled down into the maroon-coloured chair with a subtle protest from his ribs, and set to looking through the papers once more.

Unofficially, he had been working on locating Andrea whenever he found the time since before the Spencer murders. That had yielded little beyond her leaving the hospital, venturing a few steps and then essentially vanishing for a year until the phone call on Christmas Day.

But from that day, he'd been doing his best (albeit still unofficially) with Detective Sergeant Luka Strauss' assistance, to trace the calls, of which there had been a further two, one per month, almost to the day, since Christmas, making for three in total. Each call had ended up being a non-starter in terms of precisely locating where she was holed up. Andrea's continued ability to evade them struck Drake as strange, considering the woman's mental state.

He rifled through the papers, eventually finding the ones pertaining to the phones used. Strauss had found the calls were made with 'burner' phones – cheap, disposable phones loaded with pre-paid credit. The burners were still a veritable thorn in the police force's side, even in this day and age. And now with burner phone *apps* as well, it was getting silly.

Drake shook his head in disgust at the thought.

Even with the tech available to Strauss, they'd only succeeded in locating the general location where a phone had been used for the second and third calls; the second had come from the general vicinity of Ealing in west London, and the third in the borough of Newham in *east* London. They'd also ascertained which shop purchased the phones at wholesale to be sold to Andrea in the first place, with each phone being sold within the same area of each call. But questioning the staff in each place had yielded nothing; no one recalled seeing or serving any woman matching Andrea's description when he'd thrust her photo under their noses. The poor-quality CCTV hadn't shown anything of note either, as though she'd specifically targeted the shops for that reason. All in all, it was another standard frustration of the many investigations he'd taken part in over the years. And this was an investigation he wasn't even supposed to be involved in.

Drake sighed. He stood up, pacing around the bed to the small inward-opening window. A view of the courtyard far below, a tiny shrub, barely alive, at its centre. He recalled his time fruitlessly staking out random areas within Newham to no avail. Watching people go by, his stomach churning when seeing women with passing resemblances to Andrea. The stakeouts hadn't aided his battered body's recovery, and he knew in his gut she wouldn't have stayed in the area anyway. It was pointless.

Much to his chagrin, Detective Chief Superintendent Laura Miller had ruled the Whitman case to be one for CID, not for their Specialist Murder Team, largely due to the lowly level of resource they'd had available to them. And, incredibly, as it involved a different suspect to the original Family Man, it had meant Andrea's kill count was officially 'just' one, and so it didn't quite meet SMT's serial killer threshold, even with its brutality and obvious markers for further killings. To top it all, Drake knew that CID were dragging their heels on it, with Andrea having been declared officially missing in the months since her disappearance. It riled him to do so, but given his rather precarious standing in the force, he'd had to back off. Officially, at least.

Drake grunted in disgust as he leafed through the transcripts of the calls before returning to his chair.

The recordings of the second and third calls were under lock and key at Strauss' place. Drake had kept Andrea's – or Miray's – contact with him completely under wraps from both his boss and Cari. He couldn't afford to have the girl knowing her mother was in contact with him, given the mental state her mother was in; and Cari too, for that matter. The girl could be in danger if she knew the woman was close by in the same city. Andrea had almost killed her once, after all. The thought that one day he could open the door to the flat and she'd be there waiting to pounce, knife in hand, was not a new one.

The phone calls themselves were never more than a minute or two. It went without saying that she seemed completely unstable, taunting him, threatening to find him and finish what Samuel had started with Eva. How she knew what had happened, he couldn't say. Perhaps it was from the news?

Drake found it troubling that he'd not managed to speak to 'Andrea' even once. It was only ever the Miray persona in control when he got the calls. What *was* useful was that at least she seemed unaware that Cari had survived, despite her knowing what happened to him. And he'd damn well made sure he'd not given any indication to Miray either. It wasn't common knowledge that Cari was under his care. Though eventually it could be a way of getting Andrea/Miray to reveal her location, when the time was right and he could guarantee the girl's safety. He'd look to broach the subject with Miller when he was back in his boss's good books.

Putting the papers down on the bed, he heard the reedy sound of the buzzer for the flat, and one of the girls going to answer.

'Dad,' Eva called, her voice muffled by the door. 'Ellie's here to see you.'

'Coming, love. Send her up,' he answered, wincing as he rose from the chair.

Within a minute or two of waiting at the door, Ellie popped out from the lift. Drake hadn't seen her for a number of weeks, but it seemed to have done her the world of good. She appeared to be walking without any discomfort and any signs of injury were well and truly gone. He envied her for it.

'Chief,' she beamed.

He returned her smile with a slight nod. 'Ellie.'

'Sorry to come round unannounced. I thought I'd stop by and check in before the big day.'

'Big day?'

'Us starting back.'

'Oh. That.' He scrunched his nose up. 'Surprised you hadn't gone back already, what with your Wonder Woman-like healing abilities.'

'Whoa, steady on there, Drake. Don't be too enthusiastic about it or anything.'

Drake huffed. He suddenly felt very old by comparison with Ellie's burning enthusiasm. 'Yeah, well. Nothing about it will be that exciting. By all accounts it's going to be a quiet start. Might do us both some good, all things considered.'

She gave him a grin before whispering: 'About that . . . have you had any further calls from *you know who?*'

'No. Think it's too early for that, as we're only a couple of weeks into March. Think it will be next week or so.' He paused and considered the DS, wondering if she had thought of something he hadn't. 'Why? Has something come up? Is that why you're here?'

'No. Sorry.'

'Would you like to come in? Maybe go over those transcripts and see if we can figure something out? Unofficially, naturally.'

Ellie tilted her head. 'I would – unofficially.'

Drake stepped aside and let her in. She looked about the open plan kitchen, clearly impressed.

'Wow, obviously I'm at the wrong rank.'

'You really have a thing for houses and interiors, don't you? But don't worry, this one is all flash and no trousers. The walls are as thin as anything – I should know, I get to listen to the girls music whether I like it or not.'

Ellie cocked an eyebrow at him. 'Just didn't have much growing up, I guess. Anyway, Bella's not quite there yet, thankfully. Though the crap we have to watch on TV . . .'

'I shudder at the thought. My office, if you can call it that, is just through—'

Drake was cut off by the blaring of his mobile. He must have left the volume on too high.

It was Miller.

Does she have my brain tapped or something?

He answered with a gruff greeting.

'John, not long until the big day and you're back.' Miller's voice sounded as dry as the Sahara Desert; if that was her attempt at being friendly, she needed to try again. Their relationship had become strained since he'd had time off when he and Becca were estranged, and he'd left her stretched on resource. He hoped he could repair it in time, but it had been a tough few years. Perhaps things would always be broken between them.

'What is it with everyone calling it a big day?' He sighed. 'Anyway, yes, Laura. Itching to get going, if I'm being completely honest.' He kept his voice low so that Ellie didn't hear that particular comment. 'I hope you've got something lined up for me?'

Drake raised a hand in apology to his DS and pointed to the spare room. Ellie nodded and went on through, her footsteps echoing on the wooden flooring while he continued on the phone.

'Right now? Nothing directly,' Miller said. 'It will be much the same as before. You're going to be the first to check in on any murders coming in before we pass on to CID. Perhaps some sharing of DCI Collin's case load, but we'll see about that.'

'We know how that went last time.'

'Yes, well . . .' She paused. 'You know the job.'

He was about to speak when she jumped in. 'Sorry, just one second. Got another call.'

Drake hung around in the kitchen, waiting patiently until his boss came back on the line.

'John, scratch what I said before. Look, it seems you've got a chance to get back in the saddle early.' She sounded wary, as though she wasn't as happy about the news as he was.

He knew the question that would follow.

'Would you take a look at a case that's just come in from Response, seeing as we're in the firing line this week and you're so itching to get going, after all? I'll send over the address now. You'll be pleased to know details are suitably lacking.'

He smiled. 'I thought you'd never ask.'

5

'You don't mind me coming along, do you? I got the tube here and don't fancy trekking back yet. It took like an hour or so just to get here,' Ellie said as they exited the lift into the dreary underground carpark. Her shoes echoed loudly on the tarmac compared to her boss's.

'Things a little quiet at home for you or something?' Drake asked absently, pressing the key fob to unlock the car and splitting off to the driver's side.

She looked over at him as she opened the passenger door. 'No . . . Well, actually, *yes*. I like to keep busy – surprise – and these last few weeks have been a little torturous, it has to be said. Not quite DI Granger levels of admin busy work torture like last year, but torture all the same.'

Ellie closed the door and settled into her seat before giving her knee a quick rub, hoping Drake wouldn't notice. It was still a little bit too stiff for her liking.

He looked over as he put his seatbelt on. 'Things will improve, Ellie. I'm sure. "The only way is up", and all that shit.'

'Thanks. That's really convinced me, Chief.'

He gave her an amused look. 'Glad to be of service.'

Drake pulled away from the parking space and the car crawled over to the automated gate. It suddenly dawned on Ellie that she'd missed an opportunity to raise what had been troubling her: the dreams, and her feelings of guilt about what had happened to Fiona Spencer. She wanted to know if it had happened to him after such encounters, or whether he'd been having similar experiences since their latest case. She realised she'd not actually pressed him much about past cases, other than The Family Man. What else must he have been subjected to over the years that she wasn't aware of? He must have a locker full of stories. Perhaps it was for the best that she raised her worries another time, rather than dredging up the past. Or maybe never, if she had her way and blocked Len's voice out.

The solid metal gate wound up, slowly bathing them in sunlight. 'Oh, and can you do the directions, Sergeant?' Drake asked, distracted by exiting the car park.

'Really? That damn satnav still not working?' she said, pulling down the sun-visor as they passed the empty visitor parking area.

'Got it in one – you're on it today, aren't you? But yes, haven't gotten round to it quite yet.'

'All right, fine,' she groaned, taking out her phone. 'Where're we headed?'

'Somewhere near Victoria Tower Gardens. Hang on, I'll stick it in your phone – you just guide, yeah?'

'Okay.' She handed it over to him. He tapped out the address and gave it back to her.

'Oh, that's not too far. Thought it was further for some reason.'

'It's London, Ellie. You know that means sod all with the traffic round here. Plus, it's mid-afternoon and getting dark soon . . .'

She raised her eyebrows and nodded in acquiescence. 'True.'

The sunlight strobing between the buildings was becoming hypnotic, even at the slow speed they were driving, and Ellie felt her eyes drifting off as they rumbled on towards the crime scene Drake had been summoned to. She blinked several times and sat up in her seat, determined not to fall asleep. She needed to be on point. This wouldn't do.

Ellie gave Drake another direction before he muttered that he didn't need any further as he knew the rest of the way.

'Say, Boss . . . Have you heard any news about Dave?'

The last time she'd spoken with their former colleague and Drake's old friend, he was still in physiotherapy from the attack he'd helped to foil at her in-laws. Sadly, his prognosis was not quite as rosy as the doctors had initially thought. Her colleague wasn't responding to the physio quite like they'd all hoped he would.

Drake pursed his lips. 'He's still wheelchair-bound unfortunately, if that's what you're asking.'

Her heart sunk. Another thing to add to her guilt. It was down to her DS Bradfield had been injured. Dave wouldn't have been there and wouldn't have been hurt if she hadn't made the costly mistakes with the Spencers all those years ago. 'Oh no, really? Still?'

'Yes,' Drake paused as though he was trying to choose his words carefully, growling as the sun caught him in the eyes. 'Ellie, you need to try and put that behind you, okay? What happened to Dave was down to Dave, and Dave alone. He didn't have to stay and watch over your family. You didn't make him do anything he wouldn't have chosen to do himself. He's told you as much.'

'But . . .'

'No. Stop. Don't burden yourself. You can't control what

other people decide to do. How could you anticipate the absolute shit show that would follow Inspector Elgin's inaction all those years ago? You'd go insane.'

'I guess,' she said, looking down at her shoes.

'Besides, the Spencers wouldn't have turned into what they did had I caught the Man all those years ago.'

Ellie chose to drop it. Though she noticed how Drake still referred to Samuel Barrow as 'the Man'. Apparently, he'd never liked the ironic full moniker of 'The Family Man'. She couldn't say she blamed him.

Her boss glanced over at her before returning his eyes to the road, lazily palming the steering wheel. 'Are you going to his retirement party?'

She sighed. 'I still can't believe it's happening.'

'Believe me, neither can he. He's been after it for years, and all he had to do was get stabbed. If he'd known, he would've probably got in the way of a knife years ago, albeit minus the wheelchair. But, medical retirement – onto a winner there.'

She smirked. 'Chief, that's not funny.'

'Sort of is.' A large bus blocked the view on the driver's side, casting them both in shadow. 'Right, looks like we're as close as we're going to get now. Just before sunset, too.'

Drake pulled up into the rare commodity that was an empty parking bay in London and killed the engine, drumming the steering wheel for a second with his fingers before working on his seatbelt. While Ellie undid hers, a man wandered past with a comically large ladder and propped it up against some scaffolding just a few metres down from the car. It reminded Ellie of the start to some sort of comedy sketch show.

She scratched her head. 'Right, time to get back on the horse, I guess. Does Miller know I'm tagging along?'

'Nope. And you know, you're the second person to use a

horse analogy today?' Drake said, looking across at her with a hand on the door handle. 'Anyway, Miller doesn't need to know, either. We'll be in and out in no time . . . Oh, and I'll open the boot for you too. We'll need some overalls, etc. Think there's still enough there.'

'You're the boss, I'll shove the blame firmly in your direction, should I need to.' She flashed a smile, checking for cars before opening the door out into the road. 'Oh and, Chief? Don't go walking under that ladder. It's bad luck. Invites the devil into your life, supposedly.'

She received an exasperated sigh for her warning. 'Yes, Ellie.'

6

Drake headed for the Thames, east of where they'd parked up. He dodged between the sea of cars stuck in traffic, Ellie following close behind with a plastic bag stuffed full of the necessary masks, gloves and overalls. He'd given her advice short shrift and walked under the ladder and scaffolding anyway. He didn't believe in such nonsense. What next? Avoiding stepping on three drains too?

Regardless of the traffic not moving, he'd still received a few pathetic honks for holding them up, even if it was only a matter of a few feet. He'd ensured one driver had been on the receiving end of an angry glare which had quietened them soon enough.

'Supposedly it's just through here,' Drake said in Ellie's direction. He sidled past a woman and her two children passing through an ornate wrought-iron entrance gate, and entered the park. There were a good few people still milling around in the fast-descending dusk, or making their way along the mature, tree-lined path next to the river, having had their fill of the view. The immediate vicinity didn't give an indication that anything untoward had taken place, so the crime scene must be somewhere further along. Drake remembered that Miller had mentioned an underpass.

'Think it's that way, Drake. In line with where the traffic is getting heavier before the bridge.'

'I think you're right.'

They made their way along the short path through the well-tended grass to the main route lining the walled river's edge, and soon spotted a female officer in a Response uniform with a cap and fluorescent hi-vis jacket. She was remonstrating with someone Drake assumed must be a civilian. Beyond the quarrelling pair was the underpass, but it appeared to have been cordoned off for some kind of building work, owing to the number of orange traffic management barriers lining the entrance to keep Joe Public at bay.

The blonde civilian continued, '. . . Look, if I could just leave? I won't tell anyone. I just want to be on my way. Please?'

'You'll have to wait, sir. You're our primary witness and part of a crime scene. Just wait over there at that bench, as I've already said.'

'But . . .' The man hitched his glasses up his nose. 'I've got to get home.'

'Sir, *please*, we've been over this. Just move over there. Now. Someone will be along soon to talk to you.'

The irritated man made for the nearest bench by the river, hefting his laptop bag over his shoulder just as Drake was preparing to get involved.

The PC turned to them. 'This is a crime scene. You'll have to—'

'No need for that.' Drake flashed his ID, and Ellie did the same.

'Oh. Whew, makes a change. People can be so ignorant at times.' The PC hitched up her cap to scratch her forehead, revealing a flash of brown hair. 'You wouldn't believe the sheer number who don't seem to care that someone's been killed, and remain intent on moaning about how it's impacting them. Can't they see the path is closed, regardless? The bright orange barriers? It's just ridiculous.'

'Least they're not hanging around with their phones trying to get some videos for social media,' Ellie chimed in, while taking in their surroundings.

'There is that,' the PC nodded. 'Right now, though, I've just got that guy acting strangely. I think he must be in some kind of shock. He's been desperate to leave since we got here after he called it in.'

'Hmmm, think we'll need to talk to him soon. Don't let him out of your sight, please.' Drake said, peering sternly at her to hammer the point home. 'Anyway, what are we dealing with, PC . . . ?'

'Yarning.'

'Okay, PC Yarning. What can we expect ahead?'

'Not much. My colleague called it in after we got the initial call from that man, Ryan Brant. My colleague, PC Tompson, told me to stay here and cordon off this side while he worked the other. He's the only one who's been in and seen what's happened, outside of Mr Brant there.'

'Go on.'

The PC took a deep breath. 'Okay, so, it's a white male, believed to be mid-forties. The witness says he found him in the middle of the underpass resting up against a wall. As you can see, the area is not supposed to be accessible at the moment. But our gallant witness here,' she said, rolling her eyes and cocking her head in Ryan Brant's direction, 'decided that wasn't going to stop him and sneaked through anyway, coming across the victim soon after. Let's just say he didn't stick around for long after discovering the state the body was in.'

Drake frowned. 'I see. That bad?'

'Apparently so. But I'll leave you to your investigation to discover that.'

'All right. We'll be back soon. Thanks, Yarning.'

'Sounds promising, Boss,' Ellie said as they left PC Yarning to keep an eye on the cordon and her witness.

'We'll soon see. Let's take it slow – don't want to miss anything in this fading light. And we best get suited up. We don't need further contamination of the scene for SMT, CID or otherwise.'

'Sure thing.'

Fully kitted out in his "favourite" mask and gloves, complete with overalls, Drake studied the underpass access point while he waited for Ellie to finish. The walls surrounding the entrance appeared to have been hastily white-washed recently, only partially succeeding in covering up the heavy graffiti which adorned the walls beneath. The lighting seemed to be either broken or very dim from their vantage point. Perhaps that was part of the work that was supposed to be carried out, but there was no sign of any workmen milling around the cordon to confirm or deny what they'd been up to. Drake had always wondered what workmen did on the days they downed tools and seemingly left work abandoned. The pub, perhaps?

'This all seems rather ominous, don't you think, Drake?' Ellie said, taking up position next to him.

'Something like that,' he said, with a frown.

'Hey, you realise this is the first crime scene we're attending that is exclusively new for both of us?' she said, her eyes shining. 'I don't think that Family Man scene in Yorkshire counted, not really, and you beat me to it at the woods that time.'

'Heh, you're right,' he said. 'Let's go in.'

Drake rounded the orange barriers at the entrance. One of the few remaining lights flickered above, casting an ominous dim glow in the damp passage. He was surprised any light got through at all with the amount of thick, filthy cobwebs smothering it.

A few steps further along, a draft wafted through the underpass: and with it, the sudden, putrid stench of death. The smell caught in his nostrils, causing him to recoil despite himself and his mask.

Bloody hell, I hadn't prepared myself for that. At all. Wake up, man.

He put the back of his gloved hand to his nose, taking a second to acclimatise to the odour. It sounded like Ellie had just had the pleasure thrust upon her too, and was spluttering loudly behind him.

'God, Chief, that got me right in the back of the throat. Urgh, that's so grim . . . so, so grim.'

Drake decided against offering up any sage advice and continued on.

A number of wooden pallets laden with sacks of concrete, gravel and other building supplies lined both sides. They were wrapped in plastic as a means to keep them in place, and the sheer height of the pallets served to obscure a complete uninterrupted view of the underpass. There were no obvious signs of a body yet, other than the smell.

'Must be on the other side of these pallets, I guess,' he murmured.

Drake took the small torch he'd taken to keeping from his pocket and flicked it on, the stark white light at odds with the halogen above them. The beam highlighted a smattering of months' old mulched leaves and detritus amidst the rough tarmac, but still nothing of note. It suggested the crime had occurred or started from the other end.

He shone the light further ahead, and finally spotted a sign of what they were there for. A black leather shoe was protruding round the corner of a wooden pallet.

Drake glanced back over his shoulder. 'Here, Ellie. Looks like that's our man up ahead.'

'Gotcha,' she answered excitedly, a slight echo to her muffled voice. 'You lead the way.'

He rounded the pallet, minding the surrounding floor area. The shoe became a pair, which led to grey, blood-spattered trouser legs and the mutilated victim they'd come to see.

Drake winced at the sight of the slumped remains revealed by the stark light, while Ellie gasped as she rounded the pallet behind him. Above the body, an enormous smear of blood led from the whitewashed wall to the place where his remains had come to rest.

Drake's eyes narrowed as he took in the sight before him.

The man's body had been butchered; his arms hung loose at his sides, his bloody palms open and lifeless. His intestines coiled amidst his torn shirt and knees while a dark pool of blood had oozed thickly to his heels. There were no signs of restraints, though Drake imagined none were needed. The man had to have been incapacitated swiftly for this amount of violence to have been inflicted upon him. Any number of his injuries could have stopped him in his tracks. The victim's head was slumped over, his wavy white hair obscuring his face, the dark blood highlighted against the white in Drake's torchlight. The sight conjured images of the numerous Family Man scenes in his mind. Men and children at dining tables, heads slumped, hair drenched in blood.

It couldn't be . . .

Drake took a step around to the man's right. He knelt down and lifted the head up gently. He hoped he wouldn't see what he suspected, but the sight that greeted him made his stomach clench in sudden, disbelieving horror.

The dead man's mouth had been slit open, his tongue forcibly removed.

'What? Oh, shit. No! It can't be,' Ellie gasped, saying what he was thinking.

He collected his thoughts for a moment as he studied the mangled corpse, the remains exuding a ghastly aura, one which he'd hoped to never experience again in his lifetime. But that didn't necessarily mean what they thought it did. This type of butchery wasn't entirely unknown in London these days, and they needed to be patient. Thorough.

'Hang on a second, Ellie. Let's not jump to any conclusions.'

'Drake, the man's got his tongue missing, and his insides are all over the damn floor! What do you expect me to think?'

'You've got to be objective, Sergeant. We need to take our time here.'

'Okay . . . if you say so, Boss.'

He lifted the man's head further, revealing a slit throat. It wasn't a series of clean cuts either; it appeared frenzied with many superficial elements, much worse than either of the Family *Men* or Andrea's only kill scene.

'Okay, so that's three similarities so far,' Ellie said, frustration now cutting through her shock. 'What're we looking for now? His hands . . . th-they appear intact?'

Drake frowned, his heart pounding in his chest. The idea that Andrea must have been involved was front and centre in his mind. He wished it wasn't, but it had to be. She had to have killed again, this man was evidence of that. But why? She hadn't given any direct indication that she was planning to do so in her calls.

He set the man's head back down. 'Right, I'll check his hands now. Ready?'

'As I'll ever be.'

Drake took the man's stiff left arm in his clammy gloved hand. The man's hand remained intact, and didn't suddenly drop off in some grisly comedic fashion.

'Seems to be . . . attached?' Ellie observed.

Drake grunted in agreement, but he knew he needed to check further. The man's suit jacket and shirt sleeve appeared to have been damaged somehow. He carefully took hold of one wrist just above the joint, and pulled the material at the elbow to reveal the man's arm. There was a ragged wound around the circumference just below the wrist joint. It had been hacked through to the bone.

'Oh, shit.'

Drake nodded. 'Oh, shit, indeed.'

7

Drake stood deep in thought as Ellie flung question after question at him on inspecting the body herself. Her voice echoed in some middle-distance in Drake's mind, his own thoughts muting all outside noise before her final question brought him sharply back to the present.

'But this *could* be a copycat again, right?' Ellie moved away from the mangled body, having had her fill of the corpse.

Drake shook his head. He couldn't see it being anyone else, given the uptick in activity from Andrea since Christmas. 'It could, but we both know of only one "Family Man" outside of a prison cell at this moment in time, don't we, Ellie?'

'Well, yes. But, why? Why would she do this? It seems a little . . . random, don't you think?'

'As of now it does. But who knows? Once we get down into the nitty gritty of it, we may find there's something more. Remember it's not just Andrea we're dealing with, it's "Miray" too. Who knows how things have been twisted inside her head? It's been nearly eighteen months with no medication, no treatment of any kind. How is she living day-to-day? She's vulnerable.'

Truth was, Drake couldn't believe it either. It didn't make sense to him. Yes, she was violent. Yes, she was unhinged. But Ben Whitman's death had been the result of a very specific set of events which had led to her breakdown and the horrifically violent episode occurring. Why commit another murder? And why here, why this man? Why now? Something wasn't adding up.

Drake turned his head at the sound of approaching footsteps. A man in uniform, same as PC Yarning, was approaching from the unexplored end of the underpass.

'DCI Drake?' The man – PC Tompson, presumably – called out to him.

'Yes?' Drake put a hand out. 'Keep your distance, please. We'll come over to you shortly.'

The PC nodded. 'Yes, sir. Got it. But I think you'll want to see this.'

Drake looked at Ellie. Her eyes were wide above the rim of her mask.

'Please tell me there's not more,' she said.

'We can only hope. Keep behind me, and check the ground as we go, see if there's some kind of trail.'

'Got it.'

Heading in the direction of the male PC, Drake shone the flashlight around. The lights had effectively died on this side, making it harder to take everything in. However, he soon spotted more smatterings of blood on the tarmac and further light blood spray on the wall of the underpass. The man had to have had his throat slashed, then staggered this way.

The darkness gave way to cloudy moonlight as they reached the tail-end of the underpass. Drake manoeuvred through another set of orange barriers to see the PC standing expectantly at a small distance from a bench, and a decidedly more active cordon. Unfortunately, a crowd had gathered there, unlike the other side with only their witness and PC Yarning present. As Drake and Ellie appeared, phone cameras went up, and flashes illuminated the scene, together with the long continuous lights that indicated video recordings were being made. The crowd was much too close to the bench for his liking.

Shit. That's all I need. Where the hell are the reinforcements? Thank God I have a feckin' mask on.

He heard Ellie muttering "You've got to be kidding me," not far behind.

'Damn it, Tompson! You get that cordon moved further back. Now! That's an order,' Drake barked, gesticulating furiously at the man for letting the crowd build so close to the next part of the crime scene.

The PC scurried to adjust the cordon, waving and pushing where it was needed to get the crowd to move further away.

Drake scowled. 'Just what we bloody need.'

'I'll go and help him. Bit rusty, but I'm sure I've still got it,' Ellie offered.

'Good idea. Thanks. I'll take a look at the bench.'

Ellie set off toward the crowd, pulling her mask down and telling them in no uncertain terms to get back, in true Ellie style. She went to work on the part of the cordon closest to the river wall, as Drake took a slow approach to the bench. It was more well-lit, courtesy of a street lamp a little way down, but he continued using his torch, not wanting to miss a thing or carelessly step in evidence.

The blood trail seemed to lead away from a point on or around the bench. Perhaps the victim was sitting there before the attack started, Drake theorised. Had he been minding his own business, looking out over the river and taking in the view when he was attacked?

Drake narrowed his eyes at a sudden gust of wind. Hopefully

Dr Kulkarni, or whoever would do the autopsy, could give an indication as to when this all may have started. His immediate suspicion was that it probably happened the early hours of that morning, if not the previous night. He couldn't imagine the work there having been left unattended for more than a day or two, and there would have been more than one person taking a chance on using the underpass, regardless.

An icy cold feeling roiled in his stomach as he saw what was on the wooden bench. Drake knew what it was, even at a distance.

He swallowed hard, his throat tight as he approached the side of the bench, ensuring he didn't step where the victim's or suspect's feet might have trodden.

Before him on the bench lay the grotesque lump of the man's tongue. It rested on the slats, dark blood staining the surrounding wood. Above it, a crude Family Man symbol had been carved, chunky splinters littering the seat and ground beneath. This time there were no circles indicating children, only crosses.

Drake heard the rustle of overalls behind him as his partner returned.

'What is it, Chief?'

He stood aside in silence, letting her see what was on the bench.

She let out a heavy sigh at the sight. 'Is that what I think it is?'

'Yep,' Drake said, stony-faced. 'I'm going to need to get Miller down here. And pronto.'

8

Drake spotted the arrival of DCS Miller just as the news crews had finished setting up shop on *both* sides of the underpass. The brilliant beams of light from their cameras and the general hubbub gave Drake an unpleasant feeling of claustrophobia. He'd kept his mask and overalls on, despite wanting to tear them off and give the press what for, the familiar anger of recent times threatening to rear its ugly head. And who could blame him? He suspected he was in for a hell of a fight in finding Andrea and bringing an end to these crimes, once and for all.

"Back in the saddle" indeed, he thought.

SOCO were now finally in situ. They'd set up a white awning around the bench, the gusts of cold night-time air making it billow against its anchors. Much to Drake's relief, the curve of the underpass meant the body was out of sight to any would-be rubberneckers, both on this side of the river and on the other, where banks of flats overlooked the scene. He was pretty sure there would be a few expensive flats housing a telescope or pair of binoculars, at the very least.

Miller, her face drawn into a frown, edged around the orange barriers that were left in place. She stood with Drake just inside the underpass, the tunnel whistling as the wind peeled through, whipping at her black overcoat. When Drake had heard Miller was on her way, he'd left Ellie speaking with the witness, Ryan Brant, to get his version of what happened.

Her tired eyes regarded him for a moment before she spoke. 'Drake, I should really stop sending you to these crime scenes. What's that now, two out of two you've attended that have been batted our way? I'm not liking this new record of yours – not one bit,' she said irritably.

Drake pulled his mask down. 'Er, yes. Sorry about that, Laura,' he said, though he didn't see how any of it could really be his fault.

'So, this Andrea Whitman woman has finally put her head above the parapet.' Miller's grey eyes pierced him. 'Why now, though? And why this? It seems decidedly out of the blue.'

Drake knew he'd need to reveal the calls he'd been receiving, despite knowing the reveal of that *small* detail would not end well. The longer he kept it from her, the more likely her reaction would be somewhat . . . negative. She wasn't one for surprises. He kicked himself for thinking any good would come of concealing it. It was stupid. He knew it was. But the way in which the case had been treated since, with CID sweeping Andrea under the carpet the way they had, he'd felt it had been the right thing to do until he had something more solid than 'just' some calls.

He took a breath and braced himself. 'She's been in contact with me a few times. Phone calls.'

'You what!' Her drawn face was a potent mix of incredulity and anger. 'Since when?'

'Around once a month . . . since Christmas.'

'And you felt this wasn't pertinent information? Why in God's name didn't you tell me, John? For fuck's sake,' she spat.

'What the hell has gotten into you these last few years? I'm growing tired of this. I mean it.'

The quiet voices working the scene hushed completely at his boss's impressive outburst, the masked faces turning to try and snatch a glimpse of the commotion.

Drake sighed, glaring at the onlookers in disgust. 'What're you looking at?' he demanded. Go on, get back to work.'

Wisely, they did. The sounds returning as Drake paced in front of her, ordering his thoughts. He wanted to choose his words carefully; keep her on side as best he could, even if he did feel her decision-making was partly at fault for allowing this latest crime to take place. 'Laura, the case was with CID and essentially buried months ago. Particularly since you'd had to go along with the idea that it didn't belong with us anymore.' He scratched at his stubble. 'It didn't give me much appetite for leaving the calls with them too, knowing that. I wanted to get more information, maybe figure out where she was before getting anyone else involved. It was *me* she called, after all. I'm the only line into her.'

Miller shook her head. 'That's not good enough, John, and you know it. There are *rules*. Procedures to be followed. And with good reason.'

'Yeah, well, sod the rules. We both know they just get in the way,' he blurted, instantly regretting it.

She didn't respond. She didn't need to, her look of abject disgust said it all. Drake understood it wouldn't look good for her: for either of them. But he wasn't in the mood to be fanning people's egos. He wanted to resolve this. He wanted to find Andrea, and fast. Before any more people got hurt.

'And how, may I ask, is keeping it to yourself going? Have you found her yet? Is this scene just a pretence? Huh?'

'Well, no,' he admitted.

'And who have you used to try and locate her? You must have had help.'

'That doesn't matter now. What matters is that she's out there, and she appears to have developed a taste for killing.'

She pinched the bridge of her nose, eyes closed. 'If you'd spoken up. Perhaps *told me,* perhaps she wouldn't have had the chance to do so.'

Drake retorted. 'Come on, now, that's not right and you—'

'DCS Miller and DCI Drake? Well, I never.' A familiar-sounding, obnoxious voice called, interrupting their argument. A flurry of activity and flashes came from beyond PC Yarning's cordon as the man approached them, shadows dancing across the tunnel wall.

Drake turned in the direction of the voice. Silhouetted against the bright lights, the gangly frame of DI Melwood sauntered toward them, returning his former teammate's look.

Oh, great. Just what I needed. Why the hell is he here, of all people?

Melwood, seeming to have ignored the overalls requirement, was wearing his usual grey waistcoat beneath his suit jacket, his slicked-back grey hair uncovered. He came to a stop just past the dead man's body and the stepping plates which had been set out while SOCO started on taking pictures of the scene.

Clearly not reading the room, the Inspector spoke again when his greeting wasn't returned. 'Sorry, I'm late. Traffic was murder . . . heh.'

'Melwood. I didn't even know you were coming,' Drake said, brow firmly furrowed.

Miller nodded. 'His boss in CID informed me they need eyes on this, as the case was, or *is*, with them.'

Drake turned back to his boss. 'I thought it was with us now?'

'Before your little revelation, I was about to tell you it was likely going to be a joint venture. Now I'm not so sure.'

'Oh? Drake gone and done it again, has he?' Melwood said, his voice laced with sarcasm.

Miller ignored him and pulled Drake to one side, her voice low. 'Drake, I need to know I can trust you with this. Don't pull any more shit with me. I can trust you, can't I?'

'Of course you can. I'm the *only* one you can trust to do this properly, and you know it.'

She turned away, pacing a few steps before responding with a single word, her back still to him. 'Okay.'

He gave her a glimmer of a smile. 'You won't regret this, Laura.'

She turned back, face hard. 'I'd better not. Do not disappoint me. I mean it. You're on decidedly *thin* ice, John.'

Drake looked her in the eyes and nodded before turning back to Melwood, who was standing a surprisingly respectful distance away.

'So, you're on the case again with me, eh?' Drake asked.

'Yes, but solely from a CID perspective.' Melwood grinned. 'I'm not seconded to SMT this time, so you're not going to be ordering me around like you used to, regardless of your "superiority". Okay?'

Drake grimaced. 'I guess we're going to have to make it work.'

'Something like that.'

DI Melwood was an oddly hierarchical, petty man, *and* one with a confusing sense of humour at the best of times. But overall, he'd been a good addition to the previous case they'd worked together. Drake just hoped that the man didn't get ideas above his station, or start to become more of a hindrance than a help. That wouldn't aid anyone. Drake needed to get Andrea; and he needed to do it soon, lessening the likelihood of him having to involve

Cari and get her to talk her mother down somehow. It wouldn't come to that. It couldn't.

'So, who's on your team, Drake? DS Wilkinson, I take it?'

Drake looked over at Miller, who took a deep breath and gave him an almost imperceptible nod.

'Yes, maybe DS Strauss too, if I can manage it.'

'Too late. He's with me.'

'You mean *us*?'

'Oh yeah, sure. Of course, if that helps you sleep at night.'

Drake was less than convinced by that answer. 'You better not hold back from me, Melwood. I'm warning you.'

'All right, all right. I get it. I'm just messing with you, Drake. Sheesh.'

Drake pinched his forehead in frustration.

Melwood continued, 'Anyway, let me check out what we've got here, eh? I'll leave you both to it.' He nodded at Miller, uttering a respectful "Ma'am", and went to check over the dead man, making a song and dance when he saw the state of the man's body.

Drake turned back to Miller, noting a sadness within himself regarding her that he'd never felt before. The last few minutes made him feel their already strained relationship was now on its last legs, if not long for its deathbed.

He shook his head as he spoke.

'This is going to be a feckin' nightmare. I could keep a lid on him when he was under my leadership, but side-by-side?' He took a deep breath to illustrate his point. '. . . Shit.'

Miller cocked an eyebrow at him. 'I can always take you off the case, Drake.'

'Whoa, whoa. I didn't say that. I'll deal with it.'

'You better. I've not got time for any stupidity that arises from you two.'

'I promise.'

Miller rubbed at an eye, and took a slow breath. 'There's something else too, something I want kept between us. Got it?'

Drake frowned. 'Oh?'

'I mean it, John. No one.'

'I understand.'

She took a breath. 'It's about Samuel Barrow.'

He pursed his lips at the Man's name, balling one of his fists tightly. The Man's full name still triggered him instantly. 'Go on.'

'It's been decided that Jack Spencer is to be moved from HMP Belmarsh due to overcrowding. He's going to be serving his life sentence at the same prison as Samuel: HMP Wakefield.'

'You what?'

She closed her eyes slowly before opening them again. 'Look, as you and I both know, there's *no one* who knows the full story besides us and those closest to you on the Spencer case. The prison services don't know it was Samuel who murdered the Spencer's parents, Drake, nor does Jack – remember that. Besides, from our findings, when Samuel changed his ways, he didn't do any stalking. He just took his victims at random, so Samuel wouldn't have a clue either, and we kept all that from the press,' she paused, lowering her voice. 'And Jack's not even going to be on the same wing. Our friend Samuel's got his own sleeping quarters, just for him. Notoriety evidently has its advantages.'

Drake frowned. 'But surely there are rules against that sort of thing? At least, there used to be. The fact you have to keep it a secret surely rings alarm bells for you?'

'There's all sorts of serial killers, murderers and rapists intermingled at that place. It's where his kind are best catered for. You can take it up with the justice system. But as I've said, there's—'

'Ma'am,' Ellie said, springing from behind a pallet laden with building materials.

Miller turned to see Ellie behind her. 'Ah, DS Wilkinson. Any luck with the witness?'

'Not much, I'm afraid,' she said. 'He was coming back from lunch, decided to go the usual way, regardless of the work supposedly going on, and found our man there. He called the police as soon as he could.'

Melwood walked over, barging in on the conversation. 'So, he didn't recognise him, or see anything at all?'

Ellie's eyes narrowed at being interrupted. 'Melwood. Good to see you . . . And no, Mr Brant doesn't recognise the victim. He didn't see anything suspicious, nothing – to be honest, he didn't give me any strong feelings, either way. Other than his clear desire to go home and see his wife and kids.'

'I see. I might go and ask him myself, if that's all the same with you.'

'Er . . . Okay?'

Drake nodded at her. 'He's working alongside us, Ellie.'

She shrugged. 'Oh. Well, you better be quick, I told him he was free to leave.'

Their counterpart's eyes widened. 'What? Why!'

'For the reasons I just gave you . . . ?'

Melwood swore and sped off in the direction Ellie came from.

That's one way to get rid of him, Drake thought.

Miller offered another update. 'Oh, and Gemma Spencer has come out of her coma, too.'

Drake and Ellie looked at each other in surprise.

'Today's really going to be one of those days, isn't it?' he said with a sigh.

9

My forehead pressed against the tiles. I turned off the shower and watched the blood spiral away down the plughole with an unpleasant gurgling sound. The lifeblood of someone being swept away for good. It unnerved me, not that that was hard to do these days, with my "condition" being the way it was. The scenarios of what could have happened were petrifying. The idea that I could have hurt someone . . . It didn't bear thinking about.

But that didn't stop the thoughts. The constant stream of consciousness. The voices.

Whose blood was it? Were they still alive? Were they hurt somewhere? In need of help?

'Why can't I remember?' I ran my fingertips down the tiles. A few watery pink drops trickled down the polished white of the bathroom tiles, an almost-parallel shiver running down my spine. The silence grew ever starker as the plughole finally sputtered into silence. Each breath was beginning to sound like thunder in my ears, the heavy feeling that had once seemed so alien taking hold in my mind again.

* * *

I snapped into consciousness, the sheer whiteness of my surroundings disorientating me momentarily.

Something was resting on my lap.

Squinting as my eyes adjusted, I took in the sight of the white tray amidst a sea of smooth white sheets. A white rose stood in a white vase, and a boiled egg in an egg cup paired with some buttered toast had also been placed carefully on the white tray. My hands went to my hair which felt smooth and dry as I ran my fingers through it. I'd come to dressed in black silk pyjamas, not a drop of blood to be seen.

The bedroom was a familiar sight of late. A room devoid of anything but the basics. A sea of white that would one day swallow me whole.

A solitary white chair stood in the corner. A white dressing table next to it, complete with a white stool. The bed frame, white. The sheets were much the same, as were the walls and floorboards. The only things not sapped of colour were my clothing and me, though I wasn't far behind. I had no idea how long it had been, but my skin had taken on a pasty, almost translucent look.

'Welcome back.'

'Huh?' The voice sounded familiar. Dazed, I looked up, but I couldn't see where it was coming from.

'You gave me quite the scare there, you know. I thought you would never wake up.'

'W-who . . . ?' I twisted and turned, trying to find the source of the voice before giving up. 'Yes, sorry.'

I blinked heavily, my eyelids clicking as I tried to clear the brain fog. Speaking felt like an out of body experience.

'Maybe you could tell me what happened? I think it might

have been a dream. There was . . . blood. *So much blood*. I was covered in it. I had to have a shower to get it all off. There was just . . . I-It was horrible.'

'That's not for me to say, Andrea. Perhaps you should . . . speak with *her*.'

'Her?'

'Yes. Your mother.'

I winced at the painful throb in the back of my skull. 'I . . . I don't want to do that.'

'We all do things we don't want to do sometimes, Andrea. You know that more than most. Though you may not realise it.'

What did they mean? "Me more than most"? The implication was starting to scare me. What had I done?

'Now, eat up. You must be famished,' the voice smiled.

They were right, I *was* hungry.

Somehow, I had worked up an appetite.

10

'Drake! Ellie! Wait!'

Ellie heard Melwood calling over the London din. She turned back to see the man doing his best to catch up with them, and almost getting hit by a car for his troubles. He remonstrated angrily at the driver amidst the wave of red, white and amber lights before adjusting his suit jacket for the final few steps.

'Yes?' Drake said wearily.

'If we're going to be working together, I think it best that we share a base of operations, don't you?' Melwood looked up at the ladder Ellie had warned Drake about earlier.

'Not that damn broom cupboard again, I hope?' Ellie quipped.

Though the room they had used for the Spencer case had served its purpose on the previous case, it wasn't a room she was keen to revisit in a hurry. And having worked with Gemma there, Jack and Fiona Spencer's undercover sister, it held a few bad memories for her now. Plus, she couldn't say she'd miss the smell of stale coffee and mildew either.

'No, no,' he said, sounding a little out of breath. 'Managed to nab us one of the rooms in the main office in your neck of the woods.'

Drake gave him a hint of a smile. 'Oh? Good job. Seems you've a bit of clout in your day job. Thanks, Andrew.'

'Yes, something like that.' Melwood frowned, running a hand through his hair. 'I've set the team to identifying this man. He only had his phone on him, so nothing to identify him immediately, sadly. Hopefully we'll gain access soon.'

'Good man. Least someone has resource for once,' Drake said.

Melwood nodded. 'Indeed. We'll track her down before she kills again.'

'Here's hoping.'

Melwood appeared to want to talk further, but Ellie felt Drake wasn't in the mood, and she wasn't either, truth be told. Maybe it had affected her boss more than he was letting on?

'Okay, so we'll meet tomorrow morning, yeah?' she proposed.

The DI nodded. 'Sure. Sounds like a plan.'

Melwood departed soon afterwards and Ellie dived into the car, taking a deep breath before Drake opened the door. The whole afternoon had been a mind fuck to put it bluntly, and she wasn't sure how to feel about it all. When she had gone over to Drake's place earlier, she hadn't been prepared for attending an active crime scene. And she certainly hadn't been prepared to discover a whole new potential Family Man scene, nor one that she would now be on full-time. Len was going to love the news.

Oh, shit. Len.

'Problems?' Drake asked, seeing her face as he settled in.

She shifted in her seat to face him while rubbing her troublesome eye.

'Something like that, yeah. How can you take this in your stride so easily? What's your secret? Or has this bothered you more than you're letting on?'

'Oh, it *is* a surprise, don't get me wrong,' he said, giving her a look. 'But it's happened, and we have to get on with it. Try our best to treat it as we would if it were just another case. Distance yourself, remember? I'm pushing myself to do that too.'

'She's threatened you, Chief. Maybe they seemed like empty threats at the time, but now . . .'

'That's just the ravings of the Miray persona, I'm sure of it,' he said. But he didn't sound convinced.

'Okay. But please, be on your guard, yeah? Maybe you and the girls should stay somewhere else?'

'No one knows we're there apart from you, Miller, and Strauss, as far as I know.'

'Yes, but what would you say if it were me and Bella?'

He looked to be on the verge of conceding with that final point. 'Mmm, I'll think about it.'

'You better,' she said, though she knew that it would probably take a lot more prodding for him to take his own advice. He was stubborn, she knew that much.

'Boss, what would you say if I said I was planning on seeing Gemma tomorrow morning in the hospital?'

'I'd say it's a good idea, though I'd tread carefully. Her sister died, remember? Plus, she may not have all her faculties fully intact just yet. If she ever will again. I guess you'll find out soon enough.'

The dream she'd had earlier resurfaced, the sickening sound of Gemma's sister hitting the wood reverberating in her mind. Ellie had a sudden urge to tell Drake everything troubling her.

Best keep focus on the case now. That's all that matters.

'As if I could forget.' She looked away, biting her knuckle so he couldn't see her moment of weakness. She'd have to tell Gemma. Regardless of what happened, Fiona had been the ex-DC's sister. She couldn't just pretend, could she? That's why she wanted to see her, after all. To tell her what had happened. To confess. It was only right.

'Want me to come with you?'

'N-no, I'll be fine with it,' Ellie said, settling back into her seat. 'You focus on getting everything up and running with your best buddy.'

He rolled his eyes. 'Your wit knows no bounds, Ellie,' he said, as the car rumbled into life. 'I mean that.'

'Thank you.'

* * *

Ellie waved Drake off from the pavement of the quiet street, the stinking plume of exhaust soon dissipating. Normally she'd be at her front door and in the house within seconds, but something was stopping her from moving an inch. She didn't want to get into another argument with Len once she'd told him about the developments. It wouldn't help. But keeping it from him? She didn't like the slippery slope that would lead her down either.

You're better than this, Ellie. Come on, pull it together.

A few more hesitant seconds passed before Ellie steeled herself. Taking a gulp of night air, she made her way to the doorstep. The gulp inadvertently kicked off a series of gaping yawns, the last of which she was in the midst of when the door opened before she'd got her keys out.

'You're late tonight.' Len's voice was thick with suspicion as he emerged from the darkness of their house.

'Yeah, sorry. Things took a turn.'

He gave her a non-committal smile and made way for her, closing the door behind her with a thud as she removed her coat.

'Nothing too serious, I hope?'

She paused with her coat in hand as her mind flitted between two responses.

Honesty, Ellie. Honesty . . .

'Erm, no. Nothing too bad,' she said, cringing internally. 'Standard case for now – just meant I was back at the coalface earlier than expected.'

'That's good, I guess? You're not one for sitting still anyway,' he said, his hands in his back pockets as he rocked on his heels.

'Is Bella still up? I know it's late, but I thought she might have snuggled down on the sofa or something,' she asked, going to the doorway of the lounge and peering in.

'No, you missed her this time, love. Sorry.' Len clasped his hands on her shoulders. 'She's upstairs asleep.'

'Bugger.'

'Maybe next time, eh? Hey, perhaps in a few days we can both take her to school?'

'Yeah, okay. Let's aim for that.' She turned him around and nudged him towards the stairs. 'Let's get some sleep.'

He climbed the stairs, but she paused for a moment and watched him go, sadness washing over her.

Why did I lie about today? What's the matter with me?

11

Drake had tossed and turned all night. He couldn't get the image of the dead man out of his head. The blood smearing down the wall like that. The sheer amount of it. The total barbarity of what he'd had to endure at Andrea's hands. Despite the similarities to the Family Man scenes which Drake had largely grown numb to, this one hit differently; an unstable woman inflicting such pain upon another person, perhaps not knowing what she was doing.

It was sad.

That was the description that kept cropping up in his mind, amidst the flurry of blood and carnage. Sadness.

Drake pulled himself out of bed and into the en-suite bathroom. It was one of the small luxuries he'd afforded himself when viewing places for them to stay, and one that he was extremely pleased about, the stipulation justifying itself in a matter of hours. The idea of sharing a bathroom with two teenage girls struck fear into his very soul.

'Eva? Cari?' he called, emerging from the bedroom, ready to go. 'You guys better be ready for school and leaving soon. Just because you had an inset day yesterday, doesn't mean you can make up your own version today, got it?'

There was no response. No pithy remarks.

Just cold silence.

'Eva? Cari?' he frowned, listening out for any sounds of activity.

None came.

The thoughts of Andrea breaking in and grabbing Cari in the night entered his mind as he raced from his bedroom to each of the girls' bedrooms. He burst into each room in turn and each left him wanting.

Shit, shit, shit.

Frantic, he grabbed his phone, and called Eva while scrambling around the rest of the flat, looking for any tell-tale signs of forced entry or a struggle.

It had almost rung out when he heard the sound of a ringing phone and giggling. The entrance to the flat burst open, and the girls poured in.

'Jesus!' Drake roared. 'Where have you been?'

They both reeled from his outburst before Eva answered. 'Huh? Sorry, we just went out and grabbed some breakfast from the café down the road.'

'Why didn't you tell me? I was worried!'

Drake didn't know whether to laugh or cry.

'Come on . . . Dad, we're sixteen, not ten. I even grabbed you a bacon sandwich, got that gross brown sauce on it, just as you like it. No idea how you can eat that,' Eva retorted, tossing the grease-stained brown paper bag on to the kitchen counter.

Cari bowed her head, her dark hair hiding her face. 'Sorry to have worried you, Mr Drake,' she said softly.

Drake ran his hands through his still damp hair and gripped the edge of the counter before putting up a hand in a gesture of peace. 'It's all right, Cari. I shouldn't have shouted at either of you. I'm sorry.'

'Yeah . . . Erm, good,' Eva said, obviously having expected more of a fight.

Truth was, he was too relieved to admonish them further. His reaction told Drake all he needed to know about his mental state. All too clearly. They would need to move, and soon.

Drake ascended in the metal coffin to the usual floor which housed his desk space and their new investigation room. The battered old briefcase at his side containing the precious notes from the Andrea transcripts. The lift emitted a newly fixed sharp (and very, very obnoxious) *ping!* on arrival at the floor. He frowned at it as he exited to the thrum of the office, the noise loud even at this point down the corridor. He wasn't late either, it was still early. It made him almost feel guilty. Drake was pleased to see the leaks in the ceiling had been fixed since he was last there. Without a single drip bucket in sight, it was positively palatial compared to Christmas time.

Before he'd left the girls, he'd told them in no uncertain terms to let him know where they were, if they were staying out with friends, all the usual things that he shouldn't have to ask twice, but still had to on a daily basis. He hoped to God they did as he asked. He had to trust them; he couldn't keep them under lock and key until the case was over, he knew that. But knowing what he did, it was hard.

Rounding the corner, he grabbed a cup of his favourite bilge water from the coffee machine in the kitchenette, demolishing two plastic cups in short order. A DC he didn't know frowned at him as he gulped them down, uttering a friendly "Looks like you needed that." When the man received nothing more than a grunt for his troubles, he left Drake to it.

Drake leant against the counter for a short while. From his vantage point, he could see movement in Miller's office between the half-closed blinds, but he made no move to go and say good morning. After yesterday, it was probably best to give her a wide berth for a while.

'Drake, good to see you in person for a change.' A familiar voice came from the other end of the kitchenette, the slightly clipped German accent giving the speaker away.

He turned to see DS Luka Strauss, his mop of brown hair unkempt as usual; all of him was unkempt, if Drake was being truthful. The man looked like he hadn't slept in weeks.

'Strauss, same to you. And thanks again for your help with the phone calls. Shame it's come to this, though.' He pressed a button on the coffee machine again, not intending for it to be quite as loud as it was when it started up, the noise making him grimace.

The DS nodded and spoke over the din. 'Yes, quite. Who knew she would go this far?'

'Indeed.' He grabbed the brimming cup. 'You're officially on the case now anyway, I hear?'

'Yes. But now I'm – what is the saying, "caught between a rock and a hard place" –because of CID and SMT.' The corners of his mouth twitched. Strauss wasn't usually one for humour.

'Mhmm. And sorry to hear that Melwood grabbed you first,' Drake said, pausing to neck his third and final coffee. 'Perhaps I should get them to officially switch you over to us rather than you always being on a first-come, first-served basis, eh?'

'Would it be rude of me if I said, please God, yes?'

'Not at all,' Drake smirked. 'Right, I'm going to get over to the new investigation room. You coming?'

'No, I'll be a few minutes. You go ahead.'

'All right.'

Drake strode to the room that was now theirs for the foreseeable. Unlike the previous side-room down a maze of corridors, this one was quite the opposite. It took up half of one end of the main office space, encircled in internal glass windows. Closing the door behind him, he almost felt a twinge of regret for the privacy of the old room. This one felt like he was in a goldfish bowl. He could see why teams used to paper the windows. Drake was already itching to do the same.

A large TV screen took up most of one end of the room, while a table not dissimilar in size to the *Titanic*, filled the middle. A conference call unit sat at its centre, inconveniently placed so that anyone using it would need to stretch. A bank of desks on both sides of the conference table completed the room, together with a side office, which he would most definitely be appropriating before Melwood got his hands on it.

Drake had only been in the side room for a matter of minutes when he heard the clank of keys on glass on the main door, and a wheezing DI Melwood entered.

'Ah, shit.' He huffed. 'You beat me to it.'

Drake gave him a shit-eating grin. 'Yes. Yes, I did.'

Melwood inhaled sharply through his nose as if he was going to retort, but then obviously thought better of it. 'Fair play. Can't argue about it. I got stuck in traffic, was dropping my son off at school. His first year, you know.'

'Oh? You're back with your wife?'

'No, no . . . As if I would be that stupid,' he said, waving off the idea. 'I just *finally* have joint custody resolved. Get to see him so much more now, and it's really helping me clean up my act.'

Drake was a little taken aback by his frankness. 'That's good to hear, Andrew. Glad things are on the up.'

'Thanks, Drake.' Melwood gave him a tired smile. 'That actually means a lot.'

Soon the main players in the team were assembled. Drake found it strange not having the quiet, unassuming Gemma Chambers – aka Spencer – there with them, despite the reason.

They each took a seat at the conference table. He noticed Ellie seemed distracted, as though she had the weight of the world on her shoulders.

'Okay, Ellie,' he said, his voice shaking her from her thoughts. 'You've got some business to finish up, then you're with Melwood and I for the autopsy, right?'

'Yes, boss,' she mumbled.

'Good,' he said, choosing not to ask her what was up in front of the team. 'And Strauss, you're going to focus on identifying who the hell deserved to be gutted in that underpass for now, yes?'

'Indeed, I'll see what the team can shake out. There have to be witnesses somewhere, particularly with the news having caught up with this now. We could really do with someone coming forward.'

'Excellent, and I sure hope so. Andrea needs our help.'

'Help? What? She's a crazy murderer, Drake,' Melwood piped up. 'She needs locking up, and I'll happily be the one to throw away the key. I'm surprised you wouldn't want to be ahead of me in the queue.'

Drake sighed. For every step forward the man took, he took giant leaps back with that mouth of his.

'Inspector, she's a sick woman. She can't help what she's doing. To Andrea, it's not *her* doing these things.' He twisted a pen in his hands as he tried to keep a handle on his temper. 'It's a compulsion, a manifestation of her childhood, which from the limited accounts we have, was not a pleasant one,' he said through gritted teeth. 'That and those damn Family Man videos; it set a chain of events in motion that I can't even begin to imagine. Maybe have a little sensitivity to her situation, eh?'

'Not while she's out there gutting people. Who's to say she won't come back for her daughter, eh? Or you and yours, for that matter?'

Drake shook his head, his jaw set as he strove to remain calm. The mere mention of Eva made his skin prickle. 'Let's not get ahead of ourselves. We need to practice patience with this. We'll get her. We just need to be smart about it.'

Melwood leant back in his chair, wisely choosing not to put a voice to any more of what he was thinking, as Drake continued where he left off. 'The next time she calls, we need to be on it. Perhaps with a third call being traced, we can start to get more of a correlation and narrow down a real location – either way, everyone, you need to listen to the tapes again. Maybe there's something we're missing. Melwood, that includes you. You've not had a chance yet, right?'

'Well, it was only revealed to me late yesterday that there even *were* any, Drake. So, yes. I'm a little late to the party.'

'Okay, but give them a listen sooner rather than later.'

He raised his eyebrows and leant forward. 'Is that . . . an *order?*'

Drake sighed. 'No, Melwood. It's advice. I suggest you take it.'

He clenched his fists in his pockets. Flexing and closing, flexing and closing; he needed to keep his anger at bay. The thought reminded him that he had a short session with the psychologist booked for the following morning. Drake couldn't believe he was still being made to attend them. Maybe he should float the idea of finally being discharged.

He stood. 'Okay, so, if there's nothing else. I suggest we get to it.'

The team agreed and got to work.

12

Ellie sat in the hospital café, trying to pluck up the courage to speak to Gemma Spencer. It was something she had been trying to do for the past who knows how long, and through two cups of tea. She grimaced on taking a sip from the second and finding it had gone cold.

She needed to get a grip; this wasn't just about her. Someone needed to tell Gemma what had happened, if she was cognisant enough to understand. And it may as well be someone who knew her. Or at least someone who *thought* they'd known her, in some capacity.

'Fuck it,' Ellie murmured, the teacup rattling against its saucer as she stood up resolutely from the table.

Moving with purpose, she made her to way the lift, just about avoiding the hospital bed that came shooting out of its open jaws.

'Watch it, sweetheart,' the sickly woman on the bed snapped, while the hospital porter remained silent.

Good start, she thought, pressing the button for the fifth floor and watching the doors close.

Ellie turned up her nose at the strong smell of disinfectant.

The place was making her feel itchy. Hopefully it wouldn't be too long a visit, though it felt necessary. But who was it for, really? Gemma's benefit or to assuage her own guilty conscience? Would it make a difference?

Besides, the woman was a traitor. She'd wormed her way in to the team and fed on them like a parasite, misleading them and throwing investigative morsels to her siblings. It reminded Ellie of something from a film.

The doors opened and she stepped out on to the shiny vinyl floor, her footsteps overly loud to her ears. Ellie bothered a bored-looking receptionist to double check she'd got the right wing and made her way down the corridor and it wasn't long until she spotted a policeman sitting by her destination's door. She slowed her pace, suddenly feeling intensely self-conscious. Maybe the PC should be arresting *her* after she was done revealing all?

Shaking the thought from her head, she greeted the heavy-set, balding man with what felt like an overly enthusiastic "Hello".

'DS . . . Wilkinson, is it?' he said, the act of standing to greet her seemingly an enormous effort for him, judging by the large grunt he produced.

'Yes. I'm guessing they told you I was coming?'

His tired eyes flicked over her. 'Got it in one.'

Ellie crossed her arms. 'How's she doing? Is she aware? Is she talking?'

She wondered if a policeman being posted at the door had given something away to Gemma about her situation.

'She's talking. But how aware she is of what's going on? I can't say. I don't go in. I've just been posted outside since she regained consciousness yesterday.'

'Gotcha. I shouldn't be long.'

The man nodded and sat back down.

Ellie paused at the door, her hand on the handle. She closed her eyes for a split second before bracing herself and entering.

The room was clean and functional, but devoid of anything which would stimulate *anyone's* mind, let alone someone who'd been in a coma for the past few months. A number of windows to the back and side of the bed revealed only old red brick work, a flat roof with a battered-looking ventilation pipe and more hospital buildings beyond. It didn't help that the weather was overcast and miserable, casting a cold grey light on the room, making it unwelcoming and grim.

Gemma, her body and head propped up by a large set of pillows, looked emaciated compared to the healthy young woman she'd been when Ellie last saw her. The ex-DC's long blonde hair was like straw, her face gaunt and pallid. Machines encircled the bed, many of which she was still hooked up to. Her eyes were closed, but Ellie could make out the tiniest of movements beneath the lids.

Stepping up to the end of the bed, directly in front of her, Ellie gripped the frame and spoke.

'Gemma . . . ? Gemma, it's me. Ellie.'

The woman's face flinched as though she was in the midst of a bad dream.

Ellie tried again. 'Gemma, I don't know if you can hear me, or can speak. But I thought I'd stop by and see how you are.'

Gemma's mouth moved, but no sound seemed to come out. Ellie noticed a slight increase in activity on the monitor that was to the left of the bed. Gemma seemed aware, reactive.

'Ell-Ell . . . ie?' the voice came, like the crackle of old parchment.

Ellie stepped around the bed to the woman's side, the light from the window causing her shadow to fall over Gemma's face.

'Yes, it's me. Are . . . are you okay? Do you need the doctor?'

The woman moved her lips with no sound forthcoming, before finally another disjointed word. 'Wat–er.'

'Oh! Yes, let me get you some.'

Ellie grabbed the nearby jug and poured a small glass for her. She realised the woman's mouth and throat must be as dry as a desert. The intravenous drip wouldn't have solved that in a hurry.

As she turned back, a hand shot out and grabbed her wrist. It was all Ellie could do to stop herself crying out in shock, nearly dropping the glass in the process.

Gemma lay back and released her grip as quickly as she'd grabbed her.

'Jesus, don't scare me like that, Gemma. You almost gave me a frickin' heart attack!'

Ellie swore she saw an almost imperceptible smile form, if only for a second.

She took the glass over to her. 'I'm going to tilt the glass to your mouth, okay?'

The woman gave a faint nod.

Quite the change considering her movement just now, she thought. *Is she playing me?*

Gemma pushed her head forwards slightly and took a few sips, before dropping back with a pained sigh. Ellie put the glass down.

'Okay, how about this. I'll hold your hand, and you give it a squeeze. A short one for "Yes", and a long one for "No", or something like that, yeah? Be easier than talking, though you seem to have some of your strength back, you little shit.'

The woman moved a little, as though she'd tried to laugh.

Ellie took her hand, the fingers feeling bony and brittle in her grip. It would be useful to establish at least the basics to start with. Maybe she'd heat up a little as they progressed.

Here goes nothing.

'Do you remember what happened to you?'

Ellie's hand was squeezed rapidly.

Was that a double squeeze for 'No'?

'Is that a "No"?'

One short squeeze, followed by a flicker of her eyelids.

'Got it,' Ellie said, frowning. Perhaps because it was so soon after coming out of her coma, Gemma couldn't remember, or maybe she'd suffered damage to her memory. Who knew? With her history, she could even be faking it.

'Do you remember me? Ellie Wilkinson?'

One short squeeze: yes.

Okay, that's something, at least.

'Okay . . . Do you . . . Remember your brother and sister?'

One short squeeze: yes.

Ellie decided to test her. 'Your brother is called *Jack,* right? Jack Spencer?'

One short squeeze: yes — then another double: no, quickly after.

Curious. She grunted to herself. *I might have caught her in the same lie for a second time.*

Gemma appeared to be trying to open her eyes. The fluttering becoming quicker and quicker until finally they remained open, an icy blue looking back at her.

'Rob—ert.'

'No, Gemma. His name's Jack Spencer. You don't need to pretend with me anymore. I know the plan, your secret, everything.'

This seemed to cause the ex-DC some distress. Her breathing became rapid, and she balled her hands before it became apparent what she was doing. She was crying.

'I'm—I'm sorry,' she said, her eyes squeezed shut. Her voice was dry and hollow, and painfully slow, a single teardrop running down her cheek. 'I didn't . . . *want* to.'

'I know. Jack has said as much, since. How they used you once you'd started the detective job. It all fell into place for them. But you still did what you did, Gemma. You manipulated crime scenes, tampered with evidence, lied to us – lied to *me*.'

'I . . . I wanted to help people, that's why I joined. But . . .' She panted. 'I don't remember. Anything . . .' Gemma stopped to catch her breath again. '. . . after the fires.'

The fires at Clare Baker's house? That was days before the collapse at the retreat.

Ellie reminded herself she was talking to someone not long out of a coma. Gemma still appeared incredibly groggy, though she knew her former colleague had to be lying about some things. But the timing was a stretch. However, that wasn't important right now. What was important was informing her what had happened to her family . . . to her sister.

That I killed.

'Gemma—'

'What happened to the . . . the other five men?' she blurted, before Ellie had a chance to speak.

Wait, what? Five?

Ellie couldn't have heard her right. There was only Gregory and Jorge, after Clare and Peter's deaths. Who were the other three? Perhaps Gemma was still not quite with it.

'Wait, Gemma. Did you say five?'

Gemma made a face, like a child who'd said something they shouldn't have. She forced her eyes open again, panting from the exertion of talking, remembering. 'Yes. Are they . . . are they dead?'

Better go along with it for now. I need to know if we've missed something, somehow.

'Yes. Jack and Fiona killed them,' Ellie said.

'You're lying,' she said, her face turning cold and hard.

Shit.

'But, nice try. It's coming back to me a little now . . . I remember some of what happened at the retreat with those two . . . *men* who abused us.'

She stopped amidst a fit of coughing before Ellie gave her a few sips of water.

'And how is it I'm lying exactly?'

'There's actually four, not five. So, there's still two left if they killed the ones at that hellhole . . . and–and I guess you stopped my siblings, if I'm here.'

Four? she thought, *wait, so there were still a further two men out there not convicted or killed for the abuse they'd subjected the Spencers to?*

Ellie's nerves jangled at the revelation. She tried her best to remain calm with her questioning. 'Oh? And who are the other two?'

'I don't know their names. Can't really remember them at all, actually. They kept me out of all that, unless they really n-needed me.' She caught her breath. Ellie felt she couldn't keep her talking much longer. 'Like when Drake had Jack at the station. I had to do the . . . burning.' The young woman's face was consumed by a look of disgust. 'Those two were different, though. They were never there with the ones Jack and Fiona killed. But they were *particularly* awful.'

'Do you know if he kept the information anywhere? Their names, maybe their addresses, even?'

Gemma looked deep in thought, then gave a resolute, 'No. No, I don't think so.'

Because that would be too damn easy, wouldn't it? Ellie thought, her shoulders dropping. Perhaps if she gave Gemma a few days to recover further, she might be able to remember or help give a description to a facial imaging officer to put together a composite.

'Where's my brother and sister? I want to see them.'

Ellie's mind recoiled at the mention of the word 'sister'.

'What? What is it?' Gemma asked, lifting her head from the pillow. 'H-ha-have they been arrested?'

Her throat had gone as dry and tight as Gemma's must have been. Ellie was trying hard to form the words.

'Gemma. That's partly why I'm here. I thought it best I tell you, rather than some uniform you don't know. But, it's your sister. Fiona . . . she died.'

Gemma took a deep, ragged breath. Her face screwed up as she tried to process the news, her head dropping back to her pillow. The monitors picked up a sharp increase on her vitals.

'N-no, not Fi. She didn't deserve that. She'd been through so much already,' she half-croaked, tears streaming down her face. 'My beautiful sister.'

'I'm sorry, Gemma,' Ellie said, before adding: 'I couldn't . . . It all happened so fast.'

Gemma continued crying quietly. Her body didn't seem to be able to muster anything more than that. Suddenly, she turned to Ellie, her eyes wide and accusatory, giving her a hag-like quality with her gaunt features.

'Wait . . . What? It-it was you? You killed my sister? You k-killed Fi?'

'No . . . no! That's not what I meant.'

I'm such a coward.

'You're lying.' She panted. 'You . . . You murdering fucking *bitch!*'

69

13

Drake was a couple of minutes away from his next, very important meeting: lunch at the pub. The Crooked House, to be exact.

He thought it best to take the rough with the smooth until all the smooth had run its course – likely by the end of the day, knowing his luck – and all he was left with was the sharp bumps and pitfalls of the Andrea investigation. Besides, it was one of the few opportunities he had left to meet up with Dave at the place, and the man was buying too. Who was he to turn that down?

Drake looked up at the cold, uninviting grey sky. Even with the skyline of London, when the atmosphere was like this, it easily brought him down a peg or two. Just to add to it, as though someone was listening to his thoughts, a few spots of rain began peppering his face.

He quickened his pace in response, hastily dodging his way through the burgeoning lunch-time crowd, past a couple of street vendors hawking London tat and a busker covered head to toe in silver paint, appearing to float next to his cane. Drake still didn't quite understand how anyone could make a living from that, or who even came up with the bloody idea in the first place.

Soon he had reached his destination. He entered to the low murmur of a packed table at the far end, past a stout sage green and cream corniced pillar, and the clatter of a kitchen emanating from an open serving hatch set in the wall.

'John? Over here.' Drake stopped at the weakened voice of DS David Bradfield, coming from one of their usual spots round the corner. Dave must have seen him as he passed a window on the way in.

Turning the corner, Drake's heart dropped at the sight of his old friend. Dave's hand was resting on the thick oak table, and a chair had been moved to one side to accommodate his wheelchair. It brought a lump to Drake's throat.

'Dave, good to see you,' Drake clasped his shoulder before taking the seat opposite.

'You too, John. You too,' his friend said, giving him an appreciative smile. 'It sounds like I may have caught you for the final time before the shit truly hits the fan and you're buried for God knows how long. Least that's what I heard on the grapevine.'

Impressive knowledge.

Drake wondered how it was that a man not long for retirement could still have his fingers on the pulse of what was going on, and not just in his own team. He'd miss the man. The last few months had taken their toll, and not just on Dave's mobility. His heavy moustache was now almost completely devoid of colour, not just greying, and his hair was similar.

'Yes, you could say that,' Drake said. 'Though, I really do hope it doesn't come to that and Andrea hands herself in before anyone else gets hurt.'

'Aye. But the likelihood of that is . . . ?'

'A little above zero, though I still have hope.' He gave his old colleague a wry smile. 'Anyway, we're not here to talk about me. How are you? Not long until you're back on your feet?'

'What, this?' Dave slapped the arm of the wheelchair. 'No, 'fraid not. Me and this contraption are going to be seeing a lot more of each other from now on.'

Drake's stomach lurched. 'You're kidding?'

'Nope.' The man choked up a little as he spoke. 'You would have thought with all the wounds I received that it wouldn't be the small innocuous stab in the back that would have done the lasting damage.'

'Dave—'

'But here we are,' he said, looking down at the table. 'Doctor says there's only something like a ten percent chance I'll ever walk again.'

'But that's something?'

'At my age? In my condition?' He laughed. 'Who are we kidding?'

'Come on, you can beat this. I know you can.'

Dave turned slightly to the side for a moment, seemingly ashamed. 'I can't even play fucking golf, John.' He sighed animatedly, giving Drake a sideways glance and a smirk.

Drake tried not to laugh. 'Dave, you're terrible. You had me there.'

His old mate joined in with a hearty chuckle. 'Well, it *is* mostly true, though,' he said. 'But I am going to fight it. I will get better, you mark my words. I'll be walking into this damn pub by the end of the year, and on that fateful day *you* will be buying me dinner and a pint.'

'You got it, big man.'

They carried on in a similar fashion for a while, taking the piss, laughing and joking while waiting for the food and drinks to arrive. Drake opted against a pint, having knocked his fledgling drinking habit mostly on the head again after his recent hospital visit. Being beaten half to death had that effect on a man. They'd not spoken any further about the state of Jack Spencer after the fight at the retreat. Drake felt like he should, to somehow justify how it wasn't meant to go that far. About how he was doing his best to cope with his anger, now that Eva was back with him. But perhaps it was best left unsaid.

Dave speared a slice of beef with his fork, eating like a man possessed and speaking between mouthfuls. 'So, how're you and Eva faring? Oh, and Cari too, now, isn't it?'

'Please, keep the Cari part to yourself for now,' Drake said, tapping his nose. 'But yes, it's going surprisingly well. Or should I say, it *was* going well, until all this stuff started coming up now.'

Dave's ears pricked up. 'Oh?'

'Yeah, the fact Cari's Mum is going round killing people doesn't really set me up for restful times at home now.'

'True. But you'll do right by them, John. I know you will.' Dave paused. 'Have you told her? Cari, I mean?'

'God, no. She's only just acclimatising to speaking more than a few words a day, and being around someone other than Becca's aunt and wife. If I tell her, she might regress.'

'You can't keep it from her, John. It's her mother.'

'I know, but . . .'

Dave stopped eating and stared at him pointedly. If they'd been characters in a film, he could imagine the whole pub going quiet at this precise point.

'Okay, okay. I understand. I'll deal with it. Just not right now, all right?'

'You better.'

They finished off the last of their food almost in tandem, before Dave then gave him another look. 'And how are you, in yourself?'

'This is all very direct, Dave,' Drake said, shifting his weight in his chair.

'You know me. I'm a direct sort of guy. And I know you don't have many people looking out for you right now.'

Drake sighed. 'I still miss her, Dave, if that's what you mean. I miss her when I wake up, when I'm with Eva. When I'm alone . . . It's hard.'

Dave took a deep breath. 'I can't begin to imagine. If my Judy wasn't there for me, I don't know how I'd cope.'

'Indeed . . . and, well, I heard that *bastard's* name again yesterday.' He flexed his hands beneath the table. 'For the first time in a good while. It still feels like there's unfinished business there.'

'I bet. But the scumbag is locked away. There's nothing you can do, John. Justice has been served.'

'Perhaps—'

Drake's phone began buzzing in his trouser pocket. He was growing to hate the blasted thing for its untimely interruptions.

'Shit, sorry, Dave,' he said, showing his phone. 'I've got to take this.'

Dave waved him away. The man knew the drill.

'Ellie? You okay?'

'Drake, we've . . . well, there's been a development.'

'What?'

'It's the Spencers,' Ellie paused. 'They didn't kill them all. There are more of their abusers out there.'

14

Ellie arrived back at the office just after lunch, narrowly avoiding the driving rain which began as soon as she entered the building, the wind lashing the downpour against the sliding doors as they closed. She was feeling beaten down herself. The encounter with Gemma had not gone the way she'd wanted or expected. But then, what had she been expecting? Certainly not the reveal of further loose ends from her most recent case, that was for sure.

The idea that there were more of the family's abusers out there made her skin crawl. But according to Melwood and Strauss, there'd been nothing found at Gregory's place to implicate anyone else in the abuse of the Spencer children, and there definitely wasn't anything at Jack or Gemma's flats. Though they never did get a definitive location for where Fiona lived, the presumption being she lived with either Jack or Gemma, or between the two. Two of Jack's neighbours had confirmed sightings of her toward the end of the siblings' murderous revenge.

Ellie's own strange semi-confession left her frustrated. Why did she go back on it?

Maybe it's not as clear cut as I thought it was. I did want to stop her – of course – but did I really purposefully pull Fiona off the balcony to her death?

Her mind didn't know which way was up at the moment, and the way she'd reneged on her words so quickly made her question whether her subconscious was intervening in some way.

Ellie made a quick pitstop at the coffee machine before making her way over to the investigation room. She hoped she wasn't too late.

'Ah, nice of you to join us, Ellie.' Melwood looked over at her from the coat stand as she blustered in, with Drake not far behind him.

'Oh, I see. You guys thinking of leaving without me?'

Melwood cocked his head at Drake before pulling his coat on. 'I was, but Drake here wanted to give you a few more minutes.'

Her boss nodded. 'Dr Kulkarni's going to be getting impatient, and she did say she had something of particular interest to show us. Her words, not mine.'

'Colour me intrigued. It must be interesting, if she says it is?'

'Indeed.'

Ellie peered in Strauss' direction. 'You coming too?'

He turned from his laptop. 'Oh no – not my kind of thing, really. You guys go have fun.'

If that's what you can call it, she thought.

Ellie crammed herself into the backseat of Drake's car behind Melwood for the journey over. The nonsense reason which the DI had spewed for pinching her seat was, 'Ranking officers in the front', which outraged her no end. But she'd relented; unlike Melwood in his positioning of the seat, which was crushing her despite her smaller stature. Ellie felt a small pang of jealousy at the

DI taking her seat. It felt like an invasion, however childish that might seem.

They soon pulled into the coroner's office by Queen Mary's hospital in Wandsworth. The miserable weather was similar to her last visit, though the heavy rain this time gave the place an even shittier appearance, the cladding made a few shades darker by the damp. In spite of having been there once before, it didn't lessen the feeling of dread in the pit of her stomach, now that Ellie *knew* the stench of the place and the sights that awaited her. Her developing of a strong stomach for that sort of thing was still very much in its infancy.

Their now CID counterpart strode ahead of them to the reception, trying to shield his hair unsuccessfully from the rain. Neither Ellie or Drake bothered; she figured she was probably due a shower afterwards anyway, to wash away the stink of death.

'Here for the John Doe. Dr Kulkarni's expecting us,' she heard Melwood say to the receptionist as the doors closed behind them. The smell of bleach was already infiltrating her nostrils.

Ellie took a deep breath.

'You okay?' Drake glanced down at her while they waited behind Melwood, who was still yapping away to the receptionist.

'Just geeing myself up. Still not a big fan of this stuff. Not sure I ever will be.'

'You didn't have to come. And I'm not sure "fan" is the right word for anyone visiting, unless you're Tanv.'

Ellie shook her head. 'No, I know. But I think it's necessary. Just need to get better at it.'

She was just about to take a seat when the automatic door mechanism sounded, followed by Dr Kulkarni's precise accent.

'Drake. Ellie. We really must stop meeting like this. And, DI Melwood, isn't it? You too.'

Dr Tanvi Kulkarni smiled gleefully at them, reminding Ellie

of the enthusiasm the doctor had for her work. Her long hair, which Ellie had only seen worn down in the past, was now confined in a masterfully executed bun, and the doctor's latex-gloved hands were clasped as though she was trying to stop herself clapping.

'Tanv, good to see you again,' Drake said, giving her a friendly smile.

'How's my favourite DCI doing?' Tanv put a hand lightly on his forearm, leading him through the doors. 'You took quite the beating, I hear.'

Ellie followed them through. She wasn't sure if it was her imagination, but was the doctor *flirting* with him? She didn't know anything of her background, or whether she was married or not. Ellie felt compelled to ask around at the office as soon as she had the chance.

No. Stop right there, you can't be a matchmaker for your damn boss, woman!

'Good, thank you. Much better now, though not recovering as quickly as in the past. I'm getting old,' he said wearily as they made their way down the tight corridor.

'Oh shh, you're not that old,' Tanv remarked with a playful grin.

Melwood butted in as they drew near their destination. 'All right, all right. How about you get this show on the road, eh, Doc?'

'All in good time, Inspector.' She subjected him to a wilt-inducing look while she took her keycard out for the final set of double doors which led to her lab. Beyond them would be the stainless steel post-mortem tables Ellie was dreading.

Soon after, the doors opened out into the sterile laboratory. It seemed less busy than before; because there was one less body in situ, Ellie supposed. But this time their latest victim's body had been laid on his front, his feet peeking out towards the floor from the sheet covering him.

Strange. Why start that way round?

Drake must have thought the same. 'Any reason he's on his front already, Tanv?'

Before the pathologist could respond a familiar voice came from another corner of the room.

'It's because of a particular . . . *quality* that we discovered and want you to see, DCI Drake. We got started earlier today, removing the clothes and such.'

Ellie saw the contempt on Drake's face before he composed his expression and turned at Graham Reynolds's approach.

The man was bringing over a tray of tools for Dr Kulkarni's work. He wasn't wearing his usual mask, and Ellie couldn't remember the last time she'd seen him without one. His wide mouth reminded her of the Cheshire cat from Alice in Wonderland.

'Reynolds.'

The trainee pathologist greeted them, his smile seeming a little too forced. 'DCI Drake, DS Wilkinson, and?'

'Well, aren't you just a delightful little creep?' Melwood remarked, his mouth set in a thin line. 'I'm Detective Inspector Andrew Melwood.'

Reynolds flinched slightly at the cruel comment, but didn't respond.

'How's training going with the good doctor here?' Ellie asked, trying to move them on from the awkward conversation. Drake appeared to be one for holding grudges. Their meeting a few months earlier seemingly hadn't diluted his dislike for the man one iota, and now Melwood was weighing in for some reason.

'Oh, it's been very interesting.' Reynolds eyes lit up. 'Not as interesting as the bodies you and DS Wilkinson had as part of your case a while back, but still helping with my development all the same.'

Ellie managed a weak smile. 'Good.'

'Anyway, how about we get to business?' Melwood pressed. 'Anything that you can tell us, Tanv?'

'Okay. Okay. Hold your horses. I just need to get my gear on, and you all do too, for that matter.'

Once everyone had decked themselves out in the usual white surgical gowns, they were ready to see what was waiting for them under the sheet. Tanv was now wearing her clear-framed glasses that she seemed to bring out solely for examinations or close work.

Ellie was curious what it could be she was going to reveal. They'd seen everything, surely? What more could there be?

Tanv started on recording her findings, reminding the tape of the man's height, weight, (*sans* butchered organs, Ellie presumed), eye colour and so on, using a recording device that she could stop and start at the press of a button. Presumably she'd gone through a similar process when removing the clothing earlier.

'Right, here we go then,' the pathologist said. Ellie half-expected the tape device to playback a drumroll for them. The anticipation was killing her.

Tanv gripped the sheet and slowly started peeling it back, a few specks of material sticking before eventually coming away.

Ellie soon saw that the pathologist wasn't wrong that it would make for interesting viewing. The man's back had been hacked at, the skin puckered and sliced, revealing grotesque layers of fat and tissue beneath. A variety of jagged, painful-looking shapes stared back at her.

'Drake, she can't have?' Ellie said, turning her head to the side, taking the spectacle in.

'She has,' he responded, flatly.

'Sick bastard,' Melwood said.

Andrea had carved the Family Man symbol across the entirety of the dead man's back, from his shoulders all the way down to his tailbone, the base of the triangular symbol scored and sliced from hip to hip. She'd used two crosses in place of the children's usual circular symbology as per the other carvings at the crime scene. In the cold light of the lab, with the varying purples, blues and blacks due to the man's lividity as a result of being largely on his back since, it made for a brutal patchwork.

'But he was leaning against a wall when we found him, Tanv,' Drake said.

Reynolds jumped in, excitedly. 'We believe she had killed him by this point, and leant over him, pulling his shirt up as she did her work. The strokes are from bottom to top in an upwards motion, for the most part. And there are slight abrasions from the ground or wall behind him, from being man-handled when he was pushed back.'

'Really?' Melwood looked to Dr Kulkarni for a confirmation.

She nodded. 'Yes, what Graham described is how we believe it took place. The killer took her time, too. The cuts are careful and precise – though she's no surgeon – compared to the frenzied mess of the man's neck. It's almost as though two people did it.' She looked over at Drake with her last comment. 'And don't worry, they're both right-handed, before you ask.'

'Hey, don't look at me.' Drake snapped. 'It's your *assistant* who messed that up.'

Reynolds seemingly chose not to rise to the comment or respond and gestured gently to his boss with the camera he'd picked up. She nodded, and he began taking photos. For no good reason, the flash irritated Ellie.

Melwood spoke up. 'She's really hammering home that she's taken up her sick father's mantle, eh, Drake?'

'Seems that way. Though I suspect it's Miray in control with . . . all this.' He waved his hand at the cadaver in disgust.

Ellie spoke up. 'There's nothing else, I take it. Nothing we should be aware of?'

Tanv shook her head 'No, Ellie. Not that I can see.'

'Thanks Doc.'

Tanv continued recording her observations while they remained silent. Melwood appeared to be getting itchy feet and couldn't stand still, while Drake seemed deep in thought, a frown not leaving his brow.

'Okay, Graham. Let's turn him over.'

Once they'd got the body on to his back, Tanv let them know that she'd already removed the intestines, seeing as Andrea had basically done it for her anyway.

'Very kind of her,' Drake said, grimly.

'As you've already pointed out, Drake, the neck is severely damaged. Much more so than I understand was the case for the Family Man victims you've dealt with. Those injuries were more clinical in nature, even the final one of that older gentleman?'

'Yes, even the Man's son wasn't quite so savage, nor was Andrea's killing of her husband, Ben Whitman. It's as though she had some kind of pent-up rage with this particular one. I don't quite know why.'

'Better ask her for me, when you see her,' Tanv said, dryly.

'Hmm.'

A phone started ringing, the sound reverberating around the clinical room, an obnoxious tone that could only belong to one person.

Melwood put up a hand as he answered the phone. 'Sorry, *sorry*. I'll go outside, you carry on.' He began speaking in hushed tones until the doors closed behind him.

'Drake. I am sorry, you know.'

'Huh?'

Reynolds pulled down his mask and spoke again. 'The mistakes . . . the delays. It was completely unintentional, I assure you,' he said, looking genuinely remorseful.

Drake's eyes hardened. 'That doesn't make things right, Reynolds. More people may have died due to those errors. I know you're learning, and people make mistakes. But the only way to make it right is to never make those mistakes again, got it?'

Reynolds nodded. 'Got it.'

Melwood strode purposefully back into the room. 'Drake? Ellie?'

'What? What is it?'

'We've got a name for the chap on the slab, finally.'

'And?'

'It's a man by the name of Pearce Fleming. An accountant, three kids. Still married. Or was, I suppose.' He sounded out of breath. 'Wife reported him missing that morning. Then she did again that night, once she'd got scared, having seen the news.'

'Shit. Poor woman,' Ellie said.

'Poor kids, too,' Drake added. 'I take it you've got the address?'

'Of course. Strauss is sending it your way now. I was hoping you guys could take the lead on that little bit of work?' Melwood said, wincing slightly at the request.

Ellie raised an eyebrow. 'Oh? You not fancy it?'

Melwood looked at Drake, as though he was communicating something that her boss would understand more. 'I've got a school thing, it's my son. I got the call right after the one from Strauss about our man, Pearce.'

'Sure. You go do that.' Drake said, waving him away. 'We'll see you back at the office after, perhaps.'

Melwood raised his hand in thanks. 'Great, I'll grab a taxi now. You all good here?'

'Yes.' Drake nodded, scratching the back of his neck.

Ellie wondered what was going on with the man's son. She wasn't really aware of much to do with him other than what he'd overshared at the pub a few months back. Divorce, wasn't it? She hoped his kid was okay, regardless of her ongoing internal battle about whether she liked or disliked the guy.

'So, where were we . . . now you've got *your* lives in order?' Tanv said, sarcastically.

'What do you make of the hands and wrists?' Ellie asked.

'Oh, that?' She sighed as though disappointed by a student. 'Quite straightforward, really. They needed a more suitable knife to do it efficiently. Must have figured it out after they tried cutting through and weren't quite getting it done,' she said, sifting through the tools on the tray to the side of the body. 'It's strange though. Because if they'd just given it a little more time, they would have succeeded. Perhaps they were spooked, or interrupted, or just plain ran out of time?'

'Sounds about right, Tanv,' Drake agreed, then raised a finger in realisation. 'Oh, and I know we're assuming here that it's Andrea Whitman who did this, but have you retrieved anything to prove it beyond a doubt? Hairs, anything like that?'

'Yes. We've some great samples. Multiple strands of hair were found within the wounds and entrails. Shouldn't take too long to confirm, hopefully.'

'Great, thanks, Doc,' Ellie said. 'Drake beat me to the question.'

'Okay, if that's all, Tanv?' Drake asked, not waiting for an answer. 'If you don't mind, Ellie and I are going to get over to his wife now.'

'Oh, and Tanv?' Ellie said as they made moves to remove their gowns and leave.

'Yes?' Tanv looked up at her with a bone saw in hand.

'I think the poor guy will need cleaning up for official identification by the widow. You know, after you're done with all . . .' She waved a hand at the body. '. . . that.'

Tanv groaned. 'Thanks, Ellie. I would never have known.'

15

'Still can't believe there's more of those Spencer-molesting bastards out there,' Drake growled, gripping the steering wheel so tightly that the leather creaked beneath his hand.

'I know,' Ellie said. Drake saw her shoulders drop out of the corner of his eye. She wouldn't like what he had to say next either.

'And we'll need to pass that investigation on. It's not one for us, you understand. No matter how much we want it to be. There are more specialised teams for that.'

'What?' she said, raising her voice. 'But, Drake, we're involved!'

'*Were* involved,' he corrected. 'Sorry, Ellie. I don't like it either.'

Ellie hunkered down further into her car seat. 'I'm partially responsible, Drake. It's not right. Not right at all.'

Drake kept quiet; nothing he could say would make the situation feel better. But he understood. He imagined Ellie struggled with the knowledge that perhaps she could have cut the abuse short and stopped the Spencers having to mete out their own form of justice like they did. But hindsight was a destructive force in the police, and it wouldn't do for Ellie to hold herself accountable forever. He'd need to talk to her soon, though preferably not when driving to a victim's house.

Having successfully killed the conversation, he concentrated on navigating the bedlam that was London roads in silence. He was relieved when Ellie confirmed they were nearing Pearce Fleming's home. The level of concentration needed to navigate the traffic and the erratic drivers, when it was still bucketing it down *and* turning from dusk to night-time, was not something he enjoyed.

The Flemings' house was located in Notting Hill, one of the more affluent areas in London. The curb-side appeal grew progressively upmarket the closer they got, dilapidated masonry work making way for neatly trimmed hedgerows and spotlit manicured shrubs and trees. They drove past front doors fed by long paths of elaborate Victorian floor tiles with nary a leaf in sight, let alone the detritus of other, less wealthy accommodation.

'What're you expecting when we get there, Chief?'

'A fancy place, no doubt about that. Melwood mentioned he was an accountant, which probably downplays his job a little if we're in this neck of the woods. Particularly if they own the house,' Drake said, looking again at another expensive house filled with rich people. 'Sounds like the wife, Grace, was worried for her husband when the news broke.' He paused, the memory of Becca springing up. A lump formed in his throat as he remembered the moment it hit him that she really was gone. 'Have to be there for her.'

'Indeed. She must be beside herself, particularly with three children.'

He nodded but remained silent amidst the metronomic beat of the windscreen wipers battling the rain.

'Want me to take the lead?' she asked.

'Sure . . . That's *unusually* generous of you,' he said, but then a more negative line of thought occurred to him. 'Hang on, should I be taking that as a slight on my policeman's bedside manner?'

Ellie made a face. 'Oh, no-no-no. Not at all, Drake.'

'Hmm.' He pulled into a parking bay by the pavement. There was a large electric vehicle charging unit nearby.

Drake yanked on the handbrake and reached for his coat. He hoped there would be something that would give them some indication as to why the accountant had died, but he didn't have high hopes. Their last few cases had been anything but straightforward, so he would be taking an even more pessimistic stance than normal until proven otherwise.

He cursed neither of them having brought an umbrella as he got out of the car before stepping straight into a puddle.

Great.

The feeling of damp socks was not something he wanted right now. Muttering to himself, he quickened his pace as he saw the address they wanted ahead, the numbered sign attached to one of two showy pillars fronting the grand London town house. A leafy hedge gave way to a black wrought-iron fence topped with ornate, gold-painted spikes.

'What I wouldn't give for this kind of money,' Ellie said behind him as Drake set to using the thick door knocker.

It wasn't long before they heard the sound of a dog barking. A few lights were turned on by the door and a woman answered, her face drawn and free of makeup. Her blonde hair hung lank around her cheeks.

'I take it you're here about Pearce?' Her voice sounded strangely devoid of emotion.

'Yes.' He nodded. 'Mrs Fleming, I presume? I'm DCI Drake, and this is DS Wilkinson.'

She stood to one side to let them in. 'That's me. And please, call me Grace.'

They stepped into a huge cream-coloured entry hall, punctuated with tasteful black decorative mirrors and a couple of black leather form benches. A large centrepiece table with a vase of white lilies completed the room. Drake had never been a fan of the flowers; they reminded him of death and funerals. The smell was pungent.

'Please, if you could remove your shoes and come on through. And don't worry, the children are upstairs with the nanny, so they won't get in the way.'

They did as she asked, using one of the benches and padded – or squelched a little, in Drake's case – through to a side room. He wasn't sure it could be called the living room, as there were probably several of them, such was the size of the place.

'Tea? Coffee?' Grace asked, perching on the end of a black and cream chaise-longue.

'Not for me, thank you, Mrs Fleming.' Drake took a seat on an overly plump black wing chair.

'It's Grace,' the woman said tersely. She looked at Ellie, who was sitting on the edge of a similar seat. 'And you?'

'No, I won't trouble you. Thank you.'

Drake was about to let Ellie begin her questioning, when Grace spoke in clipped tones. 'Do I really *have* to go and identify him? Isn't it enough to use a photo and be done with it?'

'Not when there's been a post-mortem. I'm sorry, Grace,' he responded.

'Oh,' she said irritably.

Grace continued her oddly conflicting behaviour. Surely there should be some form of tears or emotion when the police arrive at your house to talk to you about your husband's brutal murder?

Grief could be a strange beast, Drake knew that. But perhaps there was something more at play here.

'A uniformed officer will be by in the morning to take you. I hope that's all right?' Ellie asked, pointedly enough that Drake winced inwardly.

'Yes. I suppose it will have to be, won't it?'

'I'm sorry, Grace, but I have to be honest,' Drake said, hands clasped between his knees. 'You don't appear to be particularly upset about your husband.'

'Let's just say we haven't got on these last few years.'

'Oh?'

'Yes. I won't bore you with the details, but we argued more often than not. He's a workaholic. Sorry *was* . . .' she corrected herself as though she was a teacher telling off a student. 'And a lout. It was heading towards divorce anyway. I was convinced he was having an affair, you know.'

Drake was a little taken aback by Grace's honesty. Surely, she knew she would have to be considered a suspect, saying all of this?

'What gave you that idea, Grace?' Ellie asked.

'If it wasn't work, it was some work social thing he was at, supposedly. He was never home. If that doesn't imply "affair", I don't know what does.'

'I see,' Ellie said. 'So, his recent disappearance wasn't particularly out of character?'

'Yes and no. No, in the sense that he was always out. But, yes, in that he would always tell me, more for the sake of the children, that he was here or there – so I had an answer for them. And he'd usually be home when he said he was going to be.'

'Hence the calls to the police to eventually raise the alarm.'

She nodded, her eyes not flinching. 'Yes. Accurate. It was out of character.'

Ellie asked. 'Do you have any hard evidence of any of the women he was supposedly seeing? Perhaps you've seen texts or emails corroborating your statements?'

Drake hoped there'd be a picture of Andrea she'd pull out which would then give cause to his sudden death. But he knew that would be a pipe dream.

'No, I don't. But I *know* my husband.'

But don't we all think we know the people closest to us?

Drake jumped in. 'Was he behaving more erratically? Was he stressed or worried about anything when you last saw him?'

'Nothing that I wouldn't put down to the usual work situation. He had demanding clients.' She sighed and threw her hands up. 'He'd do anything for them – suppose I should be grateful. That *willingness* got us this place, after all.'

There are worse places to be. Believe me.

Drake was irrationally jealous of her lack of emotion about her husband. He would give anything to turn off the pain from the void left by Becca for a day: not her memory, just that damnable cold, hard pain.

'Do you know of any reason your husband would have to be near Victoria Tower Gardens?'

'No, none. I'm not aware of him ever having needed to be over there – work or otherwise.'

Drake felt the line of questioning wasn't getting them anywhere. If the husband was supposedly so secretive, it was unlikely Grace had heard or seen anything directly. She was as blunt as a hammer in her openness. Perhaps searching his office or study would yield something more.

'Mrs Fleming. Would you allow me to take a look around your husband's study?' Without waiting to hear her answer, he stood up. 'I presume he has one?'

How could he not in a place like this, Drake thought.

'Of course, furthest door down the hall. Take what you need, I don't care. You'll excuse me if I don't show you myself. That room irritates me like you wouldn't believe.'

Ellie made moves to follow him, but he put out his hand for her to stay put with the "distraught" wife. He imagined she'd be thanking him later for that particular delight.

'Thank you. I shouldn't be long.'

Drake wandered out and down the marble-floored hallway, his feet slipping and sliding without his shoes on. The house felt otherworldly and decidedly sterile all at once, like a monied residential version of Kulkarni's workplace. By contrast, he half-expected the study to have a large fireplace behind a huge desk with a moose-head mounted above it. His mind was a strange place at times.

Nearing the end of the corridor was the door to the study, a heavy oak monstrosity which seemed at odds with the sparser decor preceding it. Perhaps it was more of a man cave, the one room their victim could call his own in a sea of cream and black? It could bode well for harbouring evidence that may give some clarity – or at least, direction – as to why he died.

Andrea may just have chosen randomly. Don't presume anything when it comes to her, Drake admonished himself.

Sadly, the room wasn't quite like his peculiar imagination had envisaged. There was no moose, though it did house a fireplace and desk. A large bottle green chesterfield sofa filled one side of the richly carpeted room, with the desk opposite the door and the fireplace across from the sofa. The room half-panelled throughout, with the few exposed walls decorated in a similar shade of green to the sofa. A single high window punctuated the walls of books and green paint, which did little to alleviate the study's airless quality.

Drake sidled around the side of the desk and sat down to look at what was there. A large flat screen monitor dominated the top, along with a keyboard, mouse and writing paraphernalia, while a desktop computer tower sat beneath the desk. Nothing that outwardly screamed: *This is why I'm dead, Drake!*

The one photo the man had allowed in the space was of him and his family, which stared back at Drake from a gold-frame. It threw him, seeing the accountant without any mutilation. He had bags upon bags beneath his eyes and his skin had a sickly vibe beneath the photo smile, like a man who'd spent too many hours working, mostly in front of a computer screen. At least at first glance, their victim didn't appear to be someone who could be carrying on with various women.

Drake tugged on a wheeled desk drawer and, remarkably, it opened, despite the threatening keyhole. A large number of papers presented themselves. He rifled through, the search not producing anything more than dreary accountancy documentation and some invoices. It appeared the man was earning an amount that made his mind boggle. It certainly explained the palatial surroundings. He started on the file drawer beneath, and was seeing much the same as he flipped through each in turn. He supposed he should've asked Grace, but he couldn't have imagined her turning down any requests relating to her husband.

Seeing nothing, he shoved the drawer closed with disgust, the wheels rolling the drawers into the back of the desk with a clunk.

Drake frowned. Was he imagining things or was there something *off* about the sound? He could swear it wasn't right.

Wanting to test his theory, he took hold of the drawers and drew them forwards to their original position, then rolled them – more gently this time – back into the desk.

There it was again. A metallic sound.

Why would drawers with what looked to be a wooden shell, make a metallic noise against a solid oak desk?

Drake pulled the set of drawers out from under the desk. And realised that what he saw attached to the back of them could mean his prayers might just be answered after all.

16

Drake took one of the two computer hard drives from the small leather pouch. The pouch had been attached to the back of the set of drawers by a set of Velcro strips. He supposed he should be thanking his lucky stars that the tops had been exposed enough to knock into the desk, but the hiding place was bordering on amateurish. Why would Pearce want to be hiding hard drives in such a way? Why hadn't he used a safe, or a deposit box? Had he hoped that hiding them in semi-plain sight was better somehow?

Drake wondered what could be saved on them. Maybe it wasn't meant to be quite as secretive as he thought, but it was setting off all sorts of alarm bells. Perhaps this was where the real money came from? It could go some way to explaining the long, secretive nights Grace Fleming spoke of. So many questions in need of answers. Drake hoped he got them soon.

He carefully put the drives back in the pouch and placed the drawers back in their original position, before returning to find Ellie deep in conversation with Grace.

Ellie's eyes lit up at his approach, her relief evident.

Drake tapped on the door frame, the knock echoing loudly in

the spacious living room. 'Mrs Fleming, DS Wilkinson? Can you come with me, please?'

Grace turned, a scowl on her face. 'I told you, I don't like that room.'

'Please. I need to ask you a few questions about it.'

The wife huffed. 'Fine.'

Ellie followed him through to the study without a word while Grace was close behind.

Drake sat down at the desk and made a show of pulling the drawer unit out to reveal the hard drive pouch before giving Grace a serious look. 'Mrs Fleming, were you aware of these?'

The woman's eyes finally took on a look that wasn't one of irritation or disgust. It was now one of genuine surprise. 'What . . . ? No . . . ? Why would he – I didn't know that was there.'

'This gives me a certain degree of suspicion about your husband's activities, Mrs Fleming. You have to understand that.'

'Of-of course, I understand.'

Drake plucked one of the hard drives from the pouch. 'Do you agree to us taking these, along with the desktop computer, as evidence?'

She nodded. 'Whatever you need. As I said, I'm not sure what they are or why they're there like that, I never had dealings with anything in here. It was strictly off-limits to me and the children.'

'Does he have any other rooms which are off-limits, Grace?' Ellie asked.

'No. This is the only one,' she said, perching on the arm of the sofa and looking absently around the room. 'He used to do all his work and calls here when he was working from home. He didn't like to be disturbed.'

'I see.' Drake pursed his lips. 'We'll take these into evidence as per your agreement. Thank you.'

A voice called from another room. 'Mrs Fleming, are you there? Genevieve wants you to wish her good night before she goes to sleep.'

'Sorry. Do you mind? That's the nanny,' Grace said, standing up and gesticulating towards the door.

'Go ahead. We'll see ourselves out. Unless you have any further questions, DS Wilkinson?'

Ellie shook her head. 'No. Thank you for your time, Grace.'

'Call me, if you need anything more,' she said and left the room.

Ellie turned back. 'Chief, that was quite the find. What were you doing? Crawling around on your hands and knees or something? I thought you'd been a while.'

Drake gave her a look. 'No, Sergeant. I just had a stroke of luck, shall we say.'

'Well, hopefully that continues and whatever is on those things yields us some results.'

'Maybe. Though it could just be more to do with how he made his fortune. I still can't imagine what would be on there to link him directly to Andrea. But you never know, eh?'

'Let's get Strauss on the case,' she nodded. 'I know he likes a good puzzle. I'd be very surprised if they weren't password-protected or something, being hidden like that.'

'True. Let's see what he thinks.'

* * *

'Sheiße!' Strauss grumbled.

'What is it?' Drake asked.

By the time that they had arrived back at the office, it was deathly quiet with little activity, barring the glow of Strauss' laptop on the man's face amid his furious typing. He never seemed to go home or sleep, for that matter.

It hadn't taken long for Strauss to set up the dead man's desktop computer they had brought back. He'd also hooked up the additional hard drives to Pearce's computer, rather than their own, so as to limit any potential conflicts or changes to the data contained within. A messy tangle of cables snaked around the keyboard and mouse that Strauss had set up.

'I was hoping this was going to be simple, *just this once*, you know? But, evidently I should stop hoping,' he said, scrubbing a hand through his mop of hair and gesticulating at the monitor with the other. 'This is going to take time, I'm afraid. He's encrypted the drive. It's not just straight forward user logon password protection. A few wrong guesses and everything that's on them may be long gone, if we're not careful. Or at the very least add a considerable amount of time on to our recovery efforts.'

'Okay. So, whatever is on there is not completely inaccessible and out of the question, at least?'

'No. It's just that good old thing called "time" and people with the next level of technical nous that I haven't kept up with. Sorry, Drake – and who puts stuff on mechanical hard drives these days, anyway? It's all solid state now, at the very least.'

'Don't apologise. As long as you're on it, I don't care,' Drake said with a shrug and an encouraging clap on the German's shoulder. 'Look, we just need anything and everything we can get to help us build a picture and understand if there are more to deaths to come. Or if there is a pattern – or worse, that it's just completely out of the blue and random. Whatever is on there could be completely unrelated, for all we know.'

'You never know, Chief,' Ellie said, arms folded and leaning against the glass by the door.

Strauss sighed and slumped back in the office chair. 'In other news, the team's been doing work on the CCTV in the area.'

'Oh?'

'Yeah, there's jack shit so far,' he said with a shake of his head. 'Nothing that gives a clear view of the bench or either end of the underpass. Or the area at all, really – you'd think that would be first priority these days, with safety concerns and big brother watching us. But no, seems not.'

'Patience. We just need patience,' Drake reiterated. 'Something will come. It always does, one way or another.'

Drake hoped he wouldn't live to regret those words.

17

Drake looked over at the two girls asleep on the sofa beneath a set of colourful blankets. He knew it would happen; his choice of films never went down any other way with either of them. He felt slightly hurt that they didn't have the same feeling of excitement he'd had when watching *The Game* for the first time.

Just no accounting for taste with some people, he thought with a disappointed sigh.

'Right,' he said, slapping his legs loudly to rouse them. 'Come on, you two. You've got school in the morning.'

Eva stirred first, answering with a sleepy, 'You mean sixth form, Dad. We're not kids,' as she sat up.

Cari still hadn't moved. But that all changed when Eva prodded her without thinking.

The girl instantly jumped at the touch as though she'd been jabbed with a cattle prod, screaming in the way that had become commonplace since Drake had taken her into his care. The way that could only mean she was back to the scene in her old house with her parents. No sooner was she on her feet than she collapsed back down and curled into a ball on the sofa, screaming and sobbing as she batted away invisible shapes with her hands.

Eva stood by helplessly while Drake tried his best to calm her down.

'No—No!' Cari screamed. 'Mum, no! Please! Please! No!'

'Cari . . . Cari! It's John. It's Mr Drake.' He gripped her wrists to stop her clawing at her face and neck. 'It's just a dream, Cari. It's not real. Eva and I are here with you. Please. It's just a dream.'

The girl twisted and struggled, slowly weakening in her resistance until finally she stopped struggling amidst a fit of coughs and gasps.

Awareness slowly returned to Cari's eyes beneath strands of sweat-sodden hair. 'I—I'm so sorry,' she rasped, looking at the two worried faces. 'Why can't I stop it? Why?'

Cari's hand automatically went to her throat, touching the ugly scar. For some reason, it seemed to calm her down. Drake would have thought it would have the opposite effect, and he couldn't understand why it didn't.

'Cari, it's okay, it's not your fault. We're not angry with you.'

Eva curled up next to her. 'Yeah, Cari, we're here for you.' She took Cari's hand. 'There's no one here to hurt you, okay? Maybe my dad's film choice might bore you to death, but nothing else will get you, okay?'

Cari tried her best to stifle a laugh before taking a deep breath. 'I know,' she said, despondently. 'I just . . . I just want it all to end. My life won't always be like this, will it? Something needs to change soon, right?'

'It'll work out, Cari. Don't worry. You'll be ok, you'll see,' Drake said.

Your Mum's alive by the way, he thought.

He had to tell her soon. It wasn't right. Dave had been talking sense earlier and not for the first time recently. But how? How could he tell Cari when she was like this?

18

Ellie heaved Bella up into her arms, huffing at the effort. The girl's little legs instantly wrapped around her, and Ellie staggered slightly. She was convinced her daughter had to weigh close to a metric ton and that was no exaggeration.

She glanced over at Len, his head back and mouth agape in the armchair by the sofa, and decided against waking him up just yet. They'd had enough discussions to last a lifetime. She knew he meant well, but she had to do things her own way. He couldn't fix everything.

Bella murmured something in her sleep as Ellie carefully took her upstairs and put her to bed, making sure she checked under the pillows as she did so. It was a routine that had started since the horrible 'present' her daughter had received some months earlier. The memory of discovering the Action Man with the duct-taped head still sent a chill down Ellie's spine; that, and the man on the CCTV footage who still hadn't been found. Whoever the man was, he was still out there.

Ellie's eyelid twitched, but she left it alone. She knew she wouldn't be able to rest fully until everything relating to the

Spencer case was done and dusted. Regardless of what Drake said about the case not being theirs anymore, she had to do something to speed it along. And she also needed to figure out her complex around Fiona Spencer. Until then, she knew she wasn't going to find peace.

She just knew she needed to do *something*.

They needed to be stopped, once and for all.

19

Drake walked over to the kitchen sink. The sun caught a window in the skyscraper opposite their flat, bathing the room with light. A view of a city waking up for another day.

The early morning sunshine had done wonders for his mood since the previous evening's incident with Cari. He knew he'd need to take whatever positives he could get before entering work mode, but he was worried. The way Cari had reacted to Eva's touch – and not for the first time – it showed she was still far from okay. It didn't give him much faith in her ongoing therapy sessions.

'I'm sorry about last night, Dad,' Eva said, looking over at him from her breakfast bowl. She appeared well rested considering what had happened, and for that he was pleased. She'd been sleeping better in general lately. While she was now off her anti-depressant medication, she still opted to take medication to help her sleep, which he understood. The nightmares were still something he dealt with occasionally himself, and she needed to have the energy for her schoolwork and exams.

Cari was still in her room, both of them having decided she

should stay in bed for a while longer. Though it would probably end up making her more stressed, not less.

'What? Why?'

'Because . . . it was me who forced you to take her in.'

Drake shook his head, leaning against the kitchen island. 'Eva, it was the right thing to do. I don't regret it, and you shouldn't be apologising. She's part of the family now.'

She put her spoon down. 'I know, but I've seen how you look at her. Like she's going to break at any moment.'

'That's not true. She's just troubled, and rightly so.' He sat down on a stool next to her. 'I do worry for her – of course I do. I worry she won't have the normal life we so desperately want for her.'

'I think there's more to it than that. What you said last night, about her being okay soon . . .' Her voice became a whisper. 'You know where her Mum is, don't you? That's why you've been acting weird lately.'

How the hell did she figure that out? he thought.

'What? No?' he said, barely convincing himself. 'You know I'll tell you when we find where she actually is.'

Well done. That is sort of true. We don't really know, do we?

'Anyway, you better wake her and get ready for leaving. I need to get going now, okay?'

'Got it,' she said, before adding, 'But I still don't believe you about her mum.'

* * *

Drake wound his way through the corridors in the lower levels of the offices. It was a well-worn drill now, one that he was pleased he could get out of the way early. He'd turn up, Dr Proctor-Reeves would already be in place amidst the usual old office paraphernalia that had never been cleared away. The horrendously uncomfortable chairs would still be front and centre, and she'd bash him over the head with inane questions for an hour. That was his way of looking at it, and he was sticking to it.

But if he really looked inwards, he knew that they *had* helped more than if he'd gone it alone. Speaking with someone without any skin in the game meant he could speak more openly, particularly since the Spencer case. Though he was still cagey about the specifics of his encounters with Jack, he had spoken a little about the anger he had experienced – still experienced, if he was being honest with himself – and she had listened.

Drake opened the door and saw the usual sight of Dr Helen Proctor-Reeves sitting in the chair opposite his, a ballpoint pen and notepad in her hands and ready to go. She alternated between black and purple silk shirts, he'd observed. Today was a black shirt day, her blonde hair tied back in a bun as usual. She'd also taken to wearing glasses in their last few meetings; perhaps the sight of him had caused her eyes to finally give out. He huffed to himself at the notion.

'John,' she said, looking up over her glasses. 'Good to see you. Take a seat.'

'Thanks, Doc.'

She opened her notebook and made a quick scribble. 'And how are you faring since our last appointment? It's been a while.'

'All right.'

'Just all right?' She looked over her glasses at him again; it was her latest way to make him realise he'd given an answer that was not in any way helpful or forthcoming.

He leaned back in the chair. 'Well, I've started back at work.'

'Yes, so I hear.' She tilted her head to the side. 'Tell me about that.'

'I have a feeling, or should I say, *in my experience*, it's going to be a challenging number of weeks and months.' He pinched the bridge of his nose. 'We suspect the woman who killed her husband in the style of the Family Man is back and killing again.'

Saying it out loud made his blood boil.

Way to go for keeping your emotions in check.

'And how does that make you feel?'

He hesitated while he brought himself back under control. 'Apprehensive, if I'm being honest.'

'That's understandable. It's been a challenging time for you. And you naturally associate her with what happened to Becca. This woman's daughter is still in your care, correct?'

He nodded slowly, thinking of the previous night's incident. 'Yes.'

'And does she know of the developments?'

His eyes widened. 'Oh, God, no. There's nothing to really tell, right now. It's still developing.'

'Do you not think she deserves to know?'

'Well, yes, but . . .'

She leant forwards. 'So, what is stopping you, do you think?'

'I don't want the poor girl to be living in fear. For all we know, her mother has killed this person and disappeared again for who knows how long. If not forever.'

She looked down at her notes. 'But you mentioned phone calls in our previous sessions, correct?'

'Yes – and thank you for keeping that private. But again, they weren't with her, they were with the *Miray* persona.' He chuckled morbidly. 'Someone who you would probably be fascinated to study.'

She leant back, her face taking on a look of mild disapproval. 'We're not here to talk about what would be good for me, John.'

Drake persisted in toying with her. 'Though your insight may actually help to inform the investigation, come to think of it.'

'Best save that thought for when you know more about what's going on. Though DID, or dissociative identity disorder, as it's known, is an area of interest, certainly.'

He pursed his lips. Fun and games over. 'Yes. Fine.'

She took a deep breath, took her glasses off and rested her pen alongside them on her notebook. 'I'm going to offer an opinion, John. I know this isn't really the done thing. But in this instance, I want to help more than just you.'

He gave her an inquisitive look. 'Go on.'

'You need to keep Cari informed,' she said carefully. 'It may frighten her, but she needs to know. She will only end up harbouring resentment otherwise. And if anything happens to her mother in the meantime, she will only have you to hold responsible for that.' She paused. 'You see where I'm going with this?'

Drake scratched at his stubble, recounting Dave's similar advice in his mind. 'Funny, a wise old man said pretty much the same thing to me recently.'

Proctor-Reeves frowned but didn't question him further about Dave. She rubbed her nose with an index finger and put her glasses back on. 'And how is your daughter?'

'Good. I wouldn't say she's back to her old self – I don't think she will ever be the same as before. But she's off those damn anti-depressants now, and is making a good go of her school work, though still needs a little help with her sleep.'

Proctor-Reeves gave him a rare smile. 'Excellent. You've both come a long way since she moved back with you.'

'Indeed.'

'But . . . ?'

'You're really on the ball today, Doc,' he said, sounding more sarcastic than he intended. 'But . . . I think it still angers me how this evil piece of shit robbed her of her mother, robbed her of her childhood and of any future memories of Becca. Same for Cari. The Man's taken so much of my life and tainted so many others. And Cari's nightmare is still ongoing.'

She bobbed her head. 'I see.'

He continued musing out loud. 'I guess it gives me more of a profound, first-hand insight into what victims of crimes like these go through. And since my *incident*, I'm more susceptible to . . . the bouts of anger I've mentioned.'

Nicely diminished, well done.

'Yes.'

'That's it?' he snapped. 'I say all that, and all I get is a "Yes"? Really?'

'I didn't want to interrupt.' She pursed her lips. 'However, I will say, that in light of this, and previous discussions, I won't be discharging you any time soon. I'm sorry, John. I know that's not what you want to hear, but there's still more here we have to work through.'

'You're kidding me?'

'It's this, or I recommend you're not fit for work,' she said, matter-of-factly.

Drake immediately wanted to shout at her, but thought better of it. This was precisely why she'd just said what she'd said. His immediate reaction was one of rage. Why wasn't it getting any better?

He took a deep breath. 'How can I work it out? Help me out here?'

Proctor-Reeves peered at him with weary eyes. 'I think there's still a lot of raw wounds for you, John. Despite the improvements in your home life. I think there's unfinished business in your mind.'

'Yes, I suppose you're right, Doc. The bastard is still alive, after all.'

She shook her head. 'There's nothing you can do about that, John.'

'I know.' He squeezed his hands shut, the knuckles instantly turning white. 'But by Christ, I wish I could kill the son of a bitch.'

20

Drake closed the door to Proctor-Reeves' makeshift therapy room, feeling less than enthused about the shitty news she had given him. No offence to the psychologist, but he needed rid of her and to be let off the psychological leash that Miller had inflicted upon him. Though what he wanted now, more than anything, was a moment alone to pull himself back together. And his car would have to do.

He made his way back through the maze of featureless corridors towards the carpark, feeling the familiar subtle tugs of panic building, the tightness in his chest. He tried to push them away, but was failing miserably. The only thought that entered his head was how and when he could tell Cari about her mother's not-so-pleasant reappearance.

Pull yourself out of it. Calm down, man, he pleaded inwardly. *You know what these feelings are. You need to control them.*

Still, the thoughts continued unabated. They needled at him, making him jittery and unfocused. Perhaps he should leave out the killing part, and just tell her about the phone calls? That might soften the blow, perhaps? Just that little bit?

Drake saw his car ahead and breathed a small sigh of relief. But as he increased his pace, his mind immediately flung him back to when he'd used it as a makeshift bed. It was a depressing time, and one he didn't want to dwell on. Particularly the reason why he'd made himself do it in the first place. He would do his damnedest *not* to linger on that horrific memory.

Hurriedly, he slammed the door shut behind him. He exhaled loudly before taking another deep breath, and another, gripping the bottom of the steering wheel tightly. He continued in and out, in and out, until his heart started to slow, his chest releasing the pressure slightly.

Jesus, I've not had one of those in a while—

His phone started ringing, jangling his frayed nerves further. He yanked it from his pocket and saw a withheld number calling.

Withheld? Oh no. It's not, is it? That's not following the pattern. It's too early.

He squeezed his eyes shut and answered. 'DCI Drake?'

An audible click sounded a millisecond after he answered. He heard the rustling of cloth or sheets, followed by a satisfied sigh that sounded as though it was filtered through a smile.

It had to be. It was *her*.

'DCI Drake?' he repeated, hunching down in his car seat.

'John Drake,' came the voice. 'Thank you for taking my call.'

His eyes widened. It was her; it was Miray.

The voice of Andrea's mother was strikingly different to that of Andrea. The Miray persona had a Turkish accent, with strong enunciation on each word, in line with the actual woman's childhood spent there. Andrea's accent, by contrast, was non-regional and thoroughly English, bordering on southern despite her having grown up in the Midlands and in isolation with her mother for large parts of it. It was incredibly jarring knowing that the two voices came from one person so seamlessly.

'You know you can call me whenever you need,' he said. 'I want to help, as I've said previously.'

Miray laughed. 'I don't need your help, John. Whatever gave you that idea?'

He scanned the carpark, not seeing anyone. No movement at all.

Drake knew he needed Strauss to attempt to triangulate the call, or whatever it was they did these days, to figure out where in God's name she was hiding. But how? He was in the damn car park, completely unprepared. He checked his phone and ensured it was recording the call at least.

'You've been missing for over a year,' he said, keeping his voice low to try and pacify her. She had a tendency to get angry if he didn't choose his words carefully. 'How you've managed to stay away for so long, I don't know. But you have.'

'Impressive, isn't it?'

'Yes.'

Drake looked out again at the entrance to the offices. He was so close. He knew he should try to reach Strauss and get him working on tracing the call. Maybe they'd finally strike it lucky and get an exact placement?

'How did you do it?' he continued. 'I've always wanted to know.'

Though the truth was he didn't even think she could answer him on that.

'As I said before, John, that would be telling.' He could feel the shit-eating grin ooze through the phone, the satisfaction she got from besting him.

Drake knew he had to make a dash for it. He closed his eyes for a moment, weighing his options. Somehow, he had to get up to his floor without Miray ending the call *and* without losing mobile signal. The building was a notoriously patchy black box, the Wi-Fi even less reliable. Another thing skimped on in the annual budgets.

'Why are you calling?' he asked, doing his best to keep her engaged as he considered his limited courses of action.

She remained silent as he opened his eyes, his mind made up. He had to go for it.

Drake exited the car quickly, slamming the door shut. The cool spring breeze lapped at him while he awaited a response.

'I thought you might want to . . . have a little chat,' she said finally.

A gust of wind whipped his coat up as he strode towards the entrance. The stairwell was his best bet; it ran around the periphery of the offices and had the better signal. He just had to hope it wouldn't cut out on the journey through.

'Oh? What about?' His head darted side to side as he delved into the building, dodging past a crowd of people.

'Well, how about we start with the present I left you?'

Drake turned a corner. The doors leading to the stairs were dead ahead.

Is she going to admit to killing Pearce on the call?

'What present was that?' he asked, stringing it out as best he could.

'The one in the underpass. Did . . . y— like it?' Her voice was growing faint.

Drake gripped the hand rail, stopping in his tracks. The signal was getting choppy.

Shit.

'The dead man, you mean?'

The line was suddenly silent. He looked down at the phone in panic. It was still connected. He hoped to God it didn't drop out. Drake put the phone back to his ear as he started up the stairs regardless.

'. . . Yes.' She laughed wickedly. 'It was quite fun, that one. Let's just say he *definitely* wasn't expecting it.'

Drake quickened his pace, taking two steps at a time. He was going to be out of breath before he knew it. He'd always known it would be her, but to hear her say it out loud, and with such delight, it was sickening. Is this how she felt after killing her – sorry, *Andrea's* – husband, Ben?

'You know I have to ask . . . but why? What did he do to deserve that? And why now?'

'John, John, John. Always needing a reason for this thing called *life*. S'pose it must be part and parcel of being a police detective?'

Drake barged someone out the way, putting a hand up in apology as he continued his ascent. He was getting close now, only a few more floors. He'd begun sweating; the pace, the concentration with the phone call, it was an onslaught.

'Yes, something like that,' he said, voice as blunt as a hammer. 'It's just that, in my experience, people don't go to that length for no reason, *and* for no one in particular. There's usually a reason, something driving it.' He stopped for a moment to catch his breath, so he could speak in more than measured gasps. 'What's driving you, Miray?'

There was a noise on the line as though she was shifting positions. She mumbled something unintelligible before returning to him.

'Look, John. I would love to stay and chat, but I have to go.'
Shit, no.

'Then you better give me some answers before you do, Miray. Tell me why. Show me how clever you really are.'

He bounded up the final sets of stairs. The silence on the call as she seemingly weighed up her answer was killing him. Had he pushed it a step too far?

'He deserved it,' she murmured.

Drake burst through the stairwell door, the sounds of the phones ringing and voices blaring back at him. Then seeing the glass office and, more importantly, DS Strauss within.

'Sorry, what? You have to speak up. The line is bad,' he said, in pretence, hoping the sudden influx of noise wouldn't make her hang up.

'HE. DESERVED. IT!' she shrieked.

Drake didn't react to her outburst. He just pictured what she must be doing; her springing up from the chair, or floor or bed or wherever she was, eyes crazed.

He persisted. 'To be gutted? To have his throat slit? Tongue forcibly removed?'

'YES!'

'That "he deserved it", isn't enough, Andr—Miray. Come on, give me more. There has to be more.'

Drake finally reached the door to the investigation room and burst in. Strauss immediately looking up from the work he was doing with an analyst from the support team. Making a point with his eyes, Drake gesticulated at his phone to press home the situation to Strauss.

The man's eyes widened in realisation. He nodded and immediately sprung from his chair, leaving the analyst in his wake as he sprinted out of the room to collect what he must need to try and trace the call.

Miray dropped in volume as though she hadn't been screaming into the phone just moments earlier. 'The man was scum. He was violent, he did . . . *things*.'

Drake sat down in a chair and leant forward. His eyes screwed tight in concentration as he listened.

'Things? What things?'

Miray ignored him and continued: 'I think I have a purpose in life now though, you know?'

Drake shuddered. "Purpose" reminded him of how Samuel Barrow had used the word to justify his actions. She couldn't have known about it – Drake couldn't imagine Samuel discussing it with her – but the similarity was chilling.

'To kill? To maim? That's not a purpose. Hurting people – it's sick. It isn't right, Miray.'

Drake felt the familiar churn of anger burning in his stomach. He was getting reckless. He should know better than to bait and rile her.

Strauss burst back into the room, a look of dejection on his face as he shook his head.

What? No? After all that? Fuck!

He gave Strauss a look of abject anger while Miray laughed the same twisted laugh as before. 'I enjoy it, it's very . . . freeing.'

'Miray . . .'

'I have to go now. My daughter will be back soon.'

He gripped the phone so hard he heard it creak beneath his grasp.

No! I have to keep her on the line. I have to do something to understand where she is, to hook her in. I have to. I need to stop her! I have to!

'Cari! She's alive!' he blurted

The sudden silence was deafening. Strauss stared at him, eyes wide, mouth agape.

You stupid, stupid man! What have you done?

Strauss looked down and shook his head while Drake stared ahead, the phone still silent. He was stunned at what he had just said.

Then all hell broke loose.

The phone suddenly bursting forth with static, the extreme distortion from the cacophony being thrown its way.

'What?' Miray shrieked. 'That's not true! I slit that little bitch's throat! *She bled out in front of me!'*

Keep it together now, John. Pull it back. You can undo this. You can make it right.

Belying his inner turmoil, he stated calmly. 'We saved her. You didn't kill her. She's somewhere safe. Far, far away from you – if you want her, you'll have to call again.'

'I'll find her.'

'Over my dead body.' Drake spat.

'So be it,' Miray said, and hung up the phone.

21

I watched as my mother thrashed about the room like a woman possessed. Her eyes were wild, the words coming out of her mouth worse still. The sight triggered memories of how she'd been when I was a young girl. And what she'd once again become since coming back into my life. The anger. The abuse, both verbal and physical.

From my position on the bed, I flinched while she ranted and raved, before a vivid memory deadened what I was witnessing. The woman became a blur as I withdrew into myself, recalling the memory of a time when she'd dragged me along the floor by my hair and into the bathroom.

I was just eight years old, but it was a time I remembered well because it was the one instance, the one and only day, where the teacher had awarded me a gold star for my homework. The first one I'd ever received.

It was to be the only one.

My mother had taken a pair of black-handled scissors from a drawer in the kitchen and forced me to sit in the bath. I'd gripped my legs tightly and cried while the clumps and strands of my dark hair fell around me. My head pulled every which way as she clipped and tore the hair from my head.

'Think you're clever, do you?', she'd snarled. 'Think you're *smart?* Smarter than me?' Her blood-spattered hands flashed past the corner of my eye. 'I'll show you how I reward that in *my* house. This is what people *seeing you* gets you, stupid little bastard girl.'

That's what she would always call me. "Bastard girl". I didn't understand why.

A slap around the face brought me back to the present, making me recoil and brace in the expectation of another, my hands shielding my face.

'Mum, no! Don't. Please!'

My mother froze.

What did you say to me?

'I said: Don't. Please. I don't deserve this.'

She seemed to hesitate, flinching at my words before backing down.

I'm sorry, my beautiful girl.

She sat beside me on the bed and soothed my stricken cheek with the back of her index finger. *I just had some bad news, is all.*

'Bad news?'

Yes. Nothing for you to worry about.

'Is it about Ben? Cari?'

No, no. They're fine.

'Oh, well that's good.' I smiled softly. 'You had me worried.'

Yes. Go to sleep now, my beautiful girl. Shhh . . .

She continued to stroke my cheek. Her touch making me slowly, but surely, drift away.

I was almost dead to the world when a figure entered the room.

A familiar shape in my increasingly hazy view.

It was my husband.
My Ben.

22

'Right guys, let's get—' Ellie paused mid-sentence, an analyst skirted past her and out of the door like he was in a hurry to be anywhere but there. Drake and Strauss were silent in their chairs, their expressions set as though they'd just received the worst news imaginable.

Wait . . . Have they been arguing? That might go some way to explaining why the guy scarpered out of the room so quickly.

Ellie's eyes darted between the two of them as she removed her coat. 'Erm, is everything okay? You both look like you shagged each other's sisters and only just found out.'

Drake, not turning to look at her, spoke flatly. 'Now's not the time, Ellie.'

'Indeed. It's really not,' Strauss said.

What the hell happened?

Ellie skirted around the conference room table and took a seat at the head. 'Well, I'm not going anywhere until you tell me what's up.'

Strauss shook his head, and sighed. 'DCI Drake just told

Andrea – or Miray, whatever you call her – that Cari is alive and well.'

Ellie gasped. 'You what? Chief, no! You didn't?'

Drake closed his eyes, as though he was soaking up her words. 'I had to do something, it could have been weeks, or months even. We may never have heard anything from her again. She would just go on killing and we'd be nowhere closer.'

'But, *Cari?* She's just a kid.'

Drake turned to her. His eyes were cold, though she could feel the shame radiating from him. 'I don't have to explain myself to you. Or anyone, for that matter.'

'I'm going to get a drink,' Strauss said, standing up. 'I'm sorry I couldn't help, Drake. The equipment I used before was already checked out when I got there. If I could have got it, then maybe this wouldn't have happened.'

'You did your best,' Drake said, not looking up at the man as he made for the exit.

'We'll be better prepared next time,' Strauss said, stopping at the door. 'I'll make it up to you . . . to Cari.'

With Strauss gone, it was just her and Drake in the room. Ellie needed to understand why he'd offered up Cari, effectively as a sacrifice.

'Seriously, Drake. What happened?'

He wrung his hands on the tabletop, not looking her in the eye. 'I panicked.'

'What? Why? That's not like you.'

The last time she'd seen him this way was soon after his wife, Becca, had died. He seemed bereft . . . and vulnerable. She didn't like it; he was her mentor, and it was unsettling.

'You don't know me like you think you do.'

'Okay . . .'

Ellie sat in silence. She was trying to think of the right words to say, to make a shit situation better. But how could she? She never knew what he was thinking at the best of times. Maybe what he was thinking of doing would work out, but she had her doubts. She didn't want more deaths on her conscience. Not now.

'Aren't you tired of it all?' he blurted.

She frowned. 'Tired?'

'Of all the death. Everything relating to this case and Samuel *fucking* Barrow.'

She cocked her head slightly. 'Of course, I am. It's wearing, it really is. But . . . putting Cari in the crosshairs like that, Chief? What will that solve?'

'Solve? The case, of course. I'm hoping it'll draw her out. If it works, we can put an end to this, finally.'

'And if it makes things worse?'

'Then that's a cross I'll have to bear.' He folded his arms. 'Not you. Not Strauss.'

She frowned again. 'That doesn't make it okay.'

'I know.' Her boss put a hand to his brow. 'Believe me . . . I know.'

* * *

There was a knock on the door later, soon after her boss had finished papering the middle sections of the glass windows to keep out any unwanted attention, similar to previous investigations. It meant there were now only a pair of feet and ankles and the top of a head to identify any would-be visitors. But she knew immediately who it was.

'Ma'am,' Ellie greeted her as she entered. Strauss had his headphones on and hadn't sensed that someone new had entered the room, while Melwood and Drake were deep in conversation in his side office.

Miller looked how Ellie felt. The woman's tired eyes locked on hers for a moment before taking in the room, the pictures of Pearce Fleming's face, the severity of the Family Man symbol on his back meeting her gaze.

'Can you summon the two of them for me, please, Ellie?' she asked. 'It'll save me navigating this ridiculous table.'

Strauss must have sensed Ellie stand up, and subsequently realised Miller was in the room. He snatched his headphones off, uttering a short 'Ma'am' as Ellie knocked on the door. The two men peered out and saw the DCS. Soon they were all seated at the conference table.

'So, Drake. Any progress? I would have hoped to have had an update by now.'

Drake was about to speak when Melwood interjected, much to her boss's consternation.

'We've managed to confirm in the last half hour that it is indeed Andrea Whitman's hair on Pearce Fleming's body,' Melwood said. He seemed overly pleased with himself.

Miller stared at him for a few moments, as Ellie gripped her chair.

'So.' Miller tilted her head slightly to one side. 'DI Melwood, you're telling me that you've confirmed what we knew already? That the *same* woman, the *last* known person to kill in the style of The Family Man, has indeed killed again? With that determination having come from the next person she killed in that manner?'

'Erm, when you put it that way . . . Yes.'

'Well, I never.' Miller banged the table sarcastically with a fist. 'Thank *fuck* for that. Might as well call it a day now then, eh?'

'Ma—?'

Miller pointed a finger at him angrily. 'Stop. Talking.'

Melwood shifted uncomfortably in his seat, like a schoolboy being told off by the headteacher. 'Ma'am . . . yes, ma'am.'

Ellie noticed Strauss struggling to hide a grin beneath a contemplative hand. She did enjoy seeing Melwood put back in his box, she had to admit.

Miller cast her gaze on Drake again. 'Please tell me there's more than that. There better be more than that.'

'Well . . .'

Miller breathed in sharply. 'Drake . . .'

Ellie couldn't recall seeing the DCS as apoplectic as this before. She must really be getting it in the neck from her superiors for her to be acting like this. It had only been a matter of a day or two. They needed more time, surely, she could see that?

Drake continued. 'I spoke with Andrea earlier. Her Miray 'mother' persona, I mean. She's admitted to killing Pearce Fleming. Openly revelled in it, in fact.'

'Right. Anything more come out of that discussion?'

The news didn't faze the woman at all. It was like water off a duck's back. Ellie imagined the next bit of information – if Drake was going to divulge it, like she suspected – would light her fuse, and not for the right reasons.

'And . . .We had words.'

Miller arched an eyebrow. '*Words*?'

'Yes. I believe that she will make contact again soon. And we'll be ready for her. We'll be—'

'You're telling me you've basically goaded a *serial* killer into, what? Killing again, potentially?'

'No-no, that won't happen. It—'

'Drake. Please. Give me a straight answer.'

Ellie watched him as he scratched at his stubble before running a hand through his hair. 'I'm hoping she will call back, and we'll be able to get her to come and meet us at a location, or have a video call. Something that can allow us to grab her, or to at least identify where she's holed up. I'll be needing some additional resource, either way. I was just going through the idea with Melwood when you came in.'

'Okay.'

'Okay?' Drake asked, seemingly surprised at her not blowing her top.

'Figure out what you need, and I'll see what I can do. We need to end this before she really gets going. I can't be having another Family Man killer for the next twenty goddamn years, got it?'

'Got it.'

Tap, tap.

Another set of limbs appeared at the door as a number of mobile phones in the room started ringing and vibrating. Miller put her hand up to stop anyone from answering as they all turned to see a nervous-looking constable enter the room. His eyes widened beneath his heavy brow at the sight of everyone looking back at him.

'Ma'am, I have some news.'

'Spit it out.'

The man looked at the rest of the room without saying anything.

Miller sighed irritably. 'For God's sake, don't mind them. Just speak. *Now.*'

The DC took a deep breath. 'A man has been found in a children's playground area down near Battersea Power Station.' The man paused while the mobile phones continued unabated. 'He . . . Well, he's . . . it's showing similarities to the man found at the underpass in Victoria Tower Gardens.'

23

Drake used the journey to the crime scene to try and gain some modicum of mental clarity. The day had passed in a blur of psychobabble so far; both his own, and that of the others around him as they tried to understand his wayward actions. It had left him in a bit of a funk, if truth be told. It was certainly not looking to be a good day. Not by any stretch.

He still couldn't believe he'd thrown Cari under the bus like that. Putting her front and centre for a serial killer, irrespective of the fact it was her mother, was just plain irresponsible. He wasn't a Constable not long in the job, he was a damn Detective Chief Inspector. He *knew* not to let his feelings get the better of him. But no, off he went, shooting his mouth off. But there was a twisted part of him that was glad he'd blurted what he did. Perhaps after all, there would now be an end to things. Andrea would have to go through him before he let anything happen to the girl.

Drake had said little on the way over in the car with Ellie and Melwood, and even less as they walked through the grounds to the children's play area, not far from the newly converted

Battersea Power Station flats and shops. The faint remnants of the original surroundings made him think back to his last case when he was in CID, to the dead girl found strangled nearby when it was nothing but a wasteland. It had been as though the barren ground had coughed up some little titbit it had found just beneath the surface. That was the case which had led to him being pushed into SMT in the first place. Or, more to the point, led to him being subsumed by Miller. Not that he'd needed much persuasion at the time.

Miller. He thought back to the look she had given him earlier. He owed her a lot, he supposed, in more ways than one. But Drake couldn't blame her for her reaction today; she was only doing her best to apply pressure and produce results.

'You okay, Drake?' Ellie asked.

He turned to see her face wracked with concern. Drake didn't like the way he seemed to affect those around him with his moods. Not one bit. And certainly not Ellie.

'Just thinking about what we're going to find,' he said, unconvincingly.

'Can't imagine it's going to be much of a surprise, in some respects,' she replied, casting her eyes down.

'Sheesh, and I thought *I* was the negative one,' Melwood huffed from further back. 'Maybe, just maybe, there'll be something that'll help us out, eh? Ever thought of that?'

'Not when it comes to this particular case, Andrew,' Drake stated.

'Well, I've turned over a new leaf for my boy,' Melwood said. 'So, I'll be trying my damndest. I think this one will be the making of me — sorry, I mean, *us.*'

They continued to walk through the overtly clean and new surroundings of the Battersea development. The power station loomed large overhead, the four sandstone-coloured concrete chimneys, newly constructed to mimic the originals, dominating the skyline. Their colour contrasted sharply with the brick construction of the building proper.

Drake didn't particularly approve. Surrounding the iconic (albeit redeveloped) building, all the accompanying buildings, flats and amenities were so modern and clinical in appearance. And it all looked entirely un-lived in, almost like a showroom, with a similar level of personality. By contrast, the stone pathway they were navigating to their destination seemed like something from the seventies, at odds with the general sentiment he had for the place. The colours reminded him a little of crazy paving, and the way he'd try and jump to similar colours while avoiding the cracks when he was a kid.

'Can't begin to imagine how much one of the flats in this place would cost,' Ellie mused as they rounded another smooth curve. 'Not that there's much appeal, least for me.'

Drake worried how similar they were at times, considering the age gap.

'That's London for you. Not far now, apparently,' Melwood piped up. 'Say, I take it you guys are going to the retirement thing for Dave later?'

Shit, I forgot.

There'd been an evening marked in the work calendar for weeks since the news had come out. Yet still it had slipped his mind, even though he'd seen Dave the previous day. Though Drake wondered who might actually turn up now because of the current situation. It had better be a good number, regardless. The man deserved it.

Ellie's eyes lit up. 'Yeah, of course. Though in light of all this, guess it depends a bit. May end up being cut short?'

'Shame,' Drake said, with a reluctant nod. 'But he'd understand, if the shoe was on the other foot.'

'Anyway, did she have to make it a child's playground?' Ellie said, glumly. 'That's so . . . twisted.'

Melwood looked over at her, hands in his pockets. 'Maybe it's in reaction to what Drake said to her? Her kid and all that.'

'No,' Drake shook his head. 'That was a matter of minutes prior. Don't give me that drivel.'

'Mmm, I suppose,' Melwood changed the subject slightly. 'Anyway, apparently your favourite pathologist is already here. Kulkarni, that is.'

'And why is she my favourite, exactly?' Drake turned to him, a frown etched on his face.

'Have you not seen how she is with you? You must be blind, man.'

Drake heard Ellie chuckle behind him.

What? Kulkarni? Don't be ridiculous, he thought, shaking his head in his mind's eye.

He frowned again outwardly at his colleagues and said nothing more as they finally arrived at the blandly named Prospect Place children's playground.

Drake's heart dropped at the scene before him. It was an open area, with nothing to cover the children's play equipment from the elements. SOCO had arrived before them this time round, and had obviously tried to control the open nature of the space. A sea of police tape and a number of white SOCO awnings had been erected amidst the bright, almost lurid, play area. The outlines and shapes of slides and frames poked in and out of the coverings. Drake judged that whoever had chosen the colours must have been on acid, it was the only explanation.

Drake couldn't quite make out a body from where he was standing. It meant SOCO had done a good enough job, all things considered, to keep the scene from prying eyes and the surrounding blocks of flats.

Melwood pulled a young officer managing the scene to the side and showed him his ID, saving Drake and Ellie the trouble.

Ellie glanced up at him. 'All set, Chief?'

'I will be once I've suited up in the usual SOCO crap,' he growled, nodding at a man getting into his SOCO gear by the nearby van that had parked up.

She sighed and followed him over. 'Why didn't *we* drive through too?'

Soon after, covered head to toe in human bin bags, they worked their way, snake-like, through an ever-increasing number of officers arriving at the scene. Drake almost tripped on the first floor plate that indicated they'd arrived at the correct part of the scene. The tinkle of a SOCO camera added further confirmation.

'Well, here goes,' Ellie said, her voice muffled by her mask. The awning they made their way toward was actually more tent-like, its front fully zipped. Shadows were working within its confines.

'Let's get to it,' Drake said. He raised his voice to the figures within, one of which he recognised as the familiar silhouette of Tanvi Kulkarni. 'Tanv, we're here. All right to come in?'

'Drake. What took you so long?' came an irritated reply. 'Just one moment.'

The tinkle of a SOCO camera sounded again a number of times before he finally received the all clear.

Drake braced himself and knelt to grab the zip to the door. Slowly he unzipped it, the teeth catching occasionally on the material as it revealed the grim scene beyond.

The raw dead body of a white man with short grey hair, half-laid, half-stood awkwardly before them. His intestines and viscera were splayed on the floor, still partially extending from his stomach cavity. The tattered remains of his formerly white shirt surrounded the wounds. The victim was positioned in such a way that his knees were half-bent, his back strapped at a near forty-five-degree angle to a single thick wooden beam that formed one of the triangular supports of a child's swing frame.

'Urgh, just—' Melwood gagged at the sight loudly behind him. The man never seemed to be able to take a scene in without doing so, Drake had noticed. Strange for someone in this line of work.

'It's never pleasant, that's for sure,' Ellie said, in limp agreement.

Drake remained still. His lips pursed as he took in the sight of the dead man's silent lament. The man's mouth gaped wide and ruinous, his neck slit from ear to ear. The layers of muscle and fat were prominent, much like the previous victims, amidst the copious amounts of blood which had poured from the wound and down the man's front. Drake could just make out a small tattoo beneath his ear; a badly-drawn lucky clover, all in black.

Fat lot of good that did him, Drake thought.

The dark crimson of the blood partially obscured the Family Man symbol which Andrea had chosen to carve on the poor man's front this time, the base of the symbol marking the point where she'd gutted him. Drake assumed the man's tongue was missing, but he'd soon find out, one way or another.

Taking a few moments more, he let out a sigh and stepped forward, his eyes heavy.

'So, this is what it is like, eh?' Tanv said from his left-hand side as soon as he moved. 'I feel like I'm finally joining an exclusive club, getting to see a Family Man scene in situ.'

'Tanv, come on.' Drake scowled beneath his mask. 'This isn't something to be happy about and you know it.'

'For you, maybe,' she replied with a casual shrug.

He felt an irrational need to knock her down a peg or two.

'Besides, this is Andrea,' he said. 'It's not the Man's. Not quite on par with his work.'

'All right, John, don't go spoiling everything for me. It's just professional curiosity – it *is* my job, for God's sake.'

'Well, don't go getting quite so excited by people's deaths, then. It's . . . unbecoming.'

Tanv, unusually, remained silent at his final chastisement and continued about her work.

'Lover's tiff, eh, Drake?' Ellie said, prodding him.

'Oh, Christ,' he sighed. 'Not you, too.'

She flinched slightly. 'I'll lay off.'

'Good.'

Tanv spoke up. 'This person is a man by the name of Ian Reed. Here's his ID – it was in his pocket. Though his wallet and phone are nowhere to be found.'

Drake took the card from her gloved hand. It was a driving licence, so it carried his registered address, which appeared to be in the same area of Battersea, perhaps even the flats overlooking the crime scene.

Least we won't have to go far to look into the guy.

'Thanks, Tanv.' He handed it back after taking a photo with his phone.

She didn't look him in the eye as she took the card and returned to her work. He'd probably have to apologise for how he'd spoken to her at some point.

Drake stepped closer to the body. The similarities were certainly there with the Pearce Fleming scene a couple of days earlier: the more frenzied neck and mouth cuts, the iconography. But nothing jumped out at him to make him think the killer could be someone other than Miray. Admittedly, before today's events, the thought had crossed his mind about another party being in play. His paranoia was at an all-time high, and with good reason since the case with Jonah and Samuel, and indeed the Spencers too. Multiple murderers carrying out near identical crimes. But he was confident, at least for now, that there didn't seem to be a third-party involved.

Though Miray might be considered one? he thought darkly.

Reynolds started buzzing around them with his camera. 'Sorry, Drake. Do you mind?'

'I do, actually.'

'Oh!' The trainee pathologist's eyes widened. 'Okay, my apologies. I'll wait for you to finish.'

'Good.'

'You need to grow a backbone, mate,' Melwood piped up.

'All right, Melwood. Leave him alone,' Drake said, glaring back at the DI.

That man is really pushing my buttons these last few days. Seems me being his boss on the Spencer case was the only thing that kept him from going full arsehole, Drake despaired.

Reynolds remained to the side; his eyes furrowed in a frown as he patiently waited for him to continue with his inspection.

Drake decided to take one last look at the man before attempting to find what had been done with the tongue. Despite the symbol having been carved on the victim's front, Drake still wanted to see what was on his back, if anything. He noted there had seemingly been no attempt to dismember the man's wrists this time.

He moved to the furthest plate behind the body, and crouched down to look beneath.

There's nothing here. Thank God for that. That's something, at least.

He felt a weird mix of surprise and relief. You never quite knew what to expect, but this time he was pleased to be let off the hook.

Drake was busy manoeuvring back around beneath the man's back and the wooden beams when something loomed close to his eye, making him flinch. 'Whoa!' he exclaimed, on the verge of losing his balance. His arms flailed behind him in slow motion before Reynold's hand shot out and grabbed him by the shoulder, stopping him falling on his arse and making even more of a show of himself.

'Steady,' the man said calmly.

Drake didn't reply, staring back at what had brushed his face. The thing that had almost touched his eyeball. Reynolds' glance followed his own.

The fleshy, stumpy remains of the man's tongue hung down, nailed precariously into the back of a cross-beam. Mocking him, the family man symbol had been carved close by.

'Urgh, Christ!' Drake felt a wave of bile roil up into his throat. It was all he could do to suppress it before he covered the entire crime scene in vomit.

He crouched there for as long as he could without making a scene, before clambering to his feet. His heart was still pounding from the sudden adrenaline rush.

'Tanv,' Drake said, meekly. 'I think you may have missed something down there.'

'Oh?' She turned.

'I'll let Reynolds here show you.' He exhaled heavily, still feeling green around the gills. 'Melwood, scene's all yours.'

24

Drake entered the lobby of the building where Ian Reed's flat was located, the tail-end of the daylight flooding the barren white expanse before him in a haze of burnt orange. The address given on his ID was only a five-minute walk from where the murder had occurred. It was practically on the dead man's doorstep.

The thought of Andrea turning up at his own door, and Cari or Eva answering, sent a shudder down Drake's spine. He knew the thought was irrational; very few people knew where they lived, or about the new school the girls had been attending. But it still made him itch and want to move on again. Belatedly, he realised he'd not given much thought to Eva's request about finding a new, more permanent place to live. That would most definitely have to go on the back burner until Andrea was taken into custody for good.

Drake heard Ellie mumbling on a call in the background before she abruptly ended it and came over, her footsteps echoing around behind him. He turned at her approach.

'Chief, let's see if that guy over there has some way for us to enter the flat? He might be the property manager,' she said, pointing at the property manager's office and a man standing nearby.

Drake flashed her a look and nodded as they started over. 'Whatever gave you that idea?'

Ellie ignored his witty remark. 'Strauss ran a quick check for me, and there's no immediate family for the guy in the area. Probably lives on his own, unless there's a girlfriend or boyfriend.'

'Good to know. Don't fancy dealing with another Grace Fleming-type right now, do you?'

'Can't say I do, Boss. That woman was *cold.*'

'Indeed.'

The man Ellie was keen on talking to was a gentleman in his mid-to-late sixties. He reminded Drake of poor Alan Jackson from the old Barndon store with the pair of thin-framed glasses that he wore, but the similarities stopped short at the unfettered short greying afro. The property manager sounded like he was mid-finishing his phone call as they stopped in front of him. Realising they wanted to talk, he quickly stuffed the phone in his pocket.

His rheumy eyes regarded them suspiciously. 'And what can I do for you?'

Drake offered a hand. 'I'm DCI Drake, and this is DS Wilkinson. We're looking to gain entry to a flat in this building. You may have seen the crime scene just a ways over by the playground area?'

'Gerald,' he said, shaking Drake's hand. 'Funnily enough I was just fielding a call from a *concerned* resident.'

'Oh?'

'Yes, between you and me, they were whinging about it spoiling their view.' The man tutted loudly. 'Some people.'

'Something like that,' Drake smiled.

'So, is there a way for us to gain access?' Ellie interjected impatiently.

'Oh, sure,' Gerald said, winking in that way only grandfathers appeared to get away with. 'Just let me know the number, and I'll get right on to it for you.'

'Thanks, we'll wait here,' Drake said with a nod, stepping away while Ellie showed him the dead man's licence with his address on it. He wondered if a search of the flat would provide them with more computer-based evidence, or just a dead end. He wasn't sure he was patient enough for either.

Gerald returned a few minutes later with a key. 'This should do it. Please remember to give it back once you're done.'

'Oh, I'm afraid there'll be a few more of us in need of it in the coming hours and days. You're going to be a busy man.'

The man gave them a toothy grin. 'I'm on holiday from tomorrow, not my problem for much longer.'

'Lucky you,' Drake said, giving the man another nod before heading to the lift.

A holiday. When was the last time I had a proper one of those? he pondered, then realised it would be the first family holiday without Becca. Maybe he'd put it off a little longer.

Ellie had asked what he was going to do about Cari and Eva on the way up to Ian Reeds flat, but he'd responded with 'not sure', because frankly, he wasn't. Perhaps he'd discuss it with her and Strauss soon to see what they thought.

Reaching the floor they needed, they wound through a few more characterless corridors and another lift lobby before arriving at the dead man's door.

'Would you like to do the honours, Ellie?'

'No, not this time, Chief. All yours.' She handed him the key.

'Age before beauty, eh?'

'Something like that,' she said, rolling her eyes.

Drake listened for any immediate noise in response to his opening of the door, but nothing came. No built-in alarm system, nor killers lying in wait; it was eerily quiet. He was slightly jealous. None of the flats he'd occupied in the past had provided such a luxury as bona fide peace and quiet.

As though to mock his thoughts, suddenly there was a rush of feet on the floor and a Jack Russell tore around the corner, yapping and growling at them.

'Whoa, steady now. Easy boy,' Drake said, squatting down to meet the dog.

'Hey there, little guy,' came Ellie's instantly besotted voice behind him. 'Drake, can I keep him? Please?'

The dog continued barking for a moment or two before calming at the sound of their voices. Drake beckoned him over and the dog eventually relented and tottered over to investigate tentatively, his claws tapping on the hard wood surface.

'Atta boy. Good boy,' he said, as the dog allowed his head to be patted. Drake looked up at Ellie. 'We're going to need to get on the phone for someone to take him in. He's probably going to need a new home.'

Ellie's expression dropped. 'Aww, don't say that. Hopefully there'll be some family member that'll claim him,' she knelt down and petted the dog. 'You're a good boy, aint'cha? Yes—yes, you are!'

'Keep him busy for a while, would you?' Drake stood, leaving Ellie cooing over the ferocious guard dog, while he began his rummage of the place.

The space, much like everything with this building development, was ultra-modern. It hardly even seemed lived in, as though the man had bought the place and kept it as a showroom for him and his dog. He'd always felt strangely suspicious of people like that. As though they were trying to hide something dark and sinister beneath a perfectly-tended facade. Ellie had mentioned he'd been living there for a couple of years, since the developments completion, so it should definitely look more *real* than this by now.

Drake started with the immediate area, taken up by a white table top with unpainted wooden legs. There was no place setting on the table, no notepad or anything to indicate the man worked there or ate there. The open-plan kitchen and dining area beyond was much the same in its overall feeling of sterility.

'Anything?' Ellie called from the door, the dog yapping at the sudden noise.

'Nothing so far,' Drake said, probably more quietly than intended as he perused a magazine rack to the side of the light-green sofa. Design magazines, home furnishings, nothing to spark his interest. The lounge led out onto a small balcony which presented a view of the crime scene in the middle-distance. The area was still being worked in the last remnants of daylight, the many white-overalled individuals scurrying around it like ants. Camera flashes gave brief silhouettes of what lay within the tarpaulin.

Drake's footsteps rang hollowly on the floor as he continued his sweep. He didn't find anything worth a further look until he rounded a pillar and saw a spiral staircase leading up, presumably to a bedroom or another floor entirely.

'Just going to check upstairs, Ellie,' he called out, louder this time. 'Shouldn't be long.'

'Okay. Yell if you need me, yeah?'

He climbed the stairs and came to a small landing with two doors leading off. Only a large palm tree-style houseplant in a mottled grey pot nestled between the doors lent any decoration to the sparsity of the upstairs space.

Drake entered one of the rooms, which looked to have been

used as a cross between a walk-in wardrobe and an office. He immediately hefted the bare desk to see if there was anything behind it, but to no avail. There was nothing secreted either behind it or any of the drawers.

That would have been slightly ridiculous, but worth a try, he reasoned to himself, though Strauss and the support teams would need to comb the computer for any clues, regardless. Perhaps that would yield something.

He moved on to the final room, the bedroom, the last of the sun keeping it from being completely pitch black. Drake peered and poked around: the wardrobe, nothing immediately apparent there. No space to hide anything under the bed. Lifting the mattress revealed nothing. Bedside table drawers, nothing. The whole space was a fat lot of sparse nothingness.

Why did you kill this man? Why? Damn it, Andrea.

There was nothing here. Nothing to explain it.

Drake took a deep breath, and quietly contemplated their next steps; there were scant few.

They still had the contents of the first victim's hard drives to access, though more likely than not, the storage devices would lead to nothing. Something more might come to light after Ian Reed's autopsy, or through SOCO turning this place and the crime scene over more thoroughly. But otherwise, they were still running on fumes.

He had to get Andrea out in the open somehow. And that meant he'd have to use Cari. He knew it. No matter how much he didn't want to involve her.

The familiar anger was building in his chest at the idea of having to put the poor girl in that situation, and he hated himself for it.

'There's nothing, Ellie,' he called down. 'Not a goddamn thing.'

25

'This feels weird,' Ellie said as they parked. They were only a short walk from the bar, Marxons, that had been booked for Dave's retirement party. 'You know, as in timing-wise?'

A street light made her eyes shine brightly in the darkness. Melwood had indicated he would be joining them later, which pleased Drake no end. Frankly, he didn't want the man stinking up the car with his inane crap any more. Drake couldn't argue with Ellie about the timing, but he had to admit, it might be a welcome break from the feeling of futility that had come to the fore since checking out the latest victim's home. It would never be a case of all the evidence leading to their woman's exact location, handcuffed and ready to be taken in, but he sometimes wished it would be so. He was getting tired of it. Restless, even.

'No, I know,' he said, hand on the door handle. 'Let's just test the temperature when we get there, eh? Nothing's ever going to be perfectly aligned in our line of work.'

'So wise in your old age.'

'Oi,' he said, smirking as he exited the car.

The venue, if booked in a different era, would have been

wildly inappropriate for a police retirement party, seeing as it had once been a strip club that had changed hands a few times since before eventually becoming just a bar. Drake chuckled to himself at the idea. Maybe back in the sixties and seventies that sort of thing would have been encouraged, such was the way back then. His old man's friend, an old-style bobby on the beat, would have been first in line to get inside and celebrate. His Dad, not so much. Thankfully for Drake, he'd inherited his dad's values and attitudes towards women and not his friends. Although he *had* followed the man's career path.

The stories Ryan Moore had told him of his time on the force had been so interesting and action-packed to his young ears. Chasing criminals through the streets, leaping fences, running between traffic, the story typically ending with their target meeting the business end of Moore's truncheon. It was a fantastical world to his younger self, one where he would have power and a sense of righteousness and virtue. But his mother's untimely death had tempered that desire, fashioning it more to one of selflessness and guardianship, of ridding the world of some of the worst kinds of criminals: murderers and serial killers.

'You all right there, Chief?' Ellie asked as they walked on. The sounds of car tyres peeling slowly along the cobbled side street punctuating the relative quiet.

'Ignore me,' he said. 'Just thinking back to another time in my life, is all. Happens when you get to my age. Didn't think I'd be one for nostalgia, but it's been creeping up on me more and more recently.'

'Before all this?'

'Way before, yes.'

'I wonder too sometimes, you know? Not back to bygone eras, but . . .'

'Oh?'

'I probably shouldn't be saying this, you being my boss and all, but I wonder whether I made the right decision, joining the force in the first place. Not SMT, specifically, but this world we inhabit, the things we see, witnessing what people do. How *we* react sometimes.'

This is unlike her, Drake thought. *What's causing this?*

He spoke carefully, sensing something was off. She'd been a little out of sorts since coming to his house the other day, the moments of bravado withstanding. 'Ellie, is there something you want to tell me?'

His colleague came to a halt, hesitating. He could see now, there *was* clearly something on her mind. Something nagging at her.

'Well . . . sort of. It's just—'

'John! Ellie! You made it!'

Ellie's face perked up immediately at the voice, her downbeat look from moments earlier long forgotten. He turned to see Dave poking his head around the doorway. Drake hadn't twigged how close to the bar they'd stopped. The man's feet and wheelchair were peeking out too. Drake was pleased that he'd braved navigating the cobbled entrance; the man clearly had found the knack of manoeuvring his chair already over the past few weeks. Nothing would keep him down.

'Of course. Wouldn't want you to think you should stay on the force, big man,' Ellie said. Drake noted the slight sadness behind her eyes and beaming smile. He was sure Dave would too. 'Have to ensure you leave and don't come back.'

'Soon, Ellie. Soon.' He smiled beneath his moustache. 'Let's get you both inside and a couple of pints to boot. It's quite the turn out, all things considered.'

'Glad to hear it,' Drake said, holding the side door open as they went inside.

* * *

Dave was a few sheets to the wind by the time the party started quietening down. Drake's old friend had been right, there really had been a good turnout. At Drake's last count, at least forty of Dave's colleagues, old and new, had turned up to see him off. And now, judging by Dave's behaviour, he might have had a similar number of drinks too.

'Let's say we get you home, eh?' Drake said, the two of them at a table away from the throng.

'No, not yet. It's still early. Come on,' Dave slurred.

'You're the boss, but you may need to arrange a taxi. I've got to get back for the girl's sake, soon.'

'About that.' Dave looked up from studying his pint glass on the table, and peered at him. 'I know I've been badgering you about *everything* recently.' He put his hand up at Drake's protestations. 'No, hear me out . . . I just want you to be happy, John. And I see now, those two girls are the most important things to you. I see it.' Dave paused and took a drink. 'So, if you fuck up Cari the way I hear you're going to – by using her as *bait* – then you, my friend, are a complete and utter madman.'

'Dave—'

'I mean it, John. Don't do it.'

Drake leant forwards on the table. 'She'll be protected. She'll never be in the same room as Andrea. She'll be safe. Don't worry yourself with that now, okay?'

'You won't be able to stop yourself, John. I've seen the results of that anger you have in you now. I *saw* what you did to Jack Spencer. You'll do anything to stop these people. To stop them harming those you care about. Something's changed in you since Becca, hasn't it?'

What? Why bring that up now?

He felt his guts tighten at his friend's words.

'Don't bring Becca into this.' Drake pursed his lips before continuing. 'Don't make her the reason for my behaviour – that's all on me, Dave. Just *don't*. And particularly not when you're like this.'

His friend ignored his comment. 'Then don't do what you're thinking. There will be other ways.'

'Maybe.'

'There will. Don't be an arse.'

Drake took a deep breath, trying to make himself heard over the bar's music. 'I'm just . . . I'm just so *angry*, Dave. Angry at my inability to catch these people before they hurt others. Angry at leaving Eva without a mother. Angry at Andrea doing what she did, and what she's *still* doing. How Cari is now, because of her.' He clenched his pint glass tightly. 'And most of all, I'm angry at that god forsaken *bastard*, Samuel Barrow.'

'Then use that anger the right way. But, please, don't let it cloud your judgement and make you rash, John. Don't become like those people. You're better than that.'

He took a deep breath as he considered the man's words. 'I'll try. I will.'

'You better.' He leant over and clapped Drake on the shoulder. 'Now, where's the bog?'

'You're on your own there, Dave.'

'What? Look at me? Come on . . .' his friend said, looking at him with doe eyes.

Drake shook his head with a look of feigned disgust. 'I'll get someone else. What you're after help with is *not* in my job description.'

26

Drake closed the door to the flat behind him and placed his keys on to the kitchen counter. He didn't like arriving back too late, as it meant sneaking around and checking in on the girls before he got to sleep himself. It was a habit he couldn't shake since the incidents of the previous year and Eva coming back into his life. He hoped it wouldn't always be like that. A few more years and they'd be adults, after all.

Thankfully, he heard the thrum of music coming from the direction of the girl's bedrooms. He wasn't able to make it out fully, but he discerned it to be a David Bowie track, *Sound and Vision*.

Glad to hear they're on to something a little more upbeat lately, and still not any modern crap, he thought.

Having only nursed one drink all evening, he'd decided to drive back. The thought of a hangover in the current climate, or collecting his car in the morning, were both things he didn't even want to consider. But the drive had been a nervy one all the same. He'd set himself to telling them about Andrea, on the proviso that they were still awake. And now he'd discovered they were, it was bittersweet. Drake had already played out a few scenarios, and none of them ended well. Either one or both girls were going to react badly. He couldn't blame them. He'd be the same.

He rubbed his face, physically trying to steel himself for what was to come.

It's for the best. You'll see.

He gathered his thoughts, and braced himself before striding down the corridor and knocking on Eva's door.

No answer, which seemed to be the default setting between them since the dawn of time.

He knocked again, still nothing. The momentary worry soon dispelled and replaced by relief when they both answered at the same time.

'Can you turn that off and come to the lounge, please?' Drake said without opening the door.

'Okay, coming,' came Eva's reply.

He made his way back down the corridor and stood by the window in the open-plan living area. Night-time London was still bustling, though there were markedly less cars choking up the roads. Various crane warning lights were glowing red against the night sky. The colourful lighting of the pointy end of The Shard and the surrounding skyscrapers broke up the sea of warm yellows and whites of the office blocks.

The music soon went off, followed by the sound of a door opening and hushed voices. He heard the approaching sound of feet slipping and sliding on the wooden floor, and his throat tightened.

Drake took a breath and turned, almost amused by his dread at the two near identical girls in their nightwear. Eva was in an oversized black t-shirt with a large cartoon depiction of a cat on it and Cari wore the classic yellow smiley face black Nirvana top.

Her Dad's t-shirt. That particular detail made him doubt momentarily whether he should be doing this.

No, I have to.

The two teenagers slumped down on the sofa, Cari drawing her legs into her chest and looking at the floor.

'Thank you. I thought you may have been asleep.'

'We're not party animals like you, Dad. Can smell the booze from here.'

Drake ignored the comment and got straight to the point: 'I've got something I need to tell you.'

He gripped the frame of the windowsill behind him and planted his feet. His mind screaming at him. He noticed Cari frowning slightly at his initial statement.

'Oh?' Eva raised her eyebrows.

He turned to Cari. 'It's . . . well, Cari—'

'It's my mother, isn't it?' Cari's head snapped to him instantly. 'What? What is it? Have you found her?' The sound of her voice made his own throat feel sore, such was its raspiness, and her eyes were like saucers beneath the strands of long hair. Eva, tellingly, remained quiet. It wasn't her moment.

'She . . . She's been in contact with me. Called me.'

'Is she okay?'

Drake hesitated again. What could he say to that? Even after all that had happened to the poor girl, she was asking after her mother, the person who had murdered her father and mutilated her.

Andrea wasn't okay. Far from it.

'She's . . . *confused.*'

Drake could see the girl's arms tightening around her legs as she contemplated his responses.

Cari turned her gaze back towards the floor, and spoke, her voice just above a whisper and tinged with a sadness that made

Drake crumble inside. 'She's not *there*, is she? Her condition, it's made her different, hasn't it?'

'Cari . . .'

Eva grabbed a cushion and held it tight. 'Dad, just try and be honest with her. Please.'

Your mum has brutally killed two men. I've not even been able to speak with her, just Miray, he thought.

He pinched the bridge of his nose. 'She doesn't seem to be the same person that you described, no. She's a little different right now.'

Cari lifted her eyes again. 'Please tell me she's not hurt anyone else? Please? Mr Drake?'

Drake hesitated for just a split second too long.

'Oh, no-no-no! Mum, no!' Cari started to splutter and cry, burying her head in her legs as her body quivered at the news.

Drake stayed put. Nothing he could say or do would make her feel better, but it didn't stop him feeling next to useless. 'I'm sorry, Cari. I'm so sorry.'

Eva moved in closer and put an arm around her best friend, choosing not to say a word. The girl's sobs eventually lessened and Cari looked up again at Drake, her eyes red-rimmed, her face puffy. The gash at her neck was a strange white against the reddened skin surrounding it.

'Can I speak with her?' she whispered.

Shit.

'Well, about that . . .'

27

Drake closed the door to his bedroom. The girls had gone to bed an hour or so before. Eva had insisted she sleep in Cari's room to keep her company, despite her friend irritably proclaiming she was okay. Whether they were actually asleep was another matter, but Drake was just pleased that Cari was not alone, all the same.

After the discussion about whether or not she would or even *should* be speaking with her mother, Cari still insisted that she would be fine. That it was a necessary evil, if only to stop her from hurting more people, or herself. But Eva had his nose for people. They both knew that Cari was anything but okay, despite seemingly improving after the initial shock about her mother and her condition had worn off.

But Drake was still conflicted, as he always was these days. He felt Cari could take it to some degree, but he genuinely had no idea how *Andrea* would react. She was a complete law unto herself, and without understanding the reason why she was killing, it made his job just that little bit more unpredictable and difficult.

He saw his phone vibrate on the bedside table as he was about to get undressed for bed.

What now? Give me just one minutes peace . . . Please. Just one.

He saw the grey background, the nothingness indicating it was an unknown caller.

It had to be Miray again. It had to be. She was calling back.

'Miray?' he answered, his mouth a thin line.

'Oh, how clever of you, DCI Drake,' she said, speaking with a satisfied air. 'What gave it away?'

'I don't have time for your bullshit, Miray. Have you had time to think on what I told you earlier, perhaps calmed down a little?'

'Did you like my second present, John? Nice little surprise so soon after the other one, don't you think?' She sniggered. 'I really shouldn't be spoiling you like this. But I couldn't help myself.'

'No,' he snapped, then taking a deep breath to stop himself getting carried away. 'You need to stop.'

'Why? Keeps you in a job, doesn't it? And I'm only just getting started.'

'But why? What have these people done to deserve this?' he blurted. 'How do you know them?'

He was met with nothing but distant breathing.

'How do you know them, Miray? Answer me.'

Drake listened intently, wandering over to the bedroom window, which stood slightly ajar. He swore he could hear muttering of some kind on the other end of the phone, as though she was talking to someone with her hand over it.

'Is there someone there with you, Miray?'

Silence.

'Miray!'

'Shouting won't help your case, Drake. I'm not telling you anything without seeing my *granddaughter* first.' The word 'granddaughter' spat through gritted teeth.

Drake's face hardened. 'You know that's not going to happen. I'm not letting you in the same building as her, let alone the same damn room.'

'Then this is the point where I'll be saying goodbye—'

She broke off from the phone, not hanging up. Again, it sounded like she was having a heated discussion. Perhaps it was with Andrea? Cari's mother not liking what the other personality was saying and doing?

A gentle breeze wafted across his cheek as he stared out of the window while awaiting her response.

Perhaps I could try for a middle-ground. Something that will keep both parties 'happy'. If that's even possible.

'How about a video call, Miray?' Drake said, raising his voice, hoping she could hear it, despite appearing distant from the phone. 'It's a start.'

There was a series of muffled noises for a time again. He paced the room as the silence dragged on, uncomfortably so, then Miray was back.

'Yes. Okay. We—*I'd* like that.' He felt like she was smirking again. 'I'll be able to see my handiwork.'

Drake turned his nose up in disgust. His grip tightening on the phone. The horrific scars she'd inflicted both physically and mentally on Cari were not to be joked about. 'She's just a damn kid, Miray.'

'Precisely, so who gives a shit? Anyway, tomorrow afternoon, I'll call again. And no, I'm not giving you an exact time. Beggars can't be choosers – nor can police officers, it seems.'

She laughed and hung up on him.

28

Ellie grabbed the fresh slice of toast that had just popped up, the smell making her mouth water. She quickly buttered it and snagged it between her teeth before she rushed through the morning routine, taking an occasional bite. For what was probably only the second time since the Spencer case, and her being able to walk unaided again, the stars had aligned and both she and Len were able to take Bella to school. For all Ellie knew, it could be weeks or months until the next opportunity. She had to make the most of it.

Ellie poked her head out to the hallway. 'Len, can you make sure that's everything from upstairs, please?'

'Yes, love,' he called back down.

It still seemed like such a rush, even when they'd supposedly got the majority of the routine down to a fine art. She sat down on the sofa for a moment, taking an unsatisfactory bite of her toast while thinking back to the previous evening. Ellie felt surprisingly sprightly for someone who'd drunk more than she had done in a while. She hadn't been drunk, not by any means, but it was enough for her to know she'd had a few the next day.

But she'd had fun, and it had warmed her soul that Dave had a good send-off too. God knows he'd earned it. She owed him so much.

Ellie's eyelid twinged as she thought back to the moment she'd almost confided in Drake about Fiona Spencer before Dave had interrupted. It had felt right for the first time. When would she next get the chance? Perhaps one day, things would just resolve themselves inside her brain and she'd wake up a new woman, free of any burden of guilt.

Yeah, and pigs – very, very large ones, at that – might fly, she thought, her mood taking a dip.

Ellie heard the jumping cadence of a stomping six-year-old on the stairs, followed by Len's gentler steps. Gulping down the last of her toast, Ellie snatched her work coat off the back of a dining chair and made for the front door.

'Come here, you,' she said, guiding Bella back towards the foot of the stairs so she could help her put her school shoes on.

'I can do it,' her daughter said, giggling.

'Oh, okay. I forget how grown up you are these days,' Ellie gave her a grin, and Bella returned it. She watched as her daughter did up the first shoe effortlessly, then moved on to the second.

I must be a bit slow from the night before, still. I knew she could do these things herself.

Bella made a frustrated face with the second shoe, and glanced up sadly.

'Mummy, what's wrong?'

Ellie's throat tightened. An image of her little girl being carried away by a masked Fiona Spencer flashed into her mind, making her flinch. And Dave getting a knife in the chest. Bella's kidnapping: it had been so close. She rubbed her eyes, forced a smile for Bella. 'It's nothing, honey. Let's get this shoe done and your coat on, yeah?'

Len appeared from the living room with his laptop bag, looking dapper in his glasses and a dark trench coat. Though she thought the light grey trousers were a little short in the leg.

'Ready?'

'As we'll ever be.' She nodded, squeezing Bella's shoulder and guiding her to the door.

The walk to school was a crisp one; colder than it probably should have been for the time of year, at least that's how it felt to her. Her family's breath condensed like the funnels of a steamship as they trundled along at Bella's pace. There wasn't a cloud in the sky as they followed the other families to the school, the brilliant blue of spring framing the trees and buildings in contrast to their solid mottled browns and greys.

'This is nice,' Len said, looking over at her, Bella's hand engulfed by his.

'It is, isn't it?' She returned his look with a smile. 'Feels like an age since we last did this.'

'Maybe we should try it more often,'

'Maybe once this case calms down . . . It's a little intense—' She stopped talking, slapping her hands to her mouth in her mind's eye.

Oh, shit. Yep, clearly tired. Fuck.

Len's ears pricked up. 'Calms down? I thought the case you were on was "nothing special"? *Ellie . . . ?*'

'Let's just keeping walking and drop Bella off. We'll talk after, yeah?'

Len took a deep breath and pursed his lips, choosing not to respond while they walked on.

That's the last time I lie to him. It was such a pointless one, anyway.

* * *

Ellie watched in silence with Len as Bella left them and ran over to a school friend, her loose mittens flopping around her wrists on their woollen strings. She gave them both a wave again before turning and following the waiting teacher inside.

'I can't believe how much she's—'

'All right, Ellie,' Len snapped.

'What? Come on, Len,' Ellie threw up her arms and paced towards the nearby school sign. 'It was just a *small* lie. I was tired when you asked and I just wanted to sleep. I didn't want, or need, another argument. You know my sleep is screwed enough as it is.'

'But you still did it.' He scratched the back of his head and walked over to her. 'You'd never have lied about that before your new job, and you know it.'

'That's because this job is *different*, Len. How many more times!'

He gripped her shoulders and locked eyes with her to hammer home his next point. 'It shouldn't mean you're different too, Ellie—'

Ellie stopped hearing her husband's words at the sight just beyond his shoulder. Over the road, by a bottle-green telecoms cabinet. Her eyes had to be deceiving her. It wasn't? Was it? How?

A man was leaning against the cabinet, speaking to someone on his mobile.

It was the man from the school CCTV.

The CCTV they'd reviewed as part of the Spencer case.

He was even wearing the same black hooded sweatshirt from the video they'd watched all those months ago. The video of him passing the duct-taped Action Man to Bella. It was him, she was sure of it.

'Len, be quiet a second.'

'Don't tell me to—' He saw the look on her face and stopped. 'What? What is it?'

'Call the police. Now. Tell them I need backup,' she said, stripping her coat off and shoving it on her husband. 'That I'm detaining a suspect, but he may run for it. Give them the address, the direction I may go, everything. Now.'

'Detaining a suspect? What—'

There was no time to answer Len. Ellie was off and bounding up the street, her eyes fixed on the man over the road, who had finished his call. A car sped past just as she was going to cross over and the CCTV man caught sight of her. A confused expression crossed his face as she stared him down, then one of apparent realisation.

The road now clear, she sprinted across, the man taking one final look before turning and making a run for it.

Oh no, you don't.

She'd spooked him. If only he'd seen her a few seconds later, she would have had him. Ellie couldn't say she blamed him: she must look like a woman possessed and he must have known what he'd done would catch up with him eventually.

Ellie gave chase, her feet deftly striking the pavement. The man was just short of six feet tall, which was going to make her pursuit more challenging, given her stride length compared to his. But she had stamina on her side; even with her change in career and the injury a few months back, it couldn't have altered that much. The question was, would he have similar reserves in the tank?

Just up the street, the suspect barged past an older woman, shoving her into a black bollard. Ellie reached her just as she'd gathered herself. The woman appeared unharmed, and Ellie sped on after her quarry. They both pounded down the street, passing parked car after parked car before coming to a busy junction, the sounds of mopeds, cars and beeping traffic crossings increasing in volume. The sounds of a local shopping district buzzed amidst the early morning rush; if she wasn't careful, she'd lose him in the throng and traffic.

CCTV man hesitated, seemingly unsure of where to go before making his decision and running in front of a red London bus. The driver made his feelings known at the close call, the horn sounding loudly as the man continued on toward a busy coffee shop that had a queue forming outside. A customer came out at the wrong time and the runner barged into them, sending himself and the young woman's coffee flying to the ground. Ellie was nearing the road to cross toward him. This could be her chance to catch up with him.

Ellie's heart was pumping in her chest as she gulped air, her eyes laser focused on the man. Much to her annoyance, he sprung to his feet and limped on before regaining his stride, having worked off the knock.

Shit.

They continued on, Ellie avoiding the traffic and gaining on him slightly as they reached a bridge. The man stopped again for a second.

He can't be thinking about jumping, surely? There's a damn river below.

He must have read her mind and thought better of it, sprinting on. CCTV man looked as though the run was beginning to catch up on him, and Ellie had to admit her initial bravado was fading too, the beginnings of stiffness in her leg making itself known as she began running over the hump of the bridge.

No, not now. Damn it!

The man turned sharply ahead of her, seemingly deciding his best bet was to take the stairs down the side of the bridge and on to the canal path.

He bet wrong.

Ellie peered over the side of the bridge at the stairs, seeing a younger, well-built man coming up the stairs just below, possibly out of the suspect's sight. He'd be more than a match for her runner, judging by his appearance.

'Stop that man!' she shouted, pointing above him. 'I'm a police officer!'

The younger man looked up at her with a frown as she sped down the rest of the bridge toward the stairs.

Sounds began emanating from the stairwell.

'Get out the fucking way!' Then a desperate cry of 'Please!'

'No!' came the defiant response.

Ellie pounded the stairs, and CCTV man turned just in time for her to shove him against the solid concrete of the bridge stairwell.

'Don't you move, you bastard,' she said, through gritted teeth. She seized the man's wrist and twisted it behind him, his cheek planted firmly against the wall.

'Ah! Get off! You're hurting me!'

Ellie delighted at the man's pathetic squeals.

The younger man held the suspect at the shoulder in a meaty hand. Between the two of them, he wasn't going anywhere any time soon.

'Thank you,' Ellie puffed, turning to her helper.

'No problem,' the man said, speaking with a heavy Polish accent. 'Happy to help.'

The suspect continued to squirm while Ellie shoved his wrist further into his back before she freed up one of her hands to call for a Response unit.

'Police are on their way,' she said, speaking into the man's ear. 'You better calm down, you're not going anywhere anytime soon.'

'Fuck! I didn't do anything,' he said, gasping for air. 'Please.

Let me sit down and catch my breath, at least? I promise, I won't run.'

Ellie deliberated for a moment. The man didn't have anywhere to go. Police would be here soon. She decided to let him sit. The Polish man continued to keep hold of him and pushed him to the ground. The man twisted round and sat with his legs arched, his head between his thighs while he continued panting.

Ellie grabbed a short tuft of hair and lifted his head, looking him in the eye menacingly.

'Now, you're going to tell me what the fuck is going on . . . got it?'

29

Ellie waited in the interview room for the man she'd apprehended to be brought in, her hands tightly clasped on the table. A camera peered down from the corner into the sparse space. Her knee was still throbbing, which both worried and agitated her in equal measure.

I guess this is someone up there's way of saying I'm not in my twenties any more . . . Balls.

Ellie had since prised CCTV man's name out of him: Steven Pinter. She preferred the mysterious-sounding nickname they'd given him.

Pinter was a typical re-offender. At twenty-five, he was a drug addict and infrequent homeless person, not local to Harrow where she lived. The South Harrow police station's Staff Sergeant had reeled off the man's criminal record for a good few minutes, but she'd got the message after the first couple of lines. Ellie knew the type. It was sad that there even was a type, but a type it was all the same. The man usually hung around south London, funnily enough, within a few miles of Putney and their offices, rather than Harrow in the north-western side. What were the chances?

Ellie had given a rather irate Len a ring once the Response team had arrived and got Pinter secured in their car. She tried her best to assure him everything was okay, but it hadn't quite landed how she wanted. He should have been relieved; it was one less piece of the puzzle to worry about in the Spencer case. And perhaps the man could provide them with the final fragments to fill in those last few gaps. But that was her police brain again, not understanding what it must be like for Len as a civilian to see his wife tearing off after someone. Come to think of it, he'd probably not seen her in work mode before.

Ellie was still cursing herself for only just realising that now, when Pinter was shown into the interview room. She didn't make a move to stand, instead waiting for him to take a seat. Pinter, formerly CCTV man, had been cooperative since being subdued and wasn't handcuffed as a result. It usually also helped to make people more receptive to answering questions.

Pinter sat with his head down, his eyes focused on the floor. A duty solicitor followed soon after. She was a tired-looking woman, with more grey running through her hair than brown. Ellie didn't envy her position. But the look the solicitor gave Ellie didn't exactly make Ellie warm to her, either.

'Mr Pinter.' Ellie set the recording equipment running and smiled thinly at him. 'Good to see you again.'

'Mmm,' he said, non-committal. The solicitor subtly rolled her eyes and scribbled a note.

Ellie supposed Pinter was used to the routine. No doubt he'd been in a jail cell or a police station interview room more times than he'd been in a place of work these last few years.

'Excuse the pun, but do you mind if we just cut to the chase? I know you've been through this sort of thing before.'

'Very funny,' he replied, sounding like he thought it was anything but. Still not looking up, he scratched at his arm, hitching up the black sleeve of his hoodie just enough to show his signs of drug use.

Ellie flinched slightly at the sight. She'd seen it hundreds of times, but it was still never pleasant to witness. 'Thank you.' She tilted her head and forced another smile. 'So, why did you run from me today? Hardly the actions of someone with nothing to hide, was it?'

'I guess.' He gave a faint shrug, his scratching becoming more intense. The solicitor made another note.

'Then why do it?'

'Because,' he half-mumbled, 'I saw this little black woman charging at me. What would you do? Stand there and wait for whatever was coming your way, eh?'

'If I was – as you put it – a *little* black woman, then, that's not really going to cause you much trouble, is it?'

She hoped this back and forth would stop soon. She was already growing tired of it. How she'd put up with this crap in her old role for as long as she did, she didn't know.

'I dunno, you might be after me for money or something? Maybe you were strapped. Got no idea who I owe these days, innit?'

She took a deep breath at his insinuation and let it slide. 'So, you saw me, and ran. What were you hoping would happen? That I'd just give up? Surely if I was after you and had found you there, then I'd keep coming?'

'Didn't give it much thought. I just wanted to get away,' he said meekly. Ellie felt a sudden pity for him; the way he'd just spoken, it was like he'd regressed back to his teenage years. Probably before he got on the smack.

Ellie shook her head while she thought of the state of the streets these days. The solicitor regarded her with tired eyes.

'Okay, anyway . . .' She put her hands out on the table, trying to appear open. She knew he could see her, despite his bowed head, he'd been snatching glimpses. 'I caught up with you, we're here now. I don't care what else you're in deep on. All I want to know is this, why did you give a school girl that action figure, the one with the duct-tape wrapped around its head?'

'Figure? Schoolgirl? You what?' He sat back and looked at her, giving her a look of confusion.

'Yes, a few months back now. We've got you on the school's CCTV.'

That seemed to get the solicitor's interest. The woman sat back, ears pricked.

'Think you got the wrong guy, innit?'

'No, I can assure you that's not the case. It's clear as day. It's you, Steven,' she said, staring him straight in the face. 'Look, we can go through this all day, but I *know* it was you. I'll get the video and show you, or you could just save us the time?'

'Maybe it *was* me, you know . . . ? I was probably off my face. Messing around with the kids. Scaring 'em.'

'I don't think so, Steven. What you did had purpose. You went for one kid in particular, and got their attention.'

The man sat for a moment, as though he was deep in thought. The cogs whirring for all to see. Then, he seemed to have a moment of realisation. 'The little black girl? Holy shit, that's not your daughter, is it? That's why you were there today?'

Ellie said nothing. She didn't want to bring her little girl into this discussion any more than she already had, if she could help it.

'Holy shit,' he repeated. 'What're the chances? You being there today and me too. Can't make this shit up, man. No way.'

'It's not my daughter. There's more than one black woman in this world, you ignorant fuck head.'

'Whatever you say,' he said, smiling at her sardonically.

'You're admitting it was you, now?'

'So what if I am, I didn't do anything. Didn't hurt her, did I? Only doing what I was told—'

Gotcha.

Pinter stopped talking. The solicitor put a hand on his arm and whispered in his ear. Ellie couldn't make any of it out again.

She pressed on. 'What do you mean, "only doing what you were told?"'

The man's behaviour changed instantly. Suddenly, he was scared. Really scared. He shot a look at the solicitor again.

'No, I didn't mean nothing by it.'

'Elaborate for me, please. I've no interest in anything else you may or may not have done.'

He gave his solicitor another look. She nodded.

'Okay, but please, this isn't going to go further than these walls, is it?' he said, leaning forward on the table.

'Of course,' she said, feeling an excitement building in the pit of her stomach. 'No-one outside of the investigation will know about this.'

'So, there was this guy, right? Approached me and told me to do it.'

Ellie frowned. So a man just randomly turned up and told him to do it? Was it Jack Spencer? Perhaps even Fiona, if she covered up enough? They'd made the mistake of judging her to be a man themselves, so why not a drug-addled junkie?

'Why would you do what a random stranger asked you to do?'

'He gave me money. Cash.' He whistled for effect. 'I'm hardly going to turn that down, innit?'

'Okay, but why do you seem so frightened to tell me this?'

'I ain't scared,' he mumbled, his face turning red.

'You seem scared from where I'm sitting.'

'He said he'd come back, or find me, and do me in. Don't usually get scared by that, but he had a look 'bout him.'

'What did he look like?'

'Can't really remember, I was out of it, like, waiting to meet someone for a bit of stuff, you know. Proper strung out. You get me?'

Ellie took a deep breath, shooting the solicitor a look. 'Come on, Steven. How do you know you hadn't seen him before, then?'

'Honest, like. He was wearing a hat, and like, had a scarf or snood thing or something covering up some of his face. But it didn't *feel* like someone I knew.'

Ellie stomach dropped. She wondered if that was something that they could scan for on any CCTV in the area, but doubted it, it'd been months. Probably long gone, erased or otherwise. Either way, she'd get Strauss and co to check the tapes they still had and for any others.

'You sure? You're not just making this up because you're scared?'

'No. Honest to God. It's the truth.'

Ellie wanted to punch something or someone. Just when she felt she was getting somewhere, she was basically back to square one again. For God's sake.

'Okay, but why were you back there today, then?'

'Been coming back every so often, you know . . . Thinking I might get another wad of cash for doing something else.'

'Why? Did they say they would come back?'

Pinter leant back in his chair, looking like he had won something in his mind. He gave her a shit-eating grin.

'As a matter of fact, they did, yeah . . .' He hesitated. 'But 'ent seen them since.'

Time to put the fear of God up him. If only for my own enjoyment.

She smiled to herself. 'Pinter, I'm going to be straight with you, okay?'

The man leant in again, waiting for her to confide in him. 'Oh, yeah?'

'You assisted a serial killer that day.'

Pinter looked aghast at what she was telling him. 'Shit, no way. You're kidding me, right?' He paused, eyes narrowing. 'Wait, is he going to come after me?'

'No. He's not.'

'Why? How can you be so sure?' he said, looking like he was worried that Jack Spencer would bash down the door and throttle him on the spot.

'He's in prison for life, that's why.'

'What? Shit!' The man said, wide-eyed. 'You're not going to send me down too, are you? Please! If my mum heard about that, it'd kill her.'

She looked him over once more. Taking in the sight of the man that she had been so worried about up until this interview. Now he just looked scared, almost pathetic. Not like someone who was capable of anything that she dealt with in SMT. There wasn't a calculating bone in this man's body.

She sighed, trying to make her exasperation as obvious as possible. The solicitor seemed to have a similar thought process with her client.

'Steven, I'm going to let you go, okay? No charges.' Ellie slid him her card with her details on it. 'And when you are out there – doing whatever it is you do – you're going to give me a call if you think of anything more, all right? Got it? You can do that, right?'

Pinter tutted at her. 'Why?'

'Just . . .'

Jesus Christ.

'. . . understand when you've had a close call, Steven, and that I'm feeling charitable, all right?' She pinched her brow in frustration. This was getting tedious. 'Now get out of here before I charge you with aiding and abetting a damn serial killer.'

30

I watched from the bed as Ben talked animatedly with my mother. It all felt so distant, so . . . *surreal* for some reason, and I couldn't quite put my finger on why. Like there was a shape in the distance that no matter how long you ran for or how quickly, you could never quite catch up to it and see it in its full form. Just forever a distant figment, an ethereal cloud of sorts. An enigma with no end.

And it enraged me.

My inability to think straight, to even *see* straight at times. To understand what was going on and why.

'You . . . Can't . . .' Ben said. I blinked at the words, his voice, not catching everything.

'I will,' my mother shrieked defiantly.

'No, Miray. It's not what we agreed. Please, you have to see reason.'

Reason? See reason about what?

'I have all the reasons I need,' she retorted.

I couldn't stand seeing her this way. Knowing that I would undoubtedly be on the receiving end of her temper like so many times before, her abuse more frequent and more physical. I didn't know what to do any more. She was my mother.

I turned away, not wanting to see or hear either of them chiding each other. I covered my head with the duvet as I breathed deeply and focused on anything but them.

Just focus, Andrea. Focus on the breathing. That should clear things; help you think straight.

Breathe.

My consciousness pinged to the present as something tapped my shoulder.

I didn't know how long I'd been laying there; time was a secondary element in that room. It could be night or day for all I knew. The only way to judge in any shape or form was by what food was given to me.

I stirred, but didn't move, the groggy feeling overcoming me again.

'Mmm-hmm?'

The distance voice came again. Then I felt more pressure on my shoulder.

'Andrea? Andrea . . . ?'

Suddenly the covers were yanked from me, and I was exposed. The bright light temporarily blinded me as I opened my eyes to try and react.

'Andrea, it's me. Ben.'

There was nothing and no-one else in the room. My mother wasn't there.

'Andrea . . .'

I looked around again, and there he was. My Ben.

'I was asleep. What's wrong? Is Cari okay? Are you . . . ?'

'We're fine. Cari's fine.'

'Then what? What is it?'

'I want you to come with me, again. I know you don't like it, but . . . it's,' he seemed to be choosing his words carefully, '. . . *necessary*. Your Mum can come too.'

I blinked slowly, Ben's face blurring. 'Okay.'

'Here,' he said, handing me my medication. 'This will help.'

'Thank you.'

Ben stood and made for the door. I quickly shoved the medication underneath the corner of the bed cover. Maybe that would stop my brain fog and I would finally be well enough to see Cari.

It had been too long.

My husband turned back and I smiled innocently at his loving face, taking his hand and following him out the door.

31

Drake managed to run to the café the girls liked before either had risen from the dead, and soon returned with his haul in tow: freshly-baked croissants, pain au chocolat and a bacon sandwich for himself. He'd grown quite accustomed to them these last few weeks, but looking at his burgeoning stomach, his waistline certainly wasn't. Whether it was even dad bod territory any more, he wasn't sure.

Either way, Drake knew he needed to – no, he *had* – to do everything he could to keep them in good spirits for what lay ahead. What Cari would be going through today with her mother would be extremely distressing; and for Eva, too, albeit differently. She had insisted on being nearby to support her friend with the call, despite his protestations. But Drake was worried that it might trigger his daughter somehow. She had been doing so well recently.

He knew in his bones that the video call was a bad idea. He knew it, but what more could he do? It was his job to make the hard decisions that no one else could. Though when it involved his family — and he was beginning to see Cari as family — he was wavering. But more people could die, and soon. He had to do *something*.

The plan they had devised was to sit tight with the girls at Forest Gate police station in Newham where the third call had taken place, and wait for Miray to contact them. They'd decided to cast their net of newly requisitioned interception teams as wide as they could, both in Newham and the neighbouring boroughs. There would be teams headed up by Ellie in one location, and Melwood at another; Strauss too, though he would be focused on Ealing in the west where the second contact had been made, in order to narrow down her likely location, once and for all. Miller had agreed to the additional resource for the operation, and Drake was damn well going to use it. If they couldn't pinpoint Andrea this time, they'd have to resort to something else. But he daren't even consider any other option for now. This would be their one and only — until it wasn't. But that scenario didn't bear thinking about.

Drake was just about to take the lift back up to his floor when an unexpected voice came from the direction of the lobby entrance.

'Drake, stop.'

He turned to see Melwood hurrying toward him.

'Andrew? What're you doing here? How do you—'

'I just wanted to check in and see you were all right, and ensure we're a hundred per cent on doing this.' Melwood paused, evaluating him. 'You are, right? If it were my son . . . I wouldn't be so sure.'

'It's our only option right now. We have to locate her,' Drake said flatly. He felt strangely uncomfortable about Melwood being there. The man was harmless, and some might say he was even doing his job, looking out for colleagues, but it felt like an invasion of privacy somehow. How did Melwood know where he lived? Had he asked Miller?

'Okay. Well, just know I'm here for you, if you need me. I know I can come across like a bit of an arsehole sometimes, but I mean well. You know?'

Drake frowned at the man's surprising self-awareness. There was no doubt he had the knack for coming across that way. Even more so lately, and on multiple occasions. Perhaps this could even be him turning over a new leaf, though Drake would believe it when he saw it. 'Okay. Thanks. I appreciate you coming over.'

'Cool. Well, now that's sorted, I'll be off, then,' Melwood said, giving a friendly smile. 'I'm one of the unlucky ones being shoved in the back of a van. Think of me while you're in that comfy police station, eh?'

Drake cracked a slight smile. 'Have you seen Forest Gate station? But sure, will do. Thanks, Andrew. Though, maybe just call in future, yeah?'

The DI nodded and left him to grab the glass lift, which pinged a few seconds later.

He glanced around after entering and caught a glimpse of Melwood standing and watching from the entrance to the building. Drake gave him a quick nod, but his colleague didn't reciprocate as the lift ascended.

32

It was late morning, an hour before the anxious wait for Miray's afternoon call would begin, not that anxiety wasn't rife already. The drive over to Forest Gate police station had been tense and largely silent, the atmosphere one you could cut with a knife. Eva hadn't left her friend's side for the whole morning. Drake wasn't sure if Cari really wanted that level of support, but Eva wasn't giving her much choice in the matter.

They'd been set up in a room in the far reaches of the station that Drake assumed was used for conference calls and the like, and probably storage for surplus office equipment, judging by the rusted cabinets and piles of boxes stored there, containing who knows what. A large television screen was mounted on one peeling wall, looming over the small circular table beneath it. The room was on the cosy side, and with the two girls, it was bordering on claustrophobic, even without the reason for them being there. It didn't exactly fill Drake with confidence, and it was probably more than a little unsettling for two teenagers.

'This is a bit of a shit hole, isn't it?' Eva said, stating what they were all thinking. She dusted off the table with the back of her hand, a look of disgust crossing her face when her hand returned thick with dust and unidentified crumbs.

'Welcome to my working life,' Drake said, pursing his lips.

She looked over at him as he made his way around the table now that they were inside. 'It all makes sense now. You know, why you're so miserable.'

'Thanks, love. I appreciate the sympathy.'

Cari gave a slight smile as she took a seat on a rickety vinyl chair.

Drake regretted not being able to do more for her, but they were short on time. It wouldn't be comfortable, but it would have to do.

'So, while we're here and have some time. You're clear on what you need to do, Cari? Or do you want to go over it again? It's no trouble if you do,' he said, sitting down for a moment.

'I think so. I need to try and get her to hand herself in,' she said, barely lifting her eyes to his. 'As well as try and hold her on the call long enough for you to find her?'

'Yes, that's pretty much it,' he said gently. 'Remember, if at any time you're finding it too much, leave the room and Eva will go with you, okay? Your Mum, with the way she is right now . . . Please, understand no one would be upset if it was too hard, okay?'

'You think I don't know that more than anyone?' she snapped.

Drake flinched. Obviously, she was feeling the pressure already. He really hoped Cari could keep it together for the call, but he'd completely understand if she couldn't. He was still surprised at how quickly she agreed in the first place. She certainly was made of stern stuff.

'I'm sorry, Cari. I didn't mean to patronise you. You're going to do great,' he said, putting a reassuring hand on her arm.

'Remember, if possible, please try and avoid the topic of your dad. I know it will be hard not to. But it could trigger her and make her angry.'

Cari twitched slightly at the mention of her father. 'Okay, I'll try. Sounds like her being angry is the least of your troubles, though.'

'Something like that,' Drake said, not wanting to keep the subject on Andrea a moment longer. 'Anyway, can I get you girls anything while I'm making a call? Caviar? Duck à l'orange?' he asked as he got up from the table and stood in the doorway.

Eva, humouring him, twisted round to face him. 'Duck à l'what now?'

'Never mind.'

'Just water, please, Mr Drake,' Cari whispered, her hands clasped tightly between her legs.

'Got it.'

Drake left the room and wound through the corridors of the shabby building. He knew the layout reasonably well, having had cause to stop by occasionally. He rifled around in his pocket for his phone to call Strauss, and saw that Ellie had texted him.

'Sorry, Boss. Long story. You're not going to believe this, but I'm about to interview CCTV man! Can't make your stuff with Miray right now. Sorry again. Good luck!'

Great, just great, he thought. *I'll have to get someone else on point for her detail.*

But also, it was intriguing. CCTV man? That was out of the left-field. How the hell had she cornered him? They'd had no idea who he was before today. Was it a chance encounter, or was there something she wasn't telling him? Is that why she'd seemed off recently?

He dialled Strauss' number as he reached the entrance to the cafeteria, where a few officers were gathered round a scattering of tables. The smell of food was making his stomach growl. The DS answered after a few rings.

'Drake? All set there?' Wherever Strauss was, the signal was bad.

'Just settling in, yes. How about you? You in a van too, like Melwood?'

'No, I'm in my car. Got a text from Ellie, so I've split off from the other team to take up where she would have been. Told her team to reposition a little too. More we fan out, the more likely we should be able to snap Andrea up – *if* she's calling from somewhere within our catchment, of course. With this video call, she should be on the phone a lot longer too, I hope.'

'Let's hope so. And yes, I received a message from Ellie too. CCTV man in custody? Who would've thunk it?'

The signal broke up a little again, sounding like the man was underwater. '—We have to hope she gets something out of him. Something we can use, if these other abusers are supposedly out there.'

'Not for us to do, remember?' Drake towed the party line, though he disagreed with it entirely. 'I hope she passes the case on soon. Miller would have a fit, and that's the last thing we need.'

'Hmm,' Strauss said in weak agreement.

Drake liked the man, he seemed to be cut from a similar cloth to himself. Wanting answers, wanting to solve things himself and not deferring or palming off responsibility to anyone.

'And, Drake, I've got some additional stuff to review later. Apparently, there's more footage from the first and second scenes. I'll do it after this.'

Drake nodded to himself. 'Good man. While we're on the subject, anything on the hard drives from Pearce Fleming yet?'

'Team's still working on it. Despite the man's old hardware, there's some sophisticated software protection on them. Really strange.'

'Hmm,' Drake acknowledged. He couldn't help wondering if the contents really did have something to do with Andrea, and it wasn't completely random. Or maybe he needed to take a step back to think of more "out there" theories. Could there be more to it?

Think about that later. Need to focus on the here and now, he reminded himself.

'Just to confirm, I can use the TV so we have a bigger picture when she calls, yeah?' Drake asked.

'Indeed. If you get in trouble, I'm sure one of the guys at the station can help, or your girls . . .'

'All right, all right. I'll figure it out.' He closed his eyes and took the teasing on the chin. 'Remember, you tell me the *moment* you have her location. I'll be juggling two phones.'

'Will do.' Drake could picture the man nodding, his mess of hair flopping around. 'We just have to hope she stays on the line long enough for us to find her *and* for us to get there too. I expect we're really going to be cutting it close.'

Drake scratched his cheek nervously. 'I'm sure it'll be fine. At least we'll be occupying her long enough to stop her from killing anyone for a while.'

'I hope this works out, Drake. I really do.'

'You and me both,' he said grimly, and hung up.

33

Drake and the girls fell silent as the call finally came in, the tone ringing out around the room with a sudden horrible clarity. A sharp feeling of panic hit him in the gut. He wasn't sure what state the woman would be in, how well she'd looked after herself, or how she'd behave in the presence of her daughter. All he knew for certain was that she wasn't the person Cari grew up with anymore.

The phone, configured to the TV and ready to be traced by Strauss and Melwood, continued bleating. All Drake had to do was answer.

He looked at Cari one last time for her approval. Her eyes locked with his for just a moment before she nodded her head.

Drake inhaled sharply and answered with a jab of his finger. He aimed the phone's camera at himself for the moment, to keep Cari out of sight of whatever lay on the other end.

He wasn't prepared for what he saw.

Judging by Cari's face, neither was she. The girl was seemingly stunned like a rabbit in headlights at the appearance of her mother on the TV screen.

Andrea's hair had been cut short and jagged, somewhere around chin-length with strands of grey streaking through. Her features were sharper, her skin pallid and stretched, as though she hadn't eaten properly for months. But more than anything it was her disconcerting expression that troubled Drake. The woman was smiling ear to ear in an unpleasant, crazed manner, completely at odds with that of the mother he'd seen previously at Cari's house in Barndon. This was Miray he was dealing with, no question.

Miray was in a nondescript room with few identifying features beyond its state of disrepair. Drake immediately cursed the fact there wasn't a window in shot, not even allowing him the tiniest of chances of identifying a general location from the cityscape beyond.

'Where is she?' Miray demanded, looming over the camera. The words heavily accented. Her disturbing grin dropped into something altogether sourer at the continued sight of Drake. She didn't appear to be holding on to a phone, so perhaps she'd set up everything herself on a makeshift tripod, similar to theirs. But how? He still didn't even know *how* she had access to all these phones, truth be told. Another in the long line of mysteries.

Drake felt a vibration on his leg where his secondary phone was resting. His eyes flit down for a second.

A text message from Strauss. *We're working on it, Drake.*

'She's here, don't you worry.' Drake looked over to see tears running down Cari's face.

Shit. Hold on, Cari. Please. Just a few minutes.

Miray's head tilted. 'Oh? Then why can't I see her?'

'All in good time.'

'This wasn't part of the deal, Drake. Put her on the phone now, or I'm hanging up.'

'Andrea . . .'

'It's Miray!' she shrieked. Eyes wild, then returning to normal moments later. 'You have five seconds or I'm ending the call . . . One . . .'

Cari looked to Drake and shook her head repeatedly, the girl seemed petrified.

Oh, no-no-no. Please, Cari. Don't back out now.

'Two . . .'

Drake looked Cari in the eye, trying to steady her nerves, show he was there for her however he could. Eva held her hand as the girl wept openly.

Miray sneered, her face getting closer to the camera with each count. 'Three . . .'

Cari closed her eyes, taking a deep breath, shaking her head repeatedly still.

'I'm going soon, Drake . . . Come on, show her to me . . . show her to me . . . Drake . . . FOUR . . .'

Cari wiped her eyes with her sleeve in one quick motion, smearing her eye makeup.

'Fi—'

Cari snatched the phone out of Drake's hand and stared her mother down. Her face hardening to the woman before her.

'I'm here,' she rasped. At the lack of reaction from her mother, she repeated the words. 'I'm here.'

'Good girl,' Miray said, a wicked grin spreading across the screen. Her face took up the entirety of the TV, the woman's eyes harsh and full of hate.

Another vibration on Drake's leg. His eyes flit down for a second.

We're close, Drake. Real close now.

'Where's my Mum?' Cari demanded.

'Oh, she's here, stupid girl. She's here, don't you worry,'

Miray tapped her temple, maintaining her rictus grin. 'Don't think you'll be seeing her again though. Sorry about that.'

'Mum!' Cari cried. 'Please, Mum! You've got to fight her!'

'Shut up, you little bitch!'

Cari flinched sharply at the woman's words, shoving the phone in the phone mount they'd devised on the table.

Drake intervened. 'Miray. Don't use those words with her, she's just a kid. She's your granddaughter, for God's sake.'

Another vibration.

We've got her! She's in Ilford. Melwood and I seem to be equal distance. I'll text the address! Closing in.

Drake pumped a fist tightly beneath the table in celebration. Without thinking, he nodded in Cari's direction.

What the hell are you doing, you idiot, he thought. *Don't distract her!*

Thankfully, Cari hadn't appeared to have noticed. He wouldn't do it again, in case the girl's reaction spooked Andrea.

Miray didn't respond to his granddaughter comment for what felt like forever.

No doubt she's thinking of how best to phrase them in the worst possible way.

Finally, she answered.

'Granddaughter? She's nothing of the sort. She's not my blood. She's that idiot man's. Not mine. I thought me slicing her fucking throat made it perfectly clear what my feelings on that *thing* were.'

Cari put her hand to her scar absently.

Miray sneered at the sight. 'Yes, I hope you remember the pain when I did that. The blood. The feeling of it pouring out of you, choking you, running down your chest.' She breathed in through her nostrils, as though she was savouring a memory. 'Not being able to breathe . . . The sounds you made.'

Cari flinched, Eva still gripping her other hand tightly out of shot.

Still Miray went on. 'Use it as a reminder of how much I. *Hate.* You.'

Drake wanted to intervene. Wanted to stop her saying these things. To shield Cari from hearing these vile words spewing from her mother's mouth. He couldn't begin to imagine. But they were so close to apprehending her. Stopping her for good. Drake had to hold fire, he had to.

Cari moved back from the table slightly, as though she was going to leave the room like he'd advised earlier.

No! Cari, please!

'. . . Andrea is mine, and mine alone. Not. Yours!'

Cari's hands started to tremble. She couldn't look at the phone's camera. Looking every which way but her mother's spiteful face.

'No,' Cari uttered.

Miray's eyes snapped to her. 'What did you say to me?'

'I said, *No.'*

Miray watched her in silent consideration, then demanded, 'Drake, I want you to give her to me—'

Cari spoke over her. 'I don't touch this scar and think of your hate for me.'

Miray started to say something, but Cari spoke over her again, her raspy voice growing in strength.

'I touch this scar and I think of how *strong* I have become. Of how I *survived* you. My being alive means you've *failed.* How does it feel to be a failure, *Grandmother?'*

For the first time, Miray was speechless. Cari's powerful rebuttal made Drake feel incredibly proud.

Still Miray didn't answer, her face one of pure unadulterated fury. But the woman's surprise didn't last for long. 'I am going to find you, you little cunt,' she spat. 'I am going to find you, and I am going to *gut* you just like your father.'

Miray looked like she was salivating at the thought. It was truly hateful.

'I'm going to rip out that spiteful little tongue of yours, too. Oh, yes. You mark my—'

Suddenly, a sharp bang came off camera.

Miray's head snapped round at the noise, her eyes bugging out. She snatched for something out of sight of the camera before disappearing. It was terrifying how silent she was in her movement, as though she was floating above the ground.

Who had got there first? Was it Strauss? Melwood? Both?

More noise sounded, presumably footsteps, and then Strauss appeared to the left on the screen, his eyes wide, his body set as he expected to encounter Miray. But he paused, as though he was checking out the environment. She must be hiding from him, but where?

'Drake?' Strauss shouted. 'Drake, are you there? I can't see her. There's multiple rooms leading off from here. Anything you can do to guide me?'

Oh God, no! She can't have slipped away already? Surely not?

'She was literally just there, Strauss. Be on your guard. Be careful, but don't let her escape. We must have got her cornered. Hang back at the entrance until your backup arrives.'

Drake looked over at the girls and pointed at the door. 'Leave. Now!'

They rushed from the room in a panic. Slamming the door behind them as he turned his attention back to the camera and Strauss.

Strauss took a few tentative steps further into the room. 'I think I hear her trying to escape, Drake . . .'

'Strauss, no. Stay put — don't!'

'Oh God! There's someone—'

Just as suddenly as the earlier noise, another sound came.

But this time, it was that of a woman screaming.

Miray, her body a blur, appeared on camera. She charged at the stunned DS, a knife in her hand.

Strauss reacted by lunging toward her, as though he intended to tackle her to the ground. Miray, seemingly anticipating the movement, adjusted her grip on the knife and swung it in an arc upwards, avoiding the man's outstretched arms and driving it straight up and into the man's chest.

He gasped. 'Strauss! No!'

A chill ran down Drake's spine at the sight of the impact.

The man cried out in stunned pain. His anguished cries were brutally cut short as she thrust again savagely with the blade.

'Stop! Miray! Stop!' Drake pleaded, but she stabbed Strauss again, and again, and again. 'Please, Miray! No!'

She stopped and turned to the camera.

'Thought you were clever did you, Drake?' she said, out of breath from the exertion or was it the excitement?

Miray eyeballed the camera, drops of blood running down her face, short strands of hair over her eyes. 'No. More. Fucking. Around, Drake. I'm done playing.'

With that, she turned and left, leaving the camera centred on Strauss' blood-stained body.

34

Drake sped out of the station, leaving the two girls in the hands of the desk sergeant. He'd be back as soon as he could, but he desperately needed to get to Strauss. His phone had been ringing off the hook as he gave commands left, right and centre while weaving through the London traffic. An ambulance was on its way, as were the rest of the teams. What was taking everyone so damn long? Melwood wasn't answering his phone, but he had to be closest. Surely he should be there by now? Strauss had said in his last text that they were a similar distance from Andrea. Drake hoped to God that the stabbing wasn't as bad as had appeared on the video, but who was he kidding? It wasn't looking good, not one bit. At least the address in Ilford was only a few miles east of the station he had been holed up in. Andrea had been worryingly close, after all.

He winced as he thought of the footage. *Hang in there, man!*

Drake screeched to a halt at the address just as a number of other patrol cars and un-marked vehicles arrived, everyone spewing forth from their cars like a wave of rats fleeing a sinking ship and congregating by the entrance.

The location was a tired expanse of cream-rendered three-storey flats, more wide than they were tall, with brown water stains beneath windowsills and England flags hanging beneath others. There was no activity that he could see, and it was eerily quiet. He knew Miray would be long gone by now.

Drake noted everyone around him hesitating, but he didn't have time for any more damn protocol; armed police would take too long to get there. He left the surveillance team fussing at the foot of the path while he pounded up toward the open entrance door.

Had that been Melwood or Miray who had left it open?

Drake's head flitted around as he took in the meagre surroundings. He spotted a door to the stairs and bounded up the concrete stairwell, heaving himself up two or three steps at a time with the help of the worn metal handrail. It dawned on him that he wouldn't know for sure which floor it would actually be on, but then he heard the sound of someone calling for help.

It was Melwood.

Thank God, he must have got there, after all. But had he come off worse for wear from encountering Andrea, too?

Drake reached the top floor, and yanked the hallway door open to the sounds of Melwood shouting, 'We're in here! Get an ambulance!'

It was coming from a doorway a few strides down the green-carpeted communal hallway. There was no other activity on the floor, no one poking their heads out at the cries. Was it abandoned, were people working, or did they just not care?

He made for the doorway, entering to the sight of Melwood cradling the lifeless body of Strauss between his legs. The man's arms were limp at his sides, his chest ravaged with wounds, his shirt, trousers and the surrounding floor a mess of blood.

The phone used in the fateful call set up was on a small coffee table in front of a brown sofa.

'Melwood, let go of him. Get him to the ground, for Christ's sake!'

'She did this, Drake. I can't believe it!' He cried, manoeuvring Strauss' body gently to the ground. 'That crazy bitch! She's killed him.'

Drake knelt beside the stricken sergeant and felt for a heartbeat in his ruined chest.

Nothing.

His own chest tightened, the knot that was his heart raging at what had played out before him on the call.

Again, he felt for a pulse at the man's wrist. Still nothing.

'Come on, Strauss—'

'Drake, he's gone,' Melwood said bleakly beside him. 'What's the point?'

'Don't give me that shit, Inspector.'

Drake turned his attention to the man's neck, pressing his fingers firmly against Strauss' jugular, just as the teams started rushing into the room.

'Ambulance crews just got here.' A woman's voice bellowed.

Drake, still pressing again on Strauss' neck, felt something amidst the chaos.

Wait, is that . . .

Strauss was alive.

35

Ellie turned into the Royal London Hospital as the final remnants of daylight were drawing to a close. She checked the rear-view mirror. Eva and Cari's silent faces were bathed in the warm orange glow of a streetlamp as they pulled into a parking spot in the car park.

She'd received a call from Drake just after he'd reached the hospital, requesting she collect them and bring them to him. He didn't trust anyone else to do it right now. Ellie couldn't believe what he'd told her: the phone call, the stabbing, Strauss now touch and go and in the operating theatre, and Andrea nowhere to be found.

What a disaster, an absolute shit show.

She felt another wave of guilt come over her. Strauss had covered for her. If she had been there as part of the team instead of interviewing a useless drug-addict, then maybe none of this would have happened; Andrea would have been in custody and Strauss wouldn't be fighting for his life right now.

Ellie took a deep breath, pinching her brow before turning to the girls. 'All right, your dad's just inside. I take it you want to come in?'

'Damn straight,' Eva replied, though Ellie sensed she wasn't quite as eager as she made out.

Ellie's eyes flicked to the other girl. 'Cari?'

The girl nodded without uttering a word. She'd not said anything when Ellie had collected them, nor on the journey over. And from what Drake had told her of the call with her mother, Ellie couldn't blame her. Not one bit.

'Okay then, let's go.'

Ellie peered through the thin window pane of the door, seeing Melwood sitting in a chair by Strauss. All manner of equipment and monitors connected to the broken man's body. He'd come out of surgery just an hour before. The doctor had told them the details in lieu of any family. Suffice to say, Strauss was in a bad way. He had been placed in an induced coma after a cardiac arrest, having lost four pints of blood, suffered a punctured lung and liver, and a stab wound which had just nicked his pulmonary artery. The doctor had never seen anyone pull through after such wounds. Ellie was impressed by the German; how he'd managed to hang on, no-one knew. Now it was just a matter of time and hoping that his body responded well to the surgery.

She knocked on the door and Melwood beckoned her in. The sounds of the monitors immediately setting her on edge. Strauss looked so frail and helpless. It didn't sit well with her at all.

'Stupid question, I guess. But . . . how's he doing?' she asked.

Melwood looked at her as though she'd slapped Strauss in the face before his eyes. 'I thought he was dead, Ellie. I was so useless.'

'Don't say that.' She put a hand on the man's shoulder. 'I'm sure you did everything you could.'

'I didn't, I just sat there with him. It was Drake who found he was alive.'

'But Drake wouldn't have got to Luka, nor would the ambulance guys, if you hadn't found him, right?'

'I guess,' he said, turning back to Strauss.

They remained in silence for a time, taking in the enormity of what had happened. Ellie was just about to say something when Melwood spoke once more. 'You know, me and this guy have been through a lot over the years.' He huffed. 'Still not sure if he even likes me.'

'Oh?'

Wasn't aware they'd worked together that much before.

'Yep, I was one of the people that vouched for him when he was looking to become a sergeant. Saw his potential. He reminds me a bit of me at his age.'

'He's through the worst of it now.' She put her hand on his shoulder again, giving it a tighter squeeze to drive the point home. 'I'm sure.'

'We need to get this damn Whitman woman before any more people get hurt.'

Ellie pursed her lips. 'You got that right.'

Soon afterwards, Ellie left the pair and searched out the vending machine, praying that the coffee was something resembling actual coffee. The machine noisily ground away, mining for rust for that extra flavour probably, as she stood and waited, her mind lost in thought.

I can't see an end to this. Nothing. No thread to cling on to.

Grabbing a second cup, she brought it over to her boss who was sat with a distant, tired look on his face.

'I should have been there,' Ellie said solemnly, handing Drake the cup of coffee.

Her boss took it in his large hands without uttering a word. Ellie noticed the faint remnants of blood still staining them as she sat beside him in the row of seats next to Strauss' room.

'But you weren't. And neither was I,' Drake said. His voice seemed overly loud in their surroundings, and Ellie flinched. 'Don't beat yourself up about things that can't be changed now, Ellie.'

'You're a fine one to talk, Chief,' she retorted, a little harsher than she intended.

He gave her a thin smile. 'Touché.'

They both sipped their coffee in silence while Cari and Eva sat a little further away, talking amongst themselves and keeping busy on their phones. The sounds of hospital trolleys, swinging doors and rushed footsteps occasionally punctuated the silence.

'So, what do we do now? I'm feeling a little lost here, Drake.'

'Strauss mentioned before this debacle that more footage has been received from the Pearce murder, so I've got his team on that in his absence.' Drake rubbed his eyes. 'Goes without saying that he's not going to be fit to do anything himself any time soon. Miller's even approved some overtime for them. Strauss was the equivalent of who knows how many people. His loss is certainly going to be felt hard.'

'Let's hope they find something. *Anything.*'

'Indeed. But let's just say I'm not feeling too confident about it all right now, either,' he said. 'Today's roll of the dice was just that, and I blew it. We're back to square one.'

'And Cari?' Ellie nodded slightly in the girl's direction.

'She's not doing so well.' He glanced over at Ellie, keeping his voice low. 'And I can't say I blame her. Miray was absolutely vile. The things she said . . . just the way she was with her. The separation of Miray and Andrea is something else. I can't imagine how Cari must be feeling. How conflicted she must be, having someone you both love and despise within the same person.'

'It's fucked up, is what it is.'

'And nothing came of CCTV man?' Drake asked as a man in a hospital gown was wheeled past by two hospital porters, writhing in agony. Ellie caught a glimpse of something from her angle that she really didn't want to see, and wrinkled her nose.

'Nope. Just said that a man came over to him and paid him to give the action figure to Bella on the afternoon break. Pinter, the guy from the CCTV, is not even local, he just came to the area to see a druggie mate of his and happened to be in the right place at the right time – at least, from his perspective.'

'No identifying features on the guy who gave it to him?' Drake pressed.

'Drake, I said *no*. I'd tell you if there was anything,' she said, frustrated. She felt the now familiar twinge of her eyelid.

'All right, but remember who you're taking to Ellie. I'm your boss. Don't forget that.'

'Sorry, Drake. I'm sorry, truly,' she said, feeling warmth in her cheeks. 'Just things are getting to me lately, is all.'

He arched an eyebrow. 'I had noticed.'

'Oh—' Ellie stopped and look up at Eva's approach.

The girl's shoes squeaked as she came to an abrupt stop. 'Dad – sorry to jump in, Ellie – but do you mind if we go now? Cari's not feeling so good, and I'm pretty tired.'

'Sure, love.' Drake nodded. 'Ellie, do you mind if we pick this up tomorrow sometime?'

'No—no, not at all. You guys go on,' she said, forcing a smile for Eva's sake.

That's the end of that then.

36

I came to in the bathroom again. And for the third time in recent memory – if I could even class myself as having one these days – blood was on my hands and spattered on my face. This time it was less, *much less*, but less didn't necessarily mean better. It still had to be someone else's blood, not my own.

More disturbingly to me though was my lack of surprise on seeing it. Was I getting used to this now? Was it just another strange thing in the series of strange things that were happening in my pathetic excuse for an existence? Or was my lack of medication starting to take effect?

I did feel a little more lucid than normal since waking. As though a layer of bubble wrap had been removed from my mind –though who knew how many more there were to peel away to reveal what was left beneath.

I took in the sight of my bloody handprints all over the porcelain sink, even the bathroom mirror, as the dull ache began in the back of my skull.

'Oh no you don't. Not this time. You're staying there,' I muttered.

It was then a loud, clicking sound started behind me. I turned towards the door, bumping into the sink as I backed away, my panic increasing.

Moments later, Ben entered the bathroom. He smiled upon seeing me. 'How are you feeling, my love?'

'I'm . . . I'm okay.' A lie, followed by something a little more honest. 'Just exhausted. I'm always so tired when I wake up in here.'

It really wasn't a lie either, even the faintest of breezes felt like it would send me to sleep.

'You've been busy, that's why,' he stated, as if it was common knowledge.

'Busy?'

This had happened many times now. Coming to, not knowing where I'd been or what I'd done. And that was before blood had become such a prominent feature.

'Yes. We saw Cari. She was so pleased to see you. It warmed my heart. Reminded me of us all together.'

Cari? What? Did I?

'I don't remember that. Why can't I remember, Ben? Why?'

'I don't know. You tell me, Andrea. You've been particularly unwell for months now,' he said, pacing in front of me before playing with the lock on the door. 'It's why you've been in that room for so long. You know that. For your own protection.'

'Oh,' I croaked, finding it hard to get the words out. I didn't know what to do or say. Something felt off, perhaps another layer peeling away. Some further clarity.

'But I guess I should probably leave soon, you know?' I hugged myself, my skin feeling cold to the touch. 'I'm not so sure this place is helping me anymore. Being in the bedroom all the time . . . this place. I know we wanted to keep me away from hospitals, but this is a little much.'

Ben stopped fiddling with the door lock and turned his attention back toward me, the look on his face as though I'd told him his mother had died. The colour all but drained in an instant. 'What?'

'I think I need to be outside. You know, in the daylight? All of us together, properly . . . As a family.'

'I don't think that's wise right now, honey.' His features full of worry, though whether it was of concern for me, I wasn't so sure.

He took a step toward me. 'What's brought this on? We were doing so well?'

'I . . .' The medication I'd hidden away sprung to mind. '. . . Was just thinking that maybe a different approach may be more beneficial, that's all.'

'I'll think about it,' Ben stated dismissively.

I took the hint. But there was a look in his eyes that unnerved me.

The silence was beginning to be uncomfortable.

The seconds ticked by until something in his eyes changed and he began looking me up and down like a piece of meat. 'Now, let's get you clean.'

I gripped myself tighter and frowned. 'I can do that.'

'No, allow me,' he said before he began pawing at my clothes and pulling them off roughly. Soon I was down to my underwear, my skin prickling at the cold.

Satisfied, he started to remove his clothes and before long he was completely naked in front of me. I could see what he had in mind.

'Join me in the shower,' he stated.

'I don't want to. It's only a little blood.' The statement was as weird to say as it was to hear. Washing off blood in the shower with your husband, it wasn't normal. None of this was. I knew that now.

'Come on. What is it?' he tilted his head, amused. 'What's got you so argumentative? You're not normally like this.'

'Nothing.'

His face hardened. 'Then get in the shower.'

* * *

My eyes snapped open to the white walls of the bedroom. Though this time, I didn't feel groggy like before. It seemed more rest had brought me further coherence. I felt more aware than I had in weeks, months even. More of those layers had evaporated as I slept. It was all I could do to stop myself springing out of bed and dancing round the room gleefully.

But the weight stopped me.

And an arm.

I could see the shape of my husband's hand, hanging limply off my side. Feel his breath on my back.

In stark contrast to this new found clarity, I was sore all over, as though I'd been bashed around in a tumble dryer for hours. The hot pulsing bloom of bruising.

Only I knew now what it was really.

The images flashed through my mind's eye, alarming me: a knife, blood, the shower . . . Ben.

I moved his arm carefully, placing it down in front of him as I twisted round, thinking that I should confront him about earlier, tell him that it wasn't okay what he had done.

It would never be okay.

But he didn't rouse from my movements. He just carried on breathing softly, quietly.

I studied him. His hair, his . . . face. The clarity of it all.
And my heart froze.
I need to get out of here. Fast.
It wasn't Ben.

37

Drake took a long slug of his beer and slouched further down into the sofa. He stared off into space, the wall of the lounge staring back.

What an absolute shit of a day. He sighed loudly as the coolness of the beer sunk deeper into his belly. He traced a thin paint crack with his eyes, the line winding its way up the off-white wall and into the fake cornicing of the ceiling.

Drake still couldn't quite believe how it had all gone south. How much of a disaster it all was. How much worse off he was, how much worse off *they all were*. Cari had been clearly traumatised by the whole thing, and Strauss was literally in intensive care. Even Eva, loud as she was these days, wasn't saying much or laying into him.

The different scenarios played through his head, again and again and again. What if Melwood had got there first? What if Ellie hadn't been waylaid? What if Strauss had waited for the Inspector or back-up before storming in alone like he did? Was it Drake who had influenced him into doing that? Strauss knew how desperate Drake was after putting Cari front and centre from the previous call.

Seeing the poor man attacked so brutally, Drake couldn't get the scene out of his head. The sound of the knife, the cries suddenly silenced.

He felt the flutter of panic forming once again in the pit of his stomach.

It was his fault. His. No one else's.

Miller had been very much of that point of view when she'd spoken to him at the hospital. Drake had suspected it was all she could do to stop herself from relieving him of his command right there and then. Perhaps it was only the lack of resource keeping him in a job and he'd be out the door when everything died down? If it was him in her position, he'd be planning for it right now, that's for sure.

'Dad . . . ?'

His daughter startled him. 'Eva, I didn't hear you come out of your room, love,' he said, looking up meekly.

She didn't respond and slid over to him in her slippers before curling up next to him and leaning her head on his chest. It was an action he wasn't expecting, but it felt comforting.

'Are you okay, Dad?' she asked quietly.

Her words disarmed him utterly, making his lip quiver and his eyes well up.

'No, Eva,' he said, taking a stuttering breath to compose himself, a tear running down his cheek. 'You know what? I don't think I am. Not this time.'

She glanced up at him. 'It'll be okay, you know?'

'I wish I had your optimism,' Drake said, forcing a smile. 'Are you sure it's not you that's been drinking?'

'Dad, stop. I'm being serious,' she said, putting an arm

around his chest. 'You're DCI Drake, you'll find a way. You always do.'

He reciprocated with an arm round her shoulder and smiled. 'Thank you, Eva. I really mean that. Your Mum would be so proud of how you were today, looking after Cari like you did.'

She stuttered. 'You think so?'

He put his beer down on the coffee table. 'I know so.'

'I really miss her.'

'Me too, Eva. Me too.'

* * *

They remained on the sofa in a comfortable silence until Eva eventually fell asleep on his chest, her breathing becoming heavy as her head started to droop.

'Best get you to bed,' he said, scooping her up in his arms, causing her to stir slightly.

Jesus, not so little these days, are you? He thought, struggling more than he expected as he headed for her bedroom.

Having tucked her in, Drake closed her door carefully behind him and unlocked the ramshackle office space. It still amazed him how far he and Eva had come in the few short months since they'd been reunited. When he'd been holed up in the flat for the year after Becca's murder, he'd dreamt of even having a normal discussion with her, let alone spending time with her and her living with him again.

Drake also noted the complete lack of communication from Rachel, Becca's sister, since he'd taken Eva and Cari off her hands. How could the woman be so cold? Cutting off her own niece like that, let alone Cari, the girl she'd helped nurse back to health? It was anyone's guess. It was him that Rachel should blame, not the girls. Not that she needed much encouragement in the hate department.

He looked down at the papers he'd left scattered on the bed and side-table since being distracted at Ellie's visit a few days earlier. Drake supposed they weren't much use any more, the case having moved on considerably since then. Bundling them together, he was about to toss them when he heard his phone ringing from the lounge.

Drake quietly retraced his steps and found his phone between the sofa cushions. The bright screen greeted him with a withheld number.

Miray, again? I didn't think I'd hear from her so soon, if at all?

He answered.

'Miray, turn yourself in—'

'*DCI* Drake,' the gruff voice drawled. 'Long time no speak, heh?'

The blood in his veins turned to ice in an instant at Samuel Barrow's voice.

38

Ellie finally left Melwood with Strauss and arrived at her doorstep just after midnight. The full moon's twilight shone brightly in the cloudless sky, leaving ominous shadows amidst the grey and blue hues of the street. It was so unusually bright, she wondered if it was a super moon, an altogether rarer occurrence. And probably just as rare as her being greeted by a happy husband lately.

She winced at the sounds of her keys in the lock, the sound clumsy and jarring against the quiet of the street.

'Len, I'm back,' she said, not wanting to raise her voice for Bella's sake. The small hallway was lit by a shard of twilight and little else.

'I'm in the lounge,' came the quiet reply.

Ellie put away her coat and removed her shoes slowly at the thought of another potential argument, before tentatively padding through to her fate in the lounge.

'You okay?' she asked as she entered to the sight of Len turning off the TV.

He tossed the remote on to the sofa and flopped back. 'What do you think?'

'Len—'

He gave her a look of mock seriousness and put on a deeper voice. 'Ellie.'

'I did it for the right reasons,' she blurted. 'You have to see that, right?' Before adding a grimacing 'Please?'

Len smiled. It seemed . . . *genuine.*

'Actually, I do.'

'Really?'

'Yes, I was actually quite impressed,' he said, giving her a sly look. 'Never seen you run that fast before on those little legs of yours.'

'Oi, I'm not *that* small!' she said, flopping down on the sofa, and giving him a playful poke in the ribs. Her relief was all encompassing.

'Well, you sort of are, but let's not get into the semantics,' he paused, his smile dropping into something more serious. 'I'm sorry about your colleague. Luka, wasn't it?'

'Yeah,' she said, saddened at the thought, but also the sudden dampening of the mood.

He put his hand on her leg and gave it a squeeze. 'He's going to pull through though, right? Any more news?'

She placed her hand on his. It was nice to have her husband back. Whether it was going to be a more permanent change, she'd have to wait and see. 'He's still not out of the woods yet, got more surgery in the morning and who knows what else.'

'Shit,' he said, looking at the floor. 'So, that guy today. He was the action figure guy, right?'

'Yep, the one and only.'

'Does that mean there's one less person out there wanting to fuck with us and our daughter?'

Well, the happiness was nice while it lasted . . .

She braced herself and gave him the news. 'Well, sort of. I let him go.'

'You what?' Len said, letting go of her leg and turning to face her, his features balling in confusion.

'Yeah, he's harmless. It seems he was just a clueless go-between; a spent commodity, nothing to worry about,' she said, trying her best to talk him back down. 'Please, trust me.'

'I do. Really, I do,' he said, slumping back again. 'I guess you wouldn't just do that if you thought he was any kind of threat to Bella, either.'

'Bingo. Got it in one, hun,' she said, instantly regretting the sarcastic edge it may have exuded.

Len appeared to brush it off, rubbing his tired-seeming eyes. 'So, does that mean case closed?'

'With the Spencer one? No-no-no. But I'm at a loss with it, if I'm being honest. With everything, actually.'

'Have you thought about starting again with it?'

She frowned slightly. 'What? How do you mean?'

'Like, re-reviewing everything? Going once more around it all, now you've tied up a few more bits, you know? I know doing that sort of things helps with my work sometimes. The iterative approach.'

Her husband had made a fair point, barring one small problem.

'Sadly, it's not our case anymore. So sayeth our lord, DCI Drake.'

'Come on,' he scoffed. 'From the sounds of it, that's not stopped you so far, eh?'

She smiled. 'Well, true . . . I guess not.'

Ellie thought about the facts: the Spencers were out of the picture now. CCTV man was a nobody. There were at least two more of their abusers out there, of which they'd only learned about recently. Perhaps it *would* pay to check out the evidence again, maybe even revisit the scenes of the crimes, like the retreat, or the Gregory house, with this new angle? Maybe there'd be something pointing at these new people, now she was aware of their existence? Or perhaps telling Gemma about CCTV man's capture might shake something loose?

'Thanks, Len,' she said, giving him a hug and kissing him.

'What was that for?'

'For sticking with me.'

39

Samuel cackled at Drake's surprise. 'What? Not expecting to hear from your favourite wife killer, eh? Is that it?'

'How did you get this number? How are you speaking to me now?' Drake tried his best to remain calm. His hand gripped the phone tightly, the other clenched in a tight fist. Samuel's voice had struck a strange chord in his psyche. Was it *fear?*

'It's prison, Drake. Anything's possible here, with my levels of . . . *notoriety*, shall we say.'

Samuel seemed to take particular pleasure in pointing that out. It enraged Drake. He had hoped that every day would be a living hell for the gutless cretin. But prison, it was different now. Cushy, even, if you were the right kind of criminal, and it appeared Samuel was just that.

'What do you want?' Drake said flatly, his insides roiling as he sat down on the bed.

Samuel laughed. 'I want *you*, DCI Drake.'

'What do you mean?'

'Here. This prison. I want to speak to you. In person.'

Drake frowned, the lines on his forehead deepening as he

tried to work out what possible motive Samuel could have. He drew a blank. 'Why? Why now?'

He heard Samuel take a satisfied-sounding breath. 'There's been some . . . developments, I hear.'

Developments? What possible developments could be occurring for a man with so many life sentences? Had he heard about Andrea? But how?

'Developments? What the hell are you talking about?'

'That's all I'm saying. I've got to go now,' Samuel said, shouts and calls echoing in the background and getting increasingly louder. 'You think on it.'

'But—'

The line went dead.

Drake growled in sheer frustration at his situation. How could that man be back in his life again? *How?*

It took all of his willpower to stop himself from smashing the phone against the wall.

* * *

Drake slapped irritably at the buzz of the alarm clock on his phone. It had seemingly chosen to go off *just* when his mind had finally stopped churning and allowed him to sleep. The slap had done nothing and the noise droned on, unabated. He groaned loudly, wishing he had one with a physical button he could whack like the old days. He assaulted his phone once more and seemingly succeeded, the bastard device finally silenced.

Drake lay perfectly still in bed, groaning some more, while his mind began spinning back around the same thoughts he'd had throughout the night. What the hell could Samuel want? It'd been more than a year with utter, brilliant silence. Nothing. And now this?

He had secretly hoped he'd be getting a phone call one day, but not the kind he'd received; he'd wanted to hear someone had shanked the bastard in prison, or that Samuel had lost an eye in a fight. Anything that would inflict greater pain and suffering on Samuel's time left on this earth, but obviously, that had been wishful thinking.

Drake hadn't decided whether to act on Samuel's request. It was tempting just to leave him hanging for all eternity. But the word Samuel had used, 'development', was eating away at him; his professional curiosity was worryingly close to getting the better of his emotions, in spite of all Samuel had done to ruin his life and Eva's.

Was it just Samuel wanting back in? To find a way to remind Drake of what he had taken from him, remind him of how Becca had died? Or was it something else entirely? Drake didn't know, and the timing . . . It was the last thing he or his mental state needed.

'Gotta get up, old man. Get back to it. She could be out there killing again, for all you know,' he mumbled to himself.

Heaving himself up, Drake lumbered to the shower, making sure it was a cold one, before dressing and hot-footing his way to the café. More bacon was required.

'Thank you, John,' Cari said when he got back, the paper bag rustling as she reached for the croissant within. Drake smiled to himself at her finally calling him by his name.

'Not a problem,' he said, spying an opportunity. Perhaps with Eva still in the shower, this could be the moment to ask Cari how she was after yesterday without too many people on her case, and now she'd had a chance to sleep. He waited for her to grab a plate from the cupboard and sit back at the kitchen island.

He sat down too. 'Cari, I know you may not want to talk about it – and I completely understand if you don't – but how are you after yesterday? I'm sorry I haven't asked sooner, but with the rest that was going on . . .'

'It's okay. I understand,' she said, stopping mid-way to take a bite of her croissant. 'She . . . it's not my Mum, not really. I don't see *her* that way. Miray, I mean.'

Drake understood what she was saying. 'You're trying to keep the two concepts of her separate?'

Cari nodded. 'Something like that, yes. It helps.'

She took another bite of her breakfast. 'You have to understand, John. Before all this, me and my dad . . . we'd been looking after her for so many years. Pretty much from when I was old enough to understand some of what she was going through.'

Cari's voice was cracking as she spoke. 'Dad and I were always trying to keep her from tipping over the edge. She was so terrified of going to hospital and not coming out again. And we were too, to be honest.'

Drake felt for the girl. What she must have been through over the years. The years of her childhood wracked with worry for her own mother.

'That's a lot of responsibility for a young girl to take on. Your Mum should be looking after you, Cari. Not the other way round.'

'We knew that. You make it sound like it was my dad forcing me to. But I'm just as guilty as he is, okay? She should have been in hospital years ago.' Cari's voice started to tremble. 'We thought we were doing the right thing. If only I'd known what she would become . . . my dad would still be here, and more people wouldn't have been hurt. Your colleague wouldn't be in hospital.'

Drake chose to remain silent while she wiped away a tear from her eye. 'What's going to happen to her, John? When you catch her, I mean?'

Truth was, he couldn't even picture them catching

Andrea/Miray, let alone her being taken into custody. 'Let's not worry about that, okay? Let's focus on you.'

'I don't want to focus on me,' she snapped, before composing herself again. She was beyond her years in how she spoke. The past year had aged her. Taken the joy out of what were supposed to be some of the best years of her life. 'I'm sorry. It's just . . . I need you to stop her before she hurts anyone else. Maybe when she's being treated, I'll be able to speak with my actual Mum again, the person I love. Until then, she's not my mother. She can't be. I can't cope with it any other way, it's too hard.'

She finally glanced up and looked him in the eye.

He nodded, hoping he was reassuring her more than he was himself.

'I understand. I'll get your mother back, Cari. I promise you.'

40

For the first time in a long while, Drake was happy. Happy that he had an appointment with Proctor-Reeves timed for just that morning, that is. The timing couldn't have been better for using someone completely removed from the tangle of all his messy situations. He would enjoy probing her thoughts for a change. It was about time the tables were turned, if only a little.

Drake stared at the offices, eyes glazing over, while he sat in his car for a few minutes more, having somehow ploughed through the morning rush hour in two-thirds of the time it usually took. It was another surprisingly sunny spring morning, and even a few birds were chirping, though it most definitely didn't represent his actual temperament right now. He almost wanted it to be overcast and miserable, so it would reflect his situation more accurately.

He recalled the previous couple of days: the panicked call with Andrea, flying into the office and seeing Strauss there, thinking about how sorry he had been for letting Drake down when the man had done anything but. The current situation was all Drake's fault.

Time up, he got out of the car and headed for the entrance. He had to figure out a way to make it right somehow.

'John, take a seat,' Dr Proctor-Reeves said at Drake's entrance.

'Doc.' He nodded, falling back into the seat a little heavily, having forgotten it had all the cushioning of a volcanic rock.

'I know it's quite soon after the last one, but from what Miller told me this morning, it's very much well-timed.'

Drake, still wincing from the pain in his arse cheek, frowned some more. 'You've been speaking with my boss?'

How often did they do that? He wondered. *Perhaps the doctor to Miller he could understand, but how often was Miller coming to her with an update?*

The information was almost making him want to clam up and not talk about what he wanted to discuss, after all.

'Yes. It's not a common occurrence, but she felt I should be aware of what's happened to your colleague, DS Luka Strauss,' she said, opening her notebook and resting it on her usual crossed leg. 'So, let's get right into that, shall we? How are you feeling, all things considered?'

'Where should I start?'

'Well—'

Drake gave her a look of amusement. 'That was rhetorical, Doc.'

'Of course.' She pursed her lips at her error.

'Strauss, well, suffice to say, I hold myself responsible. And so I should, he's a colleague and he's working for me. If not for me, he wouldn't have been in that situation.'

'I'm not going to disagree on that point. We all have certain responsibilities, and that only increases with higher ranks such as yours,' she said, tapping her pen lightly on a fingertip. 'However, please do remember the types of people you are gunning for in your day-to-day, and in the very nature of your work. You can't be everywhere, protecting everyone, all at once, John. You're not God.'

Drake supposed she had a point, but it didn't do much to diminish the guilt he felt in the matter. And one thing he definitely could agree on was that he most certainly was not God.

'Yes, and I would normally agree,' he started. 'But, in this instance, I should have recognised that Strauss would push himself. He appeared to be harbouring some guilt around an event in the previous days. So, perhaps normally he wouldn't have gone so far and so rashly and got hurt the way he did. I should have used my experience to recognise that and tell him it was okay.'

She scribbled on her pad furiously before looking up at him.

'John, have you heard of a little-known concept called "hindsight",' she said, placing her pen down on the notepad.

The comment stung more than it should have. 'Of course, I'm not daft. But this was . . .' He was struggling to find a reasoning that worked. 'Well . . .'

He gave up.

Fine, maybe she does have a point, he realised.

'How is the girl faring? Cari, isn't it?'

'Surprisingly well, all things considered.'

'Oh?'

'Yes, genuinely. I think having been exposed to her mum's mental woes for years, and her decline, she was more well-placed to cope than I realised. She's tough. Really tough.' He scratched at his cheek. 'But even so, there's only so much she could take. The personality that is in control of her mother, Miray, is reprehensible. Wickedly so. It beggars belief.'

'I see.' She removed her glasses and polished them with a cloth from her handbag, the imprint of the nose pads showing on her nose. 'Try and be there for her, though. It will be affecting her; she just may not be fully aware of how.'

'Of course, goes without saying. She's a member of the family now.'

He heard the smattering of water on the window, followed by a strong gust of wind.

Ominous, he thought, glancing at the window pane again. The weather had taken a turn, almost as if on cue with what he was wanting to talk about next.

'Something bothering you?' she asked, noting his distracted silence.

'Just . . . something that you would have been really useful for at the time, has come up again.'

Drake knew that wasn't a helpful sentence, but now he was there with her, he was finding it hard to actually come out and say the words. The Man's name, and everything he'd inflicted on Drake instantly conjured up the memories Drake had repressed, just so he could get through the day like any sane person would.

Proctor-Reeves remained silent. Expectant.

He chewed absently on his lower lip.

Out with it, man.

'So, I had a phone call last night, and it wasn't one I ever wanted to have.'

'Oh?' The doctor's interest was clearly piqued.

'It was . . . well, it was *Him.*'

'Him?'

'Yes, the Man. The Family Man. Samuel Barrow.'

Proctor-Reeves eyebrows raised instantly. 'And what was he wanting to speak to you about?'

'That's the thing, the bastard didn't really offer up anything.' He ran a hand through his hair. 'He's left me hanging and that angers me like you wouldn't believe.'

'I can see the effect he has on you.'

'Exactly.' Drake flung his hands up in frustration. 'The fucker is messing with me, even now.'

The psychologist shook her head at the sight of his agitation.

'Would you expect any other sort of response, John? You're only human. What he did to you and your daughter. It was catastrophic.'

'Yes, but he's behind bars now. Surely the way in which he triggers me should diminish?'

She shook her head. 'Not necessarily.'

'Why not, though? He's been brought to justice. He's going to rot behind bars for eternity.'

'But maybe it's not the justice you subconsciously – or even consciously, perhaps – think he deserves?'

'Maybe not. I would kill the bastard if I got my hands on him.' As if to hammer home the point, Drake balled his hands up and twisted them like he was wringing Samuel's neck. 'But that's not what I signed up to the police force for. I'm here to protect, not to kill and all that.'

'Doesn't mean you can't *feel* though, John,' she said, matter of fact, her face unreadable.

'I guess.' He dropped his eyes to his now open palms, remembering how they were stained with his wife's blood. Remembering how he'd cradled her with his one good arm once he was off the floor and Samuel was out cold.

Drake wondered whether he really should go and meet Samuel. What purpose would it serve? Surely it would only benefit Samuel? Samuel would know that he had a hold over him, however far away he was.

'He wants me to meet him.'

Proctor-Reeves eyes narrowed. 'Hmm.'

'Is that all you have to say?' Drake chuckled.

She ignored his remark. 'I am wondering whether that's a good idea. It could do more harm than good. Acknowledging a psychopath like him lets him in here again,' she tapped her temple. 'And you've made progress, whether you can see it or not. But . . .'

The psychologist paused for a longer time than felt comfortable to Drake. 'I'm not sure whether you're emotionally resilient enough yet to take what he could throw your way. And that's not meant as a slight on your character. No one would be. It's not even been two years.'

'He mentioned developments, it was like he was hinting at knowing something that may *help me*, somehow,' Drake said.

'That's what he wants you to think. That's his way of getting a hook into you. Surely you can see that?'

'I know,' he snapped, not meaning to, and lowered his tone again. 'I know. But I think I *need* to know. And I need to look him in the eye. It's like Cari and Miray. She stood up to her, showed her she had survived, that the woman hadn't won. Surely, I, a grown man, can do the same? *Need* to do the same?'

'There's substance there, John. Sure. But all I can say is, I would advise the utmost caution. It could tip you over the edge if you're not careful, and with the stress of your current work . . . I'd ask that you think about this some more before rushing into something you may later regret.'

Drake considered her words. She *was* right. It was a delicate equilibrium he was going to upset. His anger and grief, though still there, had been taken down a peg or two since his reconciliation with Eva. All this . . . Could it set him back?

I'll think on it further. But I can't ignore him forever. I just can't.

Drake decided to bring up the mood slightly. Though it probably sounded more ominous than he intended.

'What're you expecting will happen, Doc?' he said with a chuckle. 'That I'll kill him?

Chance would be a fine thing.

41

Drake stood in the kitchenette drinking another necessary coffee. He contemplated its contents, finding it odd how people could become conditioned to almost liking such things.

Needs must, he supposed.

'Drake?' came a tentative voice. He recognised the Scottish lilt, and turned his head to see Ellie's old boss, Police Inspector Phoebe Elgin, standing by the doorway leading to the other end of the office. The woman was in full uniform, her hair tied back in a severe ponytail that added years to her. Though the last few months probably hadn't helped in that regard, he supposed.

'Elgin? Haven't seen you since, well, since the incident a few months back,' he stated, recalling she'd been quite badly injured. 'How's the ankle?'

'Still painful. Not quite there yet, healing-wise,' she said softly. She had a guilty air about her, as though she had been caught doing something she shouldn't. 'Scars itchy as hell, the usual.'

Drake realised he'd never delved much into Elgin's involvement in the Spencer case when he'd spoken to Ellie after the dust had settled. Not that it was directly Elgin's fault, much like Ellie's situation. Perhaps he should take that thinking and apply it to his own self-blame game. After all, Elgin could only have done so much with the information she'd had at the time, and the trust she'd had for her friend – or boyfriend, or whatever the abuser, Sergeant Peter Matthews, had meant to her. She certainly didn't deserve what the Spencers had intended for her in their twisted game of revenge.

They both stood in an awkward silence for a few moments before he offered up a conversation starter. 'Seen or spoken to Ellie recently?'

'No, I think she's giving me a wide berth now these last few weeks.' The woman's eyes dropped. 'Can't say I blame her, in all fairness.'

Doing well with the conversation, John. Well done. Excellent topic. Way to kill the mood further.

Drake offered her some hope. 'I don't think she blames you. I think she's just been rattled by it all. The attempts on her family, you know?'

Elgin weighed up what he had said, and nodded. 'True, and she's not been sleeping.'

'What? What do you mean?'

'Last we spoke before the radio silence, she'd been having nightmares,' Elgin said. 'Though, maybe it's better now?' She put her empty mug down on the side. 'Hence, she's come to her senses and moved on from me.'

She never told me that. What else was she holding back? Maybe that explains her recent behaviour too, Drake thought.

'She'll come round, I'm sure. As you say, maybe she's just not one hundred percent right now?'

Elgin gave him a sad look. 'Maybe.'

'Anyway, I best be off,' he said, pushing off from the kitchen counter he'd been leaning on. 'But I'll tell her you said hello, all right?'

She forced a smile at his suggestion. 'Thank you, Drake. I'd appreciate that.'

Leaving the kitchenette, he threw the cup in the bin round the corner and proceeded on to the investigation room. Drake hoped the team had something for him. Strauss would have had something by now if he was around, he was sure of it.

Drake burst into the room, expecting a hive of activity. What he got instead was one junior analyst, Marie Neven, along with Melwood, who was sporting a puzzled look.

Where's Ellie? He wondered.

Ignoring his subverted expectations, Drake asked, 'So, what've you got for me, guys? Anything we can use?'

He loomed over Melwood at his laptop, Neven next to him, poring over the screen. The junior had wavy brown hair down to her shoulders, and a kind face. She always treated everything with a seriousness that made him feel like all the crimes were personal to her. Neven reminded him of himself when he first joined CID, always wanting to do his best to impress while not coming across like a kid. And she was largely succeeding, much to her credit.

'Funny you should say that, Drake,' Melwood said, peering up at him. The man looked tired, and Drake suspected he may have been at the hospital into the early hours, if not all night. 'I'm surprised you didn't hear me shouting across the office.'

'Go on.'

'Neven here has struck gold.'

She smiled at Melwood's compliment and took over. 'I can't take all the credit; the other guys have spent hours upon hours looking at the additional footage. It's not the best quality, but I think it's crucial.'

'Why's that?' Drake said, peering down, trying to get a good angle on the screen, but the light overhead wasn't helping.

'Because, sir. There appears to be another person with Andrea Whitman at the Pearce murder.'

What? Jesus. How can this be? Yet another case where they're not acting alone?

That was unexpected, but would explain a lot: how she was able to be undetected for so long and how she was able to function, essentially. As well as how she had a damn phone. But how had this all happened? And, more importantly, who could it be? How had she found someone who wanted to be a part of such a terrible event so readily?

'Whoever it is has tried their best to stay away from Andrea and eventually, Pearce, for as long as they could,' Neven continued. 'We received footage from a resident's doorbell cam at a nearby address, as well as a camera from across the river to corroborate they were together. You wouldn't be able to make anything out really, unless you were looking for it.' She seemed to pause for a little dramatic effect, before adding, 'but obviously, we were.'

Drake felt the single vibration of a text message in his pocket. He'd check it in a second.

'Good work, Marie. Excellent,' he said. 'Could I see, please?'

Neven nodded, tinkering with the laptop. 'Best turn that light off, though. It's pretty dark footage. Inspector Melwood here had trouble seeing it,' she said, with a smirk.

'We're getting old, Drake,' Melwood remarked.

'Don't give me that shit, Inspector,' Drake scoffed as he turned off the light, casting the room in relative darkness with some help from the papered glass.

Soon the video was sent to the television screen for them to view. Drake sat directly in front, while Melwood and Neven remained and pivoted on their seats. The footage was grainy and blocky. Even with Drake's inferior IT brain, he could see that it was low resolution. They wouldn't be identifying anyone positively without prior knowledge, that was certain.

He glanced down briefly at the text he'd received, and frowned.

Sorry, Chief. I'm not coming in today. Personal day, if that's all right. Need to get some stuff together.

What was up with her? Drake supposed he'd have to allow it, but with regret. He needed everyone he could and with this new development, it could mean the forward momentum he so wished for. But she wasn't one for taking the piss and taking off any random day she felt like.

'Ready, Drake?'

'Sorry,' he said, looking up to see their expectant faces and shoving his phone back in his pocket. 'Go ahead.'

'Okay,' Neven said and started the video. 'This is the doorbell cam first.'

Drake watched, the doorbell cam showing cars passing by, the black and white footage amplifying the whites and not doing so well with the motion of the fast-paced cars. His expectations were immediately lowered.

'Here she comes,' Melwood murmured, a sneer on his face.

Across the street from the address, Drake saw Andrea. She was hunched over, her features otherwise indiscernible, wearing a hooded coloured or grey coat of some description, along with dark trousers and shoes. The motion blurred, compared to other pedestrians, implying that she had been walking at pace. She wasn't with anyone that he could see.

Drake looked over at Neven. 'You mentioned another person? I don't see anyone?'

'Yes. Unless you watch the other footage by the underpass, you would never know they were together.'

Neven rewound the footage, and stopped at the image of a figure a few seconds before Andrea's passing, the clothing similar to her, though a hat and possibly balaclava were obscuring any defining facial features. It was hard to even tell if it was a male or female accomplice.

Drake sighed irritably at the sight. 'Okay, can we see that second set of footage next?'

'Of course, it has been manipulated by the team to get the maximum contrast and exposure to be able to see what it is that is going on.'

'Got it.' Drake squinted at the new footage. Again, it was low resolution and grainy, no faces, just blobs with limbs, and barely perceivable clothing.

Neven started the footage.

There was a view of the underpass entrance with the bench that Drake had assumed Pearce Fleming was perched on before the attack. But there was no one there at the start of the recording.

'I take it they come along soon?' Drake said, impatiently.

'Yes,' Melwood snapped. 'Just watch.'

Sure enough, soon a figure appeared and strode over to the bench and took a seat. It had to be Pearce Fleming. The man was sitting for barely a minute before Andrea made an appearance, striding over and sitting down next to him.

Drake's heart skipped a beat at seeing her about to commit an act he'd not seen since The Family Man videos. It disgusted him.

The short time between her approach and sitting down didn't indicate a conversation such as her asking to sit or similar, as she didn't stand in front or beside him. It was as though he was *expecting* her. Drake would probably need to view it again to see if his theory was right.

The video paused. 'Do you see anything here, sir?' Neven asked.

'No? I . . .' he paused, squinting at the footage further. Actually, now she mentioned it, there *was* something off. Further along the river, away from the bench and the underpass, a figure appeared to be watching. Lying or kneeling, or crouched down in some way, it was hard to tell.

'Is that the other person you mentioned, just over there?' he asked, pointing to the corner.

She gave him a toothy grin. 'Bingo.'

Drake returned an encouraging one. 'Good spot, Neven.'

'Thank you, sir.'

'Is there more? And is there anything from the Ian Reed scene?'

'Yes. Much more from this one, but the Battersea scene is proving less fruitful right now. Which is weird, considering how overlooked it was.'

She pressed play and the footage played out further.

The figures were both still until suddenly Andrea thrust at the man's neck, Drake couldn't see, but she had to have been holding a knife. Pearce reeled from the attack and started to run toward the underpass before his wound seemingly got the better of him. The accountant slowed and staggered, putting an arm up against the wall as Andrea slowly followed him like a predator watching their prey bleed out.

Her apparent accomplice then ran over and pointed at Pearce. Andrea ran to him and renewed her attack until Pearce stumbled out of view and into the underpass.

It was incredible how this was occurring with all the movement and activity of the street above. But it was, and it had.

The second figure followed slowly after, holding something in their hand.

Wait.

Drake's eyes went wide at what he was seeing. What it implied.

Not again.

'Am I imagining things, or is that figure holding a phone camera? Are they recording? Please tell me they're not recording.'

'We can't say for sure. This is as good as it gets, so it's speculation. But, there's the possibility, yes. I would be more surprised if the person wasn't.'

'Christ . . .' Drake said, shaking his head with disgust. 'It's happening again, isn't it?'

'What do you mean, Drake?' Melwood asked.

'Andrea. She's found her cameraman, just like Stan and the Man all those years ago.'

42

Ellie looked down at her phone again. The text to Drake showed as having been read within a few minutes of sending it, but she was still to receive a response or even a short acknowledgement. Was her boss angry with her? Disappointed, even?

Don't be ridiculous, you're not a kid and neither is he. He's probably just busy, she rationalised.

Perhaps it was just her guilty conscience messing with her?

Ellie never liked to take time off, and definitely not when there was nothing physically stopping her doing her damn job. All she was doing was taking her husband's advice – for once – and doing something for herself. Something she needed. Something that was necessary. Not that it was a holiday of any kind, even if she was going to be going to a retreat.

The retreat. The place where she'd killed someone.

She shook the sound of Fiona slamming into the wood from her mind, took a deep breath and turned the keys in the ignition.

Ellie took the turning off the A-road for the retreat. The anticipation of revisiting the final few moments of that fateful journey she and Drake had taken was sending shivers down her spine. And that was with a relatively sunny day backing her up. Ellie had broken free of London and outpaced its bad weather. For the moment.

The road gave way to the familiar dirt track. It was proving as bumpy as before, if not worse, as it jostled her from side to side. Ellie's car, an old silver Ford Focus, seemingly had the suspension of a battered go-kart compared to Drake's ten-ton beast. She dreaded to think what it would be like when she started on the even rougher trail leading to the basin in which the retreat was located.

A few more years, Ellie. A few more years. Then maybe you'll make DI and be able to afford something better. Or better yet, the force gives you a car allowance.

She grumbled, seeing her phone GPS signal had died on its arse. Again, much like before. But at least she knew the way now. The car struck another rut, bouncing like people were shoving each side of the vehicle.

'Easy girl, easy,' she soothed.

She continued bobbing her way down the dirt track until the familiar rickety white sign indicating the entrance to the retreat came into view, though it had fallen to the ground since her last visit. She'd heard from Melwood a while back that the shack was scheduled to be pulled down, meaning her trip may have been for naught. But she would have come anyway, to dispel her own demons, if nothing else.

A few feet before the final bend Ellie drew up to a vibrant yellow sign attached to a short metal post: *Danger - Demolition in progress.*

'Bugger. Just feckin' great,' she muttered, cursing her luck and slapping the steering wheel. 'I'm too late. I just had to be, didn't I?'

Still grumbling, she rounded the bend, and came across the familiar expanse of ground encircled by fir trees. Much to her surprise, the ruinous structure which had plagued her dreams for the past few months was still there, despite the warning sign, in all its battered glory.

The shorn-off facade of the wooden retreat stared back at her; the place where the grisly executions of Gregory and Jorge had eventually brought the balcony crashing down. The white, paint-flecked wood of the main building contrasted sharply with the torn and bare remains of the balcony doorway. Most of it had to have been removed, as it was nowhere to be seen. A JCB excavator sat off to the side of the structure, its tracks sunk deep into the thick mud. It looked frozen in a pose like that of a viper, ready to tear the sordid remains down at a moment's notice. But, much like the rest of the area, it was vacant. The demolition job had to still be in some sort of preparatory phase.

Ellie, realising she had been gawping while the car was idling, switched the ignition off.

The sudden silence enveloped her. The scene was such a stark contrast to the last time she'd been here. The grounds were devoid of noise and darkness, and the shafts of light coming through the trees were strangely enchanting. That is, until she looked back at the retreat. Knowing what had gone on there, even before their encounter with the Spencers, she could feel the pain of the place exuding a grim and malevolent aura.

Ellie wasn't sure what she would find. But, like Len had said, she should review everything again, give the place a shake for something, *anything* that may have somehow been missed, or could jolt her brain up a gear.

Snap. The memory of the paedophiles' necks breaking flashed in her mind's eye. The men's panic. Gregory swinging beneath the balcony. It was a horrific sight, now a horrific memory. But Ellie despised child abusers, and though seeing the justice wrought first-hand was unsettling and it wasn't what she stood for, it had been much deserved, had it not?

Besides, the abusers were heinous murderers too. The remains of Fiona's child had been found in the grounds as she'd described, and were verified to be that of her daughter. It hadn't been the ravings of a woman tipped over the edge by years of neglect and abuse. What the woman described had been harrowingly real.

'Get going, Ellie. No use sitting around. Make the most of the time you have,' she muttered, geeing herself up. 'Plenty more to do yet.'

She pulled on the door handle and exited the car. The sound of the wind greeted her, blasting through the tree tops, bending them to its will. The occasional bird in the distance tweeting the songs of early spring.

Ellie made her way over to the back entrance, past the yellow tape-sealed porch door. She recalled her frustration on finding it locked, then creeping on past it before entering at the back and being chased by Fiona. She could see the building had been tampered with, now she was up close. Green, blue and red graffiti daubed the side and corner of the building, while a number of small porthole windows had been smashed, the glass scattered in the grass beneath.

Kids must have come once the news had died down. Wanted to check out the spooky house in the woods for themselves.

Rounding the corner, she discovered her initial assumption of the building work was wrong. It seemed the JCB *had* been doing something; the corner of the building ahead of her was no longer in existence, while half the kitchenette had simply vanished, with a few cupboards hanging on for dear life on the remaining wall.

There was more yellow demolition warning tape in place on the door, though less than the porch. It was a pretty comical attempt at barring entry, considering she could literally walk through a gaping hole next to the doorway. Ellie peeled it back anyway and nudged the door open. It swung round a full 180 degrees, as though she'd slammed it with all her might, and struck an errant bit of timber with a rickety bang.

Ellie ignored it. She peered in and was immediately struck by the despairing feeling that she'd wasted her time coming here. The rest of the interior furnishings had been gutted. The furniture, rugs, kitchen appliances; anything that could be removed, had been removed. There appeared to be significant water damage too, the place reeking of damp and rotting wood. Maybe it had before, but she was in a different mindset back then.

Ellie took a few steps in, seeing the spot where she had crouched by the mezzanine stairs, having spied Drake motionless, beaten to within an inch of his life. She decided she'd save the trip upstairs until later, assuming it was even safe to go up there now.

Stepping down to the lounge, she felt the sodden wooden step buckling under her weight, causing her to panic and lunge down into the area that had been previously been covered by rugs. If Drake had been there, he would have laughed, there was no doubt in her mind.

The wooden floor still bore marks indicating where the furniture had been. It creaked and bowed as she crossed toward the terrible room depicted in the polaroid that had mystified both her and the team. She realised that despite everything that had happened, she'd never actually seen it in person.

The room where the Spencers abuse took place was a wreck. It was as Drake had described later in the hospital. The stained windows were nowhere to be found, the frames destroyed by the collapse, the wooden beams splintered and torn. The sorry-looking bed frame now stood away from the wall, and the stove where the baby had been so cruelly disposed of was nowhere to be found.

Ellie shuddered at the thought of what had gone on just a few short steps away from where she was standing. She had to fight a sudden urge to leave, to forget why she was there and go back to her family and cuddle her daughter.

She took another step and looked around further. Nothing jumped out at her. SOCO would have catalogued everything, would have scoured every surface, she was sure of it. The dawning realisation that the trip really could be completely pointless was starting to seep in, despite her initial positivity. She was wasting her time, wasn't she?

Removing herself from the menace of the room, Ellie carefully walked the perimeter of the living space, coming back to her original hiding spot.

I should give it a go. But at the first sign of buckling, I'll go back, she reasoned.

Readying herself, she planted a foot on the first step up to the mezzanine. It felt sturdy enough. Second, third, then fourth step. Soon she'd ascended and had made her way round to the final spot where she had fallen, the spot where she'd faced Fiona — where the woman had fallen to her death. Her stomach roiled as she held onto the remains of the balcony door frame, much like she had before, her mind's eye going through the events of that night.

Still holding the frame tightly, she tentatively peered out over the edge to the ground below. Nothing remained to show what had taken place above between her and Fiona. It was as though the falls had never happened.

'If only,' she mumbled, unable to shake the feeling of shame. 'I'm sorry, Fiona. I had to do it, I had to. For my family.'

Ellie wondered if Drake would have done the same, or Dave, or Strauss, even Melwood. She knew she wouldn't like their answers.

The realisation dawned on her, making her catch her breath, like she'd been punched in the stomach. Ellie knew now. She *knew* what she had done. Fiona charging her, knocking her like that. Yes, she was going to fall, but Ellie had *chosen* to take the woman down with her. She'd *chosen* to grab on to her. She knew what she was doing. She knew it. She'd killed her.

Ellie tore her eyes away from the ground below, fighting an irrational urge to let go of the frame again and fall. It was what she deserved.

After a few moments of hesitation, instead, she slid down the door frame until she was slumped on the ground against it, knees hunched to her chest in an attempt to calm herself down.

She wasn't sure how long she sat like that, in silence, gathering her thoughts. She may have been there a matter of minutes, or hours longer. But by the time she looked up again, the sky had darkened, along with the light inside the retreat too. The London clouds having caught up with her finally.

It was then she spotted something.

Something not in keeping with the rest of the barren interior. In the kitchenette, something that was not *right*, beyond its wrecked state. A white sliver, like the corner of a piece of paper. It was sticking out from the top of a wall-mounted kitchen cabinet. The cabinet itself was pulling away from the remains of its fixings on the wall, and it looked as though the paper had originally been tucked behind it.

Curious, she clambered to her feet, and carefully made her way back along the mezzanine and down the stairs.

'*Shit!*' Ellie's luck finally gave out and her foot plunged through one of the steps on the stairs.

'Motherfucker!' she raged as she tugged her foot awkwardly back out. Ellie checked her ankle and touched her leg, wincing at the touch of her fingers, which came back red and sticky.

Just had to happen, didn't it? One of these days I'll have a case where I don't get hurt. Chance would be a fine thing.

Limping slightly, she wiped her fingers on her jeans and did her best to walk off the pain. Upon reaching the kitchenette, she clambered carefully on to one of the few remaining countertops closest to the cabinet, which was still not as close as she'd have liked, and reached over, pulling at the suspect white corner. It was stuck tight to the wall.

More grumbling and tensing ensued as she reached at full stretch and tugged harder.

'Christ!' She yelped, toppling forward before instinctively putting an arm out to brace herself. She slammed into the cabinet, gripping it tightly so she wouldn't fall off. What she hadn't counted on was the jolt of her weight then causing the cabinet to fully shear off the wall, taking her with it.

Slamming back to the ground and into a kitchen cupboard, she groaned loudly, more stunned than hurt.

'Well done, Ellie. Really, well done. No need for the demolition team here anymore, eh.'

She took a moment to gather herself before looking up at her handiwork from the floor. She huffed, studying the place where the cabinet had been; only screws and rotten wood remained amidst a strange cavity. Was it a secret compartment of some kind?

Ellie got to her feet sheepishly and soon found what she was looking for.

She was right, it *was* paper. But not just any paper.

It was a photograph, another goddamn polaroid.

'Len, I bloody love you,' she squealed.

Ellie grabbed the picture and held it up to the fading remnants of daylight. Her excitement turned to disgust as she flinched away from the subject matter.

It was absolutely abhorrent.

A picture of a teenage Fiona and a man.

And Ellie recognised the man instantly.

43

Drake exited the office into the cold, dark early evening chill and made for his car. He'd come to a decision, and it wasn't going to be a surprise to anyone. He was going to meet with Samuel at HMP Wakefield in West Yorkshire, the prison where Samuel had been incarcerated for the past year or so. He knew not doing anything would eat away at him. The prospect of more regret and 'what ifs' was not an idea he relished, not anymore. Life was much too short. He knew that painfully well.

The drive was going to be a long one, and he'd need to get going now if he was going to make it at a reasonable time. He recalled the last drive up to that part of the world with Ellie; by the time he'd got to the hotel, he'd been absolutely knackered. He wasn't going to make that mistake again.

Unfortunately for Drake, his car lights had only just flashed to indicate the car had been unlocked when he heard a shout coming from behind him.

He turned back to see what all the fuss was about and was greeted by the sight of Melwood jogging up to him, the man's slick hair now free and flitting around his tired eyes.

'Drake! Drake, you've got to see this,' Melwood said. 'Geez, I've been trying to catch up since you got in the damn lift.'

Drake shrugged. 'What is it?'

'Pearce Fleming's hard drives, my guys have finally accessed them.'

Drake took a deep breath, locked his car again and turned back for the office. 'Well, don't just stand there. Let's go back inside.'

Drake was just about to follow Melwood back into the investigation room when he heard Miller calling his name.

Popular all of a sudden, aren't I?

'Yes, boss?' He turned to see her weaving her way toward him between a series of desks.

'Is there any further news?' She regarded him coldly. 'Please tell me there is.'

'Funnily enough, Laura. There might be something right now. Care to join us and see? I can't say for sure if it will be a development, but maybe you'll be my lucky charm.'

Her eyes narrowed as though she could think of a hundred other things she'd rather be doing, but eventually she nodded and followed him into their lair.

The room was awash with Melwood's CID colleagues and the techies Drake had left only a few minutes previously before their apparent breakthrough. They glanced up at his entrance, looking friendly enough, but then Miller followed and the room stifled instantly, like death itself had entered.

'Interrupting something?' Drake asked.

Neven poked her head around the side of a monitor. 'No, sir, ma'am. We've literally just managed to get inside the hard drives recovered from Pearce Fleming's house. We thought we'd wait until DI Melwood had brought you back so we could go through the contents.'

'And does that need everyone here?' Miller asked, looking around the room pointedly.

'For this? No, I guess not, ma'am.'

'All right, everyone out,' Miller commanded.

Drake had never seen a room empty so quickly before. Within seconds, it was just Miller, Melwood and Neven.

He tilted his head in Miller's direction. 'You really ought to teach me how to do that, Laura.'

She ignored him and sat down in front of the TV screen they had used to review the Andrea footage earlier.

'I take it you can mirror that to the TV screen, Constable?' Miller asked.

Neven returned her gaze. 'Yes, ma'am.'

'Good. Let's see what you've got. I've only a few minutes until my next call.'

'Got it.' Neven beavered away on the laptop and within seconds, the TV screen was mirroring her screen. Two hard drive icons were showing up and ready to be inspected, the two icon shortcuts directly on her desktop.

Drake sat down and squinted at the TV. 'Melwood, get the light again, would you?'

The man jumped up and soon the room was shrouded in darkness.

Neven clicked on the first hard drive icon. A series of folders and files came back, none labelled with *'See crime here'* or *'This is why I'm dead,'* which Drake found disappointing, much like when he'd been in Pearce's study. Just once, he wanted an easy life.

The contents were all seemingly categorised and organised in a methodical way to show various accounting records, spreadsheets and related documentation. Neven opened a few sample files while they watched in silence. Nothing jumped out at them, but Drake could imagine that a financial forensics team would have a field day. No one hid this kind of stuff if the transactions were all above board.

'Is this it, Drake?' Miller sighed, not looking in his direction. 'You brought me in here to look at financial records, is that it?'

'Maybe there will be something on the other hard drive? We're only halfway through,' Drake said, trying to remain calm. But truth be told, he was feeling the heat. He had hoped there would be something immediate, or something to keep her off his back at the very least. 'We need a little faith. Though, I'm not really sure what we're hoping for. Andrea has no connections to this man at all, so far.'

'Maybe second time's the charm?' Neven accessed the second hard drive and scoured each folder in turn. Once more, it seemed the same as the first. Nothing untoward.

Miller stood up and made for the door. 'I'm sorry, I don't have time for this—'

'Curious,' the analyst said, suddenly. 'There's a folder here with a series of folders within which has lots of text files numbered sequentially, but when you open them, they're garbled nonsense.'

'And?' Miller asked, looking decidedly impatient.

'I've a hunch,' Neven said. 'One second, please. Sorry.'

She fiddled around further with a variety of Windows settings, and suddenly the files changed. They were no longer showing as text files, but image files.

'Eureka!' Neven said, then lowered her voice and turned back to them. 'It's such a simple thing to do. This star accountant of ours obviously isn't very bright when it comes to this stuff. All he did was change the file extension and the file extension icon. I suppose at first glance, most people wouldn't notice. Or would just dismiss them as system files.'

Drake just nodded and agreed. Whatever she was saying, if she was happy, he was happy.

'So, what's in the files, Marie?' he asked.

Miller sat back down wordlessly and watched the screen, hands clasped firmly in front of her.

'Let's see.' Neven double-clicked a file and Drake immediately took in a sharp intake of breath, as did Melwood, who blurted out, 'What the . . . That's Fiona Spencer, isn't it?'

A teenage Fiona Spencer with long greasy blonde hair stared back at them, a terrified look on her face that would make even the strongest of men weep. She was huddled up on the same bed and in the same cursed room where all the other abuses had occurred. Only this time, it was a different man involved. Drake balled his fists, doing his best to quell the idea of Eva or Cari in that situation.

Neven keyed between more of the images, showing the man, showing Fiona. Visibly flinching as the pictures got progressively worse. He didn't want to look. And neither did Melwood by the looks of it.

'Enough for now, please, Neven,' Miller snapped.

The analyst closed the images down and scrolled the folder without opening more files. Drake stared grimly at the sight. There were hundreds of images, if not thousands. He didn't know if he could stomach looking at such vile images. Murders and death was one thing, but abuse was another thing entirely. He'd seen what it could do, how it could affect the people in the teams that specialised in abuse and all the horrific acts related to it. Many had to be moved on to other work, or eventually left the police force entirely.

This man, this abuser . . . It was Pearce Fleming.

He was one of the men that Gemma had spoken about to Ellie.

But Drake was still confused. He didn't understand. It didn't add up.

How could Andrea be involved in this enough to want to kill him? She still had no links to these men that they knew of. The only person that might have was the second person in the video footage from Pearce's murder.

But who the hell was it?

44

Ellie tried calling Drake again, but it went straight through to voicemail for what felt like the millionth time. She huffed at her phone, and decided she'd have to send a short message instead before almost walking into a nurse pushing an elderly man in a wheelchair. Embarrassed at her impressive clumsiness lately, she apologised and continued pacing down the corridors of the hospital, the sickening polaroid of Pearce Fleming and Fiona Spencer still safely stowed in her coat.

She wanted to speak to Gemma again. She needed to understand how Andrea knew who this man was, and how she could have located and killed him. Presumably the second victim, Ian Reed, was the sibling's other abuser.

Finally arriving at the right corridor, Ellie spotted the same policeman sitting outside the woman's door. She wondered how many hours he'd spent there and how he could put up with it. Some people just could, she supposed.

'Hello again.'

The man peered up at her with the same tired look from

before, instantly reminding her of their last extremely short chat. 'Oh. It's you.'

'Yes, it is. I hope it's not got you too excited. You look like you're almost ready to stand up and everything.'

'I don't think that will be necessary,' he said, dryly.

'Excellent.'

I like his style, she smirked to herself before knocking and entering without waiting for an answer.

It was early evening, so Ellie wasn't expecting Gemma to be knocked out for the night just yet. Instead, she was sitting up, a pillow bunched behind the small of her back and another behind her head, a small TV on in the corner of the dark room. Only a bedside lamp gave it any warmth at all.

The ex-DC had come on leaps and bounds in the past few days. The number of tubes and devices connected to her had at least halved by Ellie's vague recollection, and the colour was returning to her cheeks. The sickly pallor wasn't quite gone, but it was certainly nowhere near as bad as before.

'Gemma,' she said, knowing full well they didn't leave on the best terms last time, not that Ellie could blame her.

Gemma didn't turn to look at her, instead continuing to stare at the TV.

'What do you want?' she asked Ellie eventually. 'Can't you see I'm very busy?'

Her voice sounded stronger than last time.

'There's been some developments with your case.'

'Riveting.'

Ellie pulled up a chair from the corner of the room, the wood making an awkward scraping sound across the floor. She stopped at the corner of the bed, not coming up quite next to the woman. She didn't fancy Gemma grabbing at her like last time. She knew too well that looks could be deceiving.

'Do you mind?' Gemma snarled, turning up the TV.

'Can you turn that off for a bit, please?'

Gemma ignored her and continued staring off at an old re-run of *Friends*.

Okay, different approach, she thought.

'Don't make them like that anymore, eh?' Ellie remarked.

'What? Annoying and American?'

'No, the humour. Times have changed.'

'Humour is humour.'

Can't argue with that.

'Look, Gemma. Please, speak to me. It's about the two men you mentioned that were still out there.'

Gemma's eyes dropped at being reminded of them. 'I don't want to think about that. Not anymore. They've done enough already.'

'But what if I told you at least one of them was dead?'

The bed-ridden woman directed the remote at the TV and turned it off, finally meeting Ellie's gaze. 'You're joking?' Gemma tilted her head, studying Ellie's face. 'I suppose you're not. That'd be pretty fucked up if you joked about that, even for you.'

The comment stung. But she supposed she deserved anything and everything Gemma threw her way.

'No.' Ellie kept her voice low for effect to keep it as though she was divulging severely restricted information. 'And I don't think you'll be sad to know that – between you and me – they met particularly grisly ends, too.'

That should help get her on side, at least a little bit.

'Oh?'

'Yes. I'm not going to go into details, but it was . . . "intense", shall we say?'

'How do you know it was them, anyway?'

'I've found a picture. It's of your sister.'

Gemma sneered. 'Them and their damn pictures. I fucking hated that polaroid camera. It always meant they were going to be *particularly* disgusting.'

Ellie daren't imagine. She took the picture from her pocket and covered everything but Pearce's face. 'Is this one of them?'

Gemma averted her eyes immediately. 'Don't make me look at that.'

'But it could bring you some peace, knowing that he's definitely gone?'

Gemma closed her eyes. Her manner becoming timid and shy like it had been when they worked together. It was jarring seeing her old colleague as she had been, even if it had been used as a front.

'O-okay.'

Ellie showed her the covered picture again. The woman casting a quick look over it. Her eyes flinching at the image. 'Yes, yes, that's him.'

'And the other one, did he have grey hair and a shitty clover tattoo behind his ear? Irish?'

Gemma nodded. 'I think he still had some colour in his hair back then, but it was greying.'

Surely Andrea wasn't going to kill anyone else if those two men were the last of them, then?

Gemma suddenly smiled. The smile of someone who'd just had a weight lifted from them. The millstone of years of worry and suffering, knowing that those men were out there, now being removed from around her neck. If this was the one positive thing that Ellie could do for her, she'd be happy with that, despite everything Gemma had done.

'Who did it?'

Ellie shrugged. 'I was hoping you could tell me. There's a lot which I can't go into, but suffice to say, it doesn't make sense to me at all why the killer would target these men.'

'That's very vague.'

'That's the situation for me too,' she said, clasping her hands. 'Tell me, besides you and your brother and sister, was there anyone else who had the faintest idea what you were intending to do? Anyone at all?'

Gemma looked at Ellie again. Seeing the ex-Constable like this, vulnerable and tired, Ellie could see she'd aged, now looking beyond her years, rather than younger.

'No,' she replied. 'It was just us. Hardly something you spread around town, is it?'

'Then I'm at a loss,' Ellie said, sitting back. 'I have no link. No way of finding this person.'

She stood and paced the front of Gemma's bed, continuing her train of thought. 'Are you *absolutely* certain? You're saying that you guys were the only ones to stalk and kill these abusers?'

'Correct.'

'Fiona the only one to attack my family?'

Gemma nodded, exasperated. 'Yes, Ellie.'

'To threaten me with that . . . *thing* at my girl's school? You and Jack deceiving us—'

'Sorry, what?'

'What? Did I miss something out from that shit show? I'm sorry.'

'No, but, stop. I mean it. I don't know what you're on about.'

Elie frowned. 'You've lost me.'

'You said something about the thing at your girl's school? That doll?'

'Yes, the Action Man figure. The one with the duct tape wrapped around its damn head.'

Gemma pulled herself up a little further in the hospital bed.

'No. That wasn't us. Fiona and Jack didn't do any of that weird shit. I kept quiet at the time as it was a handy distraction for us – and Jack was disappointed he hadn't thought of it himself, actually. But it was never anything to do with us. I just assumed you'd caught the creep who did that by now.' She paused to cough harshly. 'And, as I said before, while I didn't know how they would kill people and stuff, for most of it, I definitely knew everything to do with *you* as I had to work with you.'

Ellie's heart quickened. 'But one of you gave the figurine to a guy on the street and paid him money to pass it to my daughter. You had to have done.'

Gemma laughed. 'That's ridiculous. I can't believe you still think we did that.'

'Yes, and the phone threats.'

'The phone calls were Jack, sure. But the Action Man figure? The random CCTV guy on the street . . .'

'Yes.'

'Sorry, Ellie. You're on your own with that one. It wasn't us. We were too busy with shitting ourselves over having to cover up Fiona's blood on the tree.'

'Then who was it?'

Gemma sniggered. 'You tell me, *Sergeant.*'

45

Drake was nearing the final hour of the drive up north to West Yorkshire and HMP Wakefield. And it felt like it was not a moment too soon. His back was aching and his arse was numb. He'd been tense ever since getting back in the car to start the journey, knowing what he was going to be inflicting upon himself in the morning. Seeing *him* again. Undoubtedly having to dredge up everything that had happened just to get a useless bit of information out of the bastard. If there even was anything in the first place.

He'd spoken with Ellie while he drove. It appeared that she'd not had a personal day at all, but had gone off-piste and done her own bit of work on the Spencer case, in direct violation of his orders.

Drake smiled to himself. Despite his misgivings, he had to admit he admired her determination. He knew his younger self would have done exactly the same if something had bugged him. But he now also recognised how bloody *annoying* it must have been to his old superiors, such as DI Sanderson and Miller. And now to top it off, the two cases were actually linked somehow through Pearce Fleming and Ian Reed. Ellie's effort hadn't been misspent and added weight to what they'd now discovered on the hard drives.

And all the more worrying was the fact that, if Gemma Spencer was to be believed, the Action Man figure she and her daughter had been threatened with hadn't come from the Spencers at all. So, who had got the CCTV man, Pinter, to do what he did? Was Gemma still keeping secrets, or had Jack Spencer deliberately withheld information from her, and he had been involved all along? Drake supposed he now had *two* reasons to be at the prison in the morning.

He'd made the call to the prison, ensuring he'd stressed the importance of seeing Jack Spencer as well, to the prison officer who'd answered. The man had sounded decidedly put out, but said it could be arranged for early afternoon, much to Drake's relief. There was no way he wanted to be away from the girls longer than necessary, no matter how safe they were in the flat.

Drake also knew Jack had no reason to cooperate. He'd beaten the young man senseless at the retreat and put Jack and his surviving sister in jail. But Jack couldn't refuse to see him, and if Drake had to sit in silence with the killer, then so be it.

He continued his train of thought as the thrum of the engine threatened to send him to sleep. Then, as though someone up above wanted to make things just that bit worse, the rain started while he sped past Sheffield up the M1 motorway. It was seemingly customary the further north he travelled; the heavy drops hammered down on the car, before a few hailstones joined the fray, turning a tired Drake into an even more irritable and testy one as the stones pinged off the car.

Sleep didn't look like it would be on the cards when he

arrived, no matter how much he wanted it to be. There was just too much to think about. Too many killers to question.

Soon he'd be face to face with the man who'd murdered his wife in cold blood.

46

I looked down at the man's limp, crumpled body on the floor.

He was out cold.

I knew it would be impossible; I knew it. I'd tried to pretend that everything was fine when I discovered that he was not *my* Ben, but it hadn't taken long for my pretence to crumble. Any answers he'd received had been short. The anger was too great. The idea of this stranger touching me again, I *couldn't*. I couldn't stand to even be in the same room as him, knowing what he'd done to me.

So no, everything was most definitely *not* fine.

It hadn't taken me long to decide to escape. To get away from wherever the hell I was, to find my husband and daughter. They'd know what was going on. They'd help me like they'd always done, and we'd be together again. Everything would be as it was, and I'd be happy.

When the time came, I hadn't meant to hit him quite so hard with the lamp.

It had shattered; not just the shade and bulb, but the base too, such was the force of the hit. I didn't know I had the strength in me, but seems I was wrong. He still seemed to be breathing though, so that was something.

My moment of elation from having bested him had soon turned into a state of panic, my heart racing as I tried to think of my next move. My desperate need to get out of there was increasing by the second. I wondered what I'd find on the other side of the door. Was it an institution? Was he an orderly? Why was I here? And how?

Dressed, I made a beeline for the door, rounding the bed and the man's body. But the door wouldn't budge. Surely to get in, the man had to have had a key?

I turned back and rifled through his pockets, being careful not to rouse him. I really had no idea how long he'd be out for. It could only be a matter of minutes, even seconds. The back of my head started to pulse as I came up trumps with the key a few moments later. I had to ignore it. *She* would just argue for me to stay, I knew she would. I needed to stay strong. Keep her at arm's length. I knew now how she'd manipulated me, how controlling she'd been.

Despite my jittery fingers, the key worked in the lock, the audible click incredibly satisfying.

I'd made it. My time here would be at an end. I just needed a few minutes more. I had to push on.

It was a shock to suddenly be flooded with colour after being in a room so devoid of any for so long. And the hallway I found myself in wasn't a hospital or a clinic, or anything like that. Instead, what confronted me was a worn blue carpet that spanned a few feet in one direction, ending in a door at one end, a set of stairs at the other.

Padding to the edge of the stairs, I listened intently.

There seemed to be nothing else going on. Perhaps it was just the stranger who lived here, after all?

I started down the stairs, carefully . . . *slowly,* until I found myself in a hallway again.

It appeared it really was just a house, a terrace. Nothing more.

I turned my attention to the front door and crept over to it before gently testing the handle. Nothing. It was locked again.

'Fuck, no. No-no-no-no-no.'

There was nothing in the vicinity that might house a set of keys, no coats, no side table or dish. I rushed down the hallway to the back of the house, entering a galley kitchen. But nothing there jumped out at me either. At the front of the house to the side, there was a dining room. There had to be something there, surely?

'Please . . . Please . . . Please.'

I burst in, louder than I probably should have, but my plight was feeling increasingly desperate. The room was almost as sparse as the bedroom; just a small table and set of chairs, no family photos, nothing at all.

However, I spotted the one thing I needed.

A key.

I'd made it. It had to be it, it had to be the right key. I just knew it.

Snatching it up, I raced back to the front door, jamming it in the lock.

It worked.

Hands still shaking, I carefully opened the door, the jet-black night sky greeting me, the air chilling my skin as it rushed over me in waves.

This was it.

I was *free*.

Until a sound of rushing feet came.

Before I could react, a hand wrapped around my mouth, pulling me violently to the ground, the back of my head slapping the wooden floor and causing me to cry out beneath the man's hand.

The man bared his teeth at me, locking his eyes on mine.

'And where do you think you're going?' he hissed.

47

Drake woke in the morning to a splitting headache and his horrendous phone alarm once again threatening to cleave his head in two. He'd been right about his expectations at the hotel; sleep had not been forthcoming at all, not until at least five that damn morning. He looked over at his phone, the alarm having been set for seven.

Great. Just bloody great. Two whole hours of sleep. You must have done something bad in a past life, John, he thought miserably as he dragged himself out of bed for a cold shower.

Before he knew it, he was back in the car again and on his way to HMP Wakefield, or the "Monster Mansion" as it was known, to meet a man that had murdered his wife and countless others, and to meet a man he'd beaten bloody.

The pale yellow walls of the prison came into view. He slowed at the sight, the masonry looming over him as he took the turning for the car park. The outer walls, topped with a curved, water-stained grey concrete, seemingly stretched on for miles. Drake dreaded to think what it would be like to live and work in such a place, to be surrounded by murderers and sex offenders, all day, every day. He had always hated visiting prisons, and fortunately for him, it wasn't something he did very often. Once his prey was behind bars, more often than not he was done with them. And that suited him just fine.

Drake took a moment once he'd parked up and the engine was off. He noticed his hands trembling slightly, like an alcoholic that hadn't had a drink for a few hours. He wasn't sure whether it was from fear, or the boundless anger that had been his constant companion since his family's fateful night. And his restless sleep hadn't given him the answer, nor cast any light on how he would react when Samuel was brought into the room. All he knew was that he despised him with every fibre of his being.

Drake gripped the steering wheel one last time as he tried to focus on the task at hand before exiting the car.

It's time.

Before Drake knew it, he was being led down a corridor in the old prison by James Walker, the custodial manager for the wing that held Samuel Barrow. Drake didn't like the newer terms for the levels of prison guards, it made them sound like office workers to him, but that was the way of it now and had been for at least eight years. Thoughts like that made him realise his own advancing years.

The prison was as dilapidated and in need of updating as ever, bringing to mind the stereotypical idea of what prisons look like to the general public, with its innumerable iron bars, rolling gates and peeling cream and white brick work. The clanking of gates and distant calls and shouts of prisoners echoed around him as he passed a door that led into the wing proper. The sight of prison officers on early morning patrol walking the landings with their batons, radios and body cameras greeted him. He'd arrived well before the prisoners were scheduled to be let out to do the day's work, so at least he wouldn't be getting the evil eye from anyone other than the bastards he was here to see.

'Through here, Drake, if you please,' Walker requested, a hand directing him through another gate and down a sterile-looking corridor with a noticeboard adorning one small patch of the expanse.

'That's where you'll be.' Walker pointed to a door way down on his left and locked the gate behind them. 'If you don't mind, I have to go and get the people necessary for bringing Barrow up for you.'

Drake nodded. 'Got it. Thanks, Walker.'

'Do you need anything while I'm gone?'

'No, thanks.'

Drake continued down the corridor for a few paces and entered the room. It was largely nondescript, similar to a few interview rooms he'd seen in his time. Though, as was typical of the prison, it was styled a few decades ago in the sixties or seventies, with the same cream brick walls and a bottle green stripe at waist-height. A metal table was positioned in the centre, bolted to the ground with a ring off-centre for handcuff chains to be threaded through. A set of metal chairs were positioned either side, a couple against a wall. An old nineties-era CCTV camera sat in the top corner of the room. Charming.

Drake sat facing the door; he didn't want his back to Samuel for any part of their discussion. Trying to get comfortable, he rested his arms on the table, while his leg bobbed under the chair. His palms grew increasingly clammy as he waited, but the visible tremor of earlier had gone, at least.

Get a grip, John. For God's sake.

He took a deep breath, and held it, hoping it would give him some calm, but his heart pounded in his chest all the same. The room smelled stale, as though its air had also been imprisoned for years.

Drake heard the ominous clanking of doors, similar to the sound of the one he'd come through earlier, before slow steps echoed down the hallway, each step leading his nemesis to him.

Drake balled his fists tight, and flexed, then again, balled and flexed. His fingernails dug harder into his hands with each echoed step.

His head snapped up as a prison officer appeared at the door.

'Ready?'

Drake closed his eyes for what seemed like forever, but must have only been a split-second.

'Yes, send him in.'

Drake felt his chest burn with an intense hatred at the sight of Samuel Barrow being brought into the room. His previous fear all but turned to ash in an instant.

Samuel's dark eyes lit up at the sight of his old adversary, a wicked grin on his craggy face. 'Well . . . well . . . well . . . As I live and breathe . . . *DCI* Drake.'

Drake didn't respond as Samuel was led to his chair by a prison officer he didn't recognise. The officer undid one of Samuel's cuffs from his outstretched wrists before threading it through the table ring, and then cuffed it back to Samuel with no interference.

Samuel had aged since Drake last saw him at court; his previously well-muscled physique had thinned down, and he held himself differently. He was wearing a grey jumper and grey tracksuit bottoms, with dark shoes, a far cry from the chequered farmer's shirt and chinos of old. Drake put Samuel's different stance down to the shoulder injury Ellie had inflicted with his own knife. The thought of Samuel dealing with a continuous pain or ache warmed Drake's soul; knowing the man was in a state of permanent discomfort was pleasing. Though it was unfortunate he had retained use of the arm at all.

Samuel sat back in his chair as the door closed behind him, the grin still fixed on his face. The prison officer took a position in the corner of the room. 'So, this how it's going to be? You just sit there and I talk, that it?'

Drake regarded him with blazing eyes. He was going to have to do his best to reign himself in. Keep it professional.

'Something like that, Samuel.'

The fact Samuel was still able to sit across from him and talk, whereas his wife's voice was stilled forever, disgusted Drake. This *man* had taken her from him.

'Heh. Didn't think you'd come, you know? After all I've done to you. To Eva. But still, you're here. Back for more. Lapping it up like a little lovesick puppy.'

Drake ignored his goading, his arms still resting on the table. 'Why ask for me to come here, Samuel? What is it you wanted to tell me?'

'Come now.' Samuel smiled. 'We can't even talk like men anymore before getting down to the sordid details?'

'I have nothing to say to you,' Drake snarled.

'Really? I killed your wife in front of your only child. I slit your bitch wife's throat, and that's it? You have *nothing* to say?'

Drake felt the anger surge within his chest at the mention of Becca's death. Samuel speaking her name. Tarnishing her memory.

Keep it together. Don't let him get a rise out of you. You're better than that. It's what he wants. It's what he needs.

'How's the shoulder doing?' Drake asked, giving Samuel a thin smile.

Samuel responded with a sneer. 'It has its moments. Could still choke the life out of you if there weren't any officers here.'

'Okay.' Drake shrugged dismissively before sighing. 'And what are these developments you spoke of?'

'How's Eva doing?'

Drake made a point of sighing loudly again. 'I'm not going to discuss her with you, Samuel. Have the decency to bring your common sense to the table with you.'

'She missing her *Mummy*?' Samuel leered at him. 'I still remember her screams, John. I bet you do too, don'tcha?'

'Have you heard from Jonah lately? If you want to talk about family,' Drake retorted, wishing he hadn't resorted to Samuel's tactics. He was better than that, he knew. But reason was going out the window now. He was already sick and tired of tiptoeing around him. Samuel didn't deserve his consideration.

Samuel's face instantly changed to one of abject disgust. 'We've not spoken.'

'And your darling wife, Ann? I bet she's enjoying prison too, yes?'

'I know what you're doing, Drake. You're not going to get a rise out of me so easily.'

Drake pushed on, enjoying his moment. 'Samuel, your whole ideal and way of life is *gone*. Your family is split up, your business has failed, it's been broken up and sold for parts. There's *nothing* you can say to me that will worry me, nor upset me. I've heard all your shit before. You're nothing but a sad old man who is now behind bars for the rest of his pathetic little life.'

'Oh? And what does Andrea have to say about that? I hear she's doing rather *well*. Takes after her old man, I hear?'

What? How does he know about that?

'Andrea? She's not doing anything, Samuel.'

'Oh, come now. You think me a fool, Drake? I told you; I

know things. I have means, whether you believe it or not. Prison only does so much for a person like me.'

'Okay. I'll bite. What do you know?'

'I know she's been out there somewhere since I went inside.' He paused. 'I know she followed my ways, John. Killed her useless husband and almost got her daughter, too. She purified *herself* without needing her Daddy. I'm proud of her.'

Samuel seemed deadly serious too, his eyes taking on a horrible look of admiration.

'That's not hard to know, Samuel. It was in the news.'

'Not the means, though, eh, Drake? Not the *details*,' he said, licking his lips.

Drake supposed he was right, the manner in which Ben had died hadn't been public knowledge. But Samuel knowing what he did, it didn't take much to put two and two together. There was still nothing.

'You're going to have to do better than that, Samuel. Come on now.'

Samuel gave Drake a shit-eating grin. 'I'm only just getting started, Drake. How about we talk about those two deaths in London, eh? She had a fun old time with them, didn't she?'

Drake's stomach lurched. *What? How did he know she was involved with that? Or about the deaths at all, for that matter?*

'That's a bit of a stretch now, Samuel. Please, don't make shit up. It insults my intelligence,' he said, not giving anything away.

'And you're insulting mine, Drake. I know what's been happening in that underpass and in Battersea too. And I might just know how to help you.'

'You?' Drake laughed. 'Help *me?*'

'Yes, but I think we should leave it there for now,' he said, getting up and causing the chain constraints to scrape the table ring sharply as he hollered for the door to be opened. 'Time's up, Drake. It was good to see you.'

The door was opened by another guard outside while the attending officer left the corner of the room to go through the handcuff routine and lead their prisoner back to his cell. Samuel turned back one last time while he waited, and tapped his nose at him. 'Let's just say your friends may not be your friends, Drake.'

Drake sat dumbfounded. He felt played. Samuel was going to string him along. How he knew about the killings, he didn't know. Perhaps there was a media outlet or social media thing he'd been made aware of via the sordid prisoner's network? Or worse, there was a leak, and Samuel had somehow tapped into it. But who would do such a thing?

Samuel didn't *know* anything, he couldn't. Drake felt it in his bones. There had to be an explanation.

'Say hi to Eva for me. I'll be in touch,' Samuel's voice echoed from the corridor.

Drake sat alone in the room, questioning what was real and what wasn't as Samuel cackled, the grotesque noise fading away into the distance.

48

Ellie sat alone in the investigation room. She didn't understand where her boss was, but then, she supposed he had the right to his privacy. And she probably deserved it after having gone off-grid the day before with her lame excuse. Either way, Drake had certainly seemed pleased with the outcome of her excursion, with her discovery providing further weight to the underpass and Battersea murders and their involvement with the Spencer siblings, so there was at least a *reason* for their deaths. But they still didn't have a clear motive in terms of their perpetrator, Andrea.

However, the unexpected revelation from her meeting with Gemma had left Ellie in a difficult position. The notion that a mystery person, who had already threatened her family, was still out there was a terrifying one. Was the person who'd been with Andrea related to her own predicament in some way? She'd floated the idea to herself that Andrea's accomplice could be the same person who had paid Pinter, but it didn't make any sense. How would they have found Andrea, *and* then brought her round to their way of thinking? And why go on to kill the

Spencer's targets if they had nothing to do with them? And how would this person even know who they were? If they hated Ellie so much to have threatened her family, wouldn't they have sent Andrea around immediately to butcher them all? Why kill the abusers instead?

There were so many unanswered questions, it was making her head hurt.

In her new state of panic, Ellie had tried to get in contact with Pinter again to see if she could give her informant a shake and get something out of that drug-addled brain of his. But she was having no luck in getting hold of him. Ellie had even contacted Elgin to see if she could get patrols to be on the lookout for him. Her former boss had promised to do what she could, but warned Ellie not to get her hopes up.

For all Ellie knew, Pinter might have pulled the wool over her eyes and it had been him all along. But she'd never had any dealings with him previously, and that just didn't ring true.

He better surface out of whatever drug's den he's in soon. Stupid bastard.

Ellie had realised she needed to work through everything that was going on, and speak to someone about the Spencer incident so, she'd decided to get in contact with Dave. With Strauss out of action, Melwood being Melwood and having failed with Drake twice now, Dave had felt like the right choice. He'd happily obliged, offering to meet her at a nearby coffee shop.

Ellie had only just arrived and grabbed the last remaining table in the bustling café when she saw him wheeling past the window, the top of his head visible. She gave him a smile as he entered, and moved the opposing chair out of the way so he could settle in.

The stormy mid-morning weather had caused the café to put

their lights on, somehow making the chintzy polka dot table clothes even more garish.

'Dave, my hero,' she said, jokingly, but also feeling quite sincere about the comment. He had saved her daughter, after all.

'You know I'm only a phone call away, Ellie.' Dave rested his arms on the table. 'Now more than ever. I'm already sort of bored. What was I thinking, agreeing to early retirement?'

'I don't think you really had all that much choice in the matter, did you?'

'You may have a point there.' He smiled warmly at her.

Ellie grabbed a tea for herself and a coffee for Dave – as well as a generous portion of cake in Dave's case – and brought it all back to the table. His eyes immediately lit up at the size of the slice of Victoria sponge.

Brandishing a fork, he got to work on it while Ellie told him about the developments, icing sugar dusting his moustache.

'That's not good, Ellie. Not good at all.'

'You're telling me,' she said, taking a sip of her tea, her heart beating faster and the irritating twitch of her eye making itself known. She began rubbing it as she built toward her reason for bringing him to the café. 'And I'm not sure how you'll take this, but I dragged you out here because there's stuff I wanted to talk about . . . it's to do with the Spencer's case.'

'Oh?'

Ellie dropped her gaze to her cup, a finger still working her eye absently. As she'd done with Drake, now she was about to say it out loud, she was having doubts again. Ellie wasn't sure if she would be so understanding in his shoes. In her eyes, what she'd done was tantamount to murder.

'What's wrong, Ellie? You can tell me, I'm not here to judge.' He put a napkin to work on his moustache. 'We've been through a lot these past few months, you and I.'

'It's just . . . God, I'm not sure if this is really the right environment to say it. It's really serious.'

Dave frowned and looked her in the eye. 'You're worrying me now, what is it?'

'I . . . Dave, I think I deliberately killed Fiona Spencer,' she said, almost under her breath.

It was enough for him to get the idea. His eyes widened. 'What? Where did you get such a daft idea from?'

Ellie felt irrationally angry that he didn't remonstrate with her and demand she take herself down the station to hand herself in that very instant.

'It's true, Dave. You weren't there.'

'But she attacked you?'

'Yes, but I pulled her down with me, when I fell.'

'So? That's just reactions, you were probably wanting to stop yourself.'

'No . . . I mean, yes. But I wanted to stop her too. She was threatening my family. I didn't *have* to grab her, Dave. But I made damn sure I did.'

'Fine, say you did do what you're *implying*,' he said, pausing for a moment. 'You couldn't know for sure that she'd die, Ellie.'

He had a point, she supposed. But it wasn't the crux of what she was admitting to; the intent was there all the same. She'd wanted Fiona to be stopped. She'd wanted her to die. *Needed* her to. Ellie had been hell bent on stopping anyone from harming her family. She knew that.

'I don't agree,' she stated succinctly.

'Sounds to me like you're being overly harsh on yourself, Ellie. You did what anyone would do in that scenario. Your life was under threat, your *family* too. Don't persecute yourself,' he said, shaking his head. 'This has got to be some sort of PTSD talking. Remorse. There is no murder here, come on.'

The noise of the café became a distant drone as she took on board what he was saying. The sound of the young woman hitting the wood reverberated through her head again. Her dead eyes.

'Ellie?'

'Sorry, Dave. I suppose so.'

'That wasn't very convincing,' he said, tilting his head slightly, intent on understanding how her brain was working. If only she knew.

She tried taking another sip of her tea, and found herself almost repulsed by it, setting it down on the saucer a little too hard. 'Dave, look . . . I can't sleep, I can't focus. When I do sleep all I see is her face, hear the sounds of her dying,' she blurted, tears coming to her eyes.

'Hey, Ellie. Hey,' he said, putting out a hand. 'Calm down, okay? It sounds like maybe you should speak with someone professionally. They're really good these days, they can help you.'

A tear ran down her cheek. 'I don't deserve help. I don't. I killed her.'

He squeezed her hand tightly. 'Of course you do, don't be ridiculous. It was just something that happened. One of those things, you know? You're a good person, Ellie. You did the *right* thing. Please, remember that.'

Maybe he was right, but it was too much for her to handle right now. She needed to focus on work, on stopping any and everything related to these damn cases. Maybe then she'd be free.

'I—I've got to go. I'm sorry, Dave. Thank you for listening.'

'Ellie. Don't go,' he pleaded as she stood. 'Please. You're not alone, remember that.'

Ellie, her eyes blurry with tears, hurried away from the table and left.

49

Drake hadn't been in the staff cafeteria for long when James Walker appeared from a side room. A pool table stood unused at one end of the place, which Drake found to be criminal; if they had one at theirs, he would have been using it all the time. It would have helped him think. He'd just about given into temptation to give it a go and maybe grant a welcome distraction from his thoughts, when the custodial manager put paid to that notion. 'Your next guest is ready for you, DCI Drake.'

'Thank you again for doing this at such short notice.'

The man shrugged, creating an extra chin. 'Makes for a more interesting day, put it that way.'

'Well, I appreciate it all the same.'

Walker led Drake down another series of painted brick corridors, the musty smell from earlier growing more pervasive with every step. As if sensing Drake's thoughts on the smell, the man commented. 'This is one of the older wings, where the new guys go.'

'I see. Does it always smell like this?'

'Like what?' Walker looked back at him with a frown. 'I got used to it so long ago, can't say I notice anything.'

Drake huffed. 'Fair enough.'

Walker unlocked another series of gates, passing more sets of prison officers bedecked with body cams and incapacitant spray before Drake was directed to a final corridor, one that was remarkably similar to every other corridor.

'Down and on the right,' the man said, nodding in the door-way's direction. 'We'll do the same as before. Give us a few minutes, all right?'

'Sure. Thanks.'

Drake made himself comfortable in the room where he was soon to meet Jack Spencer. It was largely the same as the previous one, albeit with a dark blue stripe painted along the wall at waist-height instead of the bottle green colour from the other wing. Drake marvelled at the opulence.

He still wasn't entirely sure what to make of Samuel's crowing from earlier. Was he just toying with him, making him question those around him, or was there really something more sinister at play? Drake needed to get back to the team pronto to see what he could flush out. He'd speak with Ellie and Melwood and plan accordingly, to see how they could figure out any potential leak. He couldn't believe that such a thing could have occurred. And with Samuel, of all people. But with the case being related to Samuel, through Andrea and the method of killing, Drake supposed it made sense that some weirdo might have attempted to contact him.

He heard a similar set of sounds and footsteps, and soon after Jack Spencer entered the room.

The man had healed well since their encounter, though he had acquired a small scar on his nose where Drake had broken it. His shock of blonde hair was no more, having been shaved off, and he looked tired: drained, even. The grey prison clothing hung off him, as though it was a size too big.

Jack didn't say a word and sat down; wrist outstretched while the prison officer worked the cuffs much like with Samuel earlier.

'Jack,' Drake said in greeting. He held no real animosity toward the man, he was just another in a long line of sadistic killers he'd had to deal with, albeit in a more hands on capacity than before. Drake felt a certain thrill when he thought back to fighting him. The feeling alarmed him.

Jack blinked slowly as he started to speak. 'So, what do you want?'

'I want to talk.'

'Well, yeah, I can see that. But unless you can get me out of here, I haven't got anything to say to you.' The man's voice was devoid of anything resembling emotion.

Drake could see this was going to be arduous. He just wanted to get answers so he could move on and get out of this dump, away from Samuel.

'DS Ellie Wilkinson.'

Jack looked him in the eye. 'What about her?'

'You threatened her, right?'

'Yes, you know all this. You know why.'

'Did you pay someone to scare her and her little girl? Give her daughter an Action Man figure with duct tape around its head?'

The man didn't respond, his eyes narrowing slightly. Like he was thinking of the perfect answer.

'So what if I did?'

So he did do it, despite what Gemma said? Interesting. Drake thought, wondering what else he hadn't told Gemma or maybe even Fiona.

'Give me a straight answer, Jack.'

'Nah, I think I'll leave you hanging, if it's all the same to you. I may have done it, or maybe I didn't. What does it matter?'

'Jack . . .'

It sounded as though some kind of commotion was happening nearby; prisoners were banging and hollering at some activity or another. A riot would be the last thing he needed.

Jack laughed at him. 'Oooh, the guy's still out there, threatening more little girls with action figures, that it? Scary. They got you on the big cases these days, Drake.'

'No, that's not what I'm saying.' Drake shook his head in frustration. No wonder he'd been so wound up at the retreat. 'Was it you, or was it someone else you've been working with?'

'Why the fuck would I tell you?'

Drake played his trump card. 'Because, I've got information about the two guys you hadn't killed yet.'

The prisoner frowned. 'What? What guys?'

'Pearce and Ian.'

Jack looked down at the floor at the mention of their abusers' names. 'How do you know about them?'

'That's not how this works, Jack. Give me something.'

'You first.'

Drake didn't have time for this. 'All right. They're both dead.'

Jack's eyes lit up. 'You're kidding me. How?'

'That's not for me to say. But they're dead. You can sleep easy.'

'That . . . That was the last of them.' Jack sat in stunned silence. He looked genuinely baffled at the news. 'That's incredible. I don't understand, though, we were the only ones that were abused. I should know, I had to sift through enough *stuff* online to verify everything. You wouldn't believe all the websites and private groups out there. It's beyond disgusting.' He seemed to shudder at the thought, before adding, 'I still don't know why we were so damn special to them, but we were.'

Drake didn't want to rake up any more of the man's memories, regardless of his situation. Jack didn't deserve that. He refocused the conversation. 'So, was it you, the figure?'

The man smiled, his eyes darkening. 'All right. It was me.'

'You sure on that?'

'Of course. Was hardly going to do it myself, was I? I'm not stupid.'

There you have it. Ellie, you can rest easy, Drake thought, breathing a sigh of relief himself.

But in closing one door, it still left one open and gaping. Who was with Andrea when she killed Pearce Fleming?

'One more thing,' Jack said, shuffling in his chair.

Drake's eyes narrowed. 'Yes?'

'How is my sister doing? Please? You've got to tell me. She's all I have left.'

'You're going to have to ask DS Wilkinson, she's been speaking to her. All I know is that she's awake.'

Jack shook his head in frustration. 'How can I do that in here?'

Drake's phone rang. He was surprised he'd got any signal at all, considering he was in a brick tomb. 'I'm sure you have your ways,' he said, distractedly. Seeing it was Miller, he had to answer it. He got up and went to the corner of the room, hoping it was out of earshot of Jack.

'Laura? What is it? I'm kind of in the middle of—'

'Drake, you're not going to believe this.'

'What? Out with it.'

There was a slight pause. 'It's Samuel's son, Jonah. He's been murdered in prison.'

50

'It's not protocol, Drake,' James Walker said, looking up at him from his desk in the side office. 'I'm sorry. You've seen him once today already.'

Drake paced the space in front of his desk, scratching at his cheek. 'You need to make an exception; I need to speak with him before anyone else does. This could be my one chance to get him to open up about a case I'm working. *Please.*'

Walker stared straight through him for a moment. Drake could see the cogs whirring in the man's head.

Weighing up whether it's worth the ball ache, I bet.

Finally, the man sighed heavily. 'Fine. Let me see what I can do.' He picked up the old-fashioned phone receiver on his desk and dialled a number.

'Thank you, James. Thank you.'

Walker put up a finger to shush him and had a conversation which lasted for a few minutes. Drake couldn't make out much of what they were saying, the custodial manager's voice nothing more than a mumble.

Walker hung up. 'All right, it's a go. And this better be it, Drake.'

'Oh, it will be. I promise you that.'

'Mm-hmm.'

Soon they were making the same journey down to the wing as before, the doors grating open and shut interminably slowly for the third time in the space of a day. Drake tried to be professional and suppress the unsavoury, almost gleeful satisfaction he was feeling about what he was about to do. Informing the serial killer who had killed Drake's wife that his own son was dead would be intensely gratifying. So much had happened, and it was barely midday.

He sat at the same table as before, awaiting Samuel's return.

Footsteps sounded in the distance, amid the opening and closing of further iron gates and doors. Drake could hear someone cheerfully whistling, followed by an irritated chastisement from a prison officer.

Samuel entered the room again and flashed him the same wicked grin as before. 'Drake, really? Wasn't one time enough for ya? I told you I had nothing more to say right now.'

Drake waved a hand dismissively. 'Look, Samuel. I've got some bad news for you. I'll just cut to the chase.'

Samuel leant back in his chair, hand cuffs now attached to the table as the prison officer closed the door and took the same spot in the corner as he had earlier that day. 'Oh, really? And what's that?'

'Yes. It's about your son. About Jonah.'

Same shit-eating grin. 'Oh?'

'I'm sorry—'

'Ah, yes.' Samuel cocked his head. 'Dead, isn't he?'

'Wait, what?' Drake did a double take. Samuel already knew? How?

'Throat slit in the shower, I hear.'

'Y—yes, how did you . . . ?'

'You just don't get it do you, Drake? I know . . . everything. I *hear* everything. I'm in control. Of. *Everything.*'

'But—'

'I've had enough of your shit, Drake. You come in here, your tail feathers all up, cocky as you like, clearly revelling in the fact that my damn *son* has died, and you expect me to just take that from you?'

Drake couldn't believe what he was hearing. Then it dawned on him, the grim reality of what this monster before him was still capable of.

'Oh, bravo,' Drake clapped, scarcely able to believe what had happened. 'Jesus. It was you, wasn't it? You had your son killed. Your own flesh and blood. You sick bastard.'

Samuel cackled, each successive laugh making Drake's chest tighten that little bit more.

'I ain't telling you shit. But you know what I've said all along, Drake,' Samuel said, jabbing a finger in Drake's direction. 'He's weak, always has been. I can't be condoning that. Andrea, she's the strong one. She's my blood now. And you better watch your words with me, Drake. I'm warning you.'

'You're threatening me from here, of all places?'

'Why don't you talk to your buddies, DS Strauss and DI Melwood,' Samuel said, standing and hollering for the prison officer again.

Drake raised a hand to stop the approaching guard while he stared at Samuel. 'What do you mean? What have they got to do with this? Now I know you're just screwing with me.'

Strauss? Melwood?

Then the realisation dawned on him.

No, it couldn't be. Surely not?

But someone had been telling Samuel about the case. Could Strauss or Melwood really be the leak?

'Oh, which one could it be, eh?' Samuel said, giving him a grotesque smirk. 'Anyway, we're done here, Drake. For good this time. It's been fun, you know. This little back and forth today. Kept me entertained like you wouldn't believe. Maybe I'll think of Becca when I'm alone tonight in my cell—'

'You son of a bitch!' Drake leapt across the table at Samuel as he turned to head out the door.

Without a moment's hesitation, he slammed his fist into Samuel's temple, sending him clattering to the floor. Samuel landed with a thud before the laughter started up again. Drake set upon him, punching him again and again in a blind rage as the lone prison officer tried to stop him while more clamoured to get into the room. Samuel's head thumped the hard floor for a second time with a sickening thud, and the laughter stopped.

Seconds later, Drake was swarmed. More arms hooked under his arms, pulling him back into the furthest corner of the room while others wrestled a dazed Samuel out into the hallway and slammed the door shut.

51

My head turned slowly, like it was moving through treacle, honing in on the sounds of excited gossip. The bedroom, devoid of colour, greeting me as my tired, groggy eyes struggled to open. Had it all been a dream? The colours I saw outside the room, the night sky, the cool air on my skin . . . the strange man in my bed?

It all seemed so long ago, so distant; the memory like fallen leaves being swept away by autumnal winds. The image brought back memories of the bench overlooking Barndon, the place where my mother had come back to me.

The place I felt safe, secure.

Whole.

I blinked once more; the effort more than it was worth.

My sight was once again becoming cloudier, less focused.

The last shapes I glimpsed were that of my mother and Ben; on her face, a look of glee. His was unreadable.

Why was she so worked up? What was she going to do?

Before I could even attempt to understand, the darkness was upon me, dragging me back down into the void once more.

52

Drake's chest heaved, his heart pounding against his ribcage as the two burly prison officers finally let go of him. The pair seemed like carbon copies of each other, with their short brown hair and necks as thick as their heads.

James Walker stood over him, a look of abject disappointment plastered all over his face.

'Drake, calm down. For God's sake, man! Stop!'

He backed up to the wall, looking up at Walker from the floor with his hands up. 'Okay, okay. I'm calm, all right? I'm calm.'

'What the hell do you think you were doing, assaulting someone like that? In *my* prison, of all places?'

'I—I'm sorry, Walker.' Drake took a few more breaths. 'The man . . . he killed my wife; and he said some things as he was leaving. It just—it just flicked a switch. I'm sorry.'

'Wait, what? Did you just say he killed your wife? You're joking, right?'

'You didn't know?'

The custodial manager pinched his brow. 'No! If I did, I would never have allowed you anywhere near him. Jesus Christ!'

'I see everything is just as bad in your systems as it is in ours, then,' Drake joked.

'Yeah, and then some.'

'So, what now? Are you going to report me?'

Walker whispered something to one of the two prison officers who had restrained Drake ever so gently moments ago before dismissing them. The two men closed the door behind them as Walker pulled up a chair next to Drake while he continued his recovery on the ground.

'No,' he said, quietly. 'No, I'm not going to report you. Just count yourself lucky. If word got out that I'd even let you in here with him, I'd be screwed. So it's going to have to be our little secret, got it?'

Drake breathed a sigh of relief. 'Thanks, James. I mean it.'

'Don't thank me, thank the frankly embarrassing state of the judicial and prison IT systems.'

'Amen to that. Delete the footage, yeah?'

Walker gave him a sly look. 'What footage?'

Drake noticed the light had gone out above the lens of the camera in the room. 'And Samuel?'

'I'll have a few strong words with him. A talk about his privileges situation will resolve it, I'm sure.'

'You're a good man, Walker,' Drake said, sliding up the wall to his feet.

'Thanks.' Walker's face softened. 'I imagine you are too, under normal circumstances.'

Drake dragged himself back to his car, ashamed and satisfied in equal measure by what he had done. Ashamed for having betrayed James Walker's trust. But satisfied with his beating of

Samuel. The man had it coming and plenty more besides. It felt good to silence him, if only for a few seconds. He looked down at his hands, the knuckles only slightly grazed.

Good, he thought as he flexed them.

However, now there were bigger things to think about, more to contend with. He had to get back to London as soon as possible. Drake needed to understand what the hell was going on with Strauss and Melwood, and if there was any truth to what Samuel had told him. He hoped to God it was just Samuel's mind games and nothing more. He couldn't deal with another betrayal from within the police ranks. Not again.

Drake's eyes darkened.

His fellow officers and he needed to have words, face to face.

53

Ellie still felt jittery from her discussion with Dave as she rode the lift down to the ground floor to meet Drake. For some reason, he insisted she come out and meet him at his car. It was all very secretive and she didn't know why.

The lift pinged, and some people whom she didn't know emptied out, leaving her alone for the final few floors. Ellie had felt guilty just leaving Dave like that in the coffee shop, but she couldn't stay. She just couldn't. She knew she'd panicked – something so completely unlike her. She didn't like what she was in danger of becoming.

But there had been progress too, once she'd had time to calm down and think. Dave's words were ringing true. She'd just been protecting her family. Ellie didn't know Fiona would die for sure. It was just something that happened. She couldn't – *shouldn't* – blame herself. But now her family were at risk again with this man who'd pushed Pinter to do what he did. Would she do it again if called upon?

That troubling thought was still with her as she reached the ground floor and headed out into the carpark. Drake's car was just ahead of her, the engine still running.

Good. It's bloody cold out here, so at least the car will be warm.

She put a hand up in greeting as she inched round the side of the car and got in the passenger seat.

Her boss looked tired, even for him. The bags under his eyes were dark, his face drawn; a man with a lot on his mind. He must have had an eventful day, whatever he'd been up to.

'Ellie, thanks for coming down.'

'No problem, Chief,' she said, giving him a glimmer of a smile. 'But what's all this secrecy about?'

'I'll get to that. But first, I thought it best to tell you in person that I had a chance to speak with Jack.'

She felt a flutter in her chest. 'And?'

'He's admitted to being the guy who did all that stuff with your guy, Pinter.'

Ellie felt her shoulders immediately relax. 'Drake, thank you, that's great news! You wouldn't believe how good it is to hear you say that.'

'Anytime.'

'Did you have to give him anything in exchange?'

'Just gave him the family news, you know. The two guys being dead.'

Ellie nodded. 'That was decent of you. In spite of all he's done, he deserved to know.'

'Indeed.'

The engine idled, occupying the silence for a few moments as the magnitude of what Drake had told her sunk in. She was free, she wouldn't have to worry about Bella or Len again. With the discussion earlier, and this news, could she finally give herself a break?

Ellie turned to her boss. 'Now, what's digging away at you? I can tell there's something you're holding back on?'

'I was told something by the Man. In person.'

'Samuel? What! You're kidding me?' she said, giving Drake an incredulous stare. 'Samuel feckin' Barrow has been talking to you? When? How?'

'He's been in touch, somehow got a mobile phone in prison. You know how it is these days. So, I went up to see him. That's where I've been.'

Sadly, she did know how it was these days. It was ridiculous what could be smuggled in now, how small the phones could be made, how clever the criminals continued to be and how corrupt some of the staff were.

'But I'm surprised you could even speak to the guy. What he did to you . . . I would have been raging at him in seconds.'

'Believe me, I did my best not to,' Drake said.

Ellie felt he was holding back something, but considering the subject matter, she didn't push. It wouldn't do to rake up his wife's murder right now.

'So, this is why you wanted to speak to me?'

'No, it's what he told me that's more important.' Drake rested an arm on the door. 'He knows about the Andrea murders, Ellie.'

'Jesus! How?'

Just when I thought this day was improving, she thought.

'He made out that he has an informant in the police force. I suppose it makes sense – I mean, he did have a lot of dodgy dealings before going inside anyway. What's to say he didn't have a few policemen on the take, too?'

She gave him a mischievous look. 'Hang on, you don't think it's me, do you?'

'No—no, of course not. Don't be ridiculous.'

She smirked. 'Good, just testing.'

'The Man mentioned both Strauss and Melwood, though.'

'You've got to be *kidding* me!'

Drake scratched at his cheek. 'Nope.'

She sighed loudly. 'I could kill Strauss, if he wasn't already at death's door. But I can't understand why he would do that. He doesn't strike me as the type. Melwood, though . . . no, I'm not sure he could either.'

'You and me both, Ellie.' He glanced at her to hammer home the point. 'But we need to give them the benefit of the doubt, hear their sides of the story. It could all be bullshit. Samuel trying to get us at odds with each other, or perhaps a trap of some kind.'

Ellie relented slightly in her visions of jabbing Strauss with a hot poker. Not so much Melwood. 'True.'

'Any word as to whether Strauss is out of his coma yet?'

'I'm sure you'd be told before me, Chief. But no, I've not heard anything. I don't think induced comas last all that long, like a few days, so maybe we'll get some answers soon.'

'Good. We need answers, that's for sure,' Drake said. 'And Melwood, is he in the office? I think we need to get his version of events. Strauss and he have worked together closely in the past, and for all we know, either of them – even both – could have been feeding the Man info for years.'

'No, our favourite DI left early, about an hour ago. Said he had something to do with his son. Seems to be all he does these days.'

Her boss shook his head. 'He's genuinely happy to be seeing him more. Don't be hard on him, Ellie. I'm sure you'd be the same. Put yourself in his shoes, if it's true, that is . . . perhaps it's a front, now that I think about it.' Drake looked distracted again, clearly thinking through more permutations of how Samuel's revelations could all pan out. 'Anyway, you ready?'

She frowned. 'What? Ready for what?'

'Melwood, of course. I need to be doing something – I want answers, and I need his explanation. I'm impatient, and there's only one way to find out quickly. From the horse's mouth.'

'Okay.' She gave her boss a reluctant nod. It was going to be a long day. 'You can do directions.'

'Nice try, Ellie. But that's on you.'

The journey was further than Ellie expected, down in a place she'd never heard of called Oxted. The light slowly left them as they drove south into Surrey toward the North Downs. She'd need to tell Len not to wait up for her. Her fears of it being a long day were all but confirmed now, the longer they drove and the more traffic they met.

Apparently Melwood had only moved to the area recently, giving up his London flat to be closer to his son and his ex-wife. Another reason she would prefer if Len didn't ever give up on her: the travel, living arrangements, split responsibilities. All things she would have hated, and that was before considering not being with her husband any more.

She was on the fence as to whether either of her colleagues could really be on the take. Strauss seemed like a guy that loved his job and was on the straight and narrow. So, to do that? Ellie couldn't imagine him taking the risk. And despite her misgivings of the man, Melwood didn't seem quite right either.

Ellie glanced at Drake. 'Looks like he's not far out from the train station. We should be passing that soon.'

'Okay, good,' he replied, his face lit up by some passing headlights.

'Do you really think Melwood or Strauss could do something like this?'

'I don't know any more, Ellie. After the last incident with Gemma, it does make me wonder about a lot of people.'

'Not really a reason, though, is it?'

His lips formed a thin smile. 'No, suppose not. Can't tar everyone with the same brush.'

'Okay, just round the corner now. First detached house on the left,' she said, before adding, 'Len and I clearly don't get paid enough. All you guys with your fancy detached houses.'

'All right, Ellie. All in due time.'

Ellie spotted Melwood's car on the incline of the steep driveway. The house had a couple of exterior lights on and was a half-brick, half-wood cladded structure with a well-tended garden at the front. A small blue and green bike lay abandoned out on the grass alongside a football. The place wasn't huge by any stretch, but anything wider than a large car was a veritable palace when compared to hers. Though her house was homely enough, she supposed. She worried what Melwood's place looked like inside. If she was judging on his clothing and hair style choices, an old Victorian saloon, probably?

'The man better have some answers for us,' Drake said. He undid his seatbelt and opened the door to a blast of cold air.

'Mm-hmm. Be mindful of his son though, yeah? With us turning up out of the blue.'

Drake gave her a look. 'Of course, what do you take me for?'

'I won't answer that.'

Ellie followed Drake to the front door and waited while he rang the doorbell.

She stood listening intently at the door. She was getting impatient and wanted answers.

Drake must have sensed it as he rang the doorbell again.

A few more moments passed before he conceded. 'Well, can't

stand here forever. Let's check out the back. He must be cooking in the kitchen or something.'

'Okay,' Ellie agreed. She didn't need telling twice.

Her boss kindly let her go ahead onto the grass, and they walked around the garden, following a low hedgerow. Turning a corner, another outside light was on, a spider spinning a web in its glow between it and the nearby window.

Ellie peered in, spotting her colleague immediately, the brightly-lit room highlighting the outline of the man.

She gasped.

Melwood stared back at her. The Inspector's throat was slit, mouth gaping and ruinous, his blood still dripping from the table to the floor.

54

'Drake!' Ellie hissed at him, the glow of the light casting shadows across her face.

He stopped in his tracks. 'What? What is it?'

She beckoned him over silently and moved out of the way while he stepped over and looked in the window to see what all the fuss was about.

'Oh my G—Jesus Christ! Andrew, no . . .'

Drake's heart sank upon seeing the ravaged body of his colleague in the dining room. He couldn't believe it. He'd only spoken to him earlier that day about Jonah Barrow's death. They may not have seen eye to eye on some things, but he didn't deserve to be butchered like that. No one did. Curiously though, Andrea had left Melwood's little boy alive. He must only be around five years old. The boy was sitting off to the side in his booster seat, tied up, blindfolded and crying for his father. The only thing Drake could be thankful for was that the boy might still be too young to remember the horrors he would have been party to in future years.

Drake tore his eyes away, realising something vitally important. 'Ellie, what about Andrea? She could still be here, couldn't she? Melwood can't have been home more than what . . . an hour? His boy could be bait if she heard us arrive.'

He realised he didn't even know the boy's name. Melwood may have told them, but he now felt guilty as hell for not being able to recall if he even had or not.

Ellie's eyes bulged in realisation. 'Shit, what're we going to do?'

'Firstly, we're damn well sticking together,' he whispered. 'Secondly, I'd say we take the back door. If she's here, we've already alerted her by ringing the doorbell.'

She nodded. 'You're right. Let's go.'

Drake took the lead and they stole further around the back of the house, his stomach roiling at the image he'd just seen and the adrenaline of what they were about to do. The area was so quiet besides the muted cries of the boy that it was making him more hesitant than normal, more aware of every single sound they made.

'You ready?' He grabbed the white UPVC door handle and tested it carefully. It was unlocked. Perhaps Andrea was already gone, the door her exit point?

'As I'll ever be,' Ellie breathed.

Drake gently pushed the handle down and opened the door. The little boy's shrill cries and wails instantly louder. They crept into the back of the dining room. The macabre scene was chilling, like they'd stepped into the footage of an old Family Man scene, but this was real. Very real. The coppery smell of blood hung thick in the air.

He slowly continued toward the dining table and Melwood's mutilated body, grimacing at the sight, and peered carefully into the kitchen which led straight from where they were situated.

There was no one there.

The boy's cries quietened down; he must have heard their movements. Perhaps he sensed they were on his side.

'Okay,' he said, looking back at Ellie. 'I think we just need to clear the lounge and then the hallway before working our way upstairs.'

She gave him a weak smile. 'Got it. You sure you didn't work in Response at all?'

Ellie led through the other door into the brightly-lit lounge. Again, there was nobody there. Just a television which had been muted, and some of the boys' toys, wooden blocks and Marvel figures, together with a white fabric sofa and two matching armchairs. Now that they'd left him alone, the boy's cries started again.

'I'm getting the impression she's already gone, Drake,' she said, looking back at him. 'I don't *feel* anyone here.'

'Mmm,' he grunted, noncommittal. He waved her on towards what he presumed would be the hallway and stairs.

His guess proven correct, he put a hand on her shoulder and indicated he would lead next. The boy's crying continued on in the background. Drake felt guilty leaving him there, but if they'd calmed him further, it could alert Andrea that they were inside the house now.

Drake peered up the stairs, seeing a dark landing. No lights appeared to be on at all. Which could either mean she was up there and hiding, or, of course, that there was no one there. He questioned himself, not knowing which option he preferred right now, seeing as he was in the thick of it with a serial killer.

He crept up the stairs into the darkness, Ellie holding by the banister at the foot of the stairs while he got a few steps ahead. Arriving at a mini-landing and turn in the stairs, he made out three closed rooms directly in front and to his right. There could be more out of sight to his left, but they were obscured by the stairwell wall. The room farthest to his right did appear to actually have a dim light on, the closed door glowing out of the murk.

Shit.

Drake gestured to Ellie, indicating there might be someone in there, and she climbed a few more stairs in support.

He made his final ascent, one stair creaking slightly before he arrived at the top of the stairs. He could see one other room to his left, also closed and dark, and he decided to leave the lit one until last. Drake figured he'd light each room up before attempting that last one. He didn't want to fall for the possibility that she was trying to trick him, lying in wait in one of the seemingly unoccupied ones instead. He'd been ambushed too many times already these past few months, recalling Alex Ludner's house in the Spencer case and the nasty bump on the back of his head that he'd received for his troubles.

He started with the room directly in front of him. Taking a sharp breath, he flicked the light switch on momentarily to reveal a room which was completely empty of any furniture, barring some suitcases and boxes. One column was high enough to give him pause for just a moment.

'Well, Drake?' Ellie whispered from the mini-landing.

Drake shook his head enough for her to see.

He followed the same procedure for a sparse bedroom, presumably Melwood's, and finally a bathroom on the far-left side of the landing. Each flick of the room's switches sparked some momentary tension, followed by an immediate sigh of relief. He wasn't sure how much more tension he could take.

That left only one more room to go. Could she really still be in the house?

'Ready?' he asked, his palms feeling clammy at what may lay ahead.

'Yes, Chief. If you are . . .' Ellie whispered back.

Drake nodded slightly. He leant up against the side of the door and did an internal countdown before shoving it open. The door immediately hit against something or someone, and he put an arm out to stop it closing on him again.

But there was no sudden movement, no crazed woman jumping out to attack him. Giving it a moment or two, he stepped inside cautiously and was only greeted by a cool draught. The room was painted dark-blue with a large rocket soaring toward a moon. A single child-size bed sat in the corner with a scattering of comics and a colouring book on the floor, alongside a large open window, the curtain undulating in time with the night's breeze.

Drake breathed a conflicted sigh of relief, and moved further into the room. The door had banged into an open cardboard packing box containing various items and a framed photo on top. Melwood and his son beamed back at him from the image, beside his ex-wife.

I'm sorry, Andrew, Drake thought with a disconsolate shake of the head before waving for Ellie to enter.

Drake pushed the curtain to the side and peered out the window, pursing his lips at the sight of the metal drain pipe and trellis that wound its way down from the window.

Andrea was long gone.

55

Drake had been mulling over why Melwood was killed and why Andrea had chosen to spare the man's son for the entirety of the drive home, and ever since he'd dropped off a worn-out Ellie, hours after the grisly discovery.

Neither he nor Ellie had understood what she'd done. And although Drake was surprised by very little any more, it still hadn't made any sense. Melwood didn't fit in with any logical pattern; all of the Spencer abusers were dead, that had been confirmed by both Gemma and Jack, so why target Melwood? What had he done, or what had he known that would put him in the firing line like that? Was it just guilty by association with Drake? Did it mean Samuel had been in contact with Andrea somehow? That didn't seem to be the case, judging by how he'd spoken of her, though. And he'd be actively *not* mentioning her at all to protect her, if that were true. Andrea, his only child now – the strongest child, as Samuel saw it – was important to him, so she'd warrant his protection.

The local SOCO team had arrived soon after Ellie had called it in. The place had been lit up by police and other official vehicles while the scene was cordoned off and the team began their work. It had seemed so surreal. Drake kept expecting Melwood to turn up at any moment and make some inane comment or other that would press his buttons, but that wouldn't happen again. Andrea had seen to that.

Ellie had kept Melwood's son occupied in Drake's car, having managed to calm him down once they'd deemed the house to be safe. She had been particularly affected by the boy, as she'd been the one to remove him from his seat at the table, covering him in a blanket and whisking him away from the horror of his father's end. Drake had to admit the boy's cries were still playing on his mind whenever he thought back to what they'd witnessed.

Miller had arrived just before SOCO, her face registering shock as she exited her car. Her presence was intended more to shore up and assuage any concerns and show respect. The death of an Inspector was not a common occurrence.

Drake had left the doorstep and met her halfway on the pavement.

'Drake, what the *hell* happened?'

'You tell me, Laura. We just came here to follow up on leads with him and found him like this.'

Drake chose not to mention anything about Samuel or the potential leaks. He didn't need her on his case anymore than she already was. He was still on very thin ice with Strauss' stabbing and the lack of progress.

'But why did Andrea kill him, of all people?'

'We honestly don't know. I'm at a loss.'

'CID are going to be coming down on us like a ton of bricks,' she'd said, looking strangely panicked. This was a woman who didn't *do* panic, and it had thrown Drake seeing her like that. He was still curious about it, hours later.

'They won't, Laura. There's nothing we could have done from our side. Obviously, no one saw it coming.'

'I hope you're right. For both our sakes.'

Drake had changed the subject. 'We need to inform the boy's mother. He shouldn't be here.'

'Already on it.'

He'd spoken to her little after that, as she'd been waylaid by press and other duties.

Melwood himself had been brutalised to the same exacting standard as the original Family Man killings, and Andrea's subsequent take on her own husband. However, this time there had been no symbol carved on the wall or body, and no time for the hands to be removed. Drake imagined she would have wanted to do that as she'd been in a private place, for the first time since her husband's death, which led him to believe they *had* interrupted her. But why hadn't she stayed anyway? Surely in her frenzied state of mind, she would have loved to have taken them both on. Was the accomplice with her? Did he or she ensure Andrea left without a fight?

Naturally, no one had seen or heard anything nearby, much to Drake's chagrin. It was such a common theme these days. The public was so insular. He despaired at the state of society in general and neighbours in particular. No doorbell cams were present on nearby properties, and what few security cameras there had been were not pointed at the road, nor in the direction of Melwood's house. The team would take what footage they could get anyway, just in case.

Drake's thoughts became increasingly frustrated and disarrayed as he finally arrived home, finding both girls fast asleep in bed. He was envious of them. He'd been exhausted since the initial drive back from Yorkshire, let alone after deciding to make the fateful decision to tap up Melwood for his input.

Turning the light on in his bedroom, he'd undressed and crashed in a matter of seconds.

* * *

Drake woke to the sound of his mobile vibrating on his bedside table in the retreating darkness of dawn.

In a bleary-eyed panic, he snatched at the phone, blinking a few times as he tried to focus on who it was. The bright light seared his eyeballs in the darkness.

Unknown caller . . . when will this end?

He didn't know how many more calls like this he could take. And the more he received, the worse things were getting.

He inhaled sharply, his heart pounding in his ears, and answered. 'DCI Drake.'

'Ah, John,' a gravel-edged voice smirked. 'I'm so, *so* sorry to wake you at such an hour.'

'What the hell do you want, Samuel?'

Samuel stayed silent for a moment. 'Let's just say, I didn't take too . . . *kindly* to your treatment of me yesterday.'

'You deserved every goddamn second of it, you bastard,' Drake spat.

'I know *you* think that. But do you think *Eva* deserves to be punished as a result of your actions, hmm? Maybe I'll make her relive the worst moments of her life, eh? How about that?'

Drake looked around the room frantically, his free hand balling the duvet cover as his chest constricted at the mention of her name. 'What do you mean? What's Eva got to do with this?'

'You know, before today my answer would have been "nothing". That is . . . until yesterday.'

'You're in prison.' Drake squeezed his hand tighter, struggling to contain himself. 'You can't do shit. Don't give me that.'

'We'll see about that,' Samuel said, and hung up.

Eva!

Drake leapt out of bed and scrambled for his daughter's room. He had to be sure she was safe.

Calming himself down as best he could, he opened her door carefully and peered in. Sure enough, there she was in bed, fast asleep. It appeared Samuel's empty threats were just that.

Drake relaxed slightly, his relief palpable. He turned toward Cari's room to check on her. Just in time to hear a sharp intake of breath, and feel the sudden impact of a savage blow to his head.

He slammed to the floor in a heap, out cold.

56

Stifling a yawn, Ellie entered their headquarters at what felt like an ungodly time. Why had she decided to disregard Drake's orders to come in later, and instead turn up *early?* Her eyes burned and she yawned heavily again, her body clearly in agreement that it was a bad idea and she should head home, back to bed. It was barely light outside as it was.

But she hadn't been able to sleep, thinking of Melwood's boy (who they'd since been told was named Charlie) and his wails as they'd entered his father's house. The sight of him sitting there, tied up, alone and vulnerable, amidst all that carnage was beyond heartbreaking. She had to keep pushing the idea of Bella in the same position from her head.

So, she'd decided to push on with as little let up as possible, burying her thoughts and feelings – a completely healthy approach, if ever there was one. But a colleague had *died*. She needed to stop Andrea; and she needed to do it soon, no matter what.

Ellie decided to continue her successful approach of iterative re-review from the Spencer case, and check all the relevant camera footage pertaining to Pearce Fleming, as well as the footage of Andrea, Cari and Strauss. She'd not had the chance to study the footage yet in any great detail of her own volition, only flashes on a screen the previous day, but in her defence, she'd been busy – successfully - nailing the crossover remnants of the Spencer case.

Before starting, Ellie grabbed a cup of coffee, irritated that the tea bags *still* hadn't been replenished, and hotfooted it over to the investigation room. While it *was* early, she did enjoy the office not being quite so active, and the light now shining in through the windows was warming her soul. She looked out over the undulating Thames below; in her opinion, the view the battered building afforded them was worth every penny.

Ellie opened the door to the investigation room and was immediately greeted by Maria Neven sat at a laptop, which the young woman shut immediately, a strangely guilty look on her face.

'Oh!' Neven said, looking up at Ellie's entrance.

'Neven,' she responded. Quietly disappointed that she didn't have the space to herself after all. 'Wasn't expecting anyone to be in just yet. What are you doing here?'

Ellie took a seat at the desk she'd commandeered a few days back, and set about starting up her laptop.

Neven smiled. 'Like you, I guess. Just trying to get ahead of the day, you know?'

'Nice to see someone's keen.'

'Something like that,' she said, and leant over toward Ellie. 'Between you and me, I'm just really trying to push for DS this year.'

Ellie gave her a tired smile. 'Oh, really? Good on you. Need a few more women about the place. A lot of testosterone here.'

'Speaking of which, I'm sorry about DI Melwood,' the

younger woman said, eyeing Ellie curiously. 'I heard it was you that found him?'

Mm-hmm.' Ellie frowned slightly. 'Yeah, not the best of things to find.'

'What was it like?' the DC blurted.

'Huh?'

'Sorry – too much, too soon?'

'No. More like *never*, Maria,' Ellie shot back. 'He was a colleague. I'm not going to glorify any of it. You'll see soon enough when all the photos, etc. are released later.'

'Sorry,' Neven said, not sounding particularly sorry at all. 'I didn't work with him much, so I guess it's not affected me the same way.'

Ellie didn't really know what to say to the woman. A man had died, a police officer. He may not have been her cup of tea personally, but Melwood was still a colleague, and he'd worked damn hard on the cases they'd worked together.

She stopped herself from lashing out any further at the attempt at gossip. It wouldn't help anyone.

'Neven, could you send over all the footage you have from the Fleming murder and the Strauss phone attack too, please?'

Neven eyed her suspiciously. 'Why do you want those now? Surely you've already seen them?'

'Please, Maria.' Ellie bit her tongue. 'Just do it, if you'd be so kind.'

'Okay.'

Ellie received the footage a while later and decided to move desks, so she was in a corner away from Neven and the rest of the team, who were starting to turn up.

Drake was nowhere to be seen. She couldn't blame him. He did look shattered when she left him to continue his journey home.

She settled in and put on a set of headphones so as not to disturb anyone – in more ways than one. Ellie decided to start with the Strauss footage and work her way back from that. She'd found over the years that sometimes a different order could aid in spotting something new.

As expected, the Miray footage made for highly disturbing viewing. Ellie couldn't believe the way she had treated Cari on the call, the things she said she would do to her own daughter. And it *was* her own daughter, not granddaughter, despite her other personality's claims. As a mother, it absolutely appalled her.

Cari was so brave in how she responded to her, and even had her mother beat emotionally, Ellie thought.

But then came Strauss' fateful encounter. The stabbing, the noises of their fight. It was truly horrifying seeing Andrea do what she did to him. However, something caught her attention; one particular sentence Strauss had blurted out just before his attack. She paused and went back a few seconds to before he was stabbed:

"Oh God! There's someone—"

There, she thought. *What was that?*

She played it again, squinting as she concentrated on the words amidst the noise. *"Oh God! There's someone—"*

What did he mean when he said 'someone'?

Surely if it was Andrea, he would have said 'she' or 'Andrea'?

'Someone' implied there was *someone else there.* Ellie replayed it in slow motion, looking more closely at the footage. Unless there was some sort of trick of the light, there were two shadows coming in just before the table. She was sure of it.

Was it the accomplice from the Fleming scene? It had to be, surely?

It would explain how they had got everything set up. Ellie didn't want to entirely discount the notion that Andrea could have done that herself, but she was hardly a well woman. She may have set alarms off with anyone she had to deal with in the outside world.

So I don't think this has been picked up on yet, Ellie thought, adding a mental tick in her mind. Though it was only confirming what they'd seen on the other footage, she supposed.

Before starting the remaining footage, Ellie grabbed another coffee and snagged a free protein bar from a random basket that had appeared in the kitchenette – she never could resist a freebie.

Returning to the now quieter room, a few people down (including Neven), Ellie settled in to watch the Fleming tapes. Drake was still nowhere to be seen, which she found slightly strange considering what had happened yesterday. Ellie had assumed he would just ignore his own advice too and be in by now.

She started the next video, first seeing the door-cam events, which had now been annotated with box and arrow graphics as and when Andrea and the mystery person appeared.

Ellie replayed the section a few times, but couldn't make anything out that wasn't already in the team's domain. From what she could discern, there was nothing more to be gleaned from that set of videos. Ellie was frustrated to find the same result from the footage of the underpass taken from across the river. The shapes were largely unidentifiable, and unless you knew what was going on, it was even harder to derive anything from it.

She huffed in annoyance. Her earlier positive work wasn't bringing any further joy.

Ellie decided she would give the hospital a call, see what the status was on Strauss. With Melwood no longer around to check in on him, she felt obligated to keep in the loop about him. For Melwood, if not Strauss.

As she was dialling the number, another call came through.

It was reception.

'DS Wilkinson?'

'Hello,' the receptionist responded. 'There's a man here to see you.'

'Oh? Who?'

'He seems reluctant to give his name. Seems a bit shabby, might possibly be . . . "on something", the hard stuff, you know?'

Pinter. What did he want?

57

Drake's eyes snapped open as he came to. Desperately trying to get his bearings, he realised he was in the hallway of his flat, half-blocking Eva's door. A smattering of blood mixed with saliva had pooled on the floor. Suddenly, the realisation of why he was there rushed back.

Eva!

He pulled himself to his feet, before wobbling and collapsing in a heap. His balance and legs were failing him, and his head felt like it was going to explode at any moment, a searing white pain pulsing at his crown.

'Eva!' he shouted desperately, pushing himself up to his knees. '*Eva.*'

The pain was making it hard for him to speak, but there was no response, and the silence chilled his heart.

Drake gasped out a few breaths and pushed himself up against the wall of the hallway. He stayed there, knowing he had to take it steady and regain his balance moment by moment. A fine layer of sweat began forming on his brow and back.

Feeling a little more stable, he manoeuvred himself clumsily so that he could look into his daughter's room, the door still ajar from before. To his surprise, somehow Eva was still there, facing the wall with her back to him. She was safe.

Or was she? Something seemed wrong about her.

'Eva . . . ?' Drake eschewed any sense of caution and rushed to her side. He rolled her round to face him.

He *was* imagining things. She was unscathed. 'Eva . . . ? Eva, you're okay?'

She must have been knocked out on her sleeping meds and slept straight through all the commotion. The tears started running down his face. Tears of relief. She was fine; everything was going to be fine.

He cradled her head in his arms as he continued to gasp for air.

'Dad, what're you doing?' she said, sleepily into his chest, struggling beneath his hug.

'Dad, get off!'

His daughter looked up at him, looking as groggy as he felt. 'Oh my God . . . Dad, you're–you're bleeding!'

He tentatively put a hand to the back of his head, and pulled it away, revealing his hand covered in fresh blood. 'It's nothing, Eva. I'll be fine.'

'You don't *look* fine. It's all over your face too.'

'It's no—thing, it's just a . . .'

'Dad!'

The room began to spin as Drake became breathless. His eyes rolled to the back of his head and he passed out into darkness once more.

'Dad!'

Minutes, or moments later, he regained consciousness, his head still as woozy as before he'd blacked out.

Eva's panic had since reached fever pitch. 'Dad, please, you've got to stay with me.'

'I'm sorry, Eva,' he said, breathing heavily. 'Just . . . give me a moment . . . Can you get me some water, please? I'm so thirsty.'

His daughter vanished from view, and returned with a glass of water. She helped him up so he was sitting on the floor against the frame of her bed. His back was now soaked with sweat.

'Are you . . . are you, okay, love?' he asked, sipping from the glass. The water felt so good as it went down.

'Dad, I'm fine. Fuck! You're the one bleeding from your damn head! I don't get it, I've only been asleep a few hours and I wake up to this . . . Did you fall over or something in the kitchen?'

He winced at the volume of her voice. 'Just keep it down a little, please. Need a minute to catch my breath. It'll pass soon, I'm sure.'

'What the hell happened?'

'I don't know. One minute I was up, and the next I'd been knocked out cold.'

'But how? Why? There's no one here but you, me and Cari.'

It was then Drake realised in his semi-conscious state what was missing. Something was very, *very* wrong. The sound of Samuel's voice resonated in his head. The phone call. The threats against Eva.

'Eva, where's Cari?'

58

Ellie hopped in the lift to reception. It had completely slipped her mind that she had been pushing for Pinter to come in since speaking with Gemma about the figurine. At the time, she had wrongly – though understandably – believed there was still someone out there who had threatened her family.

What could he want now? I don't have time for his shit, she thought. *Was he just off his face, and wanted to tell her about something completely unrelated?*

The floors counted down interminably. She continued to let her mind wander until the lift came to a rattling halt and opened out, facing the double doors to reception. Ellie realised she probably should have given him an address of the local station rather than their headquarters. But it was done now.

The receptionist spotted her and pointed to a window through which she could see Pinter smoking outside.

Ellie raised a hand in thanks and exited for the car park smoking area.

Pinter was looking more dishevelled and tired than the last time they'd interacted, which was quite the feat considering she'd previously chased him across Harrow. She was glad there would be no running involved this time.

The man's hands were dirty, as though he'd been rummaging through plant pots, and his ill-fitting dark blue jeans had mud stains on the knees. Pinter's complexion had a sallow quality that hadn't been nearly as prominent the last time they'd spoken. He looked around forty years of age, not in his mid-twenties.

'Pinter?' she offered.

'A'ight.' The man took a long drag on his cigarette. 'Didn't think you'd come see me after I spoke to the receptionist. This ain't a police station, is it?'

'Well observed. I don't police the usual stuff you're involved in.'

'Serial killers and shit, innit?'

'Something like that,' she replied, squinting. The sun had come out from behind some clouds and while it was warming, it was also blinding her. 'Come with me.'

Pinter followed her over to a low brick wall that used to contain a flower bed, but was now used for nothing more than an ashtray for the few remaining smokers who hadn't switched over to vaping. Ellie sat down, encouraging him to do the same, pleased that his chain smoking was downwind of her position.

'So what was it you wanted to talk to me about?' she asked, feeling more and more irritated by his presence.

Pinter looked around, as though he was worried about something. 'I dunno if I should say without my solicitor present.'

'I'm not interested in any of your shit you've got going on, Pinter, so relax, all right?' She gave him a look. 'Unless, that is, you've killed someone.'

Pinter looked taken aback. As taken aback as a drug dealer and addict can look, she supposed. 'What you take me for? I don't go round killing people, jeez.'

'It was a joke.'

'Oh,' he said, looking dumbfounded. 'Had me there. Not quite with it today, innit.'

Ellie sat and stared at him. She felt Miller would be proud by the effect it had, the man fidgeting uncomfortably. 'So . . . ?'

He looked around shiftily, pulling on his cigarette again. 'I didn't want to say before, but that guy you talked to me about . . .'

'Yes?'

'It wasn't just the Action Man thing, you know?'

Huh?

Ellie took notice. 'Okay . . . Go on. What else was it?'

Again, he looked around nervously. 'It's been like, drugs too and stuff.'

'Drugs?'

'Yeah,' he nodded, tugging at the cuff of his black hoodie. 'It's why I didn't want to say anything the other time, innit. Was worried, regardless of what you said. But then the more I thought about it later, and what you said about crazy serial killers, more I realised you genuinely wouldn't give a shit about it. So here I am.'

'Why not come sooner, for God's sake? Details matter, Steven.'

Pinter shrugged. 'Man's got a habit . . . ya know.'

Ellie shook her head in disgust, noticing his teeth were browning.

What kind of weak arse apology was that?

If she'd still been worried about the man who thankfully had turned out to be Jack Spencer, she would have been absolutely livid with Pinter right now. Knowing she would've been panicking unnecessarily for days, Ellie wanted to throttle him. Maybe doing so would get him to get his act together.

'What kind of drugs was he after?'

'Exotic shit, like Fentanyl and Rohypnol, date rape drug stuff. Told him it takes time to get that. Not something I've really had much of before myself. Ain't going to walk round with that on me too, no way. So, we sorted a time for, like, a while later.'

Ellie supposed that was what Jack and Fiona had used to subdue their victims, though she couldn't recall that coming up in the toxicology reports. She'd need to check again, refresh her memory.

'When was this arranged for? The next meet up, I mean?'

'I told him a couple of days. He agreed to it.'

Ellie did the mental math. The duct tape killings and the appearance of the figure had happened within a day or so of each other, and the other killings and eventual capture took place a week or so thereafter. Looking back, she realised how quickly it had all escalated. But it certainly didn't seem like it at the time. It had felt torturous to her and her family.

'Okay. So, they turned up and got what they came for?'

'Yeah, same guy turned up and paid me, and I gave him his stuff. Arranged a few more times, too. Same deal.'

Ellie put her hand down on the brick wall absently, then noticing she'd narrowly avoided a fresh bird shit. She wrinkled her nose. 'Okay . . . Then you must've been pissed when they stopped turning up, right?'

'Naw. That's why I'm here too, innit?'

She sat bolt upright. 'What do you mean?'

'The guy, he turned up the other day, few days before you were chasing me. I think I remember you said he was in prison, right? Realised later and thought it was weird.'

Ellie frowned. 'No, you've got it wrong. The guy's in prison.'

'Then I must have started hallucinating and sprouting money from my arse or something.' Pinter laughed.

'Are you *sure* it was the same guy? I need you to be precise now, okay?'

'Yeah, as I said. Same amount of money, and same order. I'm not sure how many ways I can say the same thing,' he said, exasperated. 'Eh, this why you ain't caught him, being this slow and all?'

Ellie wanted to punch the guy for taking the piss. She needed a moment to think. To understand what he was telling her. It couldn't be possible. Jack was in prison. Fiona was dead. Gemma in a god damn hospital bed.

Who was lying? The banged up brutal murderer who had nothing to lose, or the sad junkie who'd had no reason to come back and tell her what he knew.

This couldn't be happening.

'*Fuck!*' she shouted, as Pinter looked on, amused.

59

Though his skull was still throbbing something rotten, Drake's mind was finally starting to focus again since they'd confirmed to their horror that Cari had been taken by his mystery assailant. Cari's room was deceptively untouched, only her bed showing any sign of disarray, as though she'd literally just got out of bed and left. But that can't have been the case; Drake couldn't imagine her giving herself up without a struggle, not any more. Not unless she'd been drugged, or subdued somehow before being taken away, presumably via the stairs at the back of the flats.

Eva paced the lounge frantically while Drake absently tended to the back of his head with a towel and some ice. His mind wandered, trying to work out how the kidnapper had got her out of the building without causing a scene.

'I can't believe she's been kidnapped, Dad! You said this place was safe!'

His daughter's concern for him had long since ebbed away, replaced by an anger he had not seen for a long time. Her worry for her best friend had taken over completely, and she was proving inconsolable. Drake couldn't blame her. He knew he had failed them both.

In his exhausted state, he stupidly hadn't realised that either Strauss or Melwood must have told Samuel where they were living now. That was the only explanation for it. It might also explain how Melwood had miraculously appeared out of nowhere a few days earlier. But who in the hell had beaten him to the ground and taken Cari? Strauss certainly couldn't. The man was still in a coma.

The thought that Samuel was working with Andrea played in his mind again, but given how Samuel had spoken about her, it didn't ring true. It was as though he *wished* he was talking to her, not that he had been doing it in secret. Drake racked his brain further; he couldn't think of anyone recently linked with Samuel who was alive and not in a prison cell themselves.

'What're we going to do?' Eva cried, shaking him from his thoughts.

'I . . . Don't— Just let me think for a minute, okay? I'm not on top form right now. And have you seen my phone? I need to get people on to finding her ASAP.'

She scoffed at him. 'I should have known, the minute she did that phone call with her Mum.'

'We don't know it's Andrea, love. We need to remain calm. Where's my damn phone . . .'

'Remain calm!'

'Yes. We'll only resolve this if we try and figure things out calmly. Please. Trust me,' Drake winced as soon as the words were out of his mouth, but thankfully she didn't bite.

Instead, she sank down onto the sofa in a fit of tears.

'Eva, please, I—'

Drake's phone rang suddenly, but it wasn't nearby.

It must have fallen out when I was knocked unconscious, he realised.

'Quickly! Get it, Dad. It might be whoever took her,' she pleaded with red-rimmed eyes.

'Okay, okay,' Drake moved to the hallway, finding his phone on the floor of Eva's bedroom.

It displayed *Unknown Caller* yet again. It had to be Samuel or the kidnapper, it had to be.

He answered. 'Where is she!'

Samuel cackled on the other end of the phone. 'What's the matter, Drake? Missing someone?'

'Bring her back, right now.'

'Heard you took a bit of a beating.' Samuel laughed again. 'Eye for an eye, I guess. How's the head?'

'Obviously fine. I'm still talking to you, aren't I? You bastard.' His head pounded in response as he sat down on the floor against Eva's bed.

'Want to know where your daughter is, I bet.'

My daughter? Does he not realise Cari's been kidnapped, not Eva?

'Where is she?'

Drake kept quiet, worried if he said anything or brought Samuel's accomplices mistake to his attention it could get Cari hurt, or worse, killed.

'Where do you think?'

'I don't have time for games, Samuel.'

Samuel roared, 'You've got as much time as I say you have, you *cunt.*'

Drake racked his brain for anything that would stand out. Anything that would mean anything to both of them, a place that Samuel would enjoy staging something to torment him.

Oh, God. It's not . . . is it?

Reluctantly he offered up a muted answer. 'It's my house in Barndon, isn't it?'

'See, Drake! You still have hopes of being a good police officer yet, even after all these years!' Samuel cackled, dark and full of venom. 'You're correct, how would you ever have guessed that? You're a fucking genius, you know that?'

Drake chose not to answer. His head was spinning again, not able to fully comprehend what was happening.

Samuel carried on, enjoying the sound of his own voice. 'Don't worry, Drake. She's nice and cosy. I hear it's almost like I never left there.'

'What do I need to do to get her back?'

'Well, simple really . . .'

Drake pinched his brow. 'Yes?'

'You just have to turn up. And then, well . . . let's just see what happens, eh, *DCI* Drake. Oh, and if you alert the police, or your bitch of a partner turns up with you, then you may as well not bother sticking around. She'll be dead.'

Samuel hung up.

Drake drove like a madman, doing his best not to pass out or kill anyone as he wove through the London traffic towards his former home. He slammed the horn as a bus cut in ahead of him, completely screwing his view of what was ahead.

If you don't slow down, you're going to crash and kill yourself. Then what good are you to either of them?

But he had to push on, he had to get to Cari back.

It was all his fault, provoking Samuel like that. Goading him, and beating him the way he did. Thinking that Samuel couldn't do anything while in prison. He just had to push him that step too far. As Samuel had so proudly declared, he was in control of everything, despite him being inside.

Drake snaked through more traffic, diving into the outside lane and pressing on, cars honking their own horns at his erratic driving as he pushed on to the M4. The motorway stretched out in front of him like a concrete snake, one that was thankfully clear of too much traffic.

He hadn't given a thought to what he would do when he got there. How he would confront the kidnapper and retrieve Cari unharmed. He wasn't known for his excellent negotiation skills in these kinds of circumstances, and certainly not when half his brain felt like it had been forcibly removed from his skull.

Drake resisted the temptation to call in backup, recalling the man's threats, but his free hand hovered over the dial button on his mobile as he drove.

How would Samuel know?

'No, can't do it. If I need to sacrifice myself, so be it,' he muttered.

Drake went back and forth between going it alone and breaking Samuel's rules at least five times more before he began winding through the lanes leading to Barndon; so familiar, yet so alien to him now. The skeletal hedgerows were smattered with the first signs of spring, the new leaves blooming. Normally, he'd find it charming. Now, he just wanted to get 'home' and stop whatever was happening in the cursed place. Regardless, Drake's chest still tightened at the thought, knowing he'd soon be back there, confronting the place he'd fled from like a coward only a few months earlier, unable to confront his demons. Incapable of staying a minute longer in the room where his wife had been so brutally murdered.

He slowed to a crawl as he entered the lane leading to the house, before deciding to stop and make the rest of the way by foot. Perhaps he could get the jump on the kidnapper, or spot a car; anything that might give him some inkling as to who had taken Cari.

Drake gripped the steering wheel for a moment to gather himself, the sounds of the cooling engine ticking in the background. He realised he might not get out of this encounter in one piece at all.

You can do it. You know you can. You've just got to focus.

Steeling himself, he got out the car and stepped up onto the grass verge before jumping a picket fence into the back of his nearest neighbour's garden, which was essentially a field. The distance between him and his neighbours had proved both a blessing and a curse. Now it was very much the latter.

Drake couldn't see a car from where he was. He needed to get a better view. He continued on, keeping low as he made his way towards his house. The side he was aiming for had only windows obscured by privacy glass on the top-floor bathroom.

As he trudged through the dewy morning grass, his balance still a little off, he suddenly paused and crouched as he spotted an unfamiliar car. It *had* to be the kidnapper's. Why would anyone else have parked outside his house?

A battered silver Vauxhall Astra, at least ten years old, judging by the number plate, was parked up by the gate. He struggled to recall seeing one in and around Barndon, or around Samuels' farm business.

I'm coming for you, Cari. Don't worry.

Drake quickened his pace and stepped over the pathetic attempt for a picket fence that he'd put up years earlier, not needing anything higher to keep that side of the house private. He noted, rather irrationally, that it needed fixing.

Soon, he'd planted himself against the wall at the side of his house. He couldn't hear Cari crying, nor any words being uttered to silence her from his position. Perhaps they weren't in the kitchen, after all? Maybe they were in another room, or even upstairs?

That wouldn't be very dramatic though, would it? Certainly not to Samuel's tastes.

Drake rounded the corner, the wall giving way to the kitchen's window panes and shattered door, still contained by a metal sheet. But now the door stood open.

The kidnapper had to have forced their way in and not closed it. He couldn't see any lights, but then there had always been enough natural light in that room for it not to need anything more before night-time.

Crouching, Drake crept his way along the wall towards the open doorway. Just as he drew closer, the door was slammed closed.

Drake froze. Had he been spotted?

He thought he could hear Cari crying as he waited patiently in a form of silent standoff, his heart pounding in his chest. The minutes ticked by. Realising he mustn't have been spotted, he crept over to the second window, the one which gave the best view of the dining table area.

Drake carefully raised himself up and quickly peered above the window sill.

His glance gave him a shocking glimpse of a brute of a man, covered head to toe in black, his back to Drake. Cari was just beyond the man, facing him, but her head had been covered by a cloth bag or pillow case.

There was only one way into the kitchen, other than through the house, and that was the smashed door Ellie had used. If he did that, he would be exposed. But what other choice did he have?

Drake came to a decision.

He'd have to play the Man's game.

60

The knife spilled from my hands as I came to, clattering noisily into the sink. Followed by a door slamming shut behind me.

Blood. It was all over me. Dried. Caked. Cracking. Smeared everywhere.

I scrambled to turn on the tap. I was so sick of this happening to me again and again. I had to get it off me. I splashed my face, hoping to regain some sort of understanding; anything to bring back the clarity I had before I was captured again. The thoughts of the colourful rooms, the night sky.

The water dripped down my face, mixing with the remnants of blood, like I was crying crimson tears. A nightmare made flesh.

I stared into the bathroom mirror, damp hair stuck to my face. Focusing, *willing* myself free.

My mother was observing me at a distance.

I cast my eyes in her direction. 'This was you, wasn't it?'

It has never been me. It's always been you.

'You lie!'

How can it be me, Andrea?

'You . . . you *use* me.'

So, if I use you, then it IS you, my daughter.

'No-no-no, don't you say that. It's not me. It can't be me. It's you. Your influence. It's not me. It can't be me. It can't.'

My fingernails clawed at my cheeks. It wasn't me that did this. Whatever *it* was.

She had done it. She had done everything. My mother. She was hateful. Oh, so hateful.

I had to stop this, once and for all. Somehow. I had to find a way. I had to put an end to it.

Panicking, I sluiced the water over my arms, ridding myself of more of the blood.

The man's blood.

A knife on skin flashed in my mind.

I glanced up at the mirror. A man's savaged and bloody face, his throat spilling blood, stared back.

I fell to the ground, scurrying back against the door as the screams filled my mind.

A man's scream.

A child's scream.

My scream.

61

Drake closed his eyes for a split second before taking the plunge and opening the door as calmly as he could.

The kidnapper reacted immediately, snatching a large knife off the table and pointing it at Drake while moving to Cari's side. The man's pale blue eyes were wide within the slit of his mouthless balaclava.

'Don't come any closer.'

While he'd been outside, Drake had planned everything out: what he was going to say, how he was going to confront the kidnapper, even a plan of how he'd stop him from hurting Cari – or him, for that matter. But on entering the room, and seeing Cari with the makeshift hood over her head and a man who was the spitting image of Samuel wielding a knife, it made him do the last thing he'd ever wanted or needed to at that moment.

He froze.

Paralysed by the scene in front of him, Drake saw his past playing out again before him in a disturbing new reality, like some grotesque play.

His words wouldn't come. His body wouldn't move, his mind stuttering to a halt at what he was seeing.

The kidnapper's head tilted. 'Did you hear what I said?'

Drake didn't respond. He just stared.

Cari shouted incoherently beneath the hood, pushing against the chair and the bindings at her wrists and chest.

'I . . . I . . .' Drake took a ragged breath, and tried again. 'I . . .'

The masked man didn't respond. He didn't make a move for Cari or for Drake; he simply stood and watched a man seemingly break down before his very eyes.

Drake backed up against a kitchen cabinet and slid to the floor. He brought his trembling hands to his face, attempting to cover his eyes and blot out the scene playing out in his mind as the sights and sounds of eighteen months ago came back to him.

He saw again the gradual slice of Samuel's knife across Becca's throat, the blood pouring down her front. Her choking in front of him with those accusatory eyes. Knowing that he'd failed her, knowing she was dead because of his inability to act. Eva's pleading screams, knowing what was happening in front of her but being powerless to do anything. Samuel's eyes burning with hate at the sight of Drake. The way Samuel had savoured every sickening second of his wife's demise.

'Becca, I . . . I'm sorry. I'm s-so sorry,' he said out loud.

The kidnapper had moved away from Cari and was now standing over him without Drake having realised. Watching him with some sort of morbid curiosity, it seemed, his head tilted further at the man on the ground, confusion in his eyes. 'What did you say?'

Drake was trapped inside his waking nightmare, seemingly unable to break free from the tidal wave of pain overflowing him. Whenever he tried to push away from it, his mind drew a blank.

If he didn't snap out of it, he was lost, Cari was lost. The Man, Samuel, would win.

What're you doing? Pull yourself together!

Cari needs you, you fucking idiot.

Time to do what you should have done when you first came in. Fight it . . . Fight him.

A small flame ignited in his belly at his thoughts. The first sensible ones he'd had since entering.

You need to get a grip. It's just a room. Just a man. It's not Samuel. What happened before, happened, you had no control over it. Now, you have the control. Now you have the power. Finish this.

A warmth surged through his body, his mind becoming crystal clear. Drake pushed himself up from the floor, his face twisting into a snarl.

'Let. Her. Go.'

The kidnapper shook his head. 'I can't do that.'

The man spoke as though he was changing his voice somehow, masking it to stop Drake identifying him. Did Drake *know* him?

'Who are you? If you tell me, perhaps there's a chance you make it out of this in one piece.'

The man looked down at the knife, hesitating slightly. As though he was having doubts at what he was doing.

'I—I can't.'

'You can't, or you *won't?*'

The masked man started back-pedalling toward Cari. The girl began struggling again as she sensed him coming back to her.

'Cari, it'll be okay.' Drake stated, his new found confidence clear. 'Don't move.'

The man froze, his eyes narrowing in the slits of his balaclava. '. . . Why did you call her Cari?'

'Because *it is* Cari.' Drake said. 'You took the wrong girl, that's not my daughter.'

The kidnapper brandished the knife in Drake's direction. 'You're lying.'

Growing more confident by the second, Drake felt the fire burn in his chest, waiting for an opening. 'See for yourself. She has a scar on her neck, and Eva doesn't have one. Cari Whitman, Andrea Whitman's daughter, does. She's Samuel's granddaughter. The girl who survived on the day he got arrested.'

Still pointing the knife in Drake's direction, the kidnapper yanked the hood off Cari's head. Her dark hair shrouded her face and for a split second, it sent Drake back to seeing Eva at the same table. He took a deep breath. The vision wouldn't stop him this time. He'd seen to that.

Cari screamed through her gag as the man brought her head up and examined her neck. The puckered scar contrasted sharply against the flush brought on by her emotions.

'Holy *shit*,' the man growled. 'I don't believe this.'

Clearly unsure, the man took a step back. Drake almost felt a ridiculous sense of pity for him.

'How was I to know you have more than one girl staying with you?' The kidnapper shook his head in disgust. '*One* fucking girl was all that was supposed to be there. *One*. That's what I was told.'

The man slammed the table with the butt of the knife. 'Regardless, I promised I'd do what was necessary. This Cari girl, Eva, whatever. It brought *you* here, so it doesn't matter now.'

Drake took a step forward. 'You can just leave. I won't follow you. Just leave and don't come back. Nothing more needs to happen.'

'You don't understand. I can't back out of this.'

'You can. Just leave. Before you get hurt.'

'Before *I* get hurt. You really think you stand a chance against me?'

'I've done worse.'

The man scoffed. 'Please . . .' He took a few steps toward Drake, closing to almost an arm's length from him. The moment for action was now.

Drake saw the kidnapper wasn't going to back down without a fight. So, a fight he would get.

'Cari, get down! Now!' he commanded. It caused the man to look in Cari's direction long enough for Drake to pick up the one solitary glass tumbler on the side and fling it at the kidnapper's head. The glass shattered at the man's temple, causing him to topple towards the wall, just like Samuel had done so long ago.

Cari did as she was asked, flinging herself over on to the floor. She scrambled awkwardly under the table, the chair still strapped to her. While she made a scene, Drake picked up one of the dining chairs and ran at the man, slamming it down on his head. The chair splintered and broke in two as the man grunted at the impact and fell to the floor. But only for a moment, as he was soon pushing himself up slowly, much to Drake's surprise.

Jesus, he's strong.

Drake roared, his anger boiling over as he charged at the brute before he'd managed to regain his footing. Drake shoved him to the wall, the man's back and head flying backwards and slamming against it with a dull thud. Still bewildered by what was happening to him, the kidnapper moved slowly to intercept Drake's next blow, but had nothing to stop Drake's other fist from connecting with his gut and winding him.

Drake punched him again and again, first in the stomach and then about the head. 'You. Will. Not. Hurt. My. *Family!*'

With a dazed groan, the man finally slumped to the floor.

Drake stood over him panting, his fists throbbing with pain.

The wooziness from before he entered the room was returning. He shook his head, trying to get rid of the feeling. He needed to know who this man was, why he had done what he'd done. What hold did Samuel have over him?

'No . . .' the man groaned, trying to bat away Drake's hands feebly.

Drake pulled the balaclava off, revealing a bloodied face with short blonde hair and blue eyes staring back at him as the man slowly came to his senses.

It was Paul Randall, the pub landlord's son from Barndon.

Drake's eyes widened with surprise. *What the . . . Why?*

He knew he didn't have much time; Paul wouldn't stay down much longer once he'd caught his breath, he was much younger and stronger than Drake.

Hurrying over to Cari, he pulled away her blindfold, revealing her terrified brown eyes, before he started undoing her bindings at her ankles. 'Cari, you've got to get out of the house,' he told her. 'Run round the front and down the lane to the next neighbour's house. Get help.'

Drake felt for the girl, realising she must be reliving her own torment; the scene echoing how it had been before her mother started her own killing spree.

He unknotted the final tie on her ankles and started on her wrists. 'Do it. Do it now.'

Gasping for breath, she nodded. She got up and ran for the door as Drake heard a groan and movement behind him. With Cari gone, it was just him and Paul.

'You shouldn't have done that,' Paul panted.

'*I* shouldn't have? You kidnapped a teenage girl, you bastard.' Drake readied himself for round two, knowing it likely wouldn't go so well for him this time. 'And now she's gone. What are you still fighting for?'

Shit. The knife! Drake had forgotten all about it in the heat of the moment, spotting it too late as Paul picked up the blade from behind him, the sound of metal scraping on tile as it brushed the floor.

'You should have stopped me when you had the chance. I can't let you out of here alive. I'm sorry.'

Sorry?

Drake put on his most confident face. 'Didn't go so well for you the first time.'

'You've ran out of dirty tactics now, Drake.'

Paul was right. There was nothing left to try, Drake realised, the sweat pouring down his back.

Before he knew what to do, Paul charged at him. Drake tried to leap across the table and away from him. He almost made it, but Paul grabbed his trailing leg and yanked Drake back, catching him awkwardly. With his other hand, he sliced downward with the knife, but Drake managed to twist away, narrowly avoiding the blade.

Drake kicked out at Paul's hand with his free leg and broke the man's grip, before rolling off on to the floor and hitting his head against a cabinet. Dazed, he only just managed to pull himself back up in time to avoid another wild slash as Paul rounded the table.

Fighting to keep going, Drake pulled in a large breath and charged one last time, grabbing at the man's arms and shoving him back toward the open doorway. Paul grunted and pushed hard against Drake's grip, the point of the knife creeping ever closer to the older man's shoulder.

The anger burned in Drake's stomach as he growled against Paul's vastly superior strength. The knife was going to impale his shoulder, slowly but surely, and he'd be dead if he didn't do something fast.

That 'something' suddenly screamed from the doorway. Drake saw Cari dive in out of the corner of his eye, brandishing a pair of garden secateurs above her head. In a split second, she'd struck, plunging the curved blades into Paul's leg.

The man howled in pain, immediately pulling away and toppling back into the corner of the doorway leading to the hall.

'Cari,' Drake panted. 'I told you to get help.'

'This *is* help!'

Despite himself, Drake gave her an approving nod before moving toward Paul. He stood over the man who was hissing at the pain as he nursed his injured leg, the colour draining from his face. Blood trickled between his fingers, spotting the floor, and his eyelid was beginning to swell from his earlier beating.

Paul looked up at his approach, putting forth a hand. 'Please. Don't hurt me. Drake . . . If you let me go, you won't ever see me again.' He panted. 'I swear it. You have my word.'

Drake ignored his plea. 'Why did you do this?' he demanded. 'What does he have on you?'

'He threatened my sisters. Said if I did this for him, he wouldn't have them hurt.' Paul gasped further. 'He still knows people. I'm just the tip of the iceberg on who he has a hold over.'

'But kidnapping a teenager, though? Attacking a police officer?'

Paul dropped his head in shame. 'I had no choice.' He continued gasping, his face turning pale. 'Please. I beg you.'

Drake was disgusted. Yet again, Samuel's influence was destroying people's lives. What he wouldn't give for Samuel to be gone for good. But he knew he couldn't let Samuel ruin another life. Not now, not even with what Paul had done. He had to do something right and be the better person. Without Paul around, his sisters would be at the mercy of their father, Michael, more than ever before.

Against his better judgement, Drake came to a decision.

He pursed his lips before uttering one word. 'Okay.'

Paul looked him in the eye, not believing what he was hearing, before looking at Cari for a split-second. She clearly couldn't believe what she was hearing either.

'What?'

'I said, "Okay". Get out of here, and get that wound seen to. I don't want to see you ever again. I mean it – if I ever hear so much as a *murmur* about you again, you're finished. You understand?' His head pounding, Drake held out an arm, grimacing at the weight of the injured man as he pulled him up.

'Drake—Th-thank you, Drake. I mean it. Thank you.' Paul hissed in pain and hobbled past them out into the garden.

'*Why would you do that?*' Cari was staring at him as though he'd slapped her in the face. 'He could have killed us both. I've been so fucking scared.'

He put a hand on her shoulder. 'Because, Cari, I believe him. Sometimes you've got to make the harder choice.'

'That doesn't make what he did go away. I thought he was going to *kill me*, John.'

'No, it doesn't. But he wasn't doing it because of us. It was because of *Him*. The same man who has tainted your mum.'

Cari looked down at her hands, the wrists red from her bindings. 'But he hurt me. And you're bleeding.'

Drake brought his hand up to the back of his head and it came back red. He really needed to see a doctor.

He shook it off as best he could, so as not to worry the girl even more. 'It doesn't mean you should hurt him in kind. Try your best to forgive him, Cari – he may look like he's an adult, but he's had a terrible upbringing. His father is a monster, and he's still like a frightened teenager himself. His sisters are probably the only good thing in his life, and Samuel threatened them.'

'But—'

'Drop it. You'll drive yourself mad otherwise.'

Her eyes hardened. 'It's not that simple. He took me back to that *place* in my head. To my Mum . . . what she did. I was terrified. I'm *still* terrified. I hate him for doing that to me.'

Drake moved over to one of the two remaining upright chairs and sat down, still out of breath from the encounter. He really *was* getting too old for this shit. He indicated for her to sit at the other remaining chair.

'I'm sorry, Cari. I know I should have protected you better. If you want someone to hate, then hate Samuel Barrow; hell, hate *me*. He instigated this because of me. I failed you.'

'You can't protect me all the time. No one can.' Cari turned away from him, gathering her thoughts before coming to a quiet conclusion, 'I don't like it, but I'll try.'

'That's all you can do, love.' Drake put his hand out across the table and she took it. He gave her cold hand an encouraging squeeze. 'That's all you can do.'

Cari left him so she could lie down and rest on the sofa in the lounge, while Drake remained in the room that held the memory of so much tragedy and pain for him. His eyes became ever more vengeful as he thought of Samuel. Of how Samuel had brought down so much misery on Cari. Of how he'd terrorised his family once again.

He clenched his fists.

One day, you bastard. One day.

62

Ellie had dragged Pinter up to their floor. She'd had to be absolutely sure that he wasn't wrong in what he was telling her. It needed to be ironclad and whatever other saying for 'not bloody wrong' she could think of.

She'd then pulled him into a side room and shown him pictures of the Spencers, the Action Man and all the abusers, anything that might make him realise what he was saying was bullshit. He had to have got it wrong; he had to. The man who had threatened her family was in prison.

'I don't recognise any of them. How many more times?'

She'd stared at him for the longest time. 'You're one hundred percent sure?'

He'd made a point of looking again before returning her stare. 'That's not him. The man I was dealing with doesn't have a scar on his forehead like that guy, and the other two are women, innit. Are they his sisters?'

Shit, she'd thought, disgusted at herself. *I can't believe it.*

'Can you come back once I've grabbed someone to put together a composite of this man's face?'

He'd not liked that request, giving her an irritated look. 'When?'

'Like tomorrow morning, if I have my way.'

'Okay, but what's in it for me?'

She'd smiled at him. 'Me not passing your name on to the drug trafficking team, how about that?'

'Sheesh lady. You're a bitch, you know that?'

'Call me that again, let's see what happens.'

'Okay, okay. I like you.' He'd laughed a nasally laugh. Ellie had got the feeling he actually meant it, too. 'I'll be back tomorrow.'

She'd taken him down and stayed in the lift while he'd swaggered out, seemingly carefree, into the daylight.

Ellie was just heading back to get a coffee when a voice called out across the floor. A demand not usually directed at her, too. Odd.

'DS Wilkinson? My office, please,' Miller requested.

God, I hope I'm not heading for a bollocking. It's been a while, I suppose.

She navigated the various desks and chairs and was soon at the doorway. Ellie thought back to when she'd first walked through the doors and seen Drake at the desk with Miller. She'd seen the look of surprise on his face, and the not-so-subtle darkening of his mood the longer the conversation had gone on. The realisation that he was going to be saddled with her. She smiled at the memory.

'Ellie, take a seat, please.'

Ellie sat down and looked across at Miller, wondering why a DCS would bother with her, even in their small team. The woman was looking more troubled than usual lately, as though the weight of the world was on her shoulders. Ellie supposed having had a DI die on a case you were sharing, a DS in a coma and a Constable who'd recently been unmasked as part of a serial killer conspiracy, could do that to a woman. And that wasn't even considering a suspiciously absent DCI with a penchant for trouble.

Miller tilted her head slightly, hands clasped on her desk. 'How are you, Ellie?'

I killed someone to protect my family, my colleague has just been murdered and my boss has gone off the radar, she thought.

Ellie answered carefully. 'I'm . . . okay.'

'That's not what I hear.'

'Oh?'

'Yes. I hear you've been going outside your remit. Working a sexual abuse case.'

Shit, the Spencer case. But it had been revealed to be linked now. Why have a go?

Ellie gripped her knees and began picking absently at the leg of her jeans. 'But my work shows it is actually linked now, ma'am.'

'Indeed, and unofficially, I would say "good work",' Miller said, nodding.

Ellie expected a 'but' and was soon awarded with one.

'But officially, you went against orders. And I can't have more people not pulling their weight in the right direction.'

'I have been, though . . .'

'And what if it hadn't worked out?'

Ellie answered back, a little too quickly. 'I took leave. And it *did* work out.'

'Yes, leave at a critical time, to work on a case not in our remit. Stepping on other departments' toes.'

'I—'

'Consider this a warning, Ellie.'

She supposed she should take it on the chin. 'Yes, ma'am.'

Miller turned to the side in her chair. She rested an arm on her desk, not looking directly at Ellie, but out of the window and over the Thames, a distant, saddened look to her features. 'Have you seen or heard from Drake? I need to speak to him further about DI Melwood's death.'

Ellie's heart sank at the comment. 'No, I haven't.'

'Don't you think that odd?'

'A little, he's not one for completely closing down. Even him.'

Miller turned back to her. 'Exactly. If you hear from him, tell me. I'm starting to get worried. It may not seem it at times, but I do care.'

Ellie had never seen or heard her be so candid before. 'Yes, ma'am.'

The words hung in the air, becoming progressively more awkward just as Ellie's phone started to ring. 'I'm so sorry, ma'am.'

'It's not a problem.' Miller stated, her face unreadable. 'We're done here, okay? Answer the phone.'

'Yes. Thank you, ma'am.'

Ellie got up and left, answering without looking at who it was, and started to wander slowly back toward the kitchenette. *Get a room, damn it.*

'DS Wilkinson,' she said nonchalantly, weaving in and out of various discussions that were taking place at people's desks.

'A'ight, police lady.'

'Pinter, what do you want? It's only been like ten damn minutes.'

'Easy.' The young man laughed. 'Thought you'd be happy to hear my voice, innit.'

'What is it? Sort of in the middle of stuff.'

'Heh, you ain't going to believe this. You should be well excited. I just saw your man. The guy you want.'

Ellie stopped in her tracks.

You've got to be fucking kidding me.

'What! How?'

'Yeah, was just having a smoke before I left, you know—'

'Pinter, get to the damn point.'

'Sheesh, okay. Sorry.' He paused for what seemed like an eternity. 'So, like, this guy came out your building, matter of fact. He was on the phone. I heard his voice and like, it seemed *real* familiar. Went over to him to say hello, see if I remembered him and he pretended he didn't know me. But I recognised him – yeah, recognised his eyes and his voice when he said to leave him alone.'

Ellie couldn't believe it. He had to be high or something. Someone coming out of *their office building?* But who?

'Where are you, right now? Is he still there?'

'Nah, he left real quick after that. Got in a car and sped off. I'm still downstairs.'

'Meet me in reception. Don't move, damn it!'

'A'ight.'

Ellie could barely contain herself as she ran to the lift and took it down to reception. She had a plan, one that would identify the damn man, one way or another. She was nearly at her wits end. Her mind was racing with the idea that someone within the police force could have threatened her. What was it with this damn place?

The lift pinged, the doors opening so slowly she felt like wrenching them open by hand before she slammed through the double doors to reception, to find Pinter standing with a cocksure grin on his face. 'You missed him though, so, what's the point?'

Without answering, Ellie turned to the receptionist. Using the sweetest, most amiable voice she could muster, she said, 'Hi. Sorry to bother you, but may I see your CCTV footage from the last few minutes?'

The receptionist – Ellie thought her name was Jill – looked up over her glasses. 'Er, yes. Of course. May I ask why?'

'Just need to identify someone. You've got it in the carpark and in here, right?'

'Yes, we do.'

'Excellent.'

Ellie manoeuvred around the side of the reception desk and gestured for Pinter to do the same, much to Jill's horror.

'It's okay. He's with me.'

'Hmm, okay. If you're sure.'

'I am.' Ellie gestured at the woman's chair. 'Do you mind?'

Jill took the hint and got up. Pinter crouched down next to Ellie, who took centre stage. This was her moment.

She looked down at Pinter, his breath stinking of cigarette smoke. 'Okay, so, just a sec. You say it was like, what . . . five minutes or so?'

'Yeah, he came right on out, like it was nothing. Can't believe that guy might work for you.'

Ellie felt an irrational need to correct him. 'There's other departments.'

'But still, innit . . .'

'All right. Concentrate.'

Ellie rewound the footage for the car park. Within a few minutes, there was a man on screen on his phone, Pinter seemingly getting in his face, and the man speeding off. It wasn't great quality.

'That's him. Come to think of it, that red hair sort of stuck out his hood one time too. I swear.'

'Now you're just making shit up, surely? You're full of useful bloody information now, aren't you? Jesus.' She scoffed. 'Let me try the other footage from inside, should be clearer. Can't make out his face in that carpark one.'

Ellie found the other footage and skimmed back through it, marrying the timestamp to Pinter's encounter and winding it back a few seconds.

She gasped at who she saw. '*Holy fucking shit.*'

You've got to be kidding me. There's no way. Surely not.

There, clear as day, was Tanv's pathologist-in-training, Graham Reynolds.

63

Drake couldn't believe what he was hearing as Ellie brought him up to speed on what had happened. Her informant, CCTV man, ID'ing her stalker in the damn car park? Graham Reynolds, the creepy little SOCO, was possibly responsible for sending her the figurine covered in duct tape. And he'd bought drugs, too. What else was he responsible for?

If what Pinter had said was true, Jack Spencer had lied to them; even in prison, the bastard was still as dishonest as when they'd first interviewed him. Maybe there was more to it, but Drake would have to wait to get to the bottom of it.

He chose not to mention the events of that morning, not wanting to muddy the situation by bringing in Samuel's involvement. Drake told himself he'd deal with Samuel later. His head was still pounding, however. He couldn't tuck that painful feeling away quite so easily.

'Ellie, slow down. Take a moment. Don't just go over there all guns blazing, okay?' Drake gesticulated at the table in his old kitchen while he tried to talk her down from doing something stupid. Which, he realised, was rich considering what he had just been through.

'I need to speak to him, Drake,' she told him.

'I know, I know – believe me, I understand, but you need to be smart about this. You can't spook him. He may not think anyone has figured him out. And, perhaps, just *maybe* your guy is wrong?'

'He's not wrong, he can't be. How many people do you see with red hair and brown eyes? How many of those do you bump into, and how many of them have you been supplying with drugs?'

'You have a point, but *my* point still stands too. At the very least, wait near his place until I get there, yeah? That's an order, Ellie.'

Drake heard his impulsive partner sigh audibly. 'Okay. I suppose that *is* the most sensible option.'

'Precisely. There could be a perfectly reasonable explanation. And this is coming from a guy who dislikes him intensely, remember?' Drake didn't quite believe the words when he said it out loud either, but what could he do? He needed more.

'I get it. I doubt it, but – fine. I'll see you there. Sending you the address for the road I'll be waiting in now.'

'Great. Thanks.' Drake hung up and looked at the address; it was between his flat and their current location. Absently, he called for Cari to come back to the kitchen while testing the back of his head for more blood. It came back with nothing, thankfully.

Good.

Cari didn't make an appearance.

'Cari?' Drake waited a moment before getting up and walking through to the lounge.

The girl was fast asleep, but at least she'd changed into the clothes he'd brought for her from her London bedroom. She'd kept her Dad's Nirvana t-shirt on, though, perhaps as comfort.

'Cari?' He crouched down, touching her shoulder gently to rouse her. 'We've got to go now.'

She twitched away from his hand and scrambled back from him. 'No—no!'

'Cari, it's me. It's John. I'm sorry, I didn't mean to frighten you. You were asleep.'

The girl calmed down almost immediately, brushing her hair away from her face. She heaved a sigh and rubbed her eyes. 'Sorry, I must have been dreaming. Probably a nightmare.'

'You okay now?'

'Yeah, think so. Thanks, John,' she said, her voice sounding hoarser than usual.

'Good.' His knees cracked as he got back to his feet. He was beginning to feel the effects from his encounter with Paul. 'Do you mind tagging along with me for a bit? I want to keep an eye on you, and it's sort of on the way. I just need to stop by and meet with Ellie about something. You don't mind waiting in the car, do you?'

'No, guess not. Beats being in my bedroom. Not going to be sleeping there too well for a while, you know?'

'I'm sorry, kiddo. You've had a tough run of it these past few days. I really hope we can bring an end to that soon for you.'

'I know. If you do ever find my mum, please try and make sure she doesn't hurt herself or anyone,' Cari said, her sad eyes blinking slowly as she looked around the room. 'The idea of her hurting anyone else, it's horrible. Not just for them, but I *know* my mum wouldn't do that if she was in control. She just wouldn't.'

'I'll do my best, Cari. I promise.'

His words hung in the air for a few seconds before he clapped his hands in an attempt to muster some enthusiasm for the next shit show he would be a part of. 'Now let's get the hell out of here. I've had it with this place.'

Drake ushered her out through the kitchen door and into the garden. He closed the door behind him without looking back.

64

By the time Drake had arrived at the road Ellie had directed him to in Willesden, north-west London, it was late afternoon. The sky had darkened, bringing with it what appeared to be the makings of a storm. He hoped it didn't come to anything; he'd had enough drama for one day, and getting soaked was not high on his list of priorities.

Drake soon spotted Ellie's car a little way down the suburban road. He expected she'd parked at least one, maybe two doors down from Reynolds home to avoid arousing suspicion. Drake had been racking his brain as to why the man would have anything against his partner, but had come up blank. Against himself, maybe, with his highlighting of the man's poor performance, but Ellie? She had barely said a word to him as far as Drake knew.

Cari had slept for most of the journey, which was a blessing. He certainly wasn't in the mood for more talking right now. The pain in the back of his head had grown worse, if that was possible, though the wooziness was lifting. And he had been trying to figure out how Paul and Samuel had known where he lived, but not known about Cari. It didn't make any sense.

The girl roused as he pulled into a parking spot. 'How long was I out for?'

'Just an hour or so, don't worry. In fact, you may as well try and get some more while I run this errand with Ellie quickly.'

She gave him a strange look. 'That might be a plan.' Her wrists clicked as she stretched.

'I promise I won't be long, okay?'

'Okay.'

'Maybe give Eva another call. That'll calm her down again, I'm sure. And it'd keep you company,' Drake suggested, giving her a smile before exiting the car and heading over to Ellie. She jumped out at his arrival, clearly impatient to get going.

'What took you so long?'

Drake growled irritably. 'Got here as fast as I could, *sergeant*.'

Ellie flinched slightly at his words. 'Ouch, someone's a little testy this afternoon.'

'Just got a rather large headache. Long story. Anyway, let's get to it, yes? Lead the way.'

'Okay. It's just a street over from here. Keep an eye out for a black VW Golf, that's his car,' she said, walking ahead. 'Can you believe he might be involved? I can't figure out why. My mind's been drawing nothing but blanks while waiting for you. He did seem to be in an awful hurry after getting away from Pinter. Never seen someone shoot out of that car park so fast.'

'Honestly, I'm stumped too.'

Ellie looked back over her shoulder. 'I'll say again, Pinter seems to be genuine. I really don't think he has a reason to lie, you know?'

His colleague's footsteps echoed along the street as they walked. It was surprisingly quiet for a London suburb. Typically, around this time, the streets would be rat runs of cars and tube commuters returning home from work.

Drake nodded. 'As I said, let's just see how it plays out. Could be some rational explanation. Though I've no idea what.'

Soon they were walking down Reynolds' road. It looked like any other street; another row of Victorian terraces, some fully rendered, some red-brick, some a mix of the two. All probably out of any normal person's price range in this day and age, regardless of size, unless they rented.

Ellie stopped. 'There's his car. Just over from his house. See it?'

Drake did. It was unoccupied. His head pounded again as he squinted. 'Now, don't go in raging, okay? We'll just try and establish the facts.'

'Drake, I'm not a child.'

'I know, but you have a lot riding on this. Your sanity for starters. Not having to look over your shoulder for yours or your family's sake.'

'True. I'll try, all right?'

Drake nodded. 'I'll take point.'

'Got it.'

Drake looked over the house as he walked up to the front door. Outwardly there was nothing to make it stand out to him, though perhaps it seemed a little more "palatial" than the surrounding terraced properties. The front was a little like the house they'd attended in Notting Hill, with a pillared front entrance and bay windows to either side.

Originally, it would likely have been two separate houses before they'd been knocked together. The two up, two down layout had probably been maintained, but on a bigger scale than the neighbouring properties. A small paved area to the front straddled either side of the path leading to a central front door.

The windows were shuttered upstairs, as were the bay windows downstairs. There was no domestic CCTV system to warn Reynolds of their visit. But there didn't appear to be any lights on. It wasn't looking promising.

If Reynolds were to answer, Drake imagined the inside of the house would be fastidiously clean, as per his SOCO ways.

'Ready?' His tired eyes glanced back over his shoulder at her.

'As I'll ever be.'

Seeing no doorbell, Drake knocked hard on the door.

No answer. He tried again.

Within a few seconds of persistent banging, a light came on above them and there was the noise of a door slamming shut.

Drake looked back at Ellie and raised an eyebrow.

The sound of a key slotting into the lock caused Drake to turn back to the entrance just as the door opened. Reynolds was facing them through a chained gap, and Drake realised he had never seen the man without some sort of hooded overall or surgical gown on. Nor had he seen his hair before. It was a deep coppery red, at odds with his deep brown eyes and brows.

'DCI Drake, DS Wilkinson. What an . . . unexpected surprise,' the man said, his wide mouth twitching into a forced smile. 'Is there something you need me for? Is Dr Kulkarni okay?'

Drake forced his own thin smile. 'She's fine, don't worry. And, yes, we need to ask you some questions. Do you mind if we come in?'

Reynolds looked put out. 'I was in the middle of something, I'm sorry. Can it wait until tomorrow?'

'We're both standing on your doorstep, Graham,' Drake said brusquely. 'What makes you think it can wait?'

'A fair point.' Reynolds unlatched the door before ushering them inside into a sparse hallway. A set of stairs to one side and a number of rooms led off left and right from the uncarpeted hall, all closed.

'Quite the place you got here. They must be paying you well,' Drake said, making awkward small talk.

'I wish. I inherited money from my parents many years ago, along with some smart investments too. You know.' Reynolds shrugged. 'Come with me, there's a table we can sit at just through here.'

The man opened a door next to the front door and led Drake and a surprisingly reserved Ellie through to a dining room. It was spartan, with just a table and chairs, as though someone had only moved in recently and put what they could in situ to fulfil a purpose for the space.

Reynolds looked at Drake as he took a seat. 'I'm in the middle of doing something with the place. Not usually so . . . barren.'

'I see.'

Ellie sat down last, but asked a question before anyone else had a chance to speak further. 'So what were you doing at our headquarters today, Reynolds?'

'There was a seminar on, a follow on from another one for my pathology training,' Reynolds said without any hesitation. 'Surprised you've not seen me before. Drake jumped in on one of the sessions a few months back and spoke with my colleague, Daryl.'

Ellie didn't outwardly react to the man's answers. Though Drake could sense she wanted to jump straight to her real questions at any moment. She seemed to get a little impulsive when it came to anything impacting her family, which he understood.

Drake couldn't remember seeing Reynolds there when he was quizzing the SOCO called Daryl about the first Spencer murder scene. But judging by how the man looked outside of work, perhaps Drake had simply overlooked him in his rush for answers at the time.

Ellie clasped her hands. 'And did someone speak to you in the car park later?'

'Yes, actually. How did—'

'And what did he say?'

'He was asking me for money. I figured he was some homeless guy who was hanging about in the car park,' Reynolds said with an exaggerated shrug. 'I've never seen him before in my life.'

'You seemed shaken by it, judging by how quickly you jumped in your car after?'

'Well, yes. I'm not like you and DCI Drake here. In my work, I deal with stuff *after* the fact. I'm not particularly good with the living. I don't like them getting in my face, it's . . . *unpleasant*. I wanted to get out of there and go home, as intended, as soon as possible.'

Drake wasn't picking up anything overly suspicious so far; Reynolds was just being the same peculiar man he always was. His answers were all seemingly straight-forward and understandable. Was this Pinter bloke just barking up the wrong tree, and it was a case of mistaken identity?

Drake tried a different angle. 'Reynolds, where were you on the day the duct-tape murders were called in?'

Reynolds brow pinched ever so slightly before returning to normal. 'It was my day off.'

'Can you be more specific? What were you up to?'

'Erm, that was a while ago now, Drake.'

'But you remembered immediately that you had a day off?'

'Yes . . . you have me there.' Reynolds smiled his usual off-smile before giving a shamed look. 'I hope you don't *judge* me for it, but I was in bed for most of it. Do you ever get that?'

Reynolds looked pointedly in Drake's direction. 'That desire to just stay in bed. This world, it's all so *depressing* sometimes, eh?'

Drake wasn't sure what the man was getting at.

Ellie jumped back in for another question, scratching at the back of her hand irritably. 'When did you first hear about the duct tape murders, Reynolds?'

'When Dr Kulkarni told me when I came in the following day.'

'So, you knew nothing about them before then?'

Drake could see Ellie was trying to establish a timeline of when and where Reynolds was. Whether it was feasible for him to have had time to hear about it, then hotfoot it to the school, having knocked up the threatening toy figure. If he'd only heard about it the day after from Tanv, then that was too late.

'No.' Reynolds shook his head. 'Look, what is this? Is this related to anything? I'm not sure how much help I'm being.'

Ellie ignored his question and pressed on. 'Do you, or have you ever, received or used Fentanyl or Rohypnol?'

Reynolds looked at them incredulously. 'No. Of course not. What do you take me for?'

The man seemed rattled, but not in the way that either Ellie or Drake was hoping for. They weren't getting anywhere. Everything was plausible. Everything was *deniable*. They needed more.

Ellie tried one final question. 'May we take a look around?'

Reynolds expression tensed. 'I don't see why. I've not done anything wrong. I invited you in of my own accord. My house is my private property. If you had probable cause, then of course, I wouldn't stand in your way, but you don't and I don't see why you *ever* would, for that matter.' The man stood. 'Now, if that was all you had to ask me, I would politely like to ask you to leave now.'

Drake stood, regretfully. Ellie looked like someone had punched her in the gut. She was clearly frustrated by the outcome. But – and Drake didn't like admitting it – Reynolds was right. Drake couldn't say he'd like people barging around his home without solid actionable evidence.

Reynolds walked out to the hallway. They followed him, Ellie wearing a deep frown. Drake could tell she was desperately trying to think of something to glean more information while they had the opportunity. But, unusually for her, she appeared to be coming up short.

'Will you be in tomorrow?' Drake asked. 'For the Melwood autopsy.'

'Of course,' Reynolds said, holding the door open. 'I wouldn't miss a Family Man killing for the world . . . Sorry, my apologies, he was a colleague. I should be more respectful.'

Drake grimaced at the man's words. He still had that quality about him that made Drake want to kick him out to the curb. 'Yes. You really should.'

Ellie stepped out into the darkness without a word, and Drake followed.

'Hey! What're you doing here, Cari?' Ellie said loudly in surprise.

What? I thought she was in the car?

Drake looked beyond Ellie to see Cari emerging from the dusky gloom at the edge of the property.

'Cari, get back to the car, please.'

Reynolds looked strangely off-kilter, even for him. 'Wh–who is that?'

'Just my daughter's friend, Cari. Sorry for this. We'll leave you now—'

Suddenly there was a shout. A noise from upstairs in the house, followed by a loud tirade of bangs and screams.

'Cari! Cari!' the voice shrieked.

Ellie stared at him, wide-eyed. 'Chief, is that . . . ?'

It was Andrea.

65

Everything happened in a blur; Ellie and Drake realising who it was calling for her daughter. And Reynolds realising what was happening, and immediately moving to shove the door in Drake's face.

Drake grappled desperately with the chained door, but Reynolds managed to jam it shut before he could keep it open.

'Reynolds, let us in. Now.' Drake pounded on the door, looking back at Ellie. 'We've got to get in there. We've got to stop him. Stop *them*!'

'Is that my Mum in there?' Cari surged for the door.

Ellie caught her before she got as far as the porch, the girl thrashing in her arms and shouting toward the house. 'Let go of me! Mum! It's me!'

Drake didn't know what to say. He needed to control the situation, to get a handle on it before it really got out of hand.

'Cari, stay back,' he said, locking eyes with hers. 'We need to keep you safe and stop your mother from hurting herself or anyone else, okay? Stay back. Leave it to us.'

'Mum!' she screamed again, but she didn't shove for the door any further. Instead, she turned away from them, her head in her hands.

Drake knew he had to move fast. It would all spiral if he wasn't careful, and the last thing he wanted was for that to happen.

'Ellie, we need to get in there. If we can, you focus on Reynolds, and I'll deal with Andrea. Got it?'

Ellie's eyes gleamed in the encroaching darkness. 'Got it, Chief. Don't worry, I've got your back.'

She turned back toward Cari. 'Cari, please. Do what he says. We don't want you to get hurt, okay, hun?'

'Okay,' Cari said weakly. She'd moved away to the gate and looked to be in a state of shock. 'But, please, *help her.*'

Drake took a few steps back before charging at the door. He slammed into it, the reverberation juddering through his bones. The door didn't budge.

'Let me try, Drake,' Ellie offered, putting her hand on his shoulder. 'Got the knack for it.'

Drake stepped aside wordlessly as Ellie geared up for her own attempt. Charging forwards, the door slammed open, glass shattering and sending Ellie careering onto the floor of the hallway.

She hefted herself back up off the glass-riddled floor with a groan. 'I'm okay.'

Drake pushed through the shattered door remnants behind her.

The noises, now muffled, were emanating from upstairs. Drake gripped the banister and made his way up as fast as he could. Soon he was at the landing, a threadbare blue carpet and two doors leading off. One had all manner of locks and bolts on it, with a padlock discarded on the floor.

Jesus Christ, has he been keeping Andrea prisoner here this whole time?

He heard Ellie pound up the stairs behind him, seemingly none the worse for her encounter with the door. Drake kept his voice low. 'They must both be in there. I don't know how we deal with this without someone getting hurt, Ellie.'

'I know, but we need to hurry, Chief. He could be hurting her – or she could be hurting *him,* for all we know.'

Drake felt like he was at a crossroads. If they waited for backup, either or both of the inhabitants might die. If they went in, it could be a bloodbath. To top it off, they were unarmed. But were Andrea and Reynolds?

'Mum!' Cari called from the hallway.

Drake grimaced at the idea of the girl being in harm's way. 'Ellie, get Cari out of here, she can't be here for this. I'll try and talk them out. There's not enough space for us to overpower them up here. And call backup too, with strict instructions not to come in all guns blazing. Got it? Now go.'

'Got it.' She nodded, shooting down the stairs.

Drake looked at the door, worried about what horrors might lie beyond it. How long had Andrea been there? What had Reynolds done to her? Had he driven her to *murder?* It was all too sick and messed up to bear thinking about right now. All Drake could do was focus on what he'd promised Cari; getting her mother back, safe.

'Is Andrea with you? Is she unharmed?' Drake raised his voice, putting his ear to the door.

'More like is *he* unharmed,' Andrea shrieked.

Reynolds spoke, his voice markedly different to that of the precise man of earlier. 'Drake . . . I'm with her. If you come in, she'll kill me. She's got a knife.'

Whether that was true, or it was the other way round, he didn't know. But he *had* to get in there somehow.

'Andrea, let him go.'

'No. You don't know what he's done. What he's *capable of.* I can't take it anymore. I can't. What he's made me do. What he's done to *me.* I . . . I . . .'

'Please, Andrea. We need you both to come out of this in one piece. Think of Cari. Your daughter. She's with us.'

There was no response to his plea. The silence grew disconcerting. Drake heard Ellie start back up the stairs beneath.

'Andrea?'

'You mean my *granddaughter*,' she snarled.

Oh god, she's switched, Drake realised.

'Miray, please. Let him go.'

Reynolds, sounding relieved, responded. 'She's let me go now, Drake. Miray would never hurt me. She loves me.'

Loves him? What in God's name?

He spotted Ellie creeping back up the stairs. Drake shrugged at the lack of progress as she returned to his side, and told her about Andrea switching over to Miray.

'Cari's back outside. She promised she won't come in again. But she's beside herself, Drake. And backups on its way, though still too far out for my liking.'

He pinched his brow. This had to be handled, and quickly, there wasn't time to waste.

Drake spoke to the pair inside once again. 'What can we do to make you drop the knife and hand yourselves over?'

'Give me *her*,' Miray said, gleefully. 'Give me my granddaughter.'

Drake grimaced. 'I can't do that, Miray. You know that. I can't let you anywhere near her, knowing what you'd do.'

'It'd be quick,' she cackled.

'You sick bitch!' Ellie blurted.

Drake hissed at her. 'What the hell are you doing?'

'I'm sorry. It's just so messed up! That's her daughter she's talking about!'

'Seriously, Ellie. Not now.'

'Well, what do you propose?'

Drake ignored her and tried a different tack. 'Look, if you don't give up soon, an armed response team will be coming down on this place like a ton of bricks. You've got nowhere to go. You're holed up in one goddamn room. Make it easy on yourselves. We can all make it out of here in one piece.'

'I'm not getting put in a prison hospital, Drake. It's not going to happen. I'd rather die. And if you touch him, I'll kill you all.'

'Then come out of there, or let us in and we'll talk,' Ellie suggested.

'Talk, talk, talk, that's *all you ever want to do.* But fine. I want to see your face when I gut you.'

There was a sound of movement and the door unlocking before it was yanked open.

A stark white room shone through beyond. Everything was either white, or had been painted white. The floorboards, the walls, the bed frame, bed linen, everything. It looked almost like a padded room used to house disturbed patients. Is that what Reynolds had been doing?

Miray stepped into the doorway. She cut a menacing figure, her dark hair contrasted sharply with the room's white walls.

The woman held a wicked-looking knife in front of her, ensuring Drake and Ellie backed away.

'We can talk downstairs,' she said, her eyes crazed, jabbing them away with the weapon. Reynolds appeared behind her as Miray made them backtrack along the hallway before indicating for them to back down the stairs.

'It doesn't have to be like this, Miray,' Drake pleaded.

'Oh, it does. It *really* does. I thought that was clear when I started murdering policemen?'

He took another step down the stairs, gripping the banister tightly. How long could this go on? It needed to stop. He'd have to make a move; see an opening, and act. 'Why kill him? Melwood had done nothing to you. You'd never even met him.'

Reynolds spoke up. 'He insulted *me*. That's why. I— *We'd* run out of our initial targets. It was time for something new, and he sprung to mind.'

'He "sprung to mind"? You're kidding me.'

Reynolds shrugged. 'There doesn't have to be deep-seated meaning in everything, Drake. Why not kill for the sport of it? I've helped Miray do *just* that. He was rude and obnoxious to me. I hadn't even done anything to have warranted his harsh words.'

'He had a young son, you sick bastard!' Ellie growled.

'And?' Reynolds shrugged again. 'Why should I care?'

Ellie muttered something Drake couldn't hear as she reached the bottom of the stairs. Moments later, he'd reached ground level too, and they backed toward the front door.

From behind Miray, Reynolds pointed to the closed door nearest the kitchen. 'In there. Now. There's so much I want to show you.'

The man pressed a button on a remote he'd pulled from his pocket and the sound of a mechanism unlocking followed. Ellie grabbed the door handle and it gave a loud ping as she opened it, as though it had been alarmed in some way. Drake's eyes widened as he looked behind him for a second to see where they were headed.

The room was decorated with countless images. *Disturbing* images; all manner of crime scenes and their victims. Blunt force trauma, stabbings, burnings. Falls. *Family Man* crime scenes, *Spencer* crime scenes, Miray's latest and greatest. Images of autopsies, and more, all plastered over the walls, leaving barely a crack visible. It was a shrine.

'Jesus Christ!' Ellie gasped. 'You twisted fuck.'

Miray sniggered as Reynolds replied. 'Why? I'm a collector. Don't you see?'

Miray indicated at the floor. 'Sit.'

Drake and Ellie sat amidst the horrors as Miray secured their wrists behind their backs with rope that was horribly similar to that from the Family Man scenes. Drake took in his surroundings, trying to see what he could use to eventually free them, but all he saw were mementos in glass cases. A skull fragment. Bloodied skin. A tongue. Elements mounted and displayed.

Drake realised he'd been right all along. The nagging thoughts he'd had about the SOCO man, about the crime scenes he'd been involved in; it all made sense. The Family Man scene in Yorkshire, the late and incorrect reports. It was *him*. Reynolds been purposefully screwing with him, toying with the SMT investigations all this time.

'You misled us, didn't you?' Drake's disgust laced every word. 'The Family Man case . . . which hand Jonah used. You knew all along, and you left it off the final report, didn't you?'

Reynolds smiled. 'That *may* have happened, yes. But I'm a trainee, Drake. I didn't know what I was doing . . .' he said, making a sarcastic angelic face. It was grotesque. 'But the earring that you found, ha! That was fun. Taking it from the scene, then planting it back there the day after, making a mockery of the process.'

My God. More people died because of him. Drake's thoughts started to race as he twisted against his bonds, thinking through the Spencer case they'd worked with him since.

'It *was* you who sent me that figure through my daughter, wasn't it?' Ellie said, her eyes boring into the man.

'Of course it was. I knew about it straight after Daryl turned up to take pictures. SOCO has a private instant messaging group, you see. Only a few of us. We send each other all sorts of stuff, trying to outdo each other. It's become a game.' Reynolds laughed. 'Again, if it wasn't obvious by now. I like playing you both. Seeing how you react. Toying with you. Throwing the cat among the pigeons, and seeing who lives and who dies.' Reynolds gripped Miray's shoulders. 'It's fascinating, let me tell you. And you blindly assuming it was the Spencers and giving scant thought to other possibilities. Brilliant. I had to hurry, but I had such fun making that figure.'

'They are fools, my love,' Miray brought her free hand to Reynolds cheek and stroked it.

'Oh, they are, Miray. So much so. But they're not so different, are they, in some ways. They thrive off suffering, as do we.'

Drake looked around the room, trying to find anything that could help them before spotting a computer in the corner, connected to a large television screen. He recalled the Fleming murder by the Thames, and the accomplice who looked like he was recording the act. 'Please tell me that's not for what I think it is.'

'Ah yes. My own little murder collection,' Reynolds said. He tapped the top of his laptop with an index finger. 'Let's say the Family Man *inspired* me to start my own. After I spoke with him on the phone – that was amazing by the way, I'm such a fan – I promised him access to Miray. He said he would give me the password for his *special* stash. The hidden extras that I found and hid from the team when I worked on his play room at the farm.'

'Jesus, you're the leak, aren't you?' Ellie shook her head in disgust.

'Of course. Blaming your poor little colleagues like that – I applaud Samuel for leading you astray,' Reynolds chuckled. 'After

Melwood, Strauss was going to be next. Though it would be a bit boring by comparison. Dying in the night, not coming out of his coma. What a shame. It would have confused you even more, though. Why would he kill his only two supposed sources of information?'

'And these two abusers, seeing as you're spilling your damn guts. Why did you kill them?' Ellie asked. Much like Drake's, her eyes were flitting around the room for any way to get out of their predicament. They were pandering to the man's ego, his desperation to show how clever he was.

'Because I found Jack's laptop up at the retreat. He had a dossier of details, addresses and so on. He'd basically crossed out all the names, barring those two. It didn't take much effort, so I thought, why not start with people who really *deserved it*, deliver some good old vigilante justice.'

Miray smiled, stroking away a hair from the man's face. 'And why don't you tell them how we came to be together, my darling? It was so romantic.'

'I was just getting to that.' Reynolds smiled. 'But it was beautiful, really. It was literally my first day in London to work with Dr Kulkarni, and I'd simply gone to the hospital to see what the child of the Family Man looked like. I only meant to watch her for a while, from afar. But then, I saw her come round the corner as I was driving in. It was like someone had gifted me this wonderful present in a hospital gown. She got in the car with me and hid in the well of the backseat. All I had to do was drive out from a different exit after a while. Then it was only a matter of giving her the medicine she liked thereafter.'

'Rohypnol?'

Reynolds shook his head in disgust. 'No, Drake. Don't be so vulgar. *Medicine.*'

Drake changed the subject, not wanting to hear any more of

the man's insanity. He'd sensed an avenue that might work in his favour, things that Reynolds must have kept from Miray to keep her in check. The SOCO had perhaps revealed just a little too much in his boasting.

Here goes nothing, Drake thought, tensing as he initiated his gambit.

'But why not come straight for me and Cari?' he asked, innocently. 'Isn't that what Miray wanted? To kill her granddaughter? To finish what she started? Perhaps finish off Eva and me too? Samuel knew where I lived. No one was supposed to have that information, but *you* did, and you gave it to him.'

Miray frowned for a split second.

'I . . .' Reynolds failed to respond in time with anything to counteract what Drake was implying.

'Is this true?' Miray said, her knife hand flopping to her side as she looked at her captor. 'You mean, you knew where that little bitch was all this time and you had me killing disgusting fucking paedophiles?'

Reynolds turned to face her. 'I—I—No-no . . . that's not it, I swear. I would never do that to you.'

'I think you kept it from her, Reynolds. I think you kept a lot from her, didn't you?' Drake went on. 'And Samuel. He didn't know Cari was staying with me, either.' He continued pushing, seeing Miray getting more worked up by the second as the realisation dawned that Reynolds had used her. He'd kept her one true desire from her, kept her from killing Cari and preventing her from purifying her family, as she saw it, for well over a year.

Reynolds backed into a corner as Drake and Ellie watched the scene unfold from their position on the floor. Miray stalked toward her supposed lover.

Suddenly, she screamed and dived at Reynolds, sending him

hurtling to the floor to avoid the wild slash of her knife. 'You bastard! I'll kill you!'

'Miray, please! No! I *love* you,' the SOCO screamed, desperately scrambling away from her.

She straddled him, the man powerless beneath the strength that appeared to take hold of the woman whenever she was Miray. Drake and Ellie strained against their bindings, desperate to stop what was about to happen, but the ropes still wouldn't give.

Reynolds crossed his arms in front of his face, anticipating her next move. 'Please, no-no! Miray!'

Suddenly, Miray stopped. Staring straight ahead as though she was in a trance. Drake had read about something similar before, but he'd never seen it in the flesh. She'd gone into a catatonic state of some kind. Was this the process that led to each personality switch?

Just as suddenly as it occurred, it had finished. Reynolds still clamped beneath her, unable to make any meaningful movement.

'Andrea?' Drake questioned.

'D—DCI Drake?'

Andrea looked down in horror at Reynolds beneath her, as though seeing him for the first time. 'You!'

The man grabbed her wrist, causing her to drop the knife before violently shoving her away. He seized the blade as Andrea stumbled to the ground, her head slapping against the wall with a sickening thud.

Andrea was losing the fight. Realising what was about to happen, Drake twisted and angled his back up against Ellies to start working on her bonds, and she tried similar. If they didn't stop Reynolds, Drake realised he'd break the promise he'd made to Cari.

But he was too slow in getting free. They both were.

As though out of thin air, Cari appeared.

'No! Don't you hurt her!' the young girl shrieked, bringing down a kitchen knife with both hands into the man's collarbone, the impact making a nauseating wet thud.

Reynolds screamed in agony. The deep wound spouted blood as he writhed away from Andrea and Cari, gasping and gagging for air. Cari turned on him once more, her eyes dark and wicked, stabbing him again, this time in the chest.

'Cari, no!' Drake pleaded, attempting to rise to his feet. But he was too late.

Reynolds jerked in pain, but that didn't stop the girl. Cari stood over him and drove the knife down, stabbing him in the stomach as he cried out. The man jerked sickeningly towards the handle of the knife before he spasmed one final time and became still.

Seemingly stunned by what she'd done, Cari dropped the bloodied weapon with a clatter at the dead man's side, her breath stuttering at the enormity of what had happened. The man's lifeblood ran down her hands and arms, her dad's t-shirt spattered and bloody.

'Cari!' Andrea cried, as Drake felt the bindings drop from his wrists, Ellie having finally worked them loose. He moved to come between the two of them. Ellie put a foot out, motioning for him to stop.

'No, Drake. Let them be. Just for a moment,' Ellie said quietly.

He couldn't believe what he had just witnessed. That poor girl. That poor *woman*. Being at the mercy of Reynolds for nearly eighteen months, subjected to who knows what. Drake eyed the knife Reynolds and Miray had used by Reynolds body, but waited while mother and daughter spoke.

'Cari, is that really you?' Andrea asked softly. 'Or, am I dreaming again?'

Cari came over to her mother and knelt beside her. 'Mum, I think it should really be me asking *you* that question.'

The two women gave each other uncertain smiles, in spite of themselves and the dark scenes around them, and hugged each other.

'What the hell have we just been a part of, Chief?' Ellie whispered as Drake finally freed her.

'Words fail me, Ellie. But don't let your guard drop. Not yet.'

Truth was, Drake had no idea what action to take for at least the third time that day. The wooziness from his head wound had returned again now the adrenaline was at a lower ebb.

The mother and daughter spoke between themselves for a moment or two longer. Andrea was saying something to her daughter, insisting on it, before Cari suddenly sprung away from her.

'M—Mum?'

Andrea started to tremble, her chest rising and falling rapidly. 'Cari, get back. Get back now. Get away from me!'

'Mum! No!' Cari cried. 'Please, don't leave me!'

'I mean it. I— I can't control her.' Andrea wrapped her arms around herself tightly. 'I can feel her. Please. She's *wicked*. I can't . . . I can't lose you. P—Please! Go!'

Cari scrabbled across the floor to Drake and Ellie, as Andrea seemed to twist and turn on herself, as though she was struggling to contain whatever was within her.

'I . . . *can't! I. WON'T. LET. YOU!*' Andrea howled, springing up from the floor and grabbing the knife by Reynolds body before bounding from the room.

'Holy shit, Ellie. We've got to stop her!' Drake cried. He bounded up and through the door after the armed woman.

66

Ellie grabbed Cari by the wrist and yanked her out of the room, slamming the door shut on the horrors of the room behind her.

'Leave the house, now. I'm going after Drake, okay!'

Not waiting for a response from the girl, she barrelled through the remnants of the front door after Drake, hearing a yell coming from the street. For a man twenty years her senior, he could still run pretty fast when he wanted to.

Ellie turned out on to the street, immediately spotting him a little way ahead. He was grasping his leg, having fallen to the ground.

Oh, God.

Andrea stood just ahead of her boss, looking around her as though she didn't know what she was doing, the knife still clutched tightly in her hand.

'Chief!' Ellie caught up to him as Andrea started running again, blood spattering the pavement. She hoped the woman hadn't done any severe damage to him on her watch.

'It's just superficial – she was trying to slow me down, not kill me. Just catch her, I think she's still Andrea. We have to stop this!' Drake waved her on, sucking in a breath as he growled at his wound.

'Okay. Okay. I'm going!'

Ellie knew what catching Andrea meant to Drake and Cari; and to herself, for that matter. She needed to bring Cari's mother back to her, and bring an end to the cycle of suffering once and for all. It might go some way to assuaging her own guilt, too.

Look what she's become because of you, Samuel. And Reynolds, you sick fuck.

Ellie sprinted down the rest of the road as fast as she could, seeing Andrea veer left where the road met the high street. If she didn't close the gap quickly, she'd lose her, and Ellie doubted she'd have a huge Polish man helping her out this time, either.

Arriving at the end of the street, her heart pounding in her chest, she surveyed the road. Her head darted this way and that as she tried to spot where Cari's mother had gone.

Come on! I can't have lost her again. Please, no!

Ellie jogged further down the road and past an alleyway. She could have sworn she saw a flicker of movement in her periphery. Stopping, she turned to take another look around, making sure Andrea wasn't anywhere she could see on the main road.

She has to be hiding down here somewhere. It's what I would do.

Ellie jogged slowly down the alleyway, past piles of bin bags that had been heaped beside a large commercial waste bin for collection. Graffiti adorned the tired red brick walls, amidst years of damp and filth. 'Andrea?' she called, as a streetlight flickered into being overhead. 'Andrea, come out. We can help you. We can stop this now.'

She slowed further. Coming to a choke point, her alley intersected with another. She could be ambushed if she wasn't careful.

Suddenly Ellie heard shouting and a commotion; Andrea, perhaps, but there was a male voice too, followed by what sounded like a car door slamming shut.

'Andrea?'

Before Ellie knew it, a car appeared from a bay somewhere further down the alley and was edging toward her. Andrea was in the driver's seat of the battered old black BMW, the male nowhere to be found.

Ellie's eyes boggled at what was about to happen. 'Oh, shit.'

The car engine revved hard, the woman's face determined. Then Andrea put her foot down.

Ellie's eyes widened. She turned and ran as fast as she could, the car barrelling toward her at a rate of knots. Andrea sounded the horn repeatedly as she got closer and closer.

Shit. Shit. Shit. Shit. Shit!

Ellie sneaked a glance behind her before she reached the entrance to the alleyway, just in time to see the car bonnet. Instinctively, she dived to one side as the car shot out and on to the road. Drivers reacted angrily at the wayward vehicle sliding out in front of them, the sound of grinding gears and spinning tyres filling the air. Getting to her feet, Ellie just caught the licence plate and model of the car before it disappeared into the depths of the city.

She balled her fists, squeezing her eyes shut in frustration. *'Fuck!'*

* * *

'I'm sorry, Drake. I've lost her.' Ellie's voice was wracked with regret as she approached him and Cari at the entrance to Reynolds' house. On her way back, she'd called to report the vehicle and get Road Policing Units to locate it as soon as possible. It was only a matter of time before Andrea was caught. Surely, with the full force of the Metropolitan Police after her vehicle, she wouldn't escape this time?

'What do you mean?'

'She stole a man's car. Nearly ran me over in the process.'

Ellie saw Drake was struggling to hide his disappointment. 'You did your best, Ellie. It's my fault for getting stabbed.'

'How is it?' Ellie pointed at his blood-soaked trouser leg.

'I'll live. It was more of a slash than a stab, thankfully. Another scar to add to the collection, I'm sure. I won't be running a marathon for a while, eh, Cari?' Drake said, trying to lift the girl's spirits.

Ellie walked over to the despondent girl.

'I'm sorry I did what I did to that man. I thought he was going to kill my Mum.'

Ellie hesitated, recalling the savagery with which Cari had killed Reynolds. But what choice did she have? 'You did what you had to, Cari. You probably saved us all with your actions.'

'I saw you guys being led in to that room, so I sneaked back in and found that knife in the kitchen.' She turned to Drake, not meeting his gaze.

'It's okay, Cari. Don't you worry,' Drake said, forcing a smile.

'We'll find her.' Ellie made an attempt to change the subject. Not her best one, admittedly. 'This is just the final few hours. She'll soon be back with you.'

'I don't think she will, you know?'

'Why do you say that? I saw you two together. It was like she was herself again, wasn't it?'

'She was.' Cari locked eyes with Ellie, her face earnest. 'She really was, but I don't know . . . she needs help. I don't want her to do something stupid.'

The girl burst into tears and Ellie put her arms around her.

'I'm sure she won't, Cari.' An armed Response unit finally pulled up, the lights flashing in Ellie's eyes. She didn't like lying, but she had to say something to make the poor girl feel better.

Truth was, everyone knew what Andrea was still capable of.

67

Finally, I was back. In more ways than one. A veil had been lifted, at long last.

A fleeting smile touched my lips as I flew through the miles of country lanes, the car window wound down, the cool air buffeting my face. I was seeing reminders of better times as concrete and skyscrapers made way for fields and villages, the images a blur in the haze of dawn.

It had been a long night of zig-zagging various back roads and hiding on foot after abandoning the first car. But finally, I was free. Free of everything, free of him. But not her. I'd never be free of *her*.

The dull ache grew in the back of my skull at the thought of my mother, and I took a deep, fortifying breath. I'd have to be strong. But there was a clarity now. A strength. Being out in the open, unshackled as I was. However, with it came feelings of regret. For my actions, both past and present.

I winced at the memory of the last woman I'd frightened into handing over her car. But I knew it would be the last. I was so close now, on the periphery of where it had all begun. So close.

The terrified woman's face intermingled with the images of my time in the white room, memories of what that man and my mother had made me do there and to those men. They jittered and flashed through my mind. I did my best to suppress them, but I knew they would soon be back. They would always come back, those images of what I had done. They would break me, given the chance.

Exiting a country lane, I saw my destination at last. I pulled over to the side of the road, riding up onto the curb. The engine silenced, I sat, eyes closed, listening to the vibrant trill of morning bird song. Taking it in like it was the first time; and maybe even, the last.

I jumped out of the car and crossed the road, inching through some park gates before following the familiar path as it wound in and around the landscape beyond. A familiar pull tugged at my soul. The anticipation of what would soon follow warmed me.

I rounded one last corner and found myself at the bottom of a set of tree-lined steps, the mature trees still spluttering into life from the dormancy of winter. The summit appeared barren and desolate by comparison to my previous visit so long ago.

The ache in my head receded as I climbed the same steep stairs as before. The pain's retreat was a welcome respite, giving me space to think. The crunching of the gravel underfoot was like strange music to my ears as I pushed on through the tunnel of wooden bones to the place that was calling me. A place that had haunted my dreams since coming to Barndon with Ben and Cari all that time ago.

The place where *she* had returned.

Seeing the spot just ahead, I deviated off the path and through the dewy grass to the bench that overlooked Barndon. The view appeared more barren and skeletal than the last time. The village was quiet, the church bell still. At least the bench appeared to have been given some care and attention since I was last here; its memorial plaque had been fixed, and any rubbish was long gone. For that, I felt glad. The uptick in appearance felt like it was an analogy for the future.

I took my place, as I'd done before.

I knew now what had happened that fateful day. How I had been manipulated. How my mother had played me, twisted my very being. Slowly chipping away at my soul and corrupting me.

She had killed him.

My beloved husband. My Ben.

And she'd nearly succeeded in killing Cari too.

But Cari had survived. She was strong, and always would be, with or without me.

But I knew I wasn't.

That I could never be as Cari was.

Looking out over the village, I felt a growing sense of knowing.

I saw clearly now.

And I couldn't risk influencing her further. She'd already *killed* because of me. Seeing her innocence taken like that had shattered what little was left of the old me.

I was broken.

I would *always* be broken.

And that was why I had to put a stop to everything.

For Cari.

For Ben.

For *me.*

A tear ran down my cheek as I looked out over the village, the church bell tolling its mournful sound one last time.

68

Drake woke to find himself on the sofa in their flat. Exhaustion must have finally beaten him down and sent him to sleep. He took in his surroundings through groggy eyes as he came to, seeing Cari curled up in the armchair nearby and Eva at the other end of the sofa. His phone lay near his daughter's feet.

The events of the previous evening were still raw in his mind. The knowledge that Cari had killed a man; that it had been the second man she'd stabbed that day. It gnawed at him. Knives had been much too prominent in his life these past few years. The painful gash in his leg attested to his most recent encounter with one; the pain from the wound had dulled to a low ebb, but it was proving troublesome. The medication was certainly not doing its job as he had hoped.

But Drake's overriding concern was that they'd lost track of Andrea in the course of the night. The woman had switched cars numerous times while she'd been tracked on CCTV, before abandoning another car and losing the team chasing her in an industrial site just before morning had broken. She'd run them in absolute circles, like a veritable modern-day Houdini. It beggared belief. But Drake was convinced it was only a matter of time; she would be found, as she would have been over a year ago if she hadn't been hidden by a deranged psychopath.

He still couldn't believe it had been Reynolds all along. How the man had been in plain sight, manipulating things just enough to be overlooked or explained away. How he had watched them. Taunted them. Murdered them.

Drake's phone vibrated at his side.

Unknown Caller. Andrea?

'DCI Drake,' he answered. He got up awkwardly, hopping into the bedroom office space and seeing the bin still full of the old Andrea conversations. How times had changed.

'*DCI* Drake. You wouldn't believe how much it pains me to hear your voice,' Samuel said. Drake imagined his face curled into a snarl. His own had reacted similarly at Samuel's words.

'Yes. Not your brightest of ideas, was it?'

'Unfortunately, I have to agree. As always, when something needs doing, you're better off doing it yourself, eh?'

Drake grunted. 'You better believe it.'

'You know, I think I may even have a new-found respect for you, Drake.'

Drake didn't believe him for one second.

'Oh? Why's that?'

'Fending off not one, but *two* people in that house of yours. It makes me feel like I should give you a break, you know?'

'Don't give me that shit, Samuel.'

'You think so little of me. Perhaps we should even call it quits, eh?'

'Now I *know* you're talking crap.'

The man cackled, loud and harsh down the phone, making Drake wince.

'Okay, okay. You got me there.'

'Oh, and Samuel?'

'Mmm?'

'I know that the leak from my team is bullshit. It's been Graham Reynolds all along.'

The line remained silent.

'And he's dead, by the way.' Drake smiled. 'So that little link into my world . . . Well, it's gone – Andrea, too.'

Samuel remained silent. The man's breath heavy on the line. Drake couldn't tell if he was angry or sad, losing access to his daughter like that. Or perhaps he was thinking of a new approach.

Drake continued. 'I know about that little stash you had up at your place in Barndon as well. That's now all accounted for, too. Reynolds had left it unencrypted for us. We've accessed the contents. Seen *everything*. You've nothing left.'

'Quite the cocky little bastard, aren't you, Drake?' Samuel spat. 'Think you're better than me, is that it?'

'Something like that.'

'Well, *Drake*. Whether you like it or not, I'm going to keep on coming at you. It may not be now, it may not be a year from now, or even five. But one day, I'll come for you, and you better be ready,' he growled, his anger and spite boiling over. 'And that's how it will be until either you or I are dead, you hear?'

'Samuel—'

Samuel hung up.

Drake stood. The silence of the room and Samuel's threats hung in the air, the idea taunting him that this could be his reality now. That Samuel Barrow could be after him, after Eva. For good. Was it all just empty threats? Posturing? He daren't take the chance.

'John?'

Drake turned to see Cari at the door. She had a look in her eyes, as though she was desperate to tell him something.

'Cari. I'm sorry, did I wake you?'

'Yes, and I heard everything.'

Drake winced. 'I— I'm sorry you had to hear all that.'

'I don't care. Something you said made me realise . . . when you mentioned Barndon. I think I know where my Mum might be. A place that she said was special for her and my grandmother.'

Drake looked at her. 'Tell me everything you know. Now.'

* * *

Soon Drake was taking a trip to Barndon for the second time in as many days. And this time, he most definitely was not taking any chances. He was too damn tired. And he bet Andrea was too.

He had called in the police as soon as he'd got into his car and out on the open road, demanding that they surround the park in Barndon and not let anyone in or out fitting Andrea's description. He needed to speak to her, to tell her Cari was okay, that she would be fine. That she'd get the help she needed, and that Cari just wanted her mother to be safe and well. How he would take care of her in Andrea's absence. Keep her safe.

Drake pulled up near the park, wincing at the sharp pain in his stiff leg as he stepped out of the car. Becca and he had also spent many hours there watching the world go by, both before and after Eva came into their lives. It looked like it was shaping up to be a beautiful morning; a hazy sunshine was pushing through, its rays burning away the remaining mist that had settled low on the village.

Police cars had encircled the main entrance to the park; he counted at least six. And he hoped there was an equal number at the other two exits as well. This had to be it, it just had to be. He pulled his ID and ducked gingerly under the cordon before showing it to a burly PC who seemed to have more equipment attached to his body than limbs.

'Constable, I need you and one other to follow at a distance. I'm going to try and talk to her, and I don't want anyone startling her or going in all guns blazing. Okay?'

'Yes, sir.'

Drake's heart surged. This could be it. Andrea's nightmare could finally be over. He knew she'd only ran because she was scared, more for Cari than herself. Seeing her daughter do something like that, even if it was in her defence, had to have stirred up many emotions. And that was if she was mentally stable, let alone in her current state.

He nodded; his eyes set. 'Let's go.'

Drake inched through the tight gate and made his way round the long winding path. It would have been a great day for a walk if he'd been there under any other circumstances and had two legs in good working order. The memory of his last time there with Becca on a picnic blanket overlooking the village stirred his soul.

He scaled the set of steps up to the highest section of the park and made his way through the tunnel of tangled branches, his shoes crunching in the rough gravel trail before, finally, he saw her.

Andrea.

She was sat on a bench, perfectly still, overlooking the village beyond. Her head was tilted slightly, as though she was deep in thought. He hoped she wasn't catatonic again. He didn't want another encounter with Miray.

Drake looked back at the two officers, putting his arm out to stop them from coming any closer.

'Andrea?' He spoke carefully, not wanting to spook her. 'Andrea, it's DCI Drake.'

He took a few steps closer.

It was then he saw the blood pooled around the concrete base.

Oh no. No-no-no. Andrea, no.

Drake hurried over to the bench. The knife from Reynolds was by her side, her wrists slit vertically in ragged gashes. Andrea's face was pale and unmoving, her eyes closed as though she was asleep, her hair moving gently in the breeze.

She looked at peace.

Drake sat down gently next to her and looked out over the village below.

'I'm sorry, Andrea.'

69

Drake worked his way round the investigation room, pulling down pictures of Fleming, Reed and Melwood before putting away the photos and papers detailing all the grotesque and exacting minutiae of the case in a labelled box. The investigation was being wound down, and he expected he would soon be needed elsewhere. Perhaps he could use this golden hour to request a new coffee machine while he was riding on a case-solving high. At least, that's how it would seem from the perspective of an outsider looking in. But he didn't feel in the mood for celebration. The cost had been much too high.

A knock came at the door. Drake looked up to see Miller enter. She looked decidedly perturbed, as was becoming the norm these last few years.

'Laura? Everything okay?'

'No, John. No. It's not. Can you come with me to my office, please?'

'I'll be along in a minute,' he said, gesturing with the papers, before returning to putting them away.

Miller didn't move. 'Now, Drake.'

Drake froze, sensing there was something decidedly wrong about her demeanour. Something else.

'Okay. Gotcha.' He put down the papers and followed her out in silence to her office.

Miller closed the blinds and took a seat behind her desk while Drake made himself comfortable opposite.

'What's this about, Laura? Please tell me there's not been something more to do with this damn case. Please. I don't think I can take it.'

'Not exactly, Drake. However, there is something.'

'Okay?'

'It's Samuel—'

'What's the bastard done now?'

'If you'd let me finish . . . John, he's been found dead this morning. Murdered. Stabbed to death in his cell at HMP Wakefield with a shank.'

Drake gasped, despite himself. That was news he was not expecting. Not at all.

'What? How?'

'Indeed.' She was studying him intently.

'Do we know who did it?' Drake asked.

'Yes. We do.' She clasped her hands on the desk. 'It was Jack Spencer.'

Jack? But how? He didn't know that the Man killed his parents. Was it a coincidence? He didn't understand.

'Laura, how is that possible?'

'You tell me, Drake. Only you, I and Melwood knew about Jack's move to that prison, and it was most definitely only your team and I who knew about the connection between Samuel and the Spencers. So, the only people who knew of both details, and who are still breathing, are you and me.' She paused, the seconds ticking by. 'And I can tell you in no uncertain terms, it wasn't me.

So that leaves you and you alone, John. And I understand you spoke to Jack, and in person by all accounts, recently too.'

'What? Hang on. No. You don't think I . . . ?'

The DCS pinched her brow. 'Tell me, Drake. Tell me what I should think? What would you think in this exact moment, having learnt of this fucking fiasco?'

'Laura, please! I would never do that. Even with Samuel having done what he did, you have to believe me.'

'Then please, tell me. How it is that Jack Spencer decided to stab Samuel to death. We have footage, he confessed. He won't say anything further. And why should he? He's got life anyway.' She sneered in irritation. 'All we have for interactions recently are you and his solicitor. Gemma has not been allowed to contact him. She's been in a damn coma and confined to a hospital bed, for God's sake.'

Drake wracked his brain. Nothing was coming to mind. Nothing that would explain the situation. He still couldn't quite believe the Man was even dead.

'You are the only person with the knowledge and the motive, Drake. Please, just admit what you did.'

'It wasn't me, Laura. It wasn't. I don't know what more I can say?'

Miller slammed her desk with a fist. 'Then tell me who could have done it? It can't have been Ellie, she didn't know where Jack had been moved to. And she had no reason to believe he was anywhere but HMP Belmarsh in London. There's no record of her having contacted him, nor does she have any real reason to want the Man dead. Unlike you.'

Drake sat in a stunned silence. He didn't know what to say, or how to get through to Miller that it wasn't him. Sure, he wanted the man dead, but he would never actively seek it out. That went against everything he stood for. Though, he had to admit whoever had done it, there was a poetic justice that had been served. The Family Man was finally dead at the hands of one of the family members whose lives he had ruined.

Miller pushed back from the desk slightly, gripping the edge with her hands. 'I'm sorry, John. But without any reasonable doubt or evidence to the contrary, I'm going to have to do something I never thought I'd have to do, despite everything over the years. But there's a line, and my God, have you crossed it with this.'

She looked to her hands, like she was having to give her next words a great deal of thought.

'Laura . . . ?'

Miller took a deep breath and looked him in the eye.

'Laura . . . no, don't—'

'John, it's been recommended that I seek your termination.'

Drake's stomach lurched at her words.

'What! No, Laura, no. Please! Don't do this!'

She remained silent at his protestations.

'I'll fight this, Laura. You know I will. There are rules, procedures . . .'

Her mouth twisted, perhaps at the irony of him quoting the rule book at her. 'You could do that,' she agreed. 'You have the right to a full investigation before any final decision is taken. It would be extensive, of course. Lengthy. And we'd make every effort to keep it out of the media.' She splayed her fingers on the desk. 'But these things . . . well, in spite of our best efforts, leaks happen, don't they?'

'You wouldn't.'

She glared at him. 'You think I wanted this? I've had your back for years, John. I stood up for you, kept the powers-that-be off your back. But this is where it ends. This is where you choose to do the right thing.' Miller's eyes narrowed. 'Or finally, for once, face the consequences without my protection.'

She continued, a strange deadness to her expression. 'Or, we can put all that . . . unpleasantness aside. I can give you the option of resigning, owing to personal reasons.'

Drake stared at his colleague, wondering how it had come to this. How she could treat him like this after all this time, even with his recent record.

'There's no use just staring at me, John,' she spat. 'That's all I can give you; my hands are tied. And you should be grateful. Truly, you should. You've left me with no other way out of this. What you've done, it sickens me. Even I didn't think you could stoop so goddamn low.'

She slammed a fist on the desk and stormed over to the window.

Drake couldn't see a way out. Who would believe him? There was nothing he could do to stem the tide. He knew that their friendship had been hitting new lows in recent years, but this? His friend and colleague was utterly lost to him.

She turned back, venom in her eyes. 'With all the issues these last few years, my superiors feel there is simply no goodwill left for you. You should be thankful your years of service mean we've even given you this as a fucking option. Frankly, you disgust me.'

Drake's surprise and fear turned immediately to anger. His eyes hardened at her words, and he squeezed his hands into white-hot fists. They think they're doing me a favour? How dare she?

Taking a deep breath, he uttered the words he never thought he'd ever say.

'Fine. I resign.'

70

Drake headed to his desk to collect the few things he had. The desk still sat as sorry and empty-looking as it always had, barring the single picture of his family next to his briefcase, partially hidden by a set of papers. No one else was around to see him leave. They must be at lunch or out somewhere working a case, he supposed. But he preferred it that way.

In spite of the ups and downs of the years in the SMT, Drake could never have believed things would play out the way they had. He was out on his heels, everything he'd done counting for naught. No more benefit of the doubt, no more consideration due to the cases he'd solved, the people he'd put behind bars. The lives he'd saved. There was nothing left but this desk, and that spoke volumes. Samuel had somehow had the last laugh. After everything.

'Everything okay there, Boss?'

Drake turned to see Ellie walking over to him. She must have seen him come out of Miller's office.

'Peachy.'

Ellie smiled through his sarcasm. 'Have you heard the news?'

News? How she phrased it, it can't have meant me and my news . . .

'No?'

'It's Luka, he's finally out of his coma. He's speaking, Drake! Isn't that great?'

Drake smiled. Despite his own circumstances, there were worse things that could have happened. He was pleased to hear the man was on the mend. 'That's great news. I'll have to go and see him soon. Apologise for getting him in the situation in the first place.'

Ellie frowned. 'He's a grown man, Drake. I'm sure he knows he's only got himself to blame for charging in like he did. And did you get the details for Melwood's funeral?'

Drake looked down at his desk and the picture of his family for a moment. Becca's beautiful smile. Eva before her Mum was taken. Deep in thought.

'Ellie . . . Do you mind coming with me for a minute, please? I need to speak to you about something.' Drake started to head for a nearby empty room that was used for conference calls.

'Of course.' She frowned again and followed him through.

Ellie closed the door behind them while Drake sat in one of the few unbroken chairs. She took one opposite.

He couldn't hold it in any longer.

'Why did you do it, Ellie? Why?'

'Chief?' she said, looking bewildered.

'Why did you tell Jack about Samuel? Why? It could only have been you. At least do me the common courtesy of being honest with me.'

She hesitated slightly. 'I . . . I didn't.'

'Don't insult my intelligence,' he hissed. He knew it was her, there was no one else it could have been. She had to have known about the situation with Jack's prison move somehow. 'Ellie, I've just had to resign. It was either that, or I would have had to have *outed* a promising young sergeant on her career-ending mistake.'

'What? No!'

'Yes, Ellie,' he said. He found it hard to even look at her any more. 'Just tell me why you did it? And how. You owe me that much at least.'

Drake could see something in her that he'd not seen before. Fear. And tears.

Ellie broke down in front of him, her tears running freely. 'I'm so, so sorry, John. I couldn't let the cycle continue. After you told me of Samuel's threats and what he'd done to Cari, and how he said he would never leave you alone. I . . . I snapped.'

'*You* snapped?' he said, looking at her incredulously. 'Something that is my problem, my goddamn issue, one that I have to deal with and be wary of. The girls I have to protect with my life, and *you* snapped?'

'Yes, John . . . You don't get it. I *killed* Fiona Spencer. I made that choice when I was falling from that damn balcony. I took her down with me. I did it for my family, and God, I've suffered for it. That choice . . . that mistake; the nightmares, I couldn't sleep, I couldn't eat. I fought with Len all the time. The guilt, it was unbearable.'

'Ellie . . .'

Drake watched in dismay as Ellie rubbed at her eye in silence, the stress of the situation clearly getting to her. What had he done to the poor woman?

'No, John. Just *no*. I've had this all building up inside of me for months. I didn't want to trouble you. I didn't want to put you out, or make it worse for you, dealing with what you've had to deal with. But since realising that I did it for my family, I've made peace with myself.' Ellie balled her fists on the table as she spoke. 'It felt *justified*. Things have been better. I've at least been able to fucking *sleep*. And then, hearing about Samuel again, I stupidly thought I was doing the right thing. Yes, I spoke with Jack. He *called me*. About Gemma. He said *you'd* told him to. He was desperate. She's all he has, and he was anxious to know how she was. How she *really* was. But they wouldn't let them speak to each other.' She paused. 'So, yes. I made him aware. I knew that Samuel and he were at the same prison. I overheard Miller tell you at the first crime scene in the underpass and played along with your little charade when you came back from seeing Samuel.'

Drake put his head in his hands. 'Ellie, my God.'

'I didn't *tell* him to do anything.' She reasoned. 'I just told him the facts.'

'Ellie, that's as good as signing the Man's death warrant and you know it!'

'So, what if it is? It's not like he didn't deserve it. I thought I could give you a rest, like I've given myself since coming to terms with it all.'

'Ellie, that's not what we *do*,' he remonstrated. 'We don't choose who lives and who dies. It's what separates *us from them*, don't you see!'

'Not in these cases, Drake. Not with these . . . "people." Sometimes you have to fight fire with fire.'

'Oh, Ellie.' Drake got up from his seat, shaking his head as he paced the small room. He couldn't believe what he was hearing. It was his fault. It had to be. Even if she hadn't overheard things, his idiotic encouragement of Jack calling her had led to this. He should have been more careful. And if only he'd listened to Ellie, made himself available, let her know he was there for her, none of this would have happened. Instead, he'd only thought about his problems. His demons. She was still inexperienced, naive. This shouldn't have come to pass.

'And why didn't you tell me, Drake? We're supposed to be a team.'

'Jesus fucking Christ.' The seconds ticked by while he thought of how to handle the enormity of the situation.

'Okay. Here's the deal,' he said, running his hand through his hair. He sat down again and looked his former partner in the eye. 'We are never going to speak of this again. I am going to keep this between us . . . And I am going to leave. I can't have your career ruined because of this.'

'Drake, no! I did this. *Me*. No one else.' Her voice became little more than a whisper. 'And it was wrong. I can see that now. But as I said, I . . . I wasn't sleeping, you know? Not thinking straight, not eating properly. I was dragging myself through the days, falling apart, bit by bit. And I just . . . I needed to make everything *stop*, Drake. For all of us.'

'This is not up for debate,' he said, raising his voice. 'Ellie, don't you get it? Regardless of how you felt, your actions . . . you could be put in *prison*. Miller went easy on me. Her last ever favour to me. I have extenuating circumstances. The Man killed my wife. Threatened Eva and Cari, *kidnapped* her, for God's sake. You don't have the same in the bank. Nowhere near.'

'I . . .'

'That's an order, Ellie.' Drake slammed the table with a fist. 'Now, you promise me, you carry on. Make yourself the best damn detective you can be. You promise me that, okay? Please? At least make it so this wasn't all for nothing.'

Ellie looked at him in stunned silence. The enormity of what she had done, maybe, just maybe, finally sinking in.

'I'm so sorry, Drake. Truly, I am,' she said, stuttering through more tears. 'Will you forgive me? Please? Drake, please – say you forgive me.'

He didn't answer. Instead, he got up and left the room without uttering a word.

'John . . . No! Please!'

71

Drake folded the lid down on the last remaining cardboard box, and slapped the top with satisfaction. That was it, nothing left to pack. Not one scrap was left that he gave a shit about. His life, his family's life; all of it was set for storage while they made their next move. He praised the god of removal men for providing their services. The idea of shifting all his stuff would have sent him crazy.

'Dad!' Eva called from her old bedroom.

'Yes, love?' Drake leaned back in his battered old desk chair amidst the piles and piles of boxes in his old Barndon study. The chair creaked in pain at his weight, maybe for the last time.

'Are you ready yet?'

'I'm just finishing, I promise. Then we'll be out of here.' Drake took the box from his lap and placed it on the top of the burgeoning pile. 'Best say your goodbyes to the house soon.'

Drake peered around the doorframe of the study, expecting to see Eva ready to drag him down the stairs. Instead, he saw Cari staring intently into the hallway mirror.

He frowned. 'Cari? Is everything—'

Eva poked her head out of her room. 'Goodbyes? Fuck that!'

Drake rolled his eyes at her language. 'Eva . . .'

'Sorry, Dad,' she said, sounding anything but, before cocking her head in Cari's direction. 'And you've not changed your mind on Cari coming too, right?'

Cari turned and gave him a slight smile.

Drake reciprocated. 'Of course she's coming.'

He left the girls to it and turned his attention back to the study. The room which had shaped his life.

For better.

And for worse.

It was about time he put it all behind him. The Man. The Spencers. Miller. His career. All of it.

The times they are a-changin', he thought, as he placed the photo of Becca and Eva on top of the final box.

For the better?

Only time would tell.

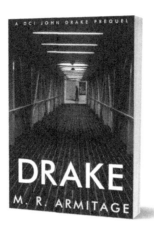

ALSO BY M. R. ARMITAGE
THE FAMILY MAN - DCI JOHN DRAKE BOOK 1

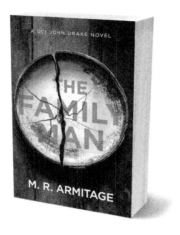

Another family dead. The mother broken, but alive. It's happening again. But how?

The Family Man died twenty years ago, cheating DCI John Drake of the chance to bring him to justice. But when a mother is found with her entire family brutally murdered at an isolated house in Yorkshire, the grim discovery bears all the hallmarks of the dead serial killer's work.

Haunted by what he'd witnessed during the original investigation, Drake knows his experience makes him the obvious choice to head the specialist team investigating these latest killings. But as the deaths move ever closer to home and the killer taunts him with sly reminders of the earlier murders, Drake's forced to contemplate the unthinkable:

Are these latest murders the work of a copycat? Or twenty years ago, did Drake make the biggest mistake of his career?

ALSO BY M. R. ARMITAGE
THE TIES THAT BIND - DCI JOHN DRAKE BOOK 2

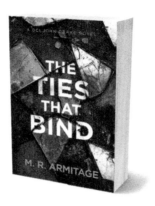

The smallest decisions can have the deadliest consequences...

His life in tatters, DCI John Drake is struggling to move past the events of *The Family Man*. But when a brutal new serial killer surfaces, he seizes the opportunity to pull himself back from the brink.

Despite her public commendation, DS Ellie Wilkinson has been sidelined into a support role. Still dealing with what she witnessed at the Whitman's house, she's determined to work with Drake again. But as their new team begins to delve deeper into this latest case, dark secrets are uncovered. And what they reveal raises the stakes for everyone involved...

Can they stop this vicious new killer? And will Drake finally confront his demons - or be consumed by them?

ABOUT THE AUTHOR

M. R. Armitage is an author hailing from Reading, England. Surrounded by a distressing number of unread books, he hopes one day he will read them all rather than just buying more.

However, now the third book is out there, the pile is frankly getting a little ridiculous.

Visit my website:

www.mrarmitage.com

And keep in touch on Facebook:

facebook.com/MRArmitageAuthor

Printed in Great Britain
by Amazon